To
Caroline,
Thankyou [illegible] g
one of the very first people
to buy a copy of –

"ACTS & MONUMENTS"

I really hope that you
enjoy it (and don't
recognise too much!)
If you do then please
do tell others
With every good wish
ALAN [illegible]

10th January 2019

14/50
AKF

Acts & Monuments

Alan Kane Fraser

Matador
9 Priory Business Park,
Wistow Road, Kibworth Beauchamp,
Leicestershire. LE8 0RX
Tel: 0116 279 2299
Email: books@troubador.co.uk
Web: www.troubador.co.uk/matador
Twitter: @matadorbooks

ISBN 978 1789016 086

British Library Cataloguing in Publication Data.
A catalogue record for this book is available from the British Library.

Printed and bound in Great Britain by 4edge Limited
Typeset in 11pt Adobe Garamond Pro by Troubador Publishing Ltd, Leicester, UK

Matador is an imprint of Troubador Publishing Ltd

For Alexis, whose innocent question
prompted the idea for this book.
And for Danielle, whose innocent question
prompted me to write it.

"People change for two main reasons: either their minds have been opened or their hearts have been broken."

Steven Aitchison

19th January 2016

Gemma Rathbone pulled up behind the gleaming sports coupé and turned her engine off. She sat for a moment, trying to summon up the courage to get out of the car. She hated this part of the job, absolutely hated it, although she would rather have been up there by the bridge than down on the carriageway below where her colleagues were helping the ambulance crew clean up the mess.

"Subaru BRZ. The SE LUX too," said Molloy as the light from the top of their vehicle momentarily washed the scene with a harsh, electric blue. "Probably a mid-life crisis. Usually is with the sports cars. 'Specially the red ones."

Gemma felt as though there was an invisible weight pressing down on her chest, stopping her from moving. In reality, it was just the fear of what she might find.

"Come on, Bones," said Molloy. "Let's get this over with."

They looked at each other, then swung out of the car in unison.

A brush of icing-sugar frost dusted the ground. Gemma led the way with Molloy following on behind; the bleak January chill quickly daubing scarlet onto their cheeks. So it was the younger constable who reached the car first, making straight for the driver's door, which had been left slightly ajar. Molloy went for the passenger side. Gemma closed her eyes as she reached the vehicle and, feeling cold chrome on her fingers, pulled the handle sharply, forcing her eyes open.

Nothing. Thank God. There was an audible exhalation of relief from both sides of the vehicle.

"Nice little motor, this," said Molloy. The moment had passed, and now he was acting as though it had never been there; as though he had never felt the slow-burning nausea that is the unspoken glue binding officers together.

Idiot, thought Gemma.

And then she noticed it. A small manila envelope on the passenger seat. She leant forward and read the message written in neat and cultured handwriting on the front: *"To whom it may concern"*.

There was something about it that touched her. Even at a time like this, someone had made the effort to write neatly and legibly. *The 'whom' is a nice touch too,* she thought. Standards were being maintained, right to the end. Gemma felt certain that this wasn't the usual tale of money troubles and relationship difficulties – she felt intuitively that this was a good person who'd simply been overwhelmed by a bad world.

"You gonna read it then?" Molloy asked. "'To whom it may concern' – that's you as much as anyone else."

Gemma shot him a glare.

"I mean, there's nothing to say we can't," Molloy added.

The gloom of a winter's day was ebbing gently into the darkness of evening, but there was still just about enough light left to read by, so she carefully removed the letter. She was pleased to see that the neat and cultured writing continued inside.

Firstly, let me say how sorry I am if I've caused anyone any trouble or put anyone out. I really didn't mean to. Please pass on my apologies if I've made a nuisance of myself – that wasn't my intention.

But I wanted to explain things.

Obviously, I'm not happy, but it's why *I'm not happy that really bothers me. It's that I seem to make the people around me miserable. I don't mean to, I just do. The people I'm supposed to be closest to actually feel the farthest away. I do care about them, but they just regard me as an inconvenience. I think they'd prefer it if I was dead, to be honest.*

It used to be so different. I was at an art college once. I had dreams; I knew what I wanted to be. But somehow I've lost sight of all that. My daughter talks to me now like I'm an idiot – when I can get her to talk to me at all. She doesn't respect me anymore. No one does. I think that's what hurts the most.

Losing our son tore us apart. When Christopher died, it pretty much ended our marriage. We don't communicate now, not really.

It's funny, because I feel I have so much love to give, but no one seems to want it. It's like money, I suppose –

you always think you want more of it, but if you keep it all for yourself, it just becomes a burden. You really need to be able to give it away, and if you can't, then frankly, what's the point? You don't have anything to live for if no one wants your love, do you?

Sorry again. Please make sure my daughter knows that I do love her. This wasn't about her; I want her to know that.

Thank you.

And then there was a signature that Gemma couldn't quite read.

What a shame, she thought. *What a lovely person.* It was a genuine tragedy that it had ended this way.

But how had it come to this? How on earth had it ever come to this?

PART 1

"Before you criticise someone,
walk a mile in their shoes."

African Proverb

WALKING THE MILE

22nd–26th October 2015

ONE

Barry Todd was a good man. It's important to make this point at the outset because it might not be immediately obvious to the dispassionate observer how someone who stole the best part of £50,000 from a charity could ever be described as 'good'; not in the eyes of most reasonable people. But, technically, although it was charity money that he'd stolen, it wasn't the charity that was out of pocket. So no homeless young people were harmed in the execution of the theft – as he would have pointed out if anyone had challenged him on that point. Which they hadn't. It was actually his employer who had ended up footing the bill, and they could afford it.

They also absolutely deserved it.

But none of that was on Barry's mind at the beginning, as he sat opposite Angela, the head of HR, in Monument Housing Association's boardroom. It contained the kind of table around which Barry liked to think evil geniuses would gather. And the high-backed leather seats that surrounded it certainly seemed indicative of a change in priorities from the days when the organisation had been run by a board of volunteers largely drawn from local churches. Back then Neville would never have countenanced spending a few thousand pounds on posh chairs. But, now, with a board of paid professionals in place, such charitable thoughts felt naïve.

Barry's pouched and jowly face craned forward in an attitude of anticipation, whilst his clammy hands sat clenched between his knees as though in prayer. Even the serene beauty of Kingsbury Water Park, visible through the huge, plate-glass windows, was not enough to distract him. *This will be it, surely,* he thought. *This is my time.*

But Angela seemed to be avoiding direct eye contact. She was looking at some notes and fiddling with her pen, rather than doing that 'leaning-forward-and-staring-benignly-whilst-tilting-your-head' thing that HR people liked to do when they were trying to reassure you. Which, Barry realised, probably meant that she *wasn't* trying to reassure him.

Angela's official job title was actually Head of People Investment, but, given that her role mainly seemed to involve sacking people, dragging them off their sick beds back into work, and relentlessly driving down their terms and conditions of employment – everything, in fact, *except* investing in them – most employees continued to refer to her as what she was (or, in the case of Kay from finance, as the Head of Grim Reaping).

A sudden chill ran down the back of Barry's neck, although he realised that might just have been the office's comfort cooling system kicking in. And then she said it.

"Well, as you can imagine, Barry, we had a lot of very good people apply for the director's job, and we've had to make some very difficult decisions."

She muttered some other stuff about his "strong application form" and "good, relevant experience" before commenting that his presentation hadn't quite demonstrated a "sufficient understanding of the business plan", and that the panel hadn't seen the kind of "innovative thinking" and "personal gravitas" they were looking for from a prospective member of the executive team.

He wanted to interrupt, to challenge her rather downbeat assessment of his capabilities. But instead, Barry found himself nodding as, with tender precision, Angela articulated his various shortcomings, echoing his assent to each. It felt like a parents' evening, but without his parents to help protect him from the brutal truth.

"So, overall, I'm afraid we don't quite feel that you meet the standard we're looking for in such a senior post."

The words washed through him like radiotherapy: silently, invisibly, killing something that he had allowed to grow inside him. Hope.

Barry slowly crumpled into his seat, like a bouncy castle being deflated at a children's party that had never happened. "Sorry," he said, as though it was somehow his fault.

"I can see that this is all rather a lot to take in at the moment," Angela said. Then she made good eye contact and started to do the 'tilty head' thing, which Barry found oddly reassuring. "But I'd be happy to offer you some more detailed feedback when you've had a chance to reflect, if you think you'd find that useful."

"Are you sure you've got the time? I mean, I know you're very busy."

"It's the least I can do."

And the way that she said it, Barry honestly believed that it was.

He'd wanted it so badly, and with everything that had happened – Christopher, his wife, the endless restructuring – he felt that he needed it. But it was not to be. Of course, Barry had always recognised that there were more dreams in the world than there were glorious destinies, so he was well practised in the art of swallowing his disappointment. And, to be honest, as long as Langley didn't get the job, he decided he could live with the outcome.

"So tell me, who did get it?"

"Well," Angela said, losing eye contact again and returning to her papers, "we've decided to give it to Langley."

"Sorry?"

"Langley. Langley Burrell."

Barry remained silent. His faced reddened and his eyes fixed Angela in a desperate stare. His breathing became heavier and he found himself involuntarily twisting his tie around his pudgy, sweaty fingers.

"Now I know that you and Langley have had your…" she searched for the right word, "issues in the past—"

"He sacked my wife, but it's not about—"

"He made your wife redundant," corrected Angela, "but that was a business decision, Barry. It wasn't personal. He acted in the best interests of Monument – he always acts in the best interests of Monument. We're facing a really challenging business environment at the moment, and Langley brings an awful lot of the kind of private-sector disciplines that Monument is going to need to face those challenges going forward."

"But he's not a housing expert. The person specification specifically said—"

"I think, in the short time that he's been here, Langley's shown that he brings a lot of other skills – the kind of skills we're looking for in a housing director. The thing is, Barry, at exec-team level we're looking for someone with good generic business knowledge of things like cost control, income generation, people management and business development. The operational side of things can be left to..."

She slowly ran out of enthusiasm before reaching the end of the sentence, as though she'd started off with a very clear idea of what she was going to say, but had gradually thought better of it.

He wanted to say something; to ask her – beg her – to reconsider. He tried to find the words to explain why Langley simply couldn't be given the director's job. The ones Barry had said to himself countless times in the bathroom mirror and when he was alone in his car. But they would not be found. They went into hiding around other people. They always did. Yet, that, of course, was precisely when he needed to find them most.

So, he simply mumbled a "thank you" and another "sorry", in what sounded to Barry like an acknowledgement of his defeat, and then he headed obediently back to his desk. Langley had been appointed and nothing Barry could say would change that fact.

Barry's desk was situated in an island along with the desks of the other members of the team he managed. Andrew, Neville's replacement as chief executive, had moved Monument into a new, open-plan office space, apparently to encourage greater interaction between staff and their managers. The consequence was that, upon returning to his desk, Barry was forced to interact with his team, when what he really wanted was to be left alone.

Lucy and Taneesha were waiting for him. As he took his seat, Barry could feel their eyes searching him for clues, but he didn't look back. He knew that if he did he would have to explain; and he couldn't explain it. Not even to himself.

Lucy was too polite and too savvy to ask her boss about his application for promotion, but Taneesha had no such qualms. "So?" she asked.

"So what?"

"The job?"

Barry noticed Lucy trying to rein in Taneesha's curiosity with a wide-eyed stare. Taneesha was having none of it, though, and simply stared back. He could see that she wasn't really in the mood to be put off.

"Oh, that. Sorry," he said. "I'm afraid I didn't get it, but thanks for asking. Now, have you got the weekly void report done yet?"

"Oh, that's a shame – although, obviously, it's good news that we get to keep you as our manager." Taneesha waited a moment to allow Barry to acknowledge her attempt at sycophancy (which he didn't) before adding, "So, who did get it then?"

Barry paused. His natural inclination was to make Taneesha wait until Angela emailed an official announcement around the office. After all, it wasn't his job to do people investment's work for them.

"I bet it's Maxine, isn't it? I really hope it's Maxine. I mean, it would have been great if you'd got it, but we really need to get a strong black woman on the exec team, and Maxine would be perfect. She really knows her stuff; everyone respects her."

Barry felt the need to stamp on Taneesha's obvious enthusiasm straight away before her wild guess reached the status of widely accepted fact.

"Actually, it's Langley, Taneesha. They've given it to Langley."

From behind him Barry heard a couple of wild whoops, and a "Yes, top result!" followed by what sounded like high-fives. From this he concluded that Area Team A were not unduly disappointed to be losing Langley as their manager.

Taneesha and Lucy, however, were both looking at him in open-mouthed horror. "You have got to be kidding me!" Taneesha said. "How can you sit there so calmly when they've just appointed that bumbaclart as your boss?"

"Sorry," said Barry again, "but that's what they've told me the decision is." He didn't know what a 'bumbaclart' was, but he sensed from Taneesha's manner that it wasn't intended as a compliment, so, whatever it was, Barry was pretty confident that Langley probably was one.

"How can they give it to him? What does he know about anything?" she said.

"I can't really say," replied Barry, although he wanted to. He wanted to say that no matter how glaring his deficiencies were to his colleagues, Langley excelled in the one skill that really was essential to get on at Monument (but that, ironically, was mentioned nowhere in the list of essential criteria for the post): he sucked up to the exec team and told them what they wanted to hear. Principally, this was that the job of front-line staff was easy, and the reason that Monument never hit any of its targets was not because the targets were unrealistic and the resources allocated to meet them inadequate, but because the people Monument employed on the front line were all lazy and useless, and needed to be kicked harder in order to get them to achieve what they were paid to. Or, failing that, fired. And the reason they were all useless was because they lacked knowledge of the basic private-sector disciplines of cost control and income generation. Langley had spent three years on the Debenhams' Graduate Management Training Programme and so he knew all about this. His favourite phrase when confronted by a missed target or a declining key performance indicator was "This would never have been tolerated at Debenhams." Fortunately, however, Barry's phone rang before he could be tempted to offer his opinion on the reasons for his new boss' unlikely elevation.

"Hi, Barry? It's Lee. I've been called out to Neville Thompson House. I think you need to come down here. It looks like we've got a problem."

"A problem…?"

"With flat twelve. He's not responding. The neighbour phoned to say she hasn't seen him for a couple of weeks; his post's not been collected from his postbox. And now there's a smell…"

"Flat twelve? Who's that?"

Lee tried to keep his fears locked up inside his mouth, but they sneaked out through a shiver in the momentary pause he left before answering. "Chris Malford."

Oh God, not him, thought Barry. Christian Malford was a young man with a troubled history, and his behaviour could sometimes be erratic. It was possible, therefore, that his absence wasn't anything more sinister than one of his periodic disappearances; one that would be followed by an equally inexplicable reappearance. But that troubled history stirred a sense of sickness in Barry's expansive stomach. "Have you spoken to the police?"

"Yeah, they'll get someone over as soon as they can. But we might need to go in. I just thought you might want to be there..."

Barry normally hated going out on site to tidy up situations that his housing officers should have been able to deal with by themselves, but Chris Malford was different. And besides, at that particular moment he was keen to avoid further probing from Taneesha on the issue of Langley's appointment. So, rather than continue with his usual raft of questions, Barry just picked up his keys.

"I'll be right over," he said, before grabbing his jacket and heading out. "Sorry, ladies, but Lee's got a problem. I've got to go over and help him out." He added a theatrical roll of the eyes to try to indicate that he didn't really want to go. He felt this would stand him in good stead when he phoned up later and said that he didn't think it was worth his while trying to get back.

Going home early would be an uncharacteristic act of rebellion on Barry's part. A small one admittedly, which (like most of Barry's actions, it seemed) would pass unnoticed by Monument's hierarchy.

But rebellions, of course, can grow.

TWO

As is often the way when you mention the words 'dead body', the police miraculously found someone from somewhere to attend the scene fairly expeditiously. Barry had tried to make sure that he wouldn't have to wait for hours for someone to turn up by offering just the slightest hint that foul play might be involved. "The neighbour says she heard a commotion late on Thursday night a fortnight ago and then someone leaving. But she's seen no one go in or come out since. It could have been an argument, I suppose," he'd ventured in an attempt to join up the dots for the police call handler.

Sure enough, a mere forty-five minutes later, a police car had pulled up and two officers had got out. One of them was so young she looked to Barry like a schoolchild who'd grabbed a police uniform out of the dressing-up box in response to the question "Now what would you like to pretend to be today, children?" Her colleague, by contrast, was older, fatter and more world-weary in appearance.

They both dawdled across the car park, appearing to be in a rather perverse race to see who could arrive at Barry's outstretched hand last. The older one lost. He shot a look over to his younger colleague to indicate his displeasure.

"Hullo. Mr Todd? I'm PC Molloy. And this is my colleague PC Rathbone. I understand you have reason to believe that there may be a body in one of your flats?"

A gust of wind sent a whisper of papery leaves scurrying around Barry's Hush Puppies as they headed toward the entrance of Neville Thompson House. It was the kind of unprepossessing 1970s, low-rise development that housing associations had flecked across the country when land was cheaper and the grant to build them was more plentiful. It was an entirely unremarkable building from a time when being unremarkable was something that social housing aspired to be. They entered the lobby as the last smear of autumnal daylight slipped through a gap in the slate-grey sky, the scent of effluent and decay murmuring of a creeping menace, of things not being as they should.

The moment they forced the door the smell of death rushed at them, as if escaping the horror inside. Barry recognised that smell. He'd smelt it before: Christopher. A tiny bubble of sadness rose from the pit of his stomach and burst into his heart.

It wasn't quite the same – there was a putrescence to this one that he didn't recall – but it was undercut by the same sickly sweetness. It hung ominously in the air, like a spirit. Behind him, Barry heard Lee retching on the landing.

They found him in the lounge, sitting on the floor with his back against a threadbare sofa. He was motionless, like a movie still; his head thrown back, eyes wide open in a ferocious and unforgiving stare. But his mouth was gaping wide in a look that was almost blissful. The scene took Barry back to his days at Dudley Art College; with his hoodie up, the body reminded Barry of Bernini's *Ecstasy of Saint Teresa*. But there was no angel and no shaft of light from heaven, only a corpse with what looked suspiciously like drug paraphernalia at his side – a spoon, some foil, a cheap lighter and a small black case. An empty Jim Beam bottle lay disconsolately on the floor a few feet away. There may have been no angel, but there was a spear, and it was sticking out of a lifeless arm.

Barry was transported back thirty years to Dr Potter's Understanding Religious Art class. He remembered St Teresa's description of her encounter with a spear-wielding angel:

"The pain was so great, that it made me moan; and yet so surpassing was the sweetness of this excessive pain, that I could not wish to be rid of it."

It probably wasn't all that different to what had been going through Chris' mind at the point that he'd stuck the needle in his arm. *It's funny the things that come back into your mind at the points of greatest stress in your life,* thought Barry.

"Well I never," said Molloy, "Chris Malford. I thought he'd given all this up. Just goes to show…" He didn't finish the sentence, but the implication was clear.

Barry was never one to succumb to fatalism about human nature. He liked to believe that people could change, could overcome their demons and improve themselves. He'd always seen Chris Malford as one of the proofs of that theory. It was fifteen years since he'd taken a chance on Chris, and had offered him a flat and some support in dealing with his drug problem. There'd been plenty of people who'd said he shouldn't have bothered; that 'people like that' were more trouble than they were worth. Admittedly, Chris' life had not been a straight line of success, but the one thing that Barry had held on to amidst all the ups and downs was that at least he had stayed clean and stayed alive, neither of which were givens when he first turned up at The Solihull Homeless Young People's Project looking for help. And yet, now, here he was: dead with a needle in his arm. Apparently, it did indeed "just go to show".

Barry felt defeated, like a little piece of him had died. *We hang on to our triumphs by so little,* he thought, *yet the grip of our failures is so firm and unrelenting.* And, in that moment, he felt the full sadness of knowing that.

"OK, Bones. Let's get this sorted," said Molloy. "Have you had to deal with one of these before? I can't remember."

"No. It's been mainly break-ins and anti-social behaviour so far."

"Right, well, we really ought to treat this as a potential crime scene," he said in the manner of someone who regarded such procedural niceties as tiresome, "so the whole area has to be kept clear of contamination. Get some police incident tape from the car and put it across the front door, would you? I'll radio for paramedics so they can confirm the poor sod's really dead."

"What about forensics?"

"Probably be good practice. But, to be honest, I don't think they're gonna find anything to indicate a crime, so it's just a matter of whether they've got anyone free. In the meantime, everyone has to stay out; nothing in, nothing out. Although it's pretty obvious what's happened, we don't want to get on the wrong side of the coroner's office, and we don't want to give them any reason to send it back to us." He fixed Gemma with a hard stare. "This is a straight 'death by misadventure' – got that?"

"Are you sure? I mean, they always taught us we shouldn't jump to conclusions."

Molloy sighed the kind of sigh that was only possible after eighteen years of following procedures that you felt were largely a waste of time. "That might be what they taught you at Hendon, Bones, but that don't mean it's true. I'm telling you, I know a 'death by misadventure' when I see one, and this is definitely a 'death by misadventure'. One hundred per cent. So we can get this one off our desks straight away and on to the coroner where it belongs."

"I guess we'll still have to inform the next of kin though, won't we?"

"You're joking, aren't you? I've nicked this guy before. He was in care," said Molloy, as though that explained everything. "Mother dead of an overdose. Dad not even on the birth certificate. No siblings."

Barry knew from his dealings with Chris over the years that PC Molloy was right. Chris Malford had been released from council care on his sixteenth birthday with only a named social worker for company. He had a solicitor, a probation officer and a tenuous link with a resettlement worker at the prison, but he didn't have a family or even a reliable friend.

"I'm sorry," said Lee, after checking the tenancy file on his tablet, "but we don't seem to have a next of kin on record."

Molloy's face broke out into what looked suspiciously like a half-smile. "Told you. We can pass this one on to social services to sort out. Go and get that tape would you, Bones?"

Gemma dutifully headed back to the car.

Barry felt, not for the first time that day, deflated. The lack of a next of kin meant that responsibility for arranging Christian Malford's funeral would indeed fall to social services. They dealt with the funerals of all the unwanted and the unloved, but, unfortunately, this was generally not a quick process. However, it was only when they were satisfied that there was no next of kin who could inherit the tenancy that they would issue the official notification allowing it to be terminated. Until then, Monument had to keep charging rent, but the council's housing benefit team would have no obligation to pay it, so the reality was that Monument would lose several weeks of rental income on flat twelve. Barry shuddered at the thought of Langley's reaction. It was, he felt sure, the kind of anachronism that would not have been tolerated at Debenhams.

Gemma returned from her brief visit back to the car with the tape. "I'm afraid we're going to have to seal the scene up now," she said.

Barry took one last look around the flat. He wanted to see what the condition of the property was and how much it was likely to cost to get it back into a lettable condition. He stopped at the bedroom door and looked in. Loneliness hung over the room like a pall: an unmade single bed, next to which there was a small cairn of scrunched-up tissues partially obscuring the cover of a porn mag. Drawing pins held up an old sheet at the window. Some clothes hung disconsolately from a bar across an alcove. And there was a second-hand dresser.

Chris had never struck Barry as a particularly organised person, but there was a filing system of sorts on the dresser. Barry wandered over out of curiosity, to see if there was anything that might help social services to speed up the whole process. Chris' most recent rent statements, along with a number of other personal papers, were all shoved rather roughly in and around a single box file. It would probably be quite useful, mused Barry. After all, it also appeared to contain bank statements and a number of other things that would probably help social services discharge their duties more quickly.

Barry knew, of course, that he should just leave them all on the dresser. But it was entirely possible that the police wouldn't be finished in the flat for a week or more – during which time rent would continue to be due, housing benefit payments would stop and social services would be unable (and not just unwilling) to progress matters.

If, however, social services had access to Chris Malford's papers (and could see for themselves that he had a grand total of £8.52 in his bank account) it might 'focus minds' on shutting down the tenancy quickly and getting the flat cleared of his personal possessions. However…

"We really ought to treat this as a potential crime scene." That's what PC Molloy had said. "Nothing in, nothing out." That included the box file, presumably, so Barry understood that he really should just leave it *in situ*. Any other course of action, however well intentioned, could technically be seen as a crime.

But, of course, the police hadn't seen the box file and so would have no reason to know it had been removed, which was perhaps why Barry then did something that he would never have dreamt of doing normally. Something that, if he'd caught Lee doing it, would have led to his instant dismissal. Barry tidied up all of the papers and tucked the box file under his arm. He then walked along the corridor toward the front door of the flat. The two police officers remained in the lounge on their radios, summoning assistance.

Barry popped his head – and only his head – round the door. "Right, well, I'd better get off then. Just drop the keys round to our offices when you've finished everything."

Molloy lifted an arm to indicate Barry was OK to leave, whilst trying to continue a conversation with someone back at the station. So Barry sauntered out of the flat and into the lobby where Lee was waiting, all the time thinking to himself – as if trying to force the idea into his mind – that as long as no one knew what he'd done then nothing could go wrong.

He had almost reached the stairs when he heard footsteps behind him.

"Excuse me! Hold on a minute!" PC Rathbone called. Barry felt his heart perform an adroit somersault and leap into his mouth. He felt like a nine-year-old caught in a teacher's glare.

"Have you got a business card I can have? I just need to check your names and contact details so we can include them in our report."

"Oh, of course. Sorry. I'm Barry Todd and this is Lee Marston. My details are on my card," said Barry, fishing a business card out of his jacket with his one free arm with as much nonchalance as he could manage under the circumstances.

PC Rathbone seemed placated. “That’s great. We’ll be in touch if we need anything,” she said, before turning and heading back into the flat.

Barry paused for a moment. He felt his heart slowly unfurl and return to his chest.

It was odd. Barry had never knowingly broken the rules before – he was one of the good guys, after all. And yet, without even trying that hard, he’d completely out-foxed the police. It felt strangely liberating, but at the same time disconcerting. After all, if he could pull the wool over the police’s eyes that easily without really thinking about it, what could he achieve if he actually set his mind to it? Barry didn’t answer that question, but it did flit through his mind for the briefest of moments.

He didn’t consider himself to have done anything criminal though. Not really. That was at the end of a very long road. But it was a road down which he was now inadvertently travelling.

THREE

Despite Barry's best intentions, he eventually arrived back at home much later than usual. The Todds' home was a modest affair on a 1980s estate of houses that had been designed with more thought for the developer's financial return than for visual appeal. Row upon row of red-brick houses sat neatly, like well-behaved schoolchildren; each primped and primed by successive owners to try to give them that most elusive of architectural properties: character. And so leaded, wood-effect, uPVC windows sat rather awkwardly with the occasional mock-Tudor beam to try to suggest historicity. Yet the day that they'd bought their home had been the proudest day of Barry's life. Moving from Dudley to a resolutely middle-class suburb like Walmley had felt to him like joining a club that he'd often read about, but never dared dream of joining. Of course, his dad didn't see it like that. He thought it was Barry leaving his roots behind; getting ideas above his station. But Barry had wanted to believe that Walmley was his station. And as he looked at the house from the drive, with its 'Hansel and Gretel' window shutters, he realised with a certain despondency that, twenty-one years on, he still wanted to.

"You're late," his wife pointed out from the lounge sofa, as he entered the hallway.

"Yeah, sorry, but I'm here now," he said, poking his head around the lounge door. As it had done every day for the last three years, a large, decorative candle burnt mutely on the hearth next to a photo of Christopher. It was meant to be a memorial, but it felt like an indictment.

"I've done you some tea. It's in the oven. I've used the last of that mince up."

"Great. Thanks," Barry replied, making his way through to the kitchen. He retrieved his meal from the oven and grabbed a beer from the fridge, with which to nurse the day's wounds. He then sat down with a heavy thud at the dining-room table. The high-backed leather chair let out a sigh and slowly relented under the force of Barry's buttocks.

"We've had a letter from the bank," his wife called through.

"What does it say?"

"I don't know. I've not read it."

"I'll read it after I've had my tea."

She waited a beat before saying, "It looks important."

"OK. I'll have a look after I've had my tea," Barry repeated.

"It's got '*Important Information Enclosed*' on the envelope." There was a pause. "It's from the mortgage people, I think," she said. "It says '*Mortgage Department*' on the back anyway."

"I'll come and have a look when I've eaten this."

"We're not in arrears, are we?"

Barry sighed. "No, but you can open it yourself if you don't believe me. It'll be addressed to both of us."

"I don't like to. You deal with all that stuff."

"OK. Just give me five minutes."

There was a further pause, during which Barry heard his wife rise from the sofa. A few seconds later she was next to him, holding the envelope. "I'm worried, Barry. What if they've found out about my redundancy?"

"We don't have to tell them every time we've had a change in circumstances. We only have to tell them if it's something that means we can't make the payments. And we *can* make the payments. We *are* making the payments."

Barry tried to concentrate on eating his tea, but the room was held in a silence that was straining to be broken. He could tell from the way she stood motionless at his shoulder, holding the letter, that she wanted to spray him with anxious words, but was fighting to hold them back, like they were a dog on a leash.

"I'd hate to think we were in arrears," she said eventually. Vermeer's *Girl with a Pearl Earring* stared down at him from the dining-room wall. It had been one of Barry's favourite paintings, but now even her gentle gaze felt as though it was accusing him.

Barry put his knife and fork down. "Give it here."

He took the letter from her and opened it roughly. As predicted, the letter was not to advise them that they were in arrears. But if this news was welcome, the letter's actual contents were less so. It was advising the Todds that the special, discounted, fixed-rate period of their mortgage had now come to an end, so, from the following month, their mortgage payments would be increasing.

"You see, we're not in arrears," he said, offering her the letter to read. "They're just telling us the discount's come to an end."

"Oh. Well, that's OK," she said, wandering back to the lounge, leaving the letter in Barry's outstretched hand.

"Have you heard about that job yet?" she called through. "The extra money would be useful if they're putting the payments up."

Barry paused. "No, we've not been told anything," he called through, before feeling the need to add, "Not officially."

"And there's Lauren's maintenance to pay for too. That's starting this month. You've not forgotten have you?"

The pause that Barry left was just fractionally too long for his subsequent denial to be convincing. His wife returned from the lounge considerably more quickly than she had departed toward it.

"It's so she can eat while she's at university, Barry!" she said in response to his blank look. "We discussed it. Over the summer. Remember?"

Barry did have a faint recollection of Lauren and her mum spending a lot of time online doing various calculations after her A-level results came through. He was also vaguely aware that he had been presented with the results of their research, but he hadn't really been paying attention because he had assumed that it wouldn't be a problem. Unfortunately, he had assumed it wouldn't be a problem because he had also assumed he would get the housing director job – and with it a hefty salary increase.

"Oh yeah, of course... How much was it again?"

"Now that I'm not working it's only two hundred a month."

Barry started. "How much?"

"Two hundred a month."

"What, *every* month? For three years?"

"Yes! Assuming you don't want her to starve."

"Of course I don't. But two hundred a month... on top of the mortgage going up."

"It's so she can eat, Barry!"

Barry sighed in acknowledgement of the superior force of her argument. "Look, I'll sort her money out when I've heard about the job. Officially."

"But you're still confident?"

"I'm absolutely confident I'm the best candidate for the job," was as much as he felt comfortable saying. And, with that, Barry went back to eating his meal alone.

He didn't like lying to her, but sometimes he felt the need to protect her from the truth. He meant it as a kindness. Like her smartphone, she carried her worries around with her all the time and constantly checked to make sure they were still there. Which is why, when she did eventually think to ask him how his day had gone, Barry decided that the most loving thing to say was simply, "Fine."

Barry got into work early the next day. He knew that at some point he would probably get called into a meeting with Langley, so he decided to grasp the nettle and pop up to see his new boss himself. He thought Langley was likely to appreciate his proactivity.

"Enter!" came a sonorous voice from within, in response to Barry's knock on the door. Barry took his cue and walked in, carefully fixing a smile of vinegary goodwill onto his face before doing so.

"Barry! To what do I owe this pleasure?"

The pot plant had gone, Barry noticed, along with the framed photo of Karen, Langley's predecessor, surrounded by the whole housing team at the previous year's Housing Heroes awards. In their place was a selection of management handbooks and a photo of Langley receiving his MBA certificate. But the biggest change was Langley himself. There was a different air about him. He sat on his seat, straight-backed and carefully poised, like it was a throne.

"Just wanted to congratulate you on the new job, Langley, and wish you all the best."

"Thank you, Barry. Umm… do you have an appointment? I didn't see one in my diary…" Langley quickly checked the online diary on his PC.

"Err… no. No, I don't. I just thought I'd swing by. 'My door is always open'; that's what Karen used to say."

Langley's face didn't flicker. "Did she really? Well, I am not Karen. I shall be establishing new disciplines for my team. Perhaps you could make an appointment with Diana on your way out?"

"Oh, right. OK. I'll just go then, shall I?"

"If you don't mind. I was hoping to catch the finance team first thing this morning. Which reminds me, is there a reason why you and Maxine get company cars, but none of the other area managers do?" Langley leant forward on his desk and steepled his fingers, a look of wry amusement carved into his face. "It's just that I've been asked to try to find some savings and I'm sure I'll get asked about it."

There was a reason, of course, which Langley knew perfectly well. When Barry had first been appointed as area housing manager, they'd all been given cars on the not-unreasonable grounds that the job required a lot of travel. Of course, it had been one of the first things that Andrew had targeted when he'd become chief executive, and so as old managers had gone, the car had been removed as part of the remuneration package for the new managers, until only Barry and Maxine still had one.

When Langley had been an area housing manager, he'd argued that if one manager got a car, they all should. Now that he had been elevated to the exec team, however (and therefore got a shiny new car anyway), he seemed to be arguing exactly the opposite.

Barry wanted to explain, but he couldn't. He knew from the look Langley gave him that there was nothing he could say. He might as well have been standing behind a huge glass wall because, no matter what he said or how loudly he shouted, Langley would never hear him. Part of him had dared to believe that the Langley of reality could not possibly be as fearsome as the Langley of his imaginings. But there he sat, his slim waist and skinny-fit shirt seemingly taunting Barry like a schoolchild, whilst his small black eyes fixed him in an emotionless stare, apparently impervious to reason or emotion.

It felt ridiculous to be intimidated. After all, Langley was practically young enough to be his son. God, his son.

"Words cannot express..." that's what people used to say. And they were right, they couldn't. Words were leaky enough vessels at the best of times without having to bear the weight of such emotion. All you could do was feel it, like a branding iron being held permanently to your heart. There was no explaining. There was just a howl of pain that went on for so long even Barry grew tired of it.

But what does Langley know of these things? Barry thought. *What does he know of pain and regret? What could he possibly know about the feeling of failure – that special feeling of failure that you get when you fail to meet the needs of your family?* But Barry had no desire to antagonise his boss, so he just muttered something about the car always having been part of his package and shuffled out, apologetically, back to his desk.

It still seemed inconceivable, though, that he would ever betray Langley. Barry would certainly have been happy to see Langley face the sack, but not for something he hadn't done, and certainly not for something Barry himself had done.

But, of course, things change. And people change too.

FOUR

"Barry! Sorry to bother you, but Iulia Nicolescu's here. Would you mind…?"

Barry had barely had time to sit back down at his desk when Lucy called over to him. Given that they were going to be discussing Iulia's imminent eviction and the situation could therefore best be described as 'potentially volatile', Barry could understand why Lucy was keen to have her manager in the interview room with her.

"OK, Luce," Barry said. "Let's see what she's got to say for herself. I know we got a possession order five weeks ago – is there anything else I need to know?"

"Have you seen the file?" Lucy lifted up a huge doorstop of a file – at least seven inches thick.

"Is there a short version?"

"Basically, she's Romanian, but she's not got proof of six months' paid work, so, since the rules for EU nationals changed in April, she's not been entitled to benefits," Lucy explained as they walked toward the interview room. "I'm sympathetic, obviously, but the fact is housing benefit are adamant she's not entitled and hasn't been for the past six months. They stopped her claim four months ago and they've claimed back the previous two months as an overpayment."

"Which they're perfectly entitled to do."

"She's made a few odd payments since then – presumably she's had bits and bobs of casual work – but she's still nearly two and half grand in debt, with no realistic chance of paying it off. I know it's a horrible thing to say, but she's got to go."

Barry knew that Lucy was right. A tenant with huge debts and no means to clear them, let alone pay the rent going forward, was not a viable tenant. But whilst, according to Monument's current policies, Lucy was absolutely correct in her rather blunt assessment of the situation, Barry couldn't help thinking that this wasn't what Neville and the local churches that had founded Monument all those years ago had set it up to do.

The interview room was a small, joyless space with no natural light. Whilst it made a few concessions to the concept of hospitality – padding on the seats, a small crate of half-broken toys in the corner for children to play with – its main talent lay in emphasising to tenants, through posters, notices and CCTV cameras, the consequences of any misbehaviour on their part.

"Good morning, Miss Nicolescu. I'm Mr Todd, the area housing manager, and you know Miss Hampton, of course. I understand you're here about your eviction notice."

The first thing that struck him was not how pretty she was but how her deep, brown eyes seemed to contain a certain Slavic sorrowfulness that undercut that prettiness. Despite her youthful years, Iulia's face spoke of a premature disappointment with the petty cruelties and compromises that life had visited upon her.

"Yes," she replied in heavily accented English, "but you have to understand – you cannot evict me. I have nowhere to go. Please, please – you must help me."

Oh dear, thought Barry. *She hasn't realised.* He hated it when people didn't realise. He had hoped that her sorrowfulness was because she was bowing to the inevitable, but she still seemed to be labouring under the delusion that Monument's charitable status might somehow provide her with some protection from the basic economic realities of the situation. In such circumstances, Barry had learnt that the best tactic was simply to let people talk through their situation for as long as they wanted until they eventually realised themselves just how hopeless it was.

"Why don't you tell us how we've got to this situation?" Barry suggested. "And, at the end, we'll see where we think that leaves us."

Iulia Nicolescu was, it transpired, a young woman from rural Romania with big dreams, who had one day been approached by a man who offered to take her to England. There would be no charge for her transport, and board and lodging would be provided, at his expense, whilst she found work. There was, he assured her, plenty of work in England – far more than in Romania – and it was far better paid too. She could pay him for her board and lodging out of her salary (along with a small contribution to help clear her original travel and accommodation costs) and the rest of the money would be hers to do with as she pleased. It all sounded almost too good to be true. Which indeed it was, as Iulia had discovered upon her arrival in Birmingham, where she had had her mobile phone and passport taken off her, and was locked up in a house and forced to have sex with as many men as she could (as were several other women who had been duped along similar lines).

Eventually, she had managed to escape and had told the police of her plight. The house had been raided; the men were arrested and ultimately sent to prison – thanks, in large part, to Iulia's testimony. In return for her bravery, Iulia was allowed to stay in England and was even provided with a flat by Monument in the comparative backwater of Coleshill.

Sadly, however, in the previous budget statement, the government had announced that they would be removing EU nationals' entitlement to housing benefit unless they were able to demonstrate that they had been working legitimately in the country for at least six months previously. Unfortunately for Iulia, her previous position had not been subject to tax and National Insurance deductions, so it counted for nought when it came to calculating her housing benefit entitlement. Consequently, Iulia was now two and a half thousand pounds in debt and that amount was going up each week as her rent continued to be charged.

"But I cannot go back to Romania," she said, almost in tears. "The men… the men who brought me here… they are there. I sent them to prison. They are looking for me already. I cannot go back, I cannot."

Barry saw in her face the haunted look of someone who knew the pain of living and knew it from the inside. It made him want to reach across the table that lay between them and hold her in a silent, tender embrace, just so she knew that he understood that pain too. Sadly, Monument's professional boundaries policy did not allow for such moments of grace, but he knew that things were not going to be as simple as he'd hoped.

"In housing for good." Monument's strapline stared down accusingly at him from a poster on the wall.

"I can see the difficulty of your situation, Miss Nicolescu. But you need to understand that we can't just let your debt carry on going up. That's not helping anyone," Barry said. "Have you got any support? Is there anyone – or perhaps a group – that can offer you advice?"

"I took a phone call the other day asking us if we had any Romanian nationals who needed help because of the benefit changes," Lucy said. "The Romanian Migrants Welfare Association, I think they were called. They might be able to help."

Iulia's eyes flared with alarm. "You must never tell them where I am! They are looking for me. They are looking to take me back to those men – the men who will kill me! Promise me you won't!"

"Well, obviously, we won't pass on your details without your consent; I promise you that," Barry reassured her. "But we need to see some money – soon. We need to see that debt going down. Is there anything you can do?"

"I have some money." Iulia took a battered brown envelope out of her jacket pocket and withdrew £400 in used bank notes. "It is not everything I owe, but it is all I have."

She was weeping now.

"Have you got work now, Miss Nicolescu?" Lucy asked, hopefully. "If you have proof of a clear source of income to pay your rent, we can reach an agreement to pay the debt."

Iulia looked Barry squarely in the eye and said deliberately, "I will do anything – *anything* – to stay in this country. I cannot go back." At which point she broke down in tears.

And so it was agreed. Lucy took the money and gave it to the cashier on reception. Barry agreed that he would hold off requesting that the court issue an eviction date for as long as Iulia continued to pay her rent every week, plus a contribution toward the arrears.

"Are you sure we've done the right thing?" Lucy asked as they headed back to their desks. "I mean, we've got no entitlement to benefit and no proof of income."

The simple answer was no, Barry wasn't sure. They had certainly not acted in accordance with Monument's policy and procedure, which, as Lucy had correctly pointed out, required them to have some proof on file of a realistic ability and intention to pay the debt before an eviction was stayed. Things could get messy if Iulia reneged on the agreement now.

"I won't tell Langley if you don't," was all he could muster in reply.

The fact was he had a horrible feeling about where that £400 had come from, and he had an even more horrible feeling about how Langley would react if he found out what Barry had just sanctioned. Yet, for all of that, it still felt like the right thing to do. Whatever the implications, Barry knew that he couldn't send her back to Romania. He was, after all, *"In housing for good."*

FIVE

When Barry returned to his desk, his attention was caught by two emails from Angela. The first was just confirming in writing what she'd told him in person the day before – he hadn't got the director's job. The second, however, was something altogether more interesting. It was headed *"Organisational Restructure: The Next Phase"*. Barry's heart sank as he read the opening paragraphs of the email, which contained all the old favourites of management-speak – *"tough operating conditions"*, *"continuing challenges"*, *"regulatory pressures"* and, of course, *"the need to focus resources on the front line"*.

But then Barry noticed something in the email that potentially offered him a way out. Yes, the exec team was looking to reduce the overall headcount of the association – but they were looking, in the first instance, to see if they could reduce it through voluntary redundancies. And so,

Angela was emailing to advise staff of Monument's intention to conduct a VR trawl. Suddenly Barry's spirits soared.

Barry was forty-eight. His salary was just over £45,000 per year. He'd been at Monument twenty-two years. Within Monument's VR policy, which didn't cap your eligible earnings or your eligible service when calculating your entitlement, all of these were good things.

Barry quickly got out his calculator and did some rough maths. It produced a figure of £22,000. By happy coincidence, this was slightly more than the outstanding balance on the Todds' mortgage.

He paused for a moment and took it in. There was no doubt that the thought of walking out of Monument without another job to go to was daunting. But the facts were that, firstly, he would be mortgage free, and, secondly, there were plenty of other housing associations in the West Midlands, all of which would be able to offer him the one thing that Monument couldn't – a workplace free of Langley Burrell.

And, in the meantime, perhaps he could pick up his art again. He decided there and then that, once his cheque came through, he would use the modest surplus to buy himself an easel and some oils, and paint a few canvasses.

He quickly scanned the email looking for instructions as to what to do next. At the end it said *"Decisions on whether to accept individual VR applications will be taken according to the needs of the business. But if you are interested in being considered, please complete the attached Expression of Interest form and return it to me by close of business next Friday."*

The other thirty-eight emails can wait, thought Barry; this was the one he intended to prioritise.

He immediately went upstairs to try to catch Angela. He wanted a bit of clarity on how decisions about the VR applications might be made and also about what his rights might be in respect of the withdrawal of his company car. But, before he could reach the people investment team, he was stopped by Saleema Bhatti. Saleema had reached that indeterminate age at which she appeared to regard it as compulsory to wear a crew-neck cardigan irrespective of the weather (although Barry also recognised that Saleema's choice may have been driven by the fact that her seat was underneath one of the vents for the comfort cooling system). With her knee-length, plaid skirt and a gold cross prominently displayed around her neck, she appeared to be affecting the look of a middle-aged widow walking home from Evensong through the pages of a Miss Marple novel.

"Barry, good morning to you. I was wondering if you could just check through the invoice for The SHYPP for me, before I send it out. I think I've got it right this time, but I could do with you having a look before it goes."

"I'm sorry, Saleema, but I just need to catch Angela first. I'll speak to you on my way back."

"Did I hear my name being mentioned in vain?" Barry was relieved to hear a familiar voice behind him and turned to address Angela directly. He was immediately deflated, however, to see that she had her coat on and was striding purposefully toward the exit.

"I'm sorry, but I've got a meeting at our solicitor's this morning. You'll have to try to catch me later, Barry."

"Perfect!" Saleema said. "It'll only take five minutes. I think I've done it right this time, but I just want to check with you. You know what Sally's like."

Barry did indeed know what Sally was like. And knowing what Sally Hedges was like meant he understood why Saleema didn't want to get the invoice wrong again. Indeed, the fact that an invoice was necessary at all was simply because of 'what Sally was like'.

The whole idea for what was to become The Solihull Homeless Young People's Project had first come to Sally almost twenty years previously. She'd wanted to develop a scheme for homeless young people in the north of Solihull and had taken her vision to Neville Thompson at Monument, whom she knew through various mutual church contacts.

They'd quickly found a derelict youth centre that had been closed a few years previously, which fitted the bill perfectly. The council had agreed to gift the site to them, but only on the understanding that the finished scheme would be run by an organisation based within the borough – which Monument wasn't.

The argument went round for a couple of years until Sally had the inspired idea of setting up a separate charity based in Solihull that could enter into a management agreement with Monument to manage the scheme on their behalf. And so The SHYPP Trust was born with Sally as its chief executive and its registered office in Solihull.

Everyone was happy. Except, as it happened, Monument, which, following Neville's departure, found themselves having a management agreement with a tiny charity run by a very annoying woman, in order to operate a housing scheme that they were perfectly capable of running themselves on a much cheaper basis. But, despite their best attempts to find a way around it, their legal advice was that they were stuck with the management agreement unless they moved their head office (and they couldn't do that because they'd already promised to maintain their head office in Kingsbury as part of a separate agreement with a different local authority).

So, although The SHYPP was owned by Monument, it was The SHYPP Trust who actually managed it on a day-to-day basis. It was they who collected the rent, took off a generous management fee and then paid the balance to Monument. But they only did that last part on production of a valid quarterly invoice, and, since the first phase of the latest organisational restructure, the task of producing that invoice had fallen to Saleema – who, unfortunately, had made rather a hash of producing her first one, despite Barry's attempts to explain in advance how the invoice sum was to be calculated. Three months on (and following an email tongue-lashing from Sally), Saleema wanted to be absolutely sure that the next quarterly invoice was right first time.

Within five minutes Barry had talked Saleema through the process and had produced a 'rent due' figure of £43,836 onto which had to be added repair costs of £4,747, giving a total quarterly invoice of £48,583. This had just been generated on the system when Barry heard an instantly recognisable nasal whine walking toward him, and detected the merest hint of sulphur in the air.

"Ah, Saleema, just who I was looking for. Marvellous."

"Oh, hello, Langley," Saleema said cheerily. "Lovely to see you – and congratulations on the new job!"

"Thank you. It's handy I've caught the both of you, actually," he said with just the slightest hint of menace. His rigorous personal training regime meant he carried himself with the taut expectancy of a wound spring. Even his clipped hair was coiled, as if waiting to pounce into action.

"We appear to be missing the quarter two payment from The SHYPP."

"We're just raising the invoice now, Langley."

"But we're in the third week of October. You mean to tell me that we haven't even issued an invoice for July, August and September yet?"

"The thing is, Langley," Barry said, "the management agreement stipulates that we can only invoice quarterly in arrears, so the account will always be behind."

"*Payment is due* quarterly in arrears, yes," said Langley, pointedly making the distinction, "but, as it happens, I've just checked the management agreement and it says nothing about when we can invoice. Unless you can point me in the direction of a clause that I've missed?" he asked, waving a sheaf of papers in Barry's direction.

This had been said with a large dollop of sarcasm, which almost certainly meant that, much to Barry's horror, Langley had actually read the agreement. This was probably because Langley had made no secret of his belief that The SHYPP should be brought under Monument's own management in order to save money, and now that he was housing director he was clearly determined to do just that.

It occurred to Barry that there might be one way in which Monument could legally cancel the management agreement, and that was if The SHYPP Trust was deemed to have breached it. Barry suspected, therefore, that Langley was hoping he could find a way to argue that The SHYPP had failed to meet the payment terms set out in the agreement, so that he could justify giving them notice. But, of course, this would require Monument to have issued an invoice in the first place.

"We're now three weeks into quarter three and the invoice for quarter two hasn't even been issued – is that what you're telling me?"

"Sorry. Yes. That's the situation," said Barry, "but if I could just—"

Barry sensed that Langley was about to cut across him with a statement about the acceptability, or otherwise, of this state of affairs to a company such as Debenhams, when Saleema cut in first.

"As far as I'm aware, we've always invoiced it this way and no one's complained. Obviously, if you want it done differently, then just let me know and I'm sure we'll be happy to oblige."

There was a brief pause during which Barry thought, for the slightest moment, that that might be the end of it, before Langley added, "And why do we include repairs on the quarterly invoice? That's not part of the management agreement. Surely we should be invoicing for repairs as we complete them? Or at least monthly. There's no reason for us to be waiting that long for the money."

"Well, because that's what Sally agreed with Neville fifteen years ago," Barry replied. "That she'd be invoiced for repairs quarterly in arrears, along with the rent."

It was, as Barry had always recognised, an arrangement designed to ease The SHYPP Trust's cash flow. There was no advantage for Monument from this arrangement, but it went back to a time when Monument was quite happy to help a smaller organisation out – even at their own expense. It was only now someone like Langley had arrived in the picture that the whole arrangement began to sound faintly ridiculous.

With this – and his VR package – in mind, Barry decided that the best course of action would simply be to agree to whatever Langley wanted. Barry felt no particular moral imperative to protect Sally Hedges and her synthetic organisation if it gave his new boss any reason to block his twenty-two grand payout.

"How would you like it to be done?" he asked.

"Well, we should issue the quarterly invoice twenty-eight days before the end of the quarter, with our usual twenty-eight-day payment terms. That's what the management agreement specifies. Is that clear?"

"As crystal," Barry replied. What was also crystal clear was that Sally would not like getting (and therefore being obliged to pay) her rental invoice six weeks earlier than had been the customary practice. Indeed, given The SHYPP's generally hand-to-mouth existence, Barry supposed that it was entirely possible that they might struggle to meet the new payment deadline. But that, of course, was precisely what Langley was banking on. Sally would almost certainly create an almighty stink in any event, but, as Barry didn't intend to be around for much longer, this was a consequence he was quite happy to live with.

"I'll make sure that's what happens in future," Saleema said.

"And, for goodness' sake, get this quarter's invoice out now. They'll be in breach in a matter of days – but I can't do anything about it unless we've actually invoiced them!"

SIX

Barry had promised Langley that the invoice to The SHYPP Trust would go out immediately. But no sooner had he done so than Ruth, Monument's finance director, had put a halt to the issuing of any further invoices until creditors had been advised of a change to Monument's banking details.

Barry well understood the reasons for this. The issue was that, as Monument had merged with other housing associations, it had begun to inherit bank accounts from them. As is often the way, tenants (and housing benefit departments) had grown used to paying their rent monies into these accounts, and so it always seemed more trouble than it was worth to shut them down. That was until the previous financial controller had worked out that having five separate bank accounts provided ample opportunity to create confusion in any event, and for this confusion to be used to cover up what was subsequently described by Andrew (in his beautifully understated email to staff explaining why the auditors were now on site, whereas the financial controller wasn't) as "*intentional fiscal leakage from the organisation*".

This had brought matters to a head, and, once the dust had settled, Ruth had agreed with Monument's regulator to reduce the number of accounts.

But the fact that Barry understood the reasons didn't mean he agreed with Ruth's decision. He didn't want Langley to be considering his VR application when he had signally failed to follow Langley's first management instruction to him.

"But Langley said he wants us to get the invoice out to The SHYPP urgently. And you agreed to do that," Barry said when Saleema had phoned him with the news.

"I'm sorry, but there's nothing I can do. Ruth says I've got to issue the notification letters first, but it shouldn't hold things up for too long. I've printed them all off and signed them already; they just need to be stuffed into envelopes and sent out. That will happen today. Then we can get the invoice out next week – I promise."

Barry sighed. "It's just that we did promise Langley—"

"I'm so sorry, Barry, but Ruth has said we can't short circuit the process for Langley or anyone else. It's essential we get those notification letters out first. It's for fraud prevention, she said, so I'm sure Langley will understand."

In due course, the irony of a fraud-prevention measure turning a previously unthinkable fraud into an eminently thinkable one would not be lost on Barry. But, as he hung up, other matters were in the forefront of his mind.

He'd been vaguely aware of raised voices coming from Langley's office a few minutes previously; the kind that were causing people out in the open-plan office space to cast glances at each other. He couldn't hear exactly what was being said, but it appeared that Langley was unhappy about some recent Tweets that referred to his appointment as housing director, the contents of which would never have been tolerated at Debenhams, apparently. Monument's new offices had been decorated with beech and chrome in order to make them look as much as possible like the headquarters of any typical modern corporation. But mostly they were made of glass. Andrew had explained that this was to emphasise the transparency of the organisation. And, indeed, the large walls of windows flooded the open-plan floor space, where Barry and his colleagues had to sit, with a fiercely invading light. Everyone and everything could now be seen. Except, ironically, the exec team. The walls of their offices, although made wholly of glass, had been covered with swirls of frosting in order, Andrew had clarified, "to maintain appropriate privacy". So Barry could not actually see who it was that Langley was berating.

For her part, Langley's interlocutor appeared to be taking with considerably less equanimity than Barry the suggestion that her company car might be withdrawn.

Suddenly, the voices died down. Then the door to Langley's office opened and Barry – along with everyone else in the office – immediately looked up to see who it was who had dared to raise their voice to a member of the exec team.

It was Maxine. She was momentarily framed in the doorway, frozen for a second, before calmly walking away. Her face was fixed in an expressionless gaze that appeared to be trying to communicate dignity. Her head was lifted up high and she was rather obviously avoiding eye contact with anyone, but her deep-brown eyes were glazed as if she were fighting back tears. Her eyes had always seemed full of defiance, yet it seemed there was still room in them for hurt. Maxine was flanked by Angela, who was walking a couple of paces behind her right shoulder. She too was avoiding eye contact, but her eyes were cast down to the floor. A pool of silence spread across the floor. The two of them reached Maxine's desk where she stopped and turned to look at Angela, as though unsure what to do.

"Just take your coat and bag for now," said Angela calmly. "You can arrange to come back and collect your other things later."

Maxine reached down serenely, and took her bag from under her desk and the jacket from the back of her chair. She took her office key fob, ID badge and work mobile phone from out of her bag and left them on her desk. And then, wordlessly, she glided majestically toward the exit door like a luxury liner sailing out of a rather grubby dock. Angela followed, like a rather embarrassed little tugboat, conscious that the office had fallen into silence and was now staring in stunned disbelief at the scene unfolding before them.

As they passed the control panel of the comfort cooling system, Maxine stopped and, in a last act of petulant defiance, pointedly increased the temperature setting despite not being the appointed system monitor for that floor. The two of them reached the door and Maxine continued through it without a backward glance. A deathly hush had descended upon the whole office. No one said anything because no one knew what to say. Except Jean. Her deep, alto voice broke the silence.

"Maxine, wait!" Without a flicker of self-consciousness, Jean grabbed her coat and dashed out.

Angela quietly turned on her heels and walked back toward Langley's office, discreetly returning the temperature on the comfort cooling system back to its default setting as she did so.

Because of the swirls of frosting over the glass wall to Langley's office, Barry couldn't tell exactly what he was up to, but the gaps were just big enough for him to see Langley executing what looked suspiciously like a celebratory fist pump, followed by a rather awkward attempt at some samba moves. Under the circumstances, it seemed reasonable for Barry to conclude that Maxine had not left Monument's employment under the generous terms of their VR scheme.

She was the second-longest serving area housing manager (after Barry) and so she was the second-most expensive person in the housing department to get rid of. If even she could be given such short shrift, then Barry felt he had good cause to be worried about Langley's intentions. He thought about the unsent invoice and about his recently-concluded agreement with Iulia Nicolescu, and recognised that either might give Langley just the excuse he appeared to be looking for to frogmarch Barry out of the door without so much as paid notice. If he had indeed been tasked with saving money, there was twenty-two grand – plus the cost of Barry's car – that he could pocket straight away.

So whilst he felt sick for Maxine, most of all Barry felt sick for himself.

SEVEN

Barry made it to 4.30pm and decided that he'd probably done as much as he was going to do for that Friday. With Angela still apparently locked in conversation with Langley, there didn't seem a huge amount of point in hanging around to try to meet with her anymore, so he logged off his computer and headed to the exit.

As he walked across the floor, he noticed Jean coming back into the office. He was a manager and she was a housing assistant, so conversation about what could be construed as a 'management issue' might be awkward, but, on a purely human level, Barry was worried about Maxine and realised that, notwithstanding his feelings of general benevolence toward her, the only contact details he had for her was the number of the mobile phone that she had deposited on her desk so theatrically forty-five minutes previously. If nothing else, he wanted to know how Maxine was.

"Not good, I'm afraid," was Jean's immediate response. "She's hurting very badly, as you can imagine. It all happened very quickly. I don't think it's sunk in yet, and, if I'm honest, I think her anger is displacing her pain at the moment. I think she needs to sit with her pain a bit more rather than avoiding it. But then again, that's easy for me to say."

That was the thing that Barry liked about Jean – she had the capacity to talk about things in a way that nobody else he knew did. In fact, she could talk about things that nobody else seemed able to talk about, and do so without sounding ridiculous.

"I guess it must all have come as a bit of a shock," Barry said. "She wouldn't have been expecting it when she came in this morning."

"I think the problem was she wanted to win," said Jean. "She knows she probably should have gone a couple of years ago – got herself a fresh start somewhere else – but she wanted to beat them, and of course, you can't. Not when you're an employee. If you try to face them down publicly, they have to fight back to protect the organisation. It just becomes unmanageable if you win. I don't think Maxine quite understood that. The company always wins, doesn't it? It has to."

She was right, as usual. Monument had shot itself in the foot, but it wasn't that simple. There were subtleties to the situation that made it more complex than a simple 'her fault/their fault' dichotomy.

"But what about you, Barry? How are you? You must be pretty disappointed to have missed out on the director's job."

Barry was caught off-guard. He'd only really wanted to find out about Maxine. Fortunately, the last twenty-four hours had given him plenty of opportunity to deliver the short script he'd mentally prepared to deflect all such enquiries. "Well, obviously, you don't go for a job if you don't think you've got something to offer, but I always knew it was a bit of a long shot. So, yes, I am a little disappointed, but not altogether surprised. I've had other promotions in my time here, so I can't really complain, I suppose."

Jean looked at him deeply, her steely blue eyes peeking out from underneath her short, grey hair and piercing something in Barry's heart. She was lovely, but she couldn't stand insincerity or a lack of honesty. Barry couldn't believe she'd stayed at Monument as long as she had.

"That's not what I asked," she said.

"Well, y'know… You've just got to pick yourself up from these things, haven't you? It can't go your way all the—"

"It's all right. You don't have to tell me if you don't want to. I didn't mean to pry."

"It's not that, it's… well, y'know…"

"I just wanted to check that you're OK. And I just wanted you to know that I'm interested, even if no one else seems to be."

Barry felt himself welling up. It was a strange sensation because it was so uncommon for him to feel it in a work context, where feelings and emotions were generally deemed surplus to requirements. But Jean had drawn his attention to a slight crack in the huge dam that he had erected to hold back his emotions. For the first time since hearing the news, Barry became aware of the sheer weight of the emotion pushing against that dam.

"I'm getting over it," he said.

"I understand," Jean replied, and the way that she said it, Barry honestly believed that she did. "Just make sure that you don't let things fester. It's better to get it off your chest."

She shut down her computer and grabbed her jacket from the back of her chair. "Talk it through with your wife this weekend; you'll feel better for it, I promise. See you Monday!"

"See you," Barry called after her.

Talk it through with my wife? Barry mused. *How would that work?*

Thirty minutes later, Barry pulled up on his drive and let out a weary sigh. For most of his journey from Monument's office in Kingsbury to his home in Walmley, Barry had been cogitating on his conversation with Jean. It was as if what she had said had turned a key in a lock, and now he felt the need to open the door.

Hence the reason for the sigh. Because what Barry had realised was that he couldn't think of anyone with whom he could have that kind of conversation anymore. It just wasn't what he did.

Lauren had left for university four weeks ago, and so Barry had hoped he and his wife would have time for each other again; time to talk about the kind of things they'd talked about when they'd first met – their hopes, their dreams, their insecurities and perhaps even how they were feeling. But somehow, in the four weeks since they'd dropped their daughter off, Barry and his wife had never quite got round to having those kinds of chats. Since

Christopher's passing, their looks were always undergirded by a silent solemnity that seemed frightened to speak. And even during the momentary flashes of pleasure since then – Lauren's eighteenth birthday; her A-level results – Barry had noticed that his wife's smile had never seemed to tell the whole story. Her face still looked as though it were just waiting for the opportunity to return to its grief, as though even her shell of happiness had a sadness at its core; so he determined that now was the time to seek to engage his wife in meaningful conversation. She would, he imagined, be delighted at the prospect of rediscovering that magical spark in their marriage.

He made a decisive leap from his car (which was not easy for a man of his size) and strode purposefully toward the house. That evening the fire in the Todds' marriage would be reignited, Barry promised himself.

He entered the lounge to find his wife sitting on the sofa staring at her tablet. She appeared to be watching a video of a cat.

"I'm home!" said Barry with unusual vigour.

His wife's gaze didn't move. "Hullo," she replied.

Silence followed. This was not an uncommon reaction to Barry entering a room, so he was neither surprised nor unduly deflated by it. He recognised that it would require a certain amount of effort to win his wife over to the possibilities now open to them in their post-Lauren weekends. He wondered if he should have bought flowers, and thought that he probably should have. But it was too late for that now; he would have to rely on his charm – the same charm with which he had won her over twenty-seven years ago at Dudley Art College.

"I wondered if you'd got any plans for the weekend?" Barry asked, sidling up to his wife on the sofa and slipping his arms around her waist, "Now that we've not got Lauren to chase after."

She removed Barry's arms from around her and stared straight at him, a look of panic in her eyes. "But she's coming back for the weekend."

"Coming back? We only dropped her off four weeks ago."

"Yes, and now she wants to come back. She's our daughter, Barry! And, anyway, aren't you worried about her?"

"Of course I am. But she's a grown adult now. She doesn't want to hang out with her parents. She's probably just coming back to sober up for a weekend, cadge some cash off us and get her washing done." As far as Barry could see, it was the only explanation that made sense.

"How could you say that? She's your daughter!"

"But don't you remember what we were like at that age?"

"I remember what *you* were like at that age – that's why I'm worried about her. I just hope she's not into drugs. She takes after you in things like that. Oh God, Barry. I couldn't cope if she was doing drugs. Anything but that, please God. I couldn't lose another one. Not to drugs."

"I'm sure she's smart enough not to do anything stupid. She'll find her own boundaries."

"But I don't want her to find her own boundaries. I want her to stay inside the boundaries we brought her up with – or, at least, the ones I did."

There was the echo of an accusation in her voice, but Barry was determined not to rise to it. It was an argument they'd never had, but which had lingered in her looks and skulked around the outskirts of every conversation. And it was an argument Barry didn't want to have because he suspected that he couldn't win it.

"I just thought it would be good for us to do something… y'know… together…"

"Well, we can do something together – together with Lauren."

"I didn't mean that; I meant together… just the two of us… Sorry."

Even as the words left his lips he realised how lame the very idea sounded. His wife's face changed from a look of simple horror to one of uncomprehending bafflement, mixed with faint disgust. "But why would we want to do that? Lauren'll be here."

In that moment, Barry realised that there was a queue for his wife's affections – and he was not at the head of it. He tried to think if there was some way in which he could stake a claim to at least a share of his wife's attention.

"Well, is she going to be here for the *whole* weekend?"

His wife shot him another glare. "I expect so. What am I saying? I hope so. I said we'd be delighted to see her. Perhaps I should have told her not to bother."

"That's not what I'm trying to say…" Indeed, it wasn't. What he was trying to say was that he now finally understood that he needed to share his frustrations with his wife. And then what he wanted to say was that he yearned to sweep her up in his arms and make mad, passionate love to her. Like he used to do when they were both younger. He'd thought that she would regard these as good things, but now he wasn't so sure.

"Anyway, I've got to clean the house. Look at it!" she said.

Barry cast his eye around the room. It all looked pretty tidy to him – or certainly tidy enough to host a visit from their daughter. Frankly, it was a good deal tidier than it had been when Lauren lived there and, Barry wagered, a good deal tidier than it would be after she'd been back for half an hour. He wanted to ask therefore, why was there this sudden need to tidy the house to accommodate her, but instead he tried to think of something less confrontational to say.

"That won't take the whole evening, surely? What about doing something together tonight? Just the two of us."

"Like what?" she said, her eyes narrowing.

"I dunno. I could get us a takeout; it'll save you having to cook again."

"But I've thawed the chicken out now."

This was clearly not going to be easy.

"Well, what do you fancy doing?"

"We could watch a DVD. I've got that David Attenborough box set we haven't watched."

Barry's face froze. He had indeed bought her a box set of David Attenborough DVDs for Christmas the previous year, and he had bought it precisely because she had suggested that she wanted to watch it. He should not, therefore, have been unduly surprised at her suggestion. But watching a DVD generally involved doing so in silence. It therefore precluded the possibility of engaging in the one thing that Barry wanted to engage in – conversation.

Nevertheless, he realised that it might have been unrealistic to expect his wife to change her patterns of engagement with him immediately. This was clearly going to be a long-term project. And the first stage of that project had to be to try to win her over to the idea that they should do things together again. If he could do that, then maybe, in time, the conversation would return. So, he realised that he shouldn't see acceding to her request as a defeat, but rather as a necessary short-term tactical retreat as part of a longer-term strategy of advancing toward his goal.

But, as the opening credits rolled and Sir David began intoning sagely about "the wonder and savagery of life on this planet", it certainly felt like a defeat.

EIGHT

Barry awoke early the next morning. Lauren's train was not due in until 11am, but, as he had no inclination to watch his wife finish cleaning the house and even less to help her do so, Barry got dressed and decided to head into Birmingham early. This would allow him some time to pop into Birmingham Museum and Art Gallery before Lauren's arrival.

The A38 was, as he had anticipated, as empty and uncluttered as their lounge was now that Lauren had moved out. Barry drove into the fists and fingers of the Birmingham skyline in barely twenty minutes, along sweeping boulevards that had been gently rinsed by early morning rain. He parked in the multistorey car park directly above Snow Hill station, the rather cold and clinically efficient 1987 building that had replaced the much-loved Edwardian building of his childhood. Barry looked at his watch: 9.50am. The museum and art gallery was only a ten-minute walk away. He could get there and back, and still have time for nearly an hour in the gallery before he had to meet Lauren. *Perfect*, he thought as he set off through the city centre, its thick and peppery air settling uncomfortably in his lungs.

The Victorian splendour of Birmingham Museum and Art Gallery came from an age that regarded public buildings as expressions of provincial civic pride. Yeoville Thomason's portico-fronted building, which in any other age would have been regarded as the zenith of municipal architecture, was actually designed merely as an extension to his earlier classical masterpiece, the Council House.

Every time Barry saw the museum and art gallery, he was struck by the sheer ambition of the whole thing. At a time when the city fathers were still struggling to ensure decent sanitation and street lighting were available to all, they thought nothing of building a majestic art gallery in the classical style, as though it was obvious that Birmingham was the natural successor to the Ancient Greeks and therefore needed an appropriate building to demonstrate that fact. There was no hint of an apology that such excellence was paid for when half the city was living in squalor.

And, as he approached the imposing steps leading up to the entrance, Barry couldn't help feeling that they were right. One hundred and thirty years on, it was still there, standing tall and proud as a symbol of all that a city could be, whilst all around it the later, more egalitarian buildings of the 1950s and 60s, for which Birmingham was famous, had come and gone. No one remembered with any great fondness the tower blocks that had brought gas, electricity, running water and inside toilets to the masses, despite the ostensibly more humane instincts that had inspired them. Meanwhile, the monuments to elitism erected by an earlier age remained a source of pride to an impoverished city that might logically have been expected to see them as hateful symbols of the oppression of the poor. Like a lot of things, Barry couldn't explain it, but he knew that it was true.

As he entered the museum and art gallery, he felt as though he was literally entering a different world – the world that it inhabited was a different moral universe to the one apparently occupied by Snow Hill station, just a few hundred metres away. Things that might have seemed audacious, bordering on the absurd, only a few minutes ago whilst he was sitting in the car park – that humanity had the capacity for genuine goodness, that the pursuit of understanding of our place in the universe was noble, and that the design of buildings and how they made you feel was as important, if not more so, than their mere functionality – here, surrounded by the delicately worked cornices and majestic Corinthian capitals of the Classical school, suddenly achieved a degree of reasonableness.

Yet something had happened in the intervening years that had made buildings like this no longer feel possible. The stone at the entrance read proudly *"By the gains of Industry we promote Art"*, and, reading it, Barry felt a sense of what it was that might have changed. It was not advances in building technology that had rendered such buildings redundant, but a loss of faith in ordinary people's ability to acknowledge a greater purpose to their daily toil than simply the accumulation of material wealth.

Barry was a man of simple tastes, so he felt no guilt about sauntering past the world-famous *The Blind Girl*

(John Everett Millais, 1856) and *Proserpine* (Dante Gabriel Rossetti, 1882), and heading straight toward the less ostentatious pleasures of L.S. Lowry.

Barry liked Lowry, though more because of his story than because of his art. Famously, Lowry had been a rent collector for The Pall Mall Property Company, and so Barry liked to think of him as, in some way, a kindred spirit.

An Industrial Town (1944) was not regarded as one of Lowry's major works, but it did contain all the familiar elements for which Lowry became famous: smokestacks belching out filth; dark, satanic mills; and, of course, the 'matchstick' figures that became his trademark, scurrying about in the shadow of the bleak industrial landscape. Barry preferred it to the ostensibly better-drafted and executed Pre-Raphaelite stuff, with which the museum and art gallery was perhaps over endowed, because it seemed to confront you with reality rather than offering you an escape from it. Instead of all those beautiful redheads with alabaster skin, staring into the middle distance whilst holding a lute, Lowry painted real people going about their ordinary lives.

His style was often described as naïve, but actually Barry had come to feel there was a brutality to Lowry's pictures that was far more sophisticated than the superficially more meaningful pictures of the Brotherhood. Lowry didn't flinch from the realities of life or pretend that things were other than what they seemed. Life was not fragrant, or mystical or pregnant with meaning; it was simply tough. No one looked up in Lowry's paintings; everyone was hunched over, staring at the ground, as if beaten down by life. And they were all faceless; anonymous bodies in a vast swarm of humanity, scurrying to and fro to nowhere very significant.

It punctured Barry's euphoria and made him melancholy because, whilst the smokestacks and mills may have gone, he sensed that this was the story of his life too.

It was all done through perspective, of course; Barry realised that. In classical paintings, perspective meant that the picture was composed in such a way as to create a single vanishing point. That vanishing point was traditionally understood to be the eye of God. So everything had a significance because it was all arranged in relation to the divine. Lowry, however, in common with most twentieth-century painters, didn't bother with perspective – it was one of the reasons critics often described his compositions as 'childish'. But maybe he was child*like;* maybe he just refused to see things that weren't there and painted the pure, unvarnished truth. Perhaps there was no ultimate significance into which all things vanished. Perhaps our sufferings were just sufferings and have no more significance than that. Perhaps the innominate figures were intended as a warning: "This is what you are – what we all are."

Barry felt, in that moment, as if Lowry was reaching out across the decades and painting just for him.

At which point his phone rang.

"Sorry," said Barry, to no one in particular whilst rummaging to get the phone out of his pocket.

It was Lauren. Her train had got in and she was waiting, somewhat irritated, at the station.

"Sorry Lol. I lost track of the time. I'll be there in ten minutes. Your mother's looking forward to seeing you… Obviously, I'm looking forward to seeing you too. Sorry."

And, with that, he hurriedly left behind the melancholy of Lowry's vision of the world and returned to the altogether different melancholy of Birmingham Snow Hill station; Yeoville Thomason's soaring vision of humanity soon just a distant memory.

NINE

She was different. Even in the four short weeks that she'd been away, Barry could see a difference in her. It wasn't just about how she looked (although she did seem to have lost a bit of weight) but how she spoke and acted; how she *was*. Her face had acquired a certain youthful swagger and indifference to her surroundings, as though the city were no longer her home, just a useful stopping off point on her way to somewhere altogether more interesting.

"Where's Mum?"

"She's at home, tidying up," said Barry as he led the way back to his car, "but she's looking forward to seeing you. I'll take you back now for some lunch, then you and your mum can come back into town for some shopping this afternoon."

"You not coming with us?" asked Lauren, her attention fixed firmly on the screen of her smartphone.

"Nah. Your mum thought you needed some mother-daughter bonding time together."

"God, we've done nothing but bond since I left! I swear she's stalking me on social media."

"She misses you. She's not used to it just being the two of us."

"Yeah, plenty of opportunities for husband-and-wife bonding time now I'm not there, eh Dad?" said Lauren, nudging her father's arm and chuckling.

Barry didn't chuckle.

"Anyway, she's looking forward to having you back for the weekend," he said.

"I know; she keeps telling me. I must have had a dozen texts last night and the same this morning, just checking I was still coming. I can't understand it – she was never this keen to see me when I lived with you."

"Yeah, well, sometimes you don't know what you've got till it's gone, do you? And after what happened with your brother…"

They continued their walk back to the car in silence. Barry was desperate to break it, not because he had anything to say, but because he could feel it growing between them awkwardly, like a balloon being inflated that might burst at any moment.

Lauren was greeted at the door by a long hug from her mum. It was the kind of hug parents gave when they re-found their child after momentarily thinking that they'd lost them in a shopping centre. But Lauren was turning into a young woman. Barry noticed it throughout the twenty-four hours or so she spent at home before returning to Warwick. He rather liked it.

His wife, in contrast, clearly hated it. The fact that Lauren was no longer their little girl disconcerted her. It was as if a pet dog had suddenly decided that she didn't need her owner to feed her anymore.

Barry's wife had a simple solution to every difficulty: food. Food, to her, was a soothing balm that could be administered to any wound. It was why she and Barry were both quite large. It was something of a bone of contention between her and Lauren, however, and, having apparently had something of a ruckus whilst they were out shopping together over the necessity or otherwise of having a cinnamon swirl with their coffee, she had decided to give up on the food angle and instead attempted to demonstrate her affection for her daughter by what Lauren took to be 'fussing'. And she asked questions – oh so many questions – about the course, about the people she'd met, about her halls of residence, about possible or actual boyfriends, about the fastidiousness of the cleaners and, of course, about the prevalence of drugs.

So, there had been conversations; small, apparently ordinary ones. But, in a house that still echoed with the howl of a death, they felt to Barry like evasions; cascades of words with no other purpose than to give the three of them something to do instead of screaming in pain.

Barry sensed Lauren's frustration pushing carefully against every word she uttered, every door she closed, every mug she put down, until finally, it tumbled out in a loud and rather dramatic argument after Sunday lunch, ostensibly about Lauren's alcohol intake. The atmosphere seemed broken, like a smashed plate, which prompted Barry to take himself upstairs until he was called down by Lauren to take her back to the station.

Barry looked into her eyes as he said goodbye on the platform, searching them for the answer to a question he couldn't articulate.

"You all right, Dad? Your face looks funny."

Barry tried to remember what his normal face looked like, but the memory of it was lost in the briars and brambles of his sorrow.

TEN

Monday started with yet another email from Angela, this one advising everybody that Maxine had decided that it was time for her "to pursue new and exciting career opportunities elsewhere" and that, therefore, she would be leaving Monument with immediate effect. The email had ended with "I'm sure colleagues will wish to join me in wishing her well for the future", which, under the circumstances, felt somewhat disingenuous at best. But, as Jean had pointed out, it was just the way these things had to be handled.

But then Barry saw another email – this one from Langley: "*I've just been told by Ruth that she's stopped the finance team issuing any more invoices until they've sorted out their bank account rationalisation. Please tell me that you managed to get The SHYPP's invoice out before she put a stop to everything. I think I was quite clear that we needed to get that one out* ASAP*!*"

Frankly, I might as well march myself to the exit door now, Barry thought.

He pulled up an email from Saleema, which had a draft version of the invoice attached. Sure enough, it contained the figures that he had agreed with her, but, frustratingly, it also contained Monument's old bank details. The thought occurred to Barry that he could post it out anyway with new payment details, and just include a note advising that they'd changed. But he didn't know what the new payment details were, and it seemed unlikely that anyone in the finance team would offer to tell him if it meant that he would circumvent Ruth's directive.

Barry printed off the invoice to The SHYPP anyway. As he did so, he heard a familiar nasal whine behind him.

"Barry, you can read my mind! I was just about to check where we were with The SHYPP invoice," Langley said. "I certainly hope you got it out before the finance team put us all in lockdown," he added with his now familiar undercurrent of menace.

"It's all in hand, Langley. I'm on the case."

"Glad to hear it. We don't want any slip-ups, do we?" Langley said, with a slightly unnerving smile.

"Oh, absolutely not, Langley."

"I was also just wondering if I could have a word with you… in my office?"

Barry wondered if he ought to pack a few of his personal effects into a box first before making his way over. He thought better of it, but still checked nervously before entering to see if Angela was waiting for him. He was relieved to see that she wasn't.

"Barry," Langley said, after the usual pleasantries had been exchanged. "We've got some challenges in the department at the moment, and I need your help, at least in the short term, to help us come through them."

This was said with the slightly forced *bonhomie* of a man who had been told how to present an unattractive proposition in a way that made it appear as though he was presenting an exciting opportunity. Barry guessed that the words had come from Angela. In any event, he was on his guard.

"As you know, Maxine has decided to move on. Now that I've been asked to fill this position, it does leave us rather low on area managers. Given your experience, we thought you would be the obvious person to ask to cover Maxine's team while we look to put some new management in place." Langley attempted to muster a smile.

"Well, thanks, Langley. It's obviously flattering to be considered for an opportunity like this, and I'm always keen to help where I can, as you know..." Barry paused for a moment, unsure quite how to put what he wanted to say.

Langley leant forward in anticipation.

"It's just that... I'm sorry, but I just wondered if... I wondered if there was any kind of additional remuneration... package... or something... Sorry."

Langley's eyes quickly flicked down to some notes on his pad.

"Well, as I'm sure you're aware Barry, the business is facing some real financial challenges at the moment, so whilst we'd love to be able to offer you something, I'm afraid at this point we've just not got the headroom."

Barry's heart sank. Even allowing for his never-failing politeness, how could they possibly have expected him to say yes? Langley's next comment seemed to provide the answer.

"Of course, with the VR trawl coming up, this should only be a very short-term arrangement. Only a couple of weeks. Probably." Then his eyes narrowed and his forehead creased. "We'll be looking at a longer-term solution when we know where we are."

Barry heard a very clear subtext to what Langley was saying. It wasn't a promise that his VR application would be approved if he did this, rather it sounded like a thinly veiled threat of what might happen if he didn't.

Under the circumstances, Barry didn't feel he could say anything other than yes, which he duly did. He even apologised for having asked about the extra money. As he did so, he reminded himself that it didn't really matter because he would be gone in a few weeks anyway. Yet, even as he tried to force that thought to the forefront of his mind, a faint whisper reminded him that he was never more than an exec-team announcement away from heartbreak.

ELEVEN

As he returned to his desk, Barry's thoughts were interrupted by a phone call.

"Oh, hi Mr Todd. It's PC Rathbone here. I was wondering if I could ask you a favour? I don't suppose you have any CCTV at Neville Thompson House, do you?"

"Yeah, we've got a few cameras."

"Brilliant. So you can go back to the last evening that anyone was heard coming out of Chris Malford's flat – two weeks last Thursday?"

"Uh, yes, I guess so. I'm sorry, but do you mind me asking what this is about? It's just that I was hoping to have had the keys back by now."

"It's probably nothing, but the lady across the hall says she heard someone coming out and we just wanted to check if there was any footage of who that was. It might just help us to fill in some blanks if we knew."

Barry didn't particularly want a late finish, but he was prepared to hang around if it meant that he would get the keys to flat twelve back quicker. On that basis, he agreed to PC Rathbone's request. When she arrived about an hour later, the footage from Neville Thompson House was available for her to view.

"That's great," said Gemma appreciatively. "Can we go back two-and-a-half weeks and have a look at the Thursday please?"

Barry whizzed through the footage of that fateful Thursday until it showed, in mid-evening, Chris Malford come up the stairs and make toward the door of his flat. Sure enough, alongside him was a companion: young, male and wearing a baseball cap that partially covered his face. As the figures stood at the door to flat twelve, both could be seen in profile, but Chris' companion had kept his cap on and was standing at Chris' shoulder, so was partly obscured.

On the screen, Chris Malford unlocked the door of flat twelve and walked in. His companion followed him and finally removed his cap – just at the point where he crossed the threshold and therefore disappeared out of sight.

"You might as well fast forward this bit," Gemma said. "Just keep going until we see someone come out."

The footage whizzed forward. Occasionally, a neighbour would be seen going into or out of one of the other flats on the landing, but the door to flat twelve remained firmly closed; 8pm, 9pm, 10pm all came and went with no movement. And then, at 11.57pm, the door finally opened and a figure with a small, black rucksack emerged – this time without his baseball cap. His face still couldn't quite be seen though, as he was looking downward. It appeared that he was stuffing something into his pocket.

"Well, that explains why we couldn't find Malford's wallet," said Gemma, with just a hint of the world-weary cynicism that Barry had found so unattractive in her colleague.

And then the figure, clearly agitated, turned to go down the stairs, taking the baseball cap out of his pocket, but facing the camera full-on for a brief moment before he put it on his head.

"Freeze it there!" Gemma said, urgently. "Back a bit... just a bit more... there. That's it."

Barry looked intently at the image on the screen.

"Oh my God! Is that Adam Furst?" PC Rathbone asked.

"Yes, I think it probably is," replied Barry.

Adam Furst was another of the lost young souls who had been washed up at The SHYPP. Barry hadn't realised that Adam had known Chris Malford, but, given that they were both 'well-known to the local police' it wasn't that much of a surprise. Indeed, the whole Furst family were notorious for being behind much of the crime in the north of Solihull, particularly in the suburb of Chelmsley Wood where they hailed from, and where The SHYPP was located.

"So you know Adam Furst?" Gemma asked.

"Yes. He lives at The SHYPP."

"The one in Chelmsley Wood?"

"Yes. That's the only one there is. Or the only one in Solihull, at any rate. There's one in South Herefordshire that we nicked the name from."

Gemma turned back toward the screen and stared intently at the small, black rucksack in Adam Furst's hand. "What's in that bag, I wonder?" she asked no one in particular.

"That, I'm afraid, I don't know," Barry replied. "Sorry."

"I'm just trying to work out if it's big enough."

"For what?"

"I don't know. It's just that when we went into the bedroom I could have sworn there was a gap in the dust on the dresser, as though someone had recently removed something. I couldn't find anything in the flat, so I wondered if someone had taken it. I'd be jolly interested to know what it was and where it's gone."

Barry felt the colour drain from his face and a film of cold sweat cover the surface of his skin. The box file. It was, he now remembered, still sitting in a small compartment in the boot of his car. Barry had deposited it there the previous Thursday in order to keep it out of sight. Unfortunately, not only was it out of sight, with everything else that had happened since, it had also been completely out of Barry's mind. He'd never actually got round to handing it over to social services as he'd intended. Now it seemed that PC Rathbone was interested in identifying its whereabouts.

"And we've found no background stuff at all. We'd normally pass all that stuff on to social services to help them, but there's nothing. I'll have to let them know we couldn't find any papers, but it's very odd."

Barry's plan to drop the box file off at social services was instantly put on hold. At the moment, they had no reason to doubt the provenance of the box file, but if the police told social services that there were no personal papers in the flat they would naturally want to know why Barry seemed to know differently.

"Anyway, thanks for letting me see that," Gemma said. "Can you download it onto disk for me? I just need to talk this through with my colleague."

"Not a problem," Barry said. "But I haven't got administrator rights, so I'm afraid I'll need to get one of the IT guys to do that for you."

"That's OK. You can just post it through," Gemma replied. "I just wish I knew what had been on that dresser, though."

"It was probably nothing," said Barry.

"You may well be right, Mr Todd, but I'd love to know who's got whatever it was now. They'd have some explaining to do. Could be looking at fifteen months for tampering with evidence."

At which point Barry decided that not only would the box file not be going to social services, it would also not be handed over to the police.

Barry didn't feel that he was like Adam Furst. Adam made his living from theft, burglary and the occasional bit of fraudulent trading. And, for the past few weeks, he'd also been dealing in drugs. The little rucksack, the contents of which contents had so intrigued Gemma Rathbone, had actually contained, not a mysterious rectangular object, but an array of powders and pills that he had begun to sell.

Even without knowing the detail of Adam Furst's latest business venture, Barry would have confidently said, without any sense of self-deception, that his misdemeanour could not be compared to those of Adam or any of his relatives. But he now realised that he had unwittingly become a criminal. His hope was that, by simply destroying the box file, he could destroy all evidence of that fact. After all, he reasoned, if there was no evidence, then surely it would no longer be true?

PART 2

"The line dividing good and evil cuts through every human being. And who is willing to destroy a piece of his own heart?"

Aleksandr Solzhenitsyn

THE LINE THROUGH EVERY HUMAN HEART

26th October – 2nd November 2015

TWELVE

Barry returned to his desk. On it, the invoice to The SHYPP sat accusingly. It was so frustrating. As Monument used a standard twelve-point Arial font across all of their software packages, it would have been a relatively simple task for him to amend the invoice if he'd known the new payment details that needed to be inserted. He could have printed them out and then pasted them onto the PDF. If he'd run the amended invoice through Monument's colour photocopier, no one at The SHYPP would have been any the wiser. It might have technically been a breach of due process, but if the association received its money more quickly, who would honestly have cared?

Just then he heard a distinctive 'ping' go off in his jacket pocket, indicating the arrival of a text. He checked his phone and saw that it was from Lauren. "*Hey Dad, I was wondering if you'd sorted out my money yet? U owe me 400 now. Thx. Lol xxx*"

"*Your mum's already said,*" he texted back. "*I'll sort something out this week. Sorry.*"

This was, if truth be told, more of an aspiration than a firm commitment. The pay freeze Monument had implemented for staff below director level, allied with his wife's redundancy and now his increased mortgage costs had severely limited Barry's scope for manoeuvre in respect of additional expenditure.

Barry felt as though he'd failed. He didn't mind failing Langley, but he did mind failing his daughter. Particularly given that he'd already failed his son. So he felt the necessity for extra income growing up around him like a creeper, wrapping itself around his chest like swaddling bands.

The simplest thing to do, of course, would just be to overwrite his own bank details onto the invoice sitting in front of him. That way he could have the £50,000 due to Monument paid directly to him. Barry chuckled at the ridiculous simplicity of the idea. Of course, he knew that, ultimately, it would be a stupid thing to do – the moment Monument failed to receive their money and spoke to the staff at The SHYPP, they would speak to their bank and discover what Barry had done.

But a small seed of an idea began to germinate in his mind. What if there was a bank account that wasn't in his name, but which he controlled? And what if he could have the money paid into that account? Then, when the money was discovered to be missing, no one would have any reason to suspect him of being involved.

He decided to have a look through Chris Malford's papers. He would do that, Barry determined, before proceeding to destroy them as planned, obviously. This would be done purely as a theoretical auditing exercise to test his hypothesis that the existence of a 'dummy' bank account could allow someone – not Barry, of course, but someone – to divert money from one party to a third party without it reaching the intended second party.

There were thirty-three unread emails sitting in his inbox, so this was not a thought experiment that he could continue at that moment. But, as part of his dedication both to his job and the company, Barry decided that he would continue it in his own time. Naturally, this required him to take both Chris Malford's box file and Saleema's draft invoice home with him for further inspection.

That evening, after he'd got home from work and had his tea, Barry took the box file up to what he grandly called the home office. Actually, it was Christopher's old bedroom with some second-hand office furniture in it (much to his wife's chagrin). Barry closed the door behind him and inspected the paperwork. He wasn't disappointed by what he found. Not only were there bank statements with Chris' sort code and account number at the top, but there was also a cheque book for the account. In addition, there was a letter headed *"Welcome to online banking"*, which contained details of the username for Chris Malford's account. The letter went on to say that when he first logged on he would be prompted to set a password. This, the letter reminded him, should not be written down or disclosed to anyone. Barry strongly suspected that Chris would be no more able to remember all of his various passwords without writing them down than anyone else. Sure enough, on the back of the letter Barry saw *"HidingMyTears82"* written in Chris' untidy scrawl.

Barry stopped for a moment. He'd never considered that computer passwords might carry emotional weight, yet Chris' password felt like the saddest one that Barry had ever seen. There was a particular poignancy, he felt, in the fact that the thing that had finally unlocked Chris and given Barry an insight into the person behind the tattoos and belligerent stare, was the one thing that Chris could never reveal.

Barry continued rifling through the box file and eventually came across another letter, this one with a grey, translucent slip at the bottom onto which was etched the PIN for Chris' debit card. He didn't have the debit card itself (which, as PC Rathbone had suggested, had probably disappeared along with Adam Furst), so he tried to log in to Chris' bank account with the intention of ordering a new one. Unfortunately, logging in required knowledge not only of Chris' username and password but also of his 'online banking access code'. Barry didn't know what this was and after three failed attempts to guess it his computer advised him that his online access had been suspended.

Barry was surprised at how frustrated he felt; after all, it was not as if he wanted to steal the money. But he was intrigued to know if he *could.* He had set himself a challenge and now he was determined to meet it. After a few moments' thought, therefore, he decided to ring the bank's customer call centre, the number for which was prominently displayed on the bank's correspondence. He put Chris' account number, sort code and then PIN into the phone when prompted by the automated system.

He was then transferred to a call handler and was quite easily able to confirm Chris' full name and address, date of birth, and the second and fourth characters of the account password. He thought he'd convinced her, but then she said, "And, finally, can you just give me the answer to your secure question?"

Barry thought for a moment that his attempt was once again doomed to fail. But then something occurred to him. Monument too had a security system that they used when divulging customer information to callers over the phone. Each tenant was asked to answer three security questions, one of which they were asked each time they called. Those details would be on Chris' account. It seemed possible – indeed, probable – that one of those questions might also be the one that he used for the bank. Barry decided to stall for time whilst he quickly tried to log on remotely to Monument's server.

"Ooh, secure question… Now, I know this. It's going to be one of three answers, because I always use one of those three questions, but I can never remember which one I've used for which account. So you might have to bear with me."

"That's quite all right, Mr Malford. I can give you three attempts anyway."

Barry's computer continued its slow progress. "Just let me check. I've got them locked away here in a drawer somewhere…"

Barry thought he heard a sigh on the other end of the line. Finally, he got onto Monument's server and quickly searched for Chris' account.

"So is it 'Aston Villa'?"

"I'm afraid not."

"'Bishop Wilson Primary School'?"

"Yes, that's the one! Thank you. So how can I help you, Mr Malford?"

Barry explained that he was no longer in possession of the debit card for the account. In response to the call handler's question, he confirmed that, yes, it may well have been stolen and that the police were aware.

"Hmm... Yes, I can see there's been a failed attempt to log in to your account online tonight, Mr Malford. No harm done, but you might want to change your online password. I'll stop the debit card for you now. Do you think the PIN's been compromised?"

"Oh, I'm absolutely sure that no one other than me knows the PIN for that card."

"Great. Well, I'll get a new card out to you straight away. It'll have the same PIN, but you can change it if you want to be absolutely sure. It should be with you by Friday."

Given that Barry had a master key for the wall of postboxes in the lobby of Neville Thompson House, it would be a relatively simple matter for him to pick up the new card. He hung up and took a deep breath.

Adopting, for a moment, the persona of a hypothetical auditor, Barry looked at the facts in front of him. He had the account details and cheque book for a bank account that was in the name of someone who was now, sadly, deceased. But the bank clearly did not know that the account holder was dead, nor would anyone know that the bank even had to be notified of his death because no one outside of the bank had any reason to know of the account's existence – except, of course, for Barry. The account would therefore continue to be operational unless and until Barry advised the bank that it needed to be closed.

He had several examples of Chris Malford's signature on documents in his tenancy file and so he could easily copy it onto a cheque if he ever felt inclined to (although he couldn't see why he would). He would shortly have a debit card for the account, and so, using the PIN that was already in his possession, he could soon withdraw money from it. To all intents and purposes, therefore, Barry concluded that he had control of Christian Malford's bank account.

For their part, an auditor would determine that a less-honest person than Barry would be able to divert funds intended for Monument into it by the simple expedient of overlaying Chris Malford's bank details onto an otherwise legitimate invoice that had been prepared by Monument. All suppliers had just been notified of an impending change to the association's payment details, so such an action wouldn't arouse undue alarm or suspicion. Any money thus diverted would therefore be under the effective control of whoever controlled Chris Malford's bank account, which, at this moment in time, just so happened to be Barry.

He felt a strange sense of exhilaration flood his body. He had done it. He'd beaten the system. And he'd not even had to lie, not really. But then a sickness rose in his stomach that reminded him of being caught copying his homework by a teacher. Surely it couldn't be that simple? It just couldn't be. Could it? But, try as he might, Barry couldn't see how anyone would be able to work out from the information that would be available, who had been responsible for the diversion of the money. Surely they wouldn't blame Barry? After all, he'd been involved with The SHYPP for fifteen years, and in that time every single quarterly payment had made its way safely into Monument's bank account.

No, if fingers were going to be pointed, it seemed natural to conclude that they would be pointed in the direction of Langley Burrell. It was he, after all, who had insisted on changing the invoicing arrangements at precisely the time that any halfway competent manager should have seen there was the potential for confusion.

So, as he typed out the sort code and account number for Chris Malford's bank account in twelve-point Arial font, Barry didn't see himself as attempting to steal £48,558. No, he actually saw himself doing Monument a favour. They would learn some important lessons from this about financial protocols that would protect them in future from people less scrupulous than Barry. And they would also learn that Langley Burrell – who was still within the probationary period for his new post – was perhaps not quite the brilliant cost-controller and income-maximiser that they thought he was.

And if Langley did happen to be blamed, would that really be so unfair? It was certainly no more unfair than the wardens of Monument's sheltered housing schemes losing their jobs despite having done nothing wrong except expecting to be paid a decent salary.

He printed off Chris' account details and cut the two numbers out precisely. He then carefully pasted the new sort code and account number into the appropriate slots in the invoice Saleema had forwarded to him for approval. He could run the amended invoice through the colour laser copier at work. That, he mused, would produce an amended invoice that would be virtually indistinguishable from a genuine one. And if it wasn't, well, he didn't have to send it, did he? And even if he did send it, Sally didn't have to pay it if she was suspicious; that was, after all, the primary purpose of the exercise – to test the robustness of the financial checks that were in place.

Barry hid Chris Malford's cheque book in his home safe. He then proceeded to destroy the rest of the papers by running them through the paper shredder under his desk. Next, he took the shredded papers outside. Recycling day was Tuesday in Walmley, so he wouldn't have to wait long before all evidence that Chris Malford's papers had ever been in his possession was taken away by the city council and pulped. As an extra precaution, he dropped the box file in the bin too.

Barry slept fitfully that night. He swam so deep in his own thoughts that he felt them pressing in on him like an ocean. He found himself repeatedly having to come to the surface of his sleep in order to gasp for air. His wife slept on, just inches from him, yet he felt as though he were about to embark on a perilous journey alone. No one knew – no one could possibly know – what it was that he was contemplating. But it felt as though he was not alone in his thoughts; as though there was an unseen companion alongside him, not judging him, but simply holding up a mirror into which he was invited to look. Yet whenever he opened his eyes there was nothing there.

He was roused at 6.45am by the sound of the recycling-collection lorry arriving in his street. He got out of bed and looked through a small gap in the curtains to see it stop a few doors from his house. A team of men in hi-vis tops got out of the lorry and spread across the street, collecting the recycling bins and bringing them back to the lorry. Sure enough, one of the men casually grabbed Barry's recycling bin and emptied its contents into the back of the truck. He then tossed the bin back in the vague direction of Barry's lawn.

That was it. It was all gone. All of the paperwork that could alert someone to the existence of Chris Malford's bank account was now not only shredded but hopelessly mixed up with the recycling of hundreds – possibly thousands – of households from Walmley and beyond. No one would ever know – and even if they suspected, they could never prove – that Christian Malford's bank account details had ever been in Barry's possession.

THIRTEEN

Barry quickly bolted down a bowlful of cereal and headed into work. His lack of sleep meant he was tired, but there was something about what he was intending to do that, conversely, made him feel wide awake. He arrived shortly after 8am, so the office was still largely empty – the ideal time to photocopy the invoice, Barry thought. The photocopier on the ground floor was next to Jean's desk, but, thankfully, she had not yet arrived at work, so Barry quickly slid his handiwork into the feeder tray and pressed the copy button. He grabbed both the amended original invoice and the copy, and slipped them into a folder, just as he noticed Jean, huddled inside a practical waterproof against the early morning rain outside, coming through the reception area and into the office.

"Morning, Barry. You're in early."

"Yes, well, I've got plenty to do," he said. "I assume

Langley's explained that he's asked me to look after the team for a couple of weeks?"

"Yes, Angela sent an email round yesterday. It'll be nice to work with you again." Then she fixed Barry with her piercing stare and asked, "But what about you? How was your weekend?"

"Fine. My daughter came home from university. It's always nice to see her. And you?"

"Oh, just church stuff, y'know," she said, placing her coat on the back of her chair.

Actually, Barry didn't know. He'd known Jean long enough to know that she went to church, but he'd never quite plucked up the courage to ask her about it. To Barry, going to church was rather like being a naturist – it was the kind of hobby that the people who had it were incredibly proud of and wanted to explain to everyone, whereas everyone else just regarded it as embarrassing. He was not minded, therefore, to explore her ecclesial interests any further. He also recognised that he was holding a doctored invoice, which Jean had just seen him photocopy. A small bead of nervous sweat formed on the fringes of Barry's hairline and ambled down his temple toward his cheek. He decided that, under the circumstances, it would be safest to make his excuses and leave.

Barry needed to make sure that his amended invoice to The SHYPP was posted out and that it wasn't duplicated by the legitimate invoice that would no doubt be produced by Saleema at some point, so he headed over to the finance team to see if Saleema had arrived at work yet.

Saleema had indeed arrived. "I am so sorry Barry, but I couldn't get your invoice out before Ruth stopped me issuing them."

"I understand. It's not a problem."

"But I can issue it now, if you're happy it's correct. Did you check the PDF I sent through?"

"Yes. It's fine. You just need to change the payment details."

"Oh, of course! Thanks for reminding me. Ruth says we have to post out all invoices, but do you want me to send a copy by email too? Just to hurry things up?"

"That won't be necessary," said Barry quickly. "Sally won't pay any attention to it anyway – she's old school. She'll want it in an envelope before she pays it."

Sending out emails was free, so fraudsters could send out thousands knowing that it only took one hard-pressed accounts assistant to rush through a payment for them to be in profit. Conversely, the sheer cost of sending out invoices by post meant that fraudsters would probably be out of pocket even if two or three people paid. So Sally deleted any invoices she received by email and was adamant that if suppliers wanted paying they would have to ensure that she received an invoice through the post.

Saleema amended the payment details on her system, printed off the invoice and slipped it into an envelope. "I'll send it out with the post tonight," she said.

"Don't worry. I'll slip it into the post room for you," said Barry.

"Are you sure?"

"Yes. I've practically got to walk past it anyway, so it's no bother."

"Oh, thank you, Barry. You are a saint."

Barry smiled. But he noticed, perhaps for the first time, that he didn't feel like one.

He made his way down to the post room. He removed the legitimate invoice from the envelope that Saleema had given him and inserted his amended invoice in its place. Then he dropped the envelope into the *"Post – OUT"* tray, where it would be franked with Monument's logo and sent out as normal with the rest of the post. He then ran the legitimate invoice and the one with Chris Malford's bank details glued on through the shredder, and returned to his desk.

Barry felt a strange sense of exhilaration as he walked back through the familiar office. He felt – and it sounded like a cliché even as he said it to himself – more alive. That first rousing from his slumbers that he'd felt as he'd walked out of Chris Malford's flat with the box file was now amplified. He was awake now, wide awake. And he hadn't even realised that he'd been asleep.

FOURTEEN

Barry headed back to his desk, where he was greeted by Taneesha. "There's a woman in reception asking for you. She says it's important. I didn't get the name, sorry! But it sounded foreign."

Barry suspected that it was Iulia. His fear was that she was going to tell him that she couldn't keep up her payments, but when he arrived at the reception desk it wasn't Iulia who was waiting for him.

"Hallo, Mr Todd," his visitor said in the same clipped Slavic tones. "My name is Teodora Oprea." She offered him her hand.

There was something about her that made Barry nervous. Her cheery tone seemed slightly too forced, and her bleach-blonde hair, white leather jacket and white patent-leather shoes didn't quite convey the air of professionalism that she clearly intended. Barry eyed her warily as he introduced himself and invited her to explain the purpose of her visit.

"You will know, of course, that the changes in benefit rules have had a big impact on many EU nationals and I am aware that some are now facing eviction," Teodora said, her breath whispering softly of cigarettes and spearmint gum.

Her English was certainly better than Iulia's, but Barry sensed an anxiety in her eyes.

"I work for an organisation that is seeking to help Romanian migrants who face – how you say? – destitution because of benefit changes."

"I see. And how do you think I can help you?"

"Well, we are very worried to hear that some of your tenants – Romanian tenants – are being told they will be evicted."

"I understand your concern Ms Oprea, but you've got to understand—"

"Oh no, I do understand Mr Todd. I am not criticising you. I understand there is nothing you can do, but we are obviously here to try to help them."

"Well, I'm happy for you to offer whatever support you can. We've got no objection to that. No one wants to evict these people, certainly not me. I'm just not sure how you think—"

"We are trying to trace a Iulia Nicolescu. We believe she's one of your tenants? We want to make contact with her, so we can support her. I was hoping you could let me have her contact details, so we can get in touch."

Teodora pulled her mouth into a milky smile that somehow omitted to communicate its joy to the rest of her face.

"Well, I'm afraid I can't divulge anything," Barry replied. "In fact, I can't even tell you whether she's one of our tenants. Data protection and all that. Sorry."

"Oh, we know she is one of your tenants. We looked through the records of County Court Judgements and saw that you took her to court – to evict her. Of course, we are very concerned by this. And Iulia Nicolescu is a Romanian name, so we are keen to help her, but we do not have her address. It was blanked out in the court papers for some reason, but if you will let me have it, then we can get over to her right away – to start helping her, of course."

"It's great that you want to help," said Barry nervously, "but even if she is one of our tenants – and, obviously, I can't confirm that – I couldn't give you her details without her consent. As I said, it's data protection."

"But we are very keen to help her, Mr Todd," Teodora insisted. "I'm sure she wouldn't mind you giving us her details so we can help her more quickly."

"Maybe not, but it's the rules, I'm afraid. And I can't break the rules." Barry felt himself wince.

Teodora looked at him with real desperation in her eyes. "Please. I need you to give me her details. We are very concerned for her welfare. It is very urgent – perhaps a matter of life and death."

The emphasis she placed on the words meant that Barry did not doubt for a moment that it was indeed a matter of life and death, although not perhaps in quite the way that Teodora was suggesting. She turned around and looked nervously over her shoulder. It was only then that Barry noticed the rather battered white Transit van parked outside the front door of Monument's offices. It was in a disabled parking bay, but when the driver got out in response to Teodora's nervous glance he appeared to have no obvious disabilities. He was a young man, perhaps in his late twenties, with short-cropped hair and a sleeve of tattoos down his muscular left arm. His scruffy T-shirt and jeans didn't seem to be obvious business attire.

"De ce nu se ia atat de mult timp? Obțineți numai insingerate detalii!"[1] he spat out as he stormed into Monument's reception area.

"Ce crezi ca incerc sa fac? Exista reguli ce stiti – nu doar dă-mi-le!"[2] Teodora replied hysterically, her professional demeanour dropping as she turned to face him.

Barry's instinct was just to show the two of them the door, but he was worried about what fate might befall Teodora if she was seen to leave the office with nothing. He had to do something to give the impression that she had at least achieved something, even if he was even less inclined to share Iulia's details with her now than he had been before.

"Obviously, Ms Oprea, I'm keen to help if I can," he said. "And it may be that I can speak to my bosses to see if, on this occasion—"

"That would be very helpful, Mr Todd. Thank you," Teodora replied, trying to regain her composure.

"It's just that I didn't quite catch who you worked for. If we had a business name, then perhaps we'd be a bit more comfortable bending the rules on this occasion."

"Of course, of course, here is my card." She reached into her clutch bag and pulled out a dog-eared business card that she handed to Barry. It looked as though it had been produced by a schoolchild on an inkjet printer. There was no postal address, landline number or website details; just

1 Why does it take so long? Just get the bloody details!

2 What do you think I'm trying to do? There are rules you know – he won't just give them to me!

a Hotmail address and a mobile phone number. And, of course, the name of the organisation.

"We are the Romanian Migrants Welfare Association. Our details are on the card. You can contact me or Costel, my colleague here."

"Thank you," Barry said. "I'll be sure to contact you the moment I get clearance from my bosses."

It wasn't intended to be a lie. It was simply a statement designed to give Ms Oprea the opportunity to paint a more hopeful picture to her belligerent 'colleague' than was actually the case. The fact was that Barry's bosses would never give him permission to divulge Iulia's details without her consent. And Iulia had already been very clear that she did not intend to avail herself of any of the services on offer from the Romanian Migrants Welfare Association. As he returned to his desk, therefore, Barry felt that he had stayed on just the right side of dishonesty.

But it was a lie – a terrible one. Barry just didn't know it yet.

FIFTEEN

High on the wall above the administrative bombsite that doubled as Sally Hedges' desk, a poster demanded that someone, somewhere *"Ban the Bedroom Tax!"* Sally liked to describe The SHYPP as a "collective community", but even if that were so (and many disgruntled ex-staff disputed it) it was more akin to Calvin's Geneva than an Israeli kibbutz. That was why all of The SHYPP's post had to be brought up to her personally. This, in turn, was why, the following day, it was Sally who opened the invoice from Monument that Barry had so helpfully taken it upon himself to send out on behalf of Saleema.

She knew before she'd even opened it what it was. It was in a neat, white, windowed envelope with Monument's logo in the bottom left-hand corner and Monument's franking mark in the top right. She knew it was about time for the quarterly invoice to come, so it seemed natural to assume that this was it. Sure enough, when she opened the envelope, there was the invoice, as expected, in exactly the same format as it was every quarter.

A less fastidious chief executive than Sally might have just passed it straight over to Marilyn, the part-time accounts clerk, for processing. But Sally was not that trusting – at least, not of Monument Housing Association. She'd had many run-ins over the years with Monument's finance team, who seemed to have only the loosest grip on what they should actually be charging her.

So she went to her filing cabinet and got out the agreed payment schedule, which she then compared with the invoice. Sure enough, in the 'rent due' column was the figure £43,836 – exactly the amount she had on her payment schedule – but Sally, being Sally, wasn't satisfied. Next, she looked at the other figure: *"Amount due for repairs carried out 1st June to 30th September 2015 (see attached schedule) – £4,747."*

Sally immediately turned to the Schedule of Repairs Completed that accompanied the invoice. There she found a list of every single repair that Monument had carried out in the previous quarter, with the exact date on which it had been completed, the number of the room where the repair had been carried out and the precise cost for that repair. Sally insisted that all repairs had to be reported to Monument through The SHYPP, and she kept her very own record of those repairs. So she was able to painstakingly check each of the repairs in her ledger against Monument's schedule, making sure that no extra jobs had been included.

Sally also insisted that all works were completed in accordance with the prices set out in the nationally recognised

PSA Schedule of Rates. Accordingly, she then took down the schedule of rates from her bookshelf and carefully checked the unit price quoted for each job. They all appeared to have been charged at the correct rate.

But still it wasn't enough. So convinced was she that Monument were trying to rob her, that Sally then proceeded to get out her calculator and add up the cost of each job, just to make sure that the total really was £4,747. And, having done that, she then checked that £43,836 plus £4,747 did indeed equal £48,583, as Saleema's invoice claimed.

It appeared that it did – so she double-checked it, with the same result. Sally sighed a slightly disappointed sigh. Everything was in order – this time. And so, she reluctantly concluded, there was nothing left to do but to pass the invoice on to Marilyn for payment. But, she consoled herself, at least she could be absolutely sure that she wasn't being robbed by those crooks at Monument.

Gemma Rathbone also had a postal delivery that morning. She opened the padded envelope and withdrew a DVD onto which was burnt the CCTV footage from Neville Thompson House. She knew she would have to convince Molloy that the footage demonstrated that there was something worth investigating, so she composed herself for a moment before sidling up to her colleague. Molloy was sitting at his desk, with a small castle of case files piled up around his computer, trying to draft an argument that would convince the Crown Prosecution Service to prosecute a rather awkward domestic-violence case they were working on. His fat fingers looked oddly out of place daintily tapping on a computer keyboard.

"I've been thinking..." Gemma said.

"Oh aye, that's always a dangerous thing. Hur hur."

Gemma decided to ignore Molloy's comment, and instead merely left a pause.

"What about?" Molloy asked, eventually.

"About the Malford case."

"I didn't realise there was a Malford 'case'. I thought we were just going to pass that one on to the coroner's office. There's no evidence of a crime," he said, continuing to type with the intense concentration of an elephant trying to balance on a beach ball.

"Yes, that's what I thought too. But then I got sent through some CCTV footage by the housing association."

"And?"

"Well, it shows Malford entering his flat with... with Adam Furst."

Molloy stopped typing and swivelled round on his seat to face Gemma. "Adam Furst?"

"Yes, and then it shows Furst leaving the flat a few hours later – alone. And it also shows that no one else went into or came out of the flat until we turned up two weeks later – including Chris Malford."

"So Furst was the last person to see Malford alive?"

"Exactly. And the times match. Remember there was that gap on the dressing table, like something had been removed? He might know something about that. Something that might help us."

"From where I'm sitting, we don't need any help, Bones.

Malford's found dead in his own flat with a syringe in his arm. There's no sign of a struggle, so I'm pretty certain toxicology will say that he's died of an overdose. There's no crime here, Bones. Let the coroner sort it out; we've got enough to do. Case closed." He turned away and went back to his typing.

"But he was the last person to see Malford alive," Gemma said. "Surely that's got to be worth taking a statement?"

Molloy sighed heavily. "OK. I suppose we can take a statement."

Gemma clenched her fist and just about managed to suppress a cry of "Yes!"

"But, Bones, that's all we're doing. We're taking a statement – like we did with the little old lady from the flat opposite. We're not interviewing him under caution; we're not digging around. We'll just see what he says and pass it on to the coroner. I don't want you doing your Columbo routine. Understood?"

"Absolutely. And, thanks, I really appreciate this."

"Do you actually know where he's living at the moment?"

"Yeah. I've checked and we've got a current address. He's moved back to Chelmsley. He's living in a flat at The SHYPP."

"Great. We can pop over tomorrow morning and catch him before he goes out."

"Oh, I'm in court tomorrow – for that assault outside The King's Head. Can we go now?"

"I've got to get this done," he said, pointing to his computer screen. "It's for the DV case. The one we agreed to prioritise. We can see Furst later in the week."

"Are you sure?"

"Yes," he snapped. "I've been trying to get this one through the CPS for weeks – I promised her lawyer I'd get it out today."

It was a lie, but Gemma didn't know that. And she had indeed insisted that they prioritise the domestic violence case. So, having won the larger war, she decided it wasn't worth trying to win a smaller battle too.

SIXTEEN

That Friday morning, Barry arrived at the office with a nauseous feeling sitting awkwardly in his stomach. The reason for his nervousness was the fact that today was the deadline for the submission of expressions of interest in the VR trawl. But there was something else lingering in the folds of his discomfort: a sense that there was something that he did not want revealed. It meant that, when he had made himself a coffee and settled down at his desk, the sudden ringing of his phone no longer felt innocent. Instead, it seemed to be sounding an alarm. He looked at the caller ID and a tide of dismay crashed over him. It was Sally.

Barry took a deep breath and grabbed the phone quickly before it diverted to voicemail. Then, putting on his most amiable telephone voice, he prepared to placate the inevitable wrath of Sally Hedges.

"Good morning. Monument Housing Association. Barry Todd speaking. How can I help?"

But there was no wrath. There was no anger. There wasn't even any of her usual brand of cruel sarcasm.

"Barry? It's Sally. Sally Hedges. I'm afraid I've got some sad news. It appears we've had a death last night, at The SHYPP. It's Shana Backley – one of the tenants."

"A death?" Barry was stunned. "But how? I mean, what happened?"

"Well, we don't know the details yet, but it looks like an overdose."

Gemma made sure that Molloy was ready to head off to The SHYPP as soon as he got in. She was keen to make sure that they caught Adam Furst before he went out. But, as they turned into the car park, they were both surprised to find it a patchwork of ambulances, police cars and flashing lights.

"Bloody hell! What's going on here?" said Molloy. "Is that Bongo's car?"

They found a parking space and got out of the car, just as PC Ali Khan came out and headed toward them.

"Hiya Bongo. What are you doing here?" Molloy asked.

"Hiya Fatty. I could ask you the same question."

Gemma felt the need to intervene. "We're here to talk to Adam Furst. It's about a case we're investigating."

"Oh yes? Not a drug overdose is it, by any chance?"

"Yes, it is actually" said Gemma, slightly unnerved by Khan's prescience. "Why?"

"Because they had one here last night. Apparently, Fursty spiked her."

"Spiked her?" Gemma asked.

Molloy sighed. "Happens in prison all the time, Bones. Basically, its injecting someone with drugs – usually heroin – either against their will or without their knowledge. It's a way of getting them hooked."

"But how can you do that?"

"Well, in prison you can get some heavies to hold them down. In a place like this, they usually just get them plastered so they can't fight back or they tell them it's something harmless – like sugared water," Molloy explained, apparently oblivious to the implications of what he was saying. "And that's what's happened here?"

"According to the CCTV footage – and a witness," Khan said. "Furst goes into the flat with two full bottles of what looks like Jim Beam. Comes out later with one empty bottle. Leaves the other bottle in there."

"Jim Beam?" A slow-dawning realisation finally began to find its way onto Molloy's face.

"Well, not quite. Actually, it's nothing more intoxicating than cold tea. That's obviously the one he's been drinking from whilst she's had the hard stuff. Looks like he's given her a shot while she's on the brink of passing out, but got his quantities all wrong. Poor girl."

"Have you got him?" asked Gemma, her voice betraying a sense of desperation.

"You're joking, aren't you? He's long gone. We won't see him for a bit."

Rathbone and Molloy looked at each other. "Shit," they said in unison.

There was going to be some explaining to do back at the station.

At about the time that Rathbone and Molloy were heading back to the station in stony silence, Marilyn, The SHYPP's part-time accounts clerk, was picking up the phone to call Barry in a considerably more convivial frame of mind.

"Oh, hi Marilyn. How are you?"

"Oh fine, thanks, Barry. Busy, you know, but I can't complain."

"Glad to hear it! Anyway, how can I help?"

"It's about this invoice you sent through earlier in the week."

Barry's heart skipped a beat. This was The Call. He felt sick. He wanted to confess – to blurt out, "It was me! It was me! It was all me! I did it!" But then he realised that Marilyn hadn't actually accused him of anything yet. He reminded himself that nothing could be traced back to him and that, even if it could, he hadn't actually stolen anything. In short, there wasn't really anything to admit *to* yet. Not really.

"Oh, well, I don't have much to do with that, I'm afraid… But, obviously, I'll try and help if I can. What's the problem?"

"Well, you've sent through the quarterly invoice, which Sally has checked, and everything seems to be in order. It's just that the payment details have changed. Is that right?"

"Yes, yes. We've consolidated our bank accounts a bit. We sent a letter out about it; didn't you get it?"

"Well, Sally did say that she'd been sent something, but she can't put her hand on it at the moment. You know what her desk's like. And she's rather busy this morning, with the police..."

"Yes, she phoned earlier... Very sad."

"So your account details *are* changing? Oh, well that's a relief. I was a bit worried. You've got to be so careful nowadays."

Barry didn't know quite how to respond. He settled for something non-committal. "Yes, I know."

"I don't suppose you could confirm the details for me could you – if I read back what's on here? It's just that the police are using Sally's office for interviews so I can't get in to check myself, and I'm supposed to finish at lunchtime today."

"Well, I don't actually have the new details to hand at the moment..."

"No, I understand. It's just that, as the letter's come from Saleema, I don't want to phone her... just in case... y'know..." Marilyn left a rather awkward pause by way of explanation.

"Oh no, I understand. No, don't bother Saleema with it. You're quite right, there."

"I mean, I'm not accusing her of anything, obviously..."

"Not at all, no," Barry said. "But you're right to want to check."

"It's just that it's quite unusual for payment details to change. And Saleema... well, she's new to this, so I don't really know her. I'd be asking her to vouch for her own work, so we both thought it best to check with you. Just as a precaution."

"That's fine. I quite understand. You're absolutely right to want to check with someone else. So, yes, I can confirm that our bank account details have changed. You can quote me on that."

"Great. Just one more question, if you don't mind?"

"Not at all."

"I got a call today from a Langley Burrell."

"Really?" Barry was intrigued.

"Yes. He seemed very keen to know when we were intending to pay the invoice. It just struck me as a bit unusual. People don't usually phone me up within a couple of days. And, with the payment details changing as well, I just wanted to check. Do you know why he'd be chasing up payment so quickly?"

"Yes, he's been pushing me and Saleema hard about this invoice. I think his point is that payment is actually due quarterly in arrears, but we don't normally invoice you until three weeks or so after quarter end – because it takes Bob that long to generate a list of all the repairs – and then you take twenty-eight days to pay. So actually, you're nearly five months in arrears by the time we get our money. You know what new people can be like; they want to be seen to make their mark in the first couple of weeks."

"Oh, right. I see. I didn't know that."

"The thing is, you should be paying the rent at the quarter end – that's what the management agreement says. So, technically, you're in breach of the agreement, which means that we can end it if you don't remedy the breach."

"Really? I've never heard mention of that before."

"No, it's not the kind of thing Neville would ever have thought of doing. But Langley has his own ideas, and he's right in one sense – it is in the agreement that breaches have to be remedied within one calendar month, or, technically, I think we can end it."

Marilyn quickly looked at the calendar on her wall.

"So that means you need paying by… the end of today?"

"Technically," replied Barry. "Are you able to do that?"

"Well, it'll be tight, but we've not got a choice, have we?" said Marilyn. "Do you think he's likely, this Langley Burrell, to try and end the management agreement if we don't pay in time?"

"I couldn't say. But he did make a point of phoning you up. Ask Sally what she thinks – she's dealt with him before."

"We'll need to raise a CHAPS payment. It's an extra twenty quid, but it's worth it if it stops us losing the scheme."

"I'm sure Langley would appreciate that."

"I'll get onto it right away. Thanks Barry."

"Not at all. Bye now."

Barry was stunned at how easy it had been. He'd not even had to lie.

SEVENTEEN

That afternoon, like most Friday afternoons, dragged – at least as far as Barry was concerned. In any other context, Barry may have felt the afternoon fly by, overwhelmed as he was by the sheer volume of work that he had to get through now he was looking after Maxine's team as well as his own. But that afternoon, work was not the focus of his thoughts.

Instead, there was only one thought in Barry's mind: had Sally authorised the CHAPS payment into Chris Malford's bank account? Nothing seemed to matter as much as that, and everything that stressed or flustered the members of his teams that afternoon seemed powerless to hurt him. That question provided a helpful protective blanket that he could wrap around himself to dull the pain inflicted by the recent blows he had suffered. It was a feeling, Barry decided, that he rather liked. It felt as though, despite all the indignities, Monument had not yet defeated him. Langley could not reduce him to worry and stress and fear as he clearly intended. And therefore he hadn't won.

Unfortunately, as he had no online access to Chris Malford's bank account, Barry couldn't check the balance on it. So, instead of flying by, the afternoon crawled to its conclusion. He tried phoning Marilyn, but he just got a voicemail message saying she was now out of the office and would be back on Tuesday. He kept looking at his phone to see if he had missed any calls from Sally asking him what he was trying to pull. He popped up to the central services floor and tried to find an excuse to idly ask Saleema if she'd had any calls from The SHYPP or the bank. But, as far as he could tell, there was nothing. No one contacted him or suggested anything was amiss.

Instead of driving home that evening, Barry decided to head over to Neville Thompson House with his master key for the wall of postboxes in the lobby. Sure enough, a brand-new debit card was waiting for him just as Barry had been promised. With it, he could check Chris Malford's account balance. Barry wasn't intending to withdraw any money. He just wanted to know that he had done it. That he'd got one over on Langley.

He assumed there would be a record of any use of the debit card, so he didn't want to use any cashpoint that would be linked too obviously to him. Equally, he had a vague sense that bank cashpoints had more security on them, so Barry opted to find an in-store machine somewhere in Chelmsley Wood. This was where Adam Furst lived, so Barry reasoned that using a cashpoint there might help reinforce the impression in PC Rathbone's mind that the debit card was in Adam's possession rather than his.

After driving around, he eventually identified a corner shop that had a *"Cash Machine Inside"* sign outside. Barry carefully parked down the road in order to avoid any CCTV that may have been immediately outside the shop, and made his way inside.

The store contained an apparently random cornucopia of household items and confectionary, with which it attempted to mask an underlying anxiety at the loss of its original purpose now that no one seemed interested in buying cigarettes or newspapers anymore. The cashpoint, which seemed symptomatic of this existential crisis, sat rather forlornly at the front of the store, just opposite the till at which a teenager sat, slouched on a chair, texting, as though she, too, had been overwhelmed by the shop's angst. She briefly sat up for a moment as Barry entered, but slumped back down when it became apparent that he only wanted to use the cashpoint.

Barry was about to approach the machine when he noticed that there was a ceiling-mounted camera behind the girl, pointing toward it. He froze for a moment, trying to work out what to do. Eventually, after a few moments of dithering, he changed direction and headed toward the till.

"Can I have a scratch card please?" he asked.

"Which one?"

Barry didn't know. He'd never bought a scratch card in his life. He didn't even realise there was a choice. He saw that there was a bright yellow one with a leprechaun on it, which seemed as good as any, so he opted for that.

"Sign of the times, eh?" asked Barry, indicating the CCTV camera.

"You what?"

"Sign of the times – the CCTV. We never used to have cameras in corner shops."

"Yeah, we've only got it 'cause of that thing," the young girl said, nodding toward the cash machine. "That's two quid, please."

"Oh, right. Uh… sorry," Barry replied, as though the request for money had taken him totally by surprise. He rummaged through his pockets trying to find some change. "I suppose it's linked up to the local police station."

"You're joking aren't you? We only have the camera 'cause the machine company insists."

"Oh. Does it go through to the bank then?"

"Nah, it's not a proper one. It's just a cheap one. It only records here. We just keep the footage for a few weeks. We could give it to the police if they asked – but they never have. They ain't bothered. We had a customer come in here a few months back saying she'd had her purse lifted out of her shopping bag with her card in it. Course, 'cause she's an old dear she'd written her PIN down too 'cause she could never remember it. Had 250 quid taken out of her account. 'Cause it happened on her way back from here and she only lives down the road, she wanted to know if they'd used our machine. My dad found the footage of them and everything. She told the police we'd caught 'em on camera. We kept the footage, but they never came round. Never heard any more about it."

"Oh, that's awful," Barry said, finding a coin and idly scratching his card. "She lost all that money."

"Well, she didn't actually. She comes in here all the time. I asked her what was happening 'cause we hadn't heard anything from the police, and she said that 'cause she'd got a crime number the bank just gave her the money back. But they didn't try and get the guys who'd done it. Told 'er it wasn't worth it for 250 quid. I think it's disgusting. Might as well not bother with the camera if they're not going to use it."

"Quite. That's terrible," said Barry. But, as he did so, a thought occurred to him; a thought that had first begun to form in his mind the previous week in Chris Malford's flat. In the absence of any conception of an all-seeing God, CCTV had become the moral police force of a secular nation. Like God in His seat of judgement, the ubiquity of CCTV would ensure that our sins were caught on camera and that we would, ultimately, face a day of reckoning.

Except that – what if it was all a con? What if no one was watching? Barry had stopped himself from using the cash machine because he'd believed he would be filmed and that someone, somewhere, would see that he had used Christian Malford's bank card. But what if, actually, no one really cared? What if the police were simply too busy to follow up on all the cases, especially ones where there was little money involved and the bank would pay it back anyway without anyone even bothering to check the CCTV?

Looked at in that light, using the cash machine to check the balance on Chris Malford's account – even in the full glare of a CCTV camera – didn't seem that risky at all. After all, checking the balance was hardly a crime. And the footage would be wiped in a few weeks anyway. *In that respect, at least,* thought Barry, *CCTV is a rather inadequate replacement for God.*

"Do I win anything?" Barry asked, looking at his scratch card in blank incomprehension.

The young girl scanned it. "Oh, you've won £3! Lucky you."

Barry took his winnings. He felt like he was on a roll, and so he turned and marched purposefully over to the cash machine. He got Chris' bank card out of his wallet and quickly checked the grey translucent slip with the PIN on. He keyed the number in and waited. He still hadn't decided to steal the money – or at least, not all of it – but he wanted to know if the transfer had happened. Just out of curiosity.

"Please wait whilst we process your request."

After what felt like an age, the message eventually changed.

"Your current balance is: £8.52."

Barry's heart sank. Of course, he knew that the odds had always been against the payment getting through. But, somewhere in his heart, he had believed that maybe – just maybe – it would. In retrospect, it occurred to him that his scratch-card winnings were not an indicator of future good fortune, but were instead a consolation prize. It was typical of his luck, Barry mused, that he would end up with £3, rather than the best part of 50,000. Barry slipped the card back in his wallet and headed disconsolately back to his car.

He was surprised at how disappointed he was. But, as he thought about it, Barry realised that what he was really trying to do was dispel the belief that had haunted him since he'd been at school and the other kids – the 'cool kids' in his class – had taken it upon themselves to flush his head down the toilet for fun. It was this: Barry was a loser. He was so obedient, so compliant with those above him, simply because he recognised that he needed their goodwill in order to survive. He was deferring to them because he recognised that they were winners and he wasn't.

He hadn't got the director's job, but, for the first time, it struck him that he was *never* going to get the director's job at Monument – or the director's job anywhere. Because people like Barry didn't win prizes like that in life. Something in the fabric of the universe decreed that they weren't allowed to. The most they could hope for was a £3 win on a scratch card.

He turned the key in the ignition of his car and drove off toward home where his wife would be waiting for him. It was enough to make him want to cry.

EIGHTEEN

Sally flopped into her chair and sighed. It had been a long day. Jamal, The SHYPP's concierge, had called her in what felt like the middle of the night to let her know he'd found a body, and she'd come straight in. And here she was, nearly fifteen hours later, still there.

But, of course, the world had not stopped turning in all that time. Emails had come in, phone messages had been left, post had been delivered – and there, in the midst of all the chaos on her desk, right on top of Sally's keyboard where she couldn't miss it, was a handwritten note and some papers with a fluorescent sticky note stuck in the middle marked: *"URGENT!"* It was from Marilyn.

Sally,

I know that you're busy at the moment and I didn't want to bother you again, but I didn't want to leave this over the weekend, so I thought you should know the following:

1. *The invoice from Monument (which you've already approved for payment) is officially due for payment at the end of the quarter. We are therefore currently in breach and we only have one calendar month to remedy breaches.*
2. *I know we usually wait until the next payment run to pay it, but the new housing director wants to do things differently and is asking for it to be paid as above; i.e. by today!*
3. *I couldn't find the letter you said you'd received, but I've checked with Barry and he's confirmed that their payment details have changed.*

Barry suggested we might want to pay now as Langley could try and use us not paying as an excuse to end the agreement – today is a month from quarter end, so, technically, we will have failed to have remedied a breach within the correct timescale, according to Barry.

Anyway, I've drawn up an authorisation letter for a CHAPS payment to be made. It's got the new payment details on, from the invoice. I've signed it, but it needs your signature too. All you have to do is sign it, scan it and email it over to our bank.

Obviously, it's your decision, but I thought it was better to be safe than sorry.

Have a great weekend. See you on Tuesday.

M

P.S. It costs £24, but it's guaranteed to be there the same day. Barry said it's your call as to whether you trust Langley or not.

Sally was annoyed at the prospect of having to pay an additional fee, but her primary concern was the choice posed by Barry – did she trust Langley or not? The answer was obviously 'not'. He'd always wanted The SHYPP to be managed directly by Monument, and now he clearly thought he'd found a way to achieve that goal.

Sally quickly checked the management agreement and confirmed that Barry was right. Payment was indeed due in arrears at the end of each quarter. Failure to make payment on the due date was classed as a 'default event'. Failure to rectify a default event within one calendar month would put the defaulting party in breach of the agreement. As it was nearly 6.30pm and she'd been in the office for fifteen hours, Sally didn't flick forward to schedule five of the agreement, which detailed what had to happen then. If she had, she would have seen that both parties had to sign up to a long and tedious process of independent arbitration before either party could terminate the agreement. Instead, she concluded that, for once, the normally useless, fat lump from Monument was actually being helpful. Langley was clearly intending to terminate the agreement if he didn't receive payment forthwith. Sally knew she could try to fight it, but her basic premise in life was to only fight the battles that she had a chance of winning and this didn't appear to be one of those.

She carefully checked the details on the CHAPS authorisation against those on the invoice and saw that they were the same. Everything appeared to be in order. Reluctantly, therefore, she signed the authorisation, scanned it and emailed it over to the bank. They'd all have gone home, she realised, but the payment could still be in

Monument's account before Langley had a chance to draft the termination notice, she assured herself. So, as she shut down her computer, Sally felt confident that she'd done enough to thwart Langley's plan.

NINETEEN

"Barry, I was wondering if you could come up to see me and Langley. We're in the boardroom," Angela said.

"Right. Sure. Not a problem," Barry replied, somewhat flustered.

It had proved to be a long weekend. One of the things that Barry had noticed was that, without Lauren in the house, there didn't seem much for him and his wife to talk about – apart from the obvious. And she didn't seem keen to talk about that at all. There was a fragility to their marriage now that surfaced whenever Christopher threatened to enter a conversation. It was as if it were a derelict house and any unauthorised intrusion by their son might cause its sudden collapse. So, they'd finished watching the David Attenborough box set in silence instead.

But the conversation that Jean had urged Barry to have with his wife still hadn't happened. If he were being honest, Barry felt she didn't seem ready for that kind of talk. Whenever he built himself up to trying to broach the subject, she looked at him with eyes that seemed filled with warnings.

He'd finally plucked up the courage on Saturday evening to tell her that he hadn't got the housing director's job, but had got no further when his wife announced that she was going upstairs. When she didn't come back down, Barry decided to follow her up to see if they could continue the conversation, but, as he walked across the landing, he heard what sounded like crying. Barry didn't want to interrupt, so he hurried back downstairs and watched *Match of the Day*. He hated football, but he preferred it to having to deal with a crying wife.

October was giving way to November, and its solemn skies spent Sunday soaking Walmley with rain of such ferocity that Barry was pinned inside the house. He didn't know what to say, and so the day was spent in carefully orchestrated manoeuvring around his wife. The hurried darkness of the late autumnal evening felt as oppressive as the summer heat, and, without the distraction of hope that Friday had provided, there was nothing to prevent Barry from fretting about what might await him at work on Monday morning.

Now, following Angela's call, it appeared he was about to find out. He hoped that he was being invited up to talk about his VR application, but, as he made his way to the boardroom, the thought did occur to him that perhaps something had been picked up at The SHYPP and he was being invited in to explain why he had attempted to use Chris Malford's bank card. His heart was pounding as he entered the boardroom, but, in order not to make himself look guilty, Barry decided to take his anxiety, wrap it up, and shove it behind the sunniest smile that he could manage under the circumstances.

"Barry, come in. Sit down," Angela said.

As Barry sat down, Langley gently swivelled his chair from side-to-side. It almost felt as though he should be stroking a white cat.

"Is this about my VR application?" Barry asked.

"Yes it is," Angela replied.

That, at least, was good news, but she was avoiding direct eye contact and instead was studying some notes in front of her intently. Even before she opened her mouth, Barry could tell what she was going to say.

"Well, as you can imagine Barry, we had a lot of good people apply for voluntary redundancy, and we've had to make some very difficult decisions."

Back at his desk, Barry flopped into his chair and let out a weary sigh. The chair beneath him expelled a wisp of air too, as though sighing in sympathy. Barry would not, it seemed, be leaving Monument under the terms of their generous voluntary redundancy scheme. Of course, Angela had emphasised all the positive things Barry brought to Monument. Langley had been less effusive. He'd merely said that, as there were currently two area manager posts vacant, they needed "boots on the ground at the moment". He didn't seem bothered about whose boots they were particularly. But Barry had taken his pointed mention of "at the moment"

to be a sign that that his current indispensability was not indefinite.

The fact that Barry had missed out on £22,000 was bad enough, but things had then got even worse. Langley had explained that he was "not comfortable" with Barry receiving a company car when the other area housing managers didn't. Angela had added that it was intended that the level of remuneration for the post would allow area managers to provide their own cars and then claim the standard mileage allowance for any business use.

Barry had asked – politely, he thought – whether the intention, therefore, was to take his company car from him.

At which point, Angela had quickly cut across Langley and said that "No final decision has been taken as yet, but we are looking to open up a consultation process with you about the issue, and that will be our proposal. Obviously, you will be entitled to present a counterproposal, but we have to consider the affordability of any arrangement to the business, Barry. And we have to be fair to all the other area managers."

It was pretty clear what that meant.

They'd asked him if he had anything to say, but he hadn't. There was nothing to say – who could argue against the concept of affordability? What counterproposal could Barry possibly table to the principle of fairness?

So, as he sat at his desk, Barry mentally scanned the horizon of his life for some good news that he could cling on to, but none was to be found. He cultivated his burgeoning sense of grievance, whilst responding to another of Langley's apparently endless stream of email queries. Everything seemed to be going wrong and it was all Monument's fault. At which point his phone rang.

"Barry. It's Sally here. Sally Hedges."

Barry's heart leapt into his mouth, but he tried to remain calm.

"Oh, hi Sally. How can I help?"

"I've just phoned to tell you that you're getting your money today – but I'm not happy."

The second part of this comment was not unexpected. But the first…

"I know exactly what Langley is trying to do," Sally went on, "and I've authorised a CHAPS payment today, solely in order to deny him the satisfaction of achieving it. So tell him he can pull that termination notice out of the post room, if he's already drafted it."

"Well, I'm not sure it's fair to say—"

"This is not what we agreed with Neville, Barry, and you know it. It's not the spirit of the agreement at all. This will cause us real cash-flow challenges, and I will be making that point forcefully to Andrew before the next quarterly invoice."

"Right. Well, I'll be sure—"

"In the meantime, if you're going to insist that we pay exactly at quarter end, can you at least issue the invoice in good time, so I don't have to pay an extra £24? It's ridiculous that we didn't even get the invoice until three weeks after the day you say we had to pay by!"

"Well, I know that's something that Langley is very keen—"

"As you know, we've got a lot to deal with here at the moment, so, on this occasion, I'm going to give Langley what he wants."

"That's very gracious—"

"But tell him from me that this is not over – not by a long chalk – so he shouldn't get any ideas that it is."

"Right. I'll pass that—"

"Your money will be with you in the next twenty minutes. Tell Langley, I hope he chokes on it!"

Before Barry had a chance to formulate a response, Sally ended the call.

He sat in stunned silence for a moment. "Your money will be with you in the next twenty minutes." Had she really just said that?

Langley had emerged from his office and was standing by Barry's desk. "Who was that? It sounded as though you were getting a real ear-chewing."

"Sally… Y'know what she's like," Barry replied, still in startled disbelief.

"Oh good, I was going to ask you about that. What's she said about our payment?" Langley asked with a hopeful look in his eyes.

"It'll be with us in twenty minutes."

"Really?"

"That's what she said."

Langley ripped up the letter he was holding. "Damn! That's a shame."

And, from the way he said it, Barry honestly thought Langley would rather the money wasn't going to be there. So he didn't feel too guilty about the fact that it wouldn't be.

TWENTY

Molloy was astute enough to have picked up that PC Ali 'Bongo' Khan hated him (although not, it seemed to Gemma, astute enough to have worked out that it was because he insisted on calling him 'Bongo'). So, he confided in his colleague, he was absolutely confident that Khan would have no hesitation in dropping him firmly 'in it' with the boss when he wrote up his report on Shana Backley's death. Gemma agreed that, although PC Khan didn't hate her, he would regard her as unfortunate, but necessary, collateral damage in his overall campaign to get Molloy into trouble. The two constables had therefore agreed that it was necessary for them to try to submit a report to their boss before PC Khan did. They would be absolutely open about what they had discovered and be clear that they had headed over to The SHYPP to question Adam Furst as soon as they reasonably could. It was just a matter of whether Inspector

Davis would interpret the forty-eight-hour delay between receiving the CCTV footage and actually attending The SHYPP as a missed opportunity to arrest Adam Furst – a missed opportunity that had contributed to Shana Backley's untimely death.

"So, you mean to tell me that you are given CCTV footage showing a known felon and suspected drug dealer leaving the flat of a man who you know subsequently died of a drug overdose, and you didn't think to go round and interview him for forty-eight hours?"

It appeared that they had their answer.

"No, sir," said Gemma after a long pause, during which it became apparent that Molloy wasn't going to say anything.

"To be fair, sir," Molloy said, "we hadn't received any toxicology reports to confirm—"

"He was found with a bloody needle in his arm!"

"PC Molloy suggested going round on Thursday, sir, but I was due in court. We went round as soon as we came on shift on Friday."

Having provided some cover for Molloy, Gemma hoped that he would return the favour and explain that she had suggested that they go round to The SHYPP immediately on the Wednesday afternoon. It was to prove a forlorn hope.

"That's right, sir. I wanted to go on the Thursday, but PC Rathbone said she wasn't available, so we couldn't get there until the Friday, sir. It wasn't until we got there that Bongo told us—"

"Who?" asked Davis.

"Bongo," Molloy replied, as though it was obvious whom he was referring to.

Inspector Davis fixed him with an uncomprehending sneer.

"PC Khan, sir," Gemma said.

"We call him 'Bongo', sir. It's 'cause his first name's Ali," Molloy added in an ill-conceived attempt to explain. "Ali Bongo," he continued. "A comedy magician from the seventies and eighties."

"Thanks for clearing that up, PC Molloy," Inspector Davis replied with barely concealed disdain.

The three of them fell silent. Davis sat back in his chair and looked out of his office window over the station's car park. Then he bowed his head, and slowly smoothed his temples with his thumb and forefinger.

"I'm going to be honest," Davis said eventually. "I had some sympathy for you at first – when I read your report. You've been honest enough to admit what happened and, to be fair, you weren't to know that Adam Furst's career as a drug lord was going to be fatally undermined by his apparent inability to distinguish between a gramme and an ounce."

"Thank you, sir," said Gemma, sensing even as she did so that Davis' short speech was building up to a monumental 'but'.

"But I'm not going to lie to you. Shana Backley is Kurt Backley's daughter—"

"Kurt Backley? You can't take him seriously, sir" said Molloy. "He practically makes his living out of suing the criminal justice system."

"That's exactly the point," replied Davis, turning back and looking his officers squarely in the face. "He's already threatening legal action. And that's *before* he finds out that we were aware of Furst's potential involvement in another fatal overdose a couple of weeks earlier. His solicitors will have a field day once they know that PC Rathbone viewed the CCTV footage on the Monday."

"But, as I also state in my report, sir—"

"Save it, PC Rathbone." There was a pause, whilst Inspector Davis leant forward, his fingers folded in front of him. He tapped his thumbs together. "I was hoping the two of you could help me here. I was hoping you would say something – *anything* – that would give me a reason to let this one slide. But what do you give me, PC Molloy? Ali Bloody Bongo. Frankly, I might as well write the cheque out now."

"Sir, I know this looks bad—" Gemma said.

"You're telling me!"

"But we've already done some work on this case. We're in touch with a guy at the housing association who knows Adam Furst, and he really wants to help us."

"I'm sorry, but this is serious. We had the information to do something and we didn't do it. Bottom line – somebody's died. I can't be seen to ignore that."

"But we couldn't have known Fursty would get his quantities mixed up," Molloy protested. "He's the one to blame, sir, not us."

"That's as may be. But there will have to be an investigation."

"You're joking!"

"The family are demanding it! Her father's already engaged solicitors."

"But, sir—" Gemma said, desperately.

"Don't worry – I'm not suspending you, but I am going to have to keep you out of the way whilst this is all looked into. I'm moving you both to traffic."

"Traffic?" Molloy said, his eyes saucering in alarm.

"Only whilst this is looked into."

Gemma was hyperventilating. The traffic unit was the police equivalent of the nonces' wing in prison. "But, sir," she said, "if I could just speak to Mr Todd. I'm sure he could explain to you. He may even know where Furst is."

"I'm sorry, PC Rathbone. But everything's being handed over to CID – Malford, Backley, Furst; the whole shebang. You won't be talking to Mr Todd again, understand? Not unless you pull him over for a traffic offence."

Little did Inspector Davis know just how wrong he would be.

TWENTY-ONE

Barry had lots to do, but he just couldn't get his thoughts straight; there was too much going on in his head. Sally's call had left his mouth feeling dry with unease. His theoretical deception was theoretical no more. Now it felt all too real, and he was faced with a decision. But an open-plan office, with its apparently never-ending stream of 'can-you-justs' and 'ooh-I'm-glad-I've-caught-yous', was not the place to make it.

"Right. I'm going down to Chelmsley Wood, Tanee. I need to catch up with Sally about what's happening at The SHYPP." After Friday's terrible tragedy, it seemed a perfectly reasonable use of his time. But Barry wasn't intending to visit The SHYPP at all.

As he walked out of the office toward his car, he was genuinely in two minds as to whether to go back to the little mini-market with the cashpoint, or just head into town and spend the afternoon wandering round the museum and art gallery. But then he saw a brand-new Jaguar XF sweep into the car park and pull into one of the executive parking bays.

"New car, Langley?" Barry asked. His subtle attempt to suggest heavy irony in light of that morning's conversation was obviously so subtle that it completely passed Langley by.

"Yes, just had to pop down to the garage to pick it up," Langley said with a beaming smile. "They did ask if I wanted Karen's old Mondeo, but I felt I wanted something with a little more... gravitas," he added, trousering his keys with a flamboyant swirl of the keyring around his index finger.

"Nice motor. Can't have been cheap."

"Are you off out?" Langley said, moving the conversation along.

"Yes, off down to Chelmsley Wood. I need to catch up with Sally at The SHYPP."

"Well, make sure you've got our money off her," Langley called out, as he headed toward the office.

"Oh, don't you worry. I will." Barry replied. "I definitely will now," he added under his breath as Langley strode through the autumnal chill toward the entrance to Monument's office.

Twenty minutes later Barry pulled up just along the road from the corner shop. He made his way back toward the shop and was pleased to see the same teenager sitting morosely on a stool behind the till, looking as though even mustering the effort to appear bored was too much for her. He went immediately to the cashpoint and inserted Chris Malford's bank card.

"Which service do you require?"

Barry asked for an on-screen account balance.

"Please wait whilst we process your request."

There was a seemingly interminable pause whilst the machine considered the matter. And then, eventually, a different message appeared:

"Your current balance is: £48,591.52.

"Do you require another service?"

Barry stared at the screen for a moment before deciding that he did indeed require another service. He would like to withdraw some cash. Not because he actually wanted the money of course, but because he wanted to prove to himself that he could do it. That he could beat them. The maximum daily cash withdrawal from Chris' account was £250, so Barry decided he would try withdrawing that. Yes, he understood that he would be charged £1.75 for this transaction. He wasn't particularly happy about it, but, under the circumstances, it seemed churlish to complain.

There was another delay whilst the machine chuntered and whirred, and then notes began to be spat out into the little tray at the bottom. Barry picked them up and, turning his back to the CCTV camera behind the till, counted out the money: £250. He took back the bank card and put it, along with the money, in his wallet. He then let out the very deep breath that he had been holding and walked over to the till.

"Can I have a scratch card, please? The one with the leprechaun, I think."

"OK," the girl replied, tearing a card off the roll and handing it to Barry. "That's two quid."

Barry handed over £2 and then scratched off the foiled area on the card that he was given.

"Have I won anything?"

The young girl scanned the card. "Not this time, no. Sorry."

"Never mind," said Barry, breezily. "You can't win every time."

But, as he turned to leave the shop, he felt, unlike the previous Friday, as though he had won a much bigger prize. It wasn't just that he'd got one over on Monument in general, and Langley in particular, it was that something fundamental had changed. No longer would he get excited about a £3 scratch-card win. No longer would he hanker after life's consolation prizes, as though they were all he could ever expect. Barry understood, for the first time, that he was just as capable as anyone else of securing the good things in life, if only he had the confidence to believe it. And, from now on, he determined he *would* have the confidence to believe it. No longer would he sit mournfully alone with his wounds in a world full of people with knives. He would pick up his own knife. He would strike back. He would actively pursue and seize those things that he wanted. His pain would matter. He wouldn't allow it to simply be lost in the vast swarm of innominate humanity, scurrying about to nowhere very significant.

Just believing that shifted something in his universe. He had made the transition from 'loser' to 'winner'. Barry Todd's life of crime had most definitely begun.

PART 3

"We know what greatness is, but we ignore it in favour of banality."

Frank Gehry

THE GREATNESS OF THE AGES

2nd November – 4th December 2015

TWENTY-TWO

Barry found himself shaking as he drove away from the mini-market with £250 in his wallet – and over £48,000 more in a bank account that he controlled. And, despite his not inconsiderable bulk, he felt weightless, as though he were floating through space. He sensed that the reason for his feeling of exhilaration was the fact that he had a secret. He'd never had a secret before, not a proper one, and he couldn't help but feel a sense of pride that he had one now, which felt so grown up. He held it close and nursed it, like a pet.

But there was something lurking behind his exhilaration that he couldn't quite see. Despite the fact that his plan had been executed flawlessly, Barry couldn't shake the sense that he might be caught. It was ridiculous – he knew that – but he couldn't quite rid himself of the feeling that it couldn't be that easy to steal nearly £50,000 of someone else's money. If it was, then why didn't everybody do it? And why, come to think of it, had he not done it before? The question flitted across his mind for the briefest of moments before scurrying off into the penumbra.

But a sense of annoyance with his employer was also spreading like a rumour within him. He was annoyed that, after twenty-two years of exemplary service, he had been denied a promotion he was clearly the best candidate for. He was annoyed too that Monument had now also denied him a fair and appropriate financial settlement to leave their employment. And, of course, he was annoyed that they were now threatening to take away his company car. So, as he drove off, he felt entirely justified in starting to think about exactly how much of the money that he had so skilfully diverted he might actually be able to access.

It would take twenty-eight days before Monument's system would flag the invoice as being unpaid. At some point shortly after that a reminder would be sent, which would no doubt provoke a furious (and immediate) response from Sally. She would contact the bank, where staff would realise the money had been diverted and contact Chris Malford's bank. They would freeze the account and return what money was left to The SHYPP. Given that he could only withdraw £250 in cash each day, Barry worked out that he would only have time to withdraw around £7,000 from Chris Malford's account. The remaining forty-one and a half thousand would therefore be returned to Monument.

Barry thought for a moment. Seven thousand pounds: that wasn't even fifteen per cent of the money he'd diverted. Fifteen per cent was the standard administration fee Monument charged its tenants on their service charges.

They were allowed to; housing benefit regulations said so. So taking fifteen per cent of the money he'd diverted wouldn't really be theft, it would simply be a perfectly reasonable administration charge for all the time and effort he'd taken to highlight the shortcomings in Monument's financial processes. They would still get eighty-five per cent of their money back, which they'd probably be quite relieved about, actually.

Going back to the office now was out of the question, but he found himself wanting to go where there was no CCTV. He knew he needed to keep his secret well hidden, like all the other contents of his heart. But he worried that the cameras might be able to see it somehow, even through the fabric of his clothes and the folds of his skin. For the first time he could recall, his heart felt strangely insecure, as though there were another key to it somewhere in the hands of someone he didn't know.

Having driven for a few minutes, he found himself approaching Solihull town centre. He decided to pull over and grab a coffee to calm his nerves.

There was a language and a certain ritual to ordering a 'bespoke' coffee that he was not fully conversant with, but that others seemed to be. This made him feel instantly ill at ease, a bit like when he walked into a church for a wedding or a funeral.

He always liked having a filter coffee back at the office, so he ordered one of those. He couldn't be certain, but Barry thought he heard a dismissive "tut" from someone behind him in the queue. As he turned his back to grab a cup and start preparing Barry's drink, Barry thought he might have seen the barista roll his eyes at one of the other staff.

He wanted to shout at them that he was a winner now; that he had joined their elite club. But he couldn't. Partly, this was because it would sound ridiculous, but mainly it was because he couldn't tell anyone what he'd done. His new-found status as a winner had to remain a secret too. In order for him to avoid detection, it was, ironically, vital that everyone still viewed him as a loser.

So far, so good, Barry mused.

In response to the barista's promptings, Barry decided that a celebratory blueberry muffin was in order. Under the circumstances, it didn't feel like an inappropriate extravagance.

As he took his seat, Barry's eye fell on a small barely-toddler in a rather fetching bear onesie on the other side of the shop. His mother, deep in conversation with a friend, was trying to keep watch over him – offering him encouragement and the occasional admonishment – whilst trying to engage hungrily in the adult conversation on offer. He toddled around the shop, somehow aware of her presence, and apparently reassured by it, but at the same time almost oblivious to it.

Everywhere the little boy went the other patrons would smile at him, make faces and offer a few words of encouragement. Without really doing anything particularly stretching, the child was the centre of everyone's attention. Somehow, there was a tacit agreement between the patrons of the shop that it was everybody's job not just to keep the child safe but to make him feel good about himself.

Of course, Barry realised, as the child grew up this sense of obligation toward him would diminish. He would slowly have to learn the lesson that he was not, in fact, the only person whose well-being mattered; there would be other people who also had wants and needs, some of which would be in conflict with his. And Barry knew from bitter personal experience that one day that child would learn the painful lesson that, when those competing aspirations came into conflict with his, sometimes he would lose.

But, for the moment, those were thoughts for another day.

Barry watched the child exploring the world with a wholly innocent belief that it was benevolent and friendly, and would always be shaped around his needs. He wondered to himself how much of his own adult life had really just been a search for a return to those long-lost days when he was the centre of someone's attention.

It was, quite literally, childish, but there was a part of Barry that needed to feel that, somewhere in his life, there was someone who cared about his hopes, dreams and aspirations as much as he did. He wanted to feel that there was someone – not everyone, obviously, but one person – who would put those things at the centre of their concerns. And who would let him put their hopes, dreams and aspirations at the centre of his concerns too.

Barry decided that he needed to go home. He needed to have that conversation with his wife, not to confess (obviously), but to try to re-establish the connection that they seemed to have lost when Christopher died. In fact, thinking about it, Barry realised that they'd lost that connection before Christopher died; it was just that his presence in their lives had masked that fact. Their conversations had become about things on the surface, whilst carrying an undercurrent of secret meanings. And then, at some point, probably because they both got tired of arguing so indirectly, their conversations had become just about things on the surface.

But Barry wanted those old conversations back – the ones they'd had when they'd first met – and he decided that now was the time to restart them. He snaffled the last bit of his muffin, got up and strode purposefully toward the door. Tonight, he resolved, would be the night.

A few minutes later, Gemma Rathbone found herself alone, slumped in the same easy chair that Barry had recently vacated, miserably sipping a skinny cappuccino. Her intention had been to have a quiet conversation with Rob, her boyfriend, about what she should do now. As a fellow officer, Rob was bound to know how she should deal with Molloy; as her boyfriend, she hoped he would offer some sympathy. However, the peace of her surroundings was being disturbed by a small child in a bear onesie. He was careering around the shop whilst his mother carried on chatting, apparently oblivious to the disturbance her child was causing to the other customers. *Selfish cow,* Gemma thought to herself. *What chance does that child stand in life with a mother like that? What kind of man will that little boy grow up into if his mother shows such casual disregard for him now? Probably one like Molloy,* she concluded.

The toddler ran about with great enthusiasm, but with no real sense of purpose. What he wanted was people's approval, but he offered them nothing in return. He wasn't interested in what they were doing or whether he was interrupting them; he just wanted them to notice him and tell him how wonderful he was. And, once they'd done that, he'd toddle off to the next person and do the same thing. The more she watched the child, the more he annoyed her, and the more he annoyed her, the more she realised that it was because he was just like Molloy.

It was hours since they had been hauled into Inspector Davis' office and had a strip torn off them, and yet, not once since then had Molloy indicated, even obliquely, that he thought an apology might be in order. But, more than that, he gave no indication of even having considered for a moment that a person who had died – Shana Backley – might still be alive if he had listened to her. The only thought that had occurred to him since they'd been advised of their enforced transfer was the impact of the whole situation on him. Even now, he was spending his lunch break in a meeting with the Police Federation rep down at the station. An innocent woman lay dead, but Molloy seemed to think that he was the principal victim. He was trying to claim a starring role in the drama, but, in doing so, was pushing the central figure to the sidelines.

Only Molloy, Gemma mused, *could try and claim that his career was more important than the life of a highly vulnerable woman.*

But it was not only Molloy at all.

TWENTY-THREE

To get from Solihull back to Walmley involved doing battle with rush-hour traffic, so the fifteen-mile journey took over an hour, but, for once, Barry wasn't frustrated. The long, slow drive meant that he didn't arrive back home too early, and he had also had a chance to think about what he might want to say to his wife. He obviously couldn't tell her about the money, but he needed to convey to her that things would be different from now on.

Barry had felt like a loser for so long that, somehow, the feeling had soaked into his bones. So it was only natural that his wife appeared to regard him with the kind of exasperation usually reserved for small puppies that refused to be housetrained. But now he wanted her to see him in a new light.

Eventually, Barry pulled up on his drive, the loose chippings crackling under his tyres. He checked his wallet.

It was still there: £250. He knew that it would be prudent to start putting some money away for the deposit on a new car. But, he decided, this first withdrawal would be spent on new art materials. The new Barry Todd was going to reward himself with something to nourish his inner life. He was going to start painting again. He would go up into the loft and see how much of his college art stuff was still useable and how much needed replacing, but, at the very least, he knew that he would need some paints.

The moment he came in, his wife jumped up from the sofa and stood, bolt upright, arms folded, like an exclamation mark at the end of a sentence. "You're home early."

There was definitely a suggestion in the tone of her voice that Barry could only be home at this point because he'd done something wrong – which, in a sense, was true, but not in the way that she seemed to suppose.

"I had a meeting in Solihull that finished early. It wasn't worth going back to the office."

"I've had Lauren on the phone." She snipped at the words like a pair of scissors.

"And...?"

Her arms dropped to her sides and she looked at him truculently, as though challenging him to prove her suspicions about him wrong. "She was in tears, Barry; in absolute floods of tears."

Barry found this very hard to believe. It felt like the kind of detail his wife would add to a story to make him feel more guilty. "Oh, that's not good. Did she say why?"

There was a slight pause, during which his wife's eyes expanded to the size of saucers.

"I can't believe you sometimes!" She slapped the words down like an accusation.

"Sorry..." was all Barry could think to say.

"You don't know, do you? You don't even know what you've done – or not done."

Barry couldn't argue with her on this point. "Sorry..."

"You've not sent her the money, Barry!"

Barry quietly closed his eyes. She had caught him bang to rights. He had indeed failed to send Lauren the money he should have – the money he had promised to send her.

"No, I haven't—"

"Oh Barry..." she said. And the space she left was filled with her silent disappointment. It spread out across the room until neither of them seemed to know quite what to do to stop it. Eventually she continued in a voice that could not have sounded more tired or more let down. "She's our daughter, Barry. She needs that money to live on."

"I know, and if you'll just—"

"You said you'd send it last week. The poor girl's running out of money!"

Barry had set his heart on some kolinsky-hair paintbrushes, but now realised that desperate times called for desperate measures.

"If you'll just let me explain," he said, withdrawing his wallet from his pocket like a magician withdrawing a rabbit from his top hat. "I had to wait until I got paid today, but I've withdrawn a couple of hundred quid in cash and I'll post it to her special delivery tomorrow. That way she won't have to wait for a cheque to clear."

"A couple of hundred? We already owe her 400!"

"Yes, and I'll withdraw another couple of hundred in cash tomorrow morning and put that in the envelope too. But there's a limit on how much you can withdraw each day," Barry explained, as though this had always been part of his plan.

There was the slightest of pauses, which suggested (to Barry, at least) that her ire might be beginning to assuage.

"Well, just make sure you do!" she said.

"I've not started tea yet," she continued, apropos of nothing in particular.

Barry realised that he was being accused of always coming in and expecting his dinner to be on the table. However, her tardiness in preparing their evening meal presented him with an opportunity, and it was one upon which he pounced like a cat on string.

"That's good actually, 'cause I was going to suggest we went out for dinner tonight."

"Out?" She looked at him as though he had suggested something strange and wondrous.

"Yeah. There's that new Indian I thought we could try. The one at the end of the road. What d'you think?"

The frown on her face slowly dissolved as she considered the idea. "I suppose so. If you want to," she replied. "But I warn you, Barry, if it's like that filthy Thai place you took me to, we're not staying."

Two-and-a-half years on, the 'filthy' (but highly recommended – and expensive) 'Thai place' still loomed large in his wife's thoughts.

"I tell you what, though," she added, a warm smile suddenly beginning its weary passage across her face. "We could ask Alun and Sue if they wanted to come with us. What do you think?"

Alun and Sue Evans were the Todds' neighbours. Alun was a retired police officer who – having spent thirty years tapping the side of his nose and muttering darkly about how, "I'd love to tell you, but you know how it is…" – now felt no need to hold back on telling people *exactly* how it was. Barry found this incredibly boring, so his immediate reaction was to demur at his wife's suggestion. Besides, the whole point of his plan was to engage in The Conversation They Needed to Have, and it was not the kind of conversation he felt he could have if Alun and Sue were there too.

But then it occurred to Barry that, in view of the legal risks associated with his recent cash withdrawal, Alun's tendency to be fabulously indiscreet to all and sundry about the inner workings of the police force might actually be quite helpful for once. And he also thought that being seen to accede to his wife's request might gain him some credit when he did eventually try to have The Conversation They Needed to Have. So he graciously agreed, and she phoned Sue to see if she and Alun were free.

"Alun's not back from the golf club yet," she said after hanging up. "But Sue says she's definitely up for joining us, so she suggests we go down now and have our starters and they'll join us for the main course – if Alun gets back in time. I've said we'll let them know how we get on. If it's no good, we're only five minutes' walk from that nice place – the one I like."

Barry declined to rise to the bait. Whatever his wife's misgivings, from his perspective, the Evans' delayed arrival sounded just about perfect. The Conversation They Needed to Have was back on.

TWENTY-FOUR

The restaurant, whilst not exactly full, was busier than one might have expected on a Monday evening. Barry took this to be a good thing – it was a sign that his proposed choice was not quite as hare-brained as wife's initial reaction had suggested. He was also reassured by the fact that the restaurant's decor was pleasingly contemporary and the waiting staff smartly dressed – it demonstrated a degree of classiness in his selection that might not have been immediately assumed by his wife.

The comforting scent of turmeric and coriander, of cardamom and paprika, warmed his nose as they were escorted to their table. He hoped she would be impressed. And, indeed, she agreed to take a velour-covered seat without protest, and had not immediately suggested going on to "that nice place – the one that I like", even after their waiter left them alone with the menus. So at least Barry's suggestion had passed the first test: Furnishings and General Ambience.

She surveyed the menu silently, casting a matronly eye over the options, withholding final judgement until she had fully apprised herself of the choices on offer. Finally, after an apparent age and without lifting her eyes from the menu in front of her, she concluded simply, "Seems nice."

Bingo! Barry knew from this that he had passed the second test. The restaurant had met her fairly exacting standards for Menu Range and Presentation. There was just one more thing she would need to check.

"I'm just popping to the ladies'."

Excellent, Barry thought. He knew, of course, that she wouldn't actually be availing herself of the facilities on offer – that would be too much to expect on a first visit to a new restaurant – but the fact that she wished to view them was a good sign.

The habitual 'visit to the ladies' served two purposes in his wife's mind. Firstly, it allowed her to satisfy herself that the toilets themselves were of an appropriate level of hygiene and general comfort. But secondly, it was also the case that in most restaurants (for practical reasons of plumbing, as Barry understood from his basic building design knowledge) the toilets tended to be next to the kitchen. This meant that whilst checking out the toilets, his wife could also cast a quick glance into the kitchen to establish the conditions under which her food was being prepared. These were the final tests to be passed before any food or drinks could be ordered.

Three minutes later, she returned and took her seat. Barry took this as a sign that she was satisfied, but he thought he'd better just check.

"Everything all right?" he asked.

"Yes. Fine."

'Fine' was OK, Barry decided. Not as good as 'good' to be sure, and certainly nowhere near as helpful as 'lovely', but 'fine' was enough for Barry to be able to catch the waiter's eye, confident in the knowledge that his wife was happy to eat there. Maybe, in time, she would even be happy to use the toilets. But that was an issue for another day. Tonight was about crossing the threshold and eating the food. And, of course, it was about the conversation: The Conversation They Needed to Have.

But sitting there, it occurred to Barry that he didn't know what he wanted to say. Or rather, he knew what he wanted to say, but there was too much of it. The Conversation They Needed to Have felt like an ocean and all he had with which to attempt a crossing was an inflatable dinghy. He didn't know where to start or how.

She began talking to him about her day; about having to go and complain to the deputy head because one of the other volunteer classroom assistants had been offered a paid post when she had not even been told there was a paid post available. Or something. Barry hadn't quite heard because he wasn't really listening. And he wasn't really listening because he was trying to work out what he needed to say.

And then, all of a sudden, as if some divine force had entered her and made her see what the problem really was, his wife completely changed tack and opened up The Conversation They Needed to Have for him.

"What do you want, Barry? Just say what you want!"

It felt like a weight had been lifted from his chest. Of course, that was it. That was what he had to tell her – what he wanted. He had to tell her about the little boy in the coffee shop. Because as soon as he told her about him she would understand. And once she understood they could go back to being like they were before, when they were so close.

But what pleased Barry even more was that he knew exactly what to say in response. He leant forward and grabbed her hands with relief.

"I want people to see me as I really am, that's all…" he said. And then, almost as an embarrassed afterthought, he added, "And I want to know that that's enough for someone to love me."

It was, he guessed, what everyone wanted really – even tossers like Langley – so it was probably what his wife wanted too. And, knowing that, they could cross the ocean that separated them and be together again – not just in proximity to each other, but together in an altogether deeper sense.

Except that it appeared that this might not be the case at all.

His wife's eyes flared in alarm and her cheeks flushed a deep red. She pulled her hands away from his and looked at Barry in horror. Her head snapped to the left.

"He'll have a samosa to start and the chicken jalfrezi to follow. He always has that."

"Very good, madam," the waiter replied, as though Barry's outburst of a few moments earlier had not happened at all.

"And I'm terribly sorry for my husband. Just ignore him." The waiter nodded discreetly and headed back toward the kitchen. "What was that all about? Are you *trying* to embarrass me?"

"Sorry," said Barry. "I didn't mean to… I just thought—"

"Thought? Thought? You were actually *thinking* when you said that? Well, you certainly weren't paying any attention. What will that waiter think of us?"

What, indeed. Barry was going to try to protest, but it would have been futile. The fact was, he hadn't been paying attention, and, yes, he had committed the ultimate social *faux pas* and embarrassed his wife in public. If she hadn't already ordered her own meal, she probably would have insisted on walking out there and then. As it was, it seemed unlikely they would be staying for dessert.

But there was something else that made him realise the futility of trying to resurrect The Conversation They Needed to Have: the look on her face at that moment. She'd looked at him as if he had admitted to some unspeakable crime. Of course, he hadn't – but he could have. He could have told her all about the money and where the £200 that he'd promised to send to Lauren had come from, as well as all the other £200s that he was proposing to send to Lauren. But that look seemed to Barry to contain a clear warning of what he could expect if he did.

Barry needed her to give him the benefit of the doubt, but her look did not suggest she would be minded to give it to him. It was the look of a woman who had heard the *second*-most intimate thing that her husband could have chosen to share with her – and had found it utterly horrifying and revolting. Her reaction if Barry had chosen to share the *most* intimate thing that he could have told her didn't bear thinking about. But what he knew was this: he had opened his heart up to her and had got a very clear response. She had seen him (very nearly) as he really was and had unambiguously declared that what he really was *wasn't* enough for her to love him.

"What do *you* want?" he asked, forlornly.

"The balti chicken bhuna," she replied. "Were you not listening?"

And she went back to talking about The Great Classroom Assistant Scandal.

And there, Barry reflected, was their relationship in a nutshell. He said, almost unthinkingly, that he loved her. But when he looked into her eyes – even really deeply – he couldn't see her soul anymore. Not since Christopher. She was impassive now, like a sphinx; giving nothing out and expecting nothing in return. The Conversation They Needed to Have was deferred indefinitely.

A few minutes later, however, her eyes did indeed light up. Sadly, she wasn't looking at Barry as they did so, but rather just over his shoulder as an ebullient voice came from behind him. "Sue! Alun! You did make it. Oh, that's wonderful!"

The Evanses had barely taken their seats and placed their orders when Alun began regaling the Todds with yet another story of police incompetence that he had, apparently, been told on good authority. Barry immediately saw his opportunity to steer the conversation on to more helpful territory.

"That's very interesting, Alun," he lied, "but I heard a story from a shopkeeper the other day and I just can't believe what she said the police told her."

"Go on then," Alun said, daring Barry to try to shock him.

"Oh, don't get him started, Barry. I get this every day," said Sue despairingly.

"Well, they had a cash machine in a shop, and they had a CCTV camera pointing straight at it, recording everything."

"Oh aye," said Alun with a knowing smile.

"You've got him started now. I told you not to get him started! Anyway, how's Lauren getting on?" And with that the two women turned their heads and began talking about their respective families.

"Anyway," Barry continued, "a little old lady has her purse taken out of her shopping bag with her bank card and PIN inside. The thieves come into the shop and use the cash machine to take £250 out of her account."

"I bet they did!" said Alun, chuckling slightly and shaking his head.

"So, the old lady goes to the police and reports the crime. She tells them the shop's got CCTV footage of the people taking her cash, so it shouldn't be too difficult to find them."

"I know what's coming next."

"Really? Because, according to the shopkeeper, who had kept the CCTV footage and everything, apparently they said—"

"That they weren't going to investigate the crime, and she should just give the crime number to her bank and get her money back off them!"

"Yes! That's exactly what they said."

"Not worth it, apparently," said Alun, with heavy sarcasm.

"But they took 250 quid out of her account – it was all caught on CCTV!"

"The CCTV's a red herring. If there's no proof of violence, 250 quid would be below the prosecution threshold. It doesn't matter that they've seen them withdrawing the cash on CCTV. If they haven't got CCTV footage of them mugging the old lady, the CPS won't authorise a prosecution."

"So you can just steal £250 and the police won't even investigate?"

"As long as you don't break in anywhere, or use or threaten violence, you can nick a lot more than that and get away with it. What's the point of the police investigating if the CPS won't prosecute at the end of it?"

Barry was both shocked and yet also relieved. He'd been worried about the possibility of being caught, but it now appeared that, even if the police traced Monument's money to Chris Malford's account and found there was a few thousand pounds missing, they wouldn't bother to investigate.

"So, stealing money isn't important anymore? It's all about whether you use violence?"

"I'm not saying it's right; I'm just telling you how it is," said Alun. "Politicians keep going on about how violent crime's dropping, as though we're all becoming more honest because of them. What they don't tell you is that white-collar crime – fraud and the like – is going through the roof! Why would you bother to run the risk of serving time for holding up a post office for maybe a few hundred quid, when you can go online and steal tens – even hundreds – of thousands of pounds and not even face the possibility of being investigated?"

"Really?" Barry couldn't quite believe what he was hearing. "So most of this white-collar crime isn't even investigated?"

"Not anymore. Of course, it was different when I came on to the force, but they've rationalised and centralised everything now. Complete waste of time, if you ask me. Just confuses the public and means that, by the time anybody actually gets round to making a decision on whether to investigate or not, it's not worth it – so they hardly ever bother. I'm not condoning it; I'm just telling it as it is. It's all about priorities now."

"So, if the little old lady isn't a priority, what is?" Barry asked. "Corporate fraud?"

"I should coco."

"But I don't understand. Why wouldn't they want to investigate corporate fraud? I mean, I can see they might not be interested in 250 quid, but corporate fraud is for thousands. And there'll be audit trails and everything."

"Well, firstly, the company may not even bother to report it to the police. They'll be too embarrassed that they've been conned, and they'll probably get told by their solicitor that it won't get investigated anyway. But let's say they do report it. Well, now you've got all this internet fraud and these foreign scams, they don't let the local coppers on to it straight away. You can't even report it to your local police force."

"Really?"

"Really! You have to report it to something called Action Fraud – or *In*action Fraud, as I call 'em!" Alun laughed at his own wit.

Barry joined in with a polite chuckle and poured Alun another glass of horribly sweet German wine to try to encourage him to continue.

"Half the time Action Fraud will just say straight out, 'I'm sorry, there's nothing we can do'. The fact is, there's hardly any resources put into fraud. There are literally thousands of these cases reported every week – over 20,000 a month – and they just haven't got the manpower to pick up on every case. If there's multiple reports of the same thing, then you're more likely to get something done. But if it's a one-off incident – and I'm just being honest with you Barry, you know me – the reality is it's almost certainly going to be ignored."

Barry's old certainties about crime and its reputed inability to pay were starting to fall away.

"But they must decide to do something about some of the cases, surely?"

"Oh yes. They pass them on to the National Fraud Intelligence Bureau."

"And they investigate them?"

"Oh good grief, no. They package the cases up – whatever the hell that means, I never found out – and then weeks later decide whether to pass them on for investigation."

"*Whether* to pass them on?"

"That's the point. When I was still on the force, they only passed on about five or six thousand a month."

"But didn't you just say there were about 20,000 frauds reported every month?"

"Exactly. And even if they do finally pass a case on to an investigative agency, like the local police force, it's them who have to decide whether to carry out an investigation."

"You're not serious?"

"Absolutely. They might decide to investigate, but, then again, they might decide that they don't have the capacity to accept the case. In which case they'll just send it back to the NFIB."

"And they'll investigate it then?"

"You're joking, aren't you? They might take some action to prevent a repeat of that specific crime going forward, but they won't try to solve the crime that's already happened. Unbelievable, isn't it?"

Indeed it was.

"So how do they decide which cases to investigate? I mean they must make a decision on something more than whether they've got capacity, surely?"

"Oh yes. They look at the degree of harm. Like I said, even if they solve a case, the CPS won't sanction a prosecution unless it's in the public interest. So there's got to be a significant degree of harm. If a business goes bankrupt because of a fraud, then they'll see that as a high degree of harm. But if it's a couple of grand nicked off some massive multinational, then they won't."

"Is that it?"

"Well, there's got to be what we call 'a viable line of enquiry'. The police will want to know that there's a reasonable chance of them solving the case before they start investigating it. Ridiculous, isn't it?"

"Ridiculous," Barry agreed.

"Oh, and then there's the biggie."

"The biggie?"

"Offender overseas. If it looks like the fraudster's abroad, the police here won't want to bother – particularly if it's a non-EU country. It all gets too complicated and expensive, and half the time the police forces in those places are as crooked as the criminals."

Barry felt he may have overdone it on the cheap German wine. He could sense that Alun was building up to one of his explosive rants about foreigners.

"I'll tell you something, Barry. If I was going to commit a fraud, I'd make sure I had a bank account open in Bongo-Bongo Land 'cause the moment the money leaves Blighty, the police here don't want to know."

Barry subtly moved the wine bottle out of Alun's reach.

"So tell me, Alun, just as a matter of interest, out of those 20,000 cases a month, how many actually end up with someone being convicted?"

"Honestly? About 800 or so."

"Eight hundred! Is that all? That's only about four per cent. That can't be right, surely?"

"I'm afraid it is. Why do you think so many people are chancing their arm? It's because they know they've got a ninety-six per cent chance of getting away with it – and they're virtually guaranteed to get away with it if they can get the money abroad. But even if they can't – from the fraud being detected, to it being reported to Action Fraud; them passing it on to the NFIB; them sitting on it for a bit, then packaging it up and sending it out to the local force; then the local force deciding whether they can investigate it or not – how long do you think all that takes?"

"I don't know – five or six weeks?"

Alun let out a hearty guffaw. "Oh Barry! I envy your naïveté! Try five or six *months* – if you're lucky."

"Five or six months? You're kidding me!"

"'Fraid not. And, by that time, any remote chance you might have had of tracing someone has probably gone. The evidence has disappeared. Under the blessed Data Protection Act, for instance, you can only keep CCTV footage for twenty-eight days without due cause, so even if the person has walked up to a cashpoint or into a bank branch and withdrawn all their ill-gotten gains in cash right in front of a prosecution-standard camera, by the time the police get round to investigating it, the footage will have been wiped."

At which point their starters arrived.

Alun carried on talking – about his latest gardening project and their son's recent promotion at work – but Barry wasn't really listening. He was trying to process what Alun had just told him and work out its consequences for him.

Barry had – up until that point, at least – always sought to stay within the law. But, actually, what Alun had suggested was that it didn't really matter. No one cared. Not even the police. And even if they suspected that he'd broken the law, they probably wouldn't bother to investigate. It was all, according to Alun, just too much bother.

All of which begged the question: why? Why did he need to bother trying to be good? Monument certainly didn't seem to bother about doing the right thing. The days when people like Neville ruled the roost were long gone. Today, all Andrew and his kind were worried about was profitability, business growth and the long-term financial viability of their associations. In short – money.

Money had become the Esperanto of moral debate; the universal, shared-language that everyone could use to decide what was right. Because you couldn't argue with money – it was a brutal arbiter in debates about who was doing the right thing. In the absence of a shared moral code, money was the last remaining thing everyone could agree on. If you had more of it, then you must be doing something right; if you had less, then it was a sign you were doing something wrong. And Barry currently had a bit more, whilst Monument would shortly discover that they had a bit less. In Barry's new-found moral universe (albeit one that was powered by Cobra Beer), that seemed fitting, even just. And, even if it wasn't, it didn't matter because he almost certainly wasn't going to get caught. Probably.

So not even Alun's long monologue about all that was wrong in the modern-day police force could dampen Barry's spirits. It had been, he decided, a good day.

As they got up to leave at the end of their meal Barry shook Alun's hand and wished him well. He then noticed Sue leaning over. She pecked Barry on the cheek, but, before he could pull away, Sue grabbed his wrist and whispered in his ear, "Look after her, Barry. She needs you at the moment."

It struck Barry as an odd thing to say. He had always tried to look after his wife, but the fact was that she had never shown a huge amount of interest in being looked after. He wanted to point out to Sue that he had been trying to have a conversation with his wife for over a week, but, as far as he could tell, 'conversation with my husband' ranked somewhere below 'cat videos on social media' and 'balti chicken bhuna' in her list of priorities. Quite why Sue felt that his wife needed him at that particular moment was a mystery. And it wasn't one that Sue seemed inclined to shed any light on as the two couples walked back up the road toward their respective homes.

TWENTY-FIVE

The next day, Barry stopped at a petrol station on his way into work and withdrew another £250 from a cash machine on the forecourt. He was aware that both he and his car registration details would be picked up by the CCTV cameras, but, after his conversation with Alun the previous night, he knew it didn't matter. Yet Barry couldn't quite shake the belief that was woven into him that it did; that it must. The boy at the till, the professional woman filling up the car opposite, the dog-walker sauntering past – Barry felt defenceless against the accusations that seemed to lurk behind their stares. They could not see – they could not possibly have seen – what he had done, but it felt as though they could see the secret that was nestled in the deepest recess of his heart.

Nevertheless, he put £400 into an envelope with a card apologising to Lauren for the delay and assuring her that there would be a further £200 with her every month from now on, without fail. Then he headed on toward Monument's offices.

Upon arriving, he decided to visit the finance team. He wanted to be absolutely sure that there were no suspicions or concerns being raised.

"Saleema, good morning."

"Good morning, Barry. And how are you this beautiful day?"

It was a dull and overcast day in early November – not the kind of day habitually described as beautiful, and certainly not by people from countries where the sun typically shone for more than two weeks a year. Barry was intrigued.

"You seem very bright this morning. Are you celebrating?"

"Yes!" said Saleema with even more enthusiasm than was her custom. "Yes, I am."

"So what's the occasion?"

"Well, really I am not supposed to tell people yet, but as it's you, I will," said Saleema in a conspiratorial whisper. "They've approved my voluntary redundancy application!"

Barry could feel his anger burning through his face. After all her mistakes, how could Saleema walk out of the door with a pay-off when Langley seemed determined to deny Barry the selfsame thing after twenty-two years of exemplary service? But the rejection of his own voluntary redundancy application was hardly Saleema's fault. Under the circumstances, therefore, Barry felt the best thing was simply to pretend to be happy for her.

"Oh, that's great news. Do you know what you're going to do?"

"Oh yes," said Saleema, excitedly. "Me and my husband are going back to Peshawar to look after my father. He's been very ill. I'm going to use the redundancy payment to pay his hospital bills and then we'll stay on so I can be near him."

"That sounds exciting. It'll be nice to spend some time with the family – if you can afford not to work for a bit."

"My husband's done all the sums and we think we can afford it. He retired last year, so we've got his pension. And his mother died a little while ago, so he needs to go over there anyway to sort out her estate. Once the funds from that are released, we'll be fine. It's such a relief to know I can be with my father. It's such an answer to prayer."

Barry didn't quite know what to say to that. Saleema was a woman of simple faith. She had no doubt prayed that her application would be successful, and it had been. In her mind, it was inconceivable that the two things were unrelated. It was equally indisputable that Barry hadn't prayed about his application and it had been unsuccessful. If Saleema had known this, then there would be only one conclusion that she could possibly have drawn. And, Barry had to concede, she might be right. But it did seem unlikely. This wasn't because he lacked faith in the power of the Almighty (although he did). It was because he lacked faith in the willingness of Monument to respond to His promptings. Andrew, Ruth and Langley did not strike Barry as the kind of people who would allow themselves to be moved by the Almighty to undertake any action that was not in the financial interests of the association.

Saleema was still talking, but, as she clearly had nothing to say about the invoice from The SHYPP, Barry concluded that it was safe to withdraw. He waited for a pause in her exposition of flight times to Pakistan, then headed back down to his desk. No one was watching him – he knew that now.

But, somehow, it still felt like everyone was.

Over the next fortnight, Barry tried to relax. He continued to withdraw the maximum of £250 every day from Chris Malford's bank account. He spread his withdrawals around as many cashpoints as possible, just so there was no obvious geographical link to him in the unlikely event that the soon-to-be-missing money was ever investigated by the police. But, each day, as he went unchallenged, he noticed himself finding the process of withdrawal slightly easier. The looks of those around him seemed less accusing, his heart less unprotected. Slowly, he found himself able to shut the door of his conscience to people's invading stares, and, when he had done so, he made sure to padlock it shut.

He knew he had to pay for Lauren's maintenance for the next three years, so each day he took £200 of his withdrawal and put it in an envelope marked with the appropriate month and year. The remaining £50 Barry set aside for his 'Art Fund'.

The question began to surface in Barry's mind, of course, as to whether he might be able to withdraw more of the money. Initially, this was merely a theoretical challenge that he set himself – he was not, after all, a common criminal – but it suddenly became more than that when the consultation on the proposal to withdraw his company car was formally begun (although, if it were possible to indicate the presence of inverted commas around the words 'consultation' and 'proposal' merely by the tone of one's voice, then Langley somehow managed to do it).

Barry was called to a meeting with Langley and Angela. Officially, the purpose was to outline the company's proposals and listen to any counterproposals from Barry. Unofficially, Barry sensed immediately that the purpose was to tell him what would be happening once they'd observed the legal niceties.

Langley outlined the rationale for the removal of the perk, and Barry reiterated his objection; the provision of a car clearly formed part of his contract. At which point, Angela said, "Well, actually, Barry, the most recent iteration of your contract makes it clear – as was always implied – that any benefits in kind provided by the company are discretionary and can be withdrawn at any point, if circumstances justify it. So, the company isn't technically altering your contract."

Barry was livid. After Neville's departure, Andrew had initiated a review of everyone's terms and conditions of service. This wasn't wholly unexpected as, because of the history of mergers, there were people working in the same organisation on a range of different contracts, and so it wasn't unreasonable to try to standardise them all. Barry (and, indeed, Maxine) had actually queried the new clause about benefits in kind being discretionary, but had been assured that their salary and benefits would remain the same: it was purely a tidying up exercise. But now it appeared that it wasn't.

Langley closed the discussion by advising Barry that the company would "carefully consider" (with more implied inverted commas) his request to keep his car and get back to him shortly.

Barry left the meeting and immediately went out to lunch to think through his options. Whilst he could have kicked up a fuss, months of arguing with Monument was not an attractive proposition. Angela had made it clear that they had taken extensive legal advice and were confident they had the right to withdraw the car, so really all they would be arguing about was the precise legal process by which Monument would enforce its will. Barry decided, therefore, not to bother getting angry; instead, he determined to get even.

If Monument were not prepared to honour their clear moral obligation voluntarily, then Barry felt less guilty about the idea of ensuring that they did so anyway. He had tried to be reasonable, he pointed out to himself, but it was clear that that approach was doomed to fail. Accordingly, he would reluctantly have to take further action himself if a fair outcome was to be assured. His fifteen per cent management fee would be increasing.

But the only way that Barry could see to access more of the money that he'd diverted within the window of time that was available was to pay it into someone else's bank account, and for them to withdraw the money and give it to Barry. In short, he needed an accomplice. But he needed an accomplice who was gullible and naïve enough to be prepared to help him without asking too many questions. Ideally, based on what Alun said, he needed an accomplice with a foreign bank account.

It seemed an impossibly tall order. Who, after all, would be naïve enough to agree to have over forty grand paid into their account without asking any questions? And, even more pertinently, who would be gullible enough to agree to simply pass that money on to Barry? No matter how many scenarios Barry ran through in his mind, he just couldn't see how it could be done.

But that was before Saleema dropped her bombshell. That would change everything.

TWENTY-SIX

"PC Rathbone? I'm DS Norton. Can I have a word?"

Gemma's heart skipped a beat. She was on a late shift, so had come in at what would normally have been lunchtime. She was not looking forward to several hours stuck in a car with Molloy. But if the prospect of that was unappealing, the prospect of being grilled by CID for several hours over what she had and hadn't done in the cases of Chris Malford and Shana Backley was even worse.

But it soon became apparent that Lindsey Norton had no interest in hauling Gemma over the coals. "It's all right," she whispered in Gemma's ear once they were out of earshot of Molloy. "There's nothing to worry about. You're not in trouble. Let's go for a coffee."

They went to a coffee shop round the corner from the station, and grabbed a couple of drinks; Lindsey even paid. She was taller and stockier than Gemma, and her look betrayed evidence of the thousand disappointments with the frailty of human nature that were the inevitable consequence of eighteen years in the police. But there was something in her manner that Gemma had always admired from afar. She seemed to fight against the fatalism that Molloy was so keen to succumb to. It meant that her smile had not entirely lost its innocence. Gemma hadn't had a chance to get changed into her uniform before Lindsey had grabbed her, so, as they settled down in two easy chairs, they just looked like two friends having a chat.

"Why did you cover for him?" Lindsey was nothing if not direct.

"What do you mean?"

"Molloy – why did you cover for him?"

Gemma squirmed in her seat. "I didn't cover for him."

"Look, Gemma, you're a good copper. I've read the file. You've done everything right – even gone 'above and beyond'. Don't feel you've got to protect Molloy." She looked Gemma squarely in the eyes. "He didn't want to go, did he? You did all that work – behind his back, I bet – and then when you went to him with what you'd found, he didn't want to know."

"It wasn't quite like that," Gemma said, but without much conviction.

"Look, we all know what Molloy's like. He's a lazy bugger who'll do the minimum possible to cover his fat backside. Don't feel you've got to take one for the team – if the roles were reversed, he'd quite happily leave you to hang. And Davis knows that."

"It's difficult. He's been trying to help me. I didn't want to... y'know."

"What?"

"Get a reputation. I'm new; it's difficult. You're expected to put up with it."

"Not by me, you're not, and not by Davis. He didn't want to put you onto traffic, but you didn't give him a choice."

Gemma didn't know what to say. She bowed her head and took a sip from her drink.

"Look, forget it now. It's gone," Lindsey continued, "and this'll all be forgotten about in six months, you mark my words."

"Really?" Gemma was not convinced.

"Really! Believe me, I know. I've been on the force long enough to see it happen loads of times. You think it's going to be a disaster, but it all blows over. And – let's be honest – you've practically solved both cases for us."

"Have I?"

"Yes! There's no way we'd have made the link between the two cases. If it had been left to Molloy, the Chris Malford case wouldn't even have been investigated. It's you thinking to check the CCTV and spotting Adam Furst that means we know what's happened. If we can get some prints off the syringe, we can probably pin this on him. If it hadn't been for you, it'd have just been forgotten about."

Gemma hadn't thought about it like that before, but now she realised that Lindsey was right. And yet… "I guess so. But does it matter? Really?"

"What d'you mean?"

"He's dead – and no one cares."

"I care!"

"Yeah, I get that. You care about the case. But it's not as if anyone's mourning him. There's no one who needs to see justice being done, is there?"

Lindsey put her coffee down deliberately and fixed Gemma with a stare that was so piercing it pinned the young officer to her seat. "Gemma, people rate you. That's why I'm here. To let you know this isn't the end for you. But you can't start thinking like that – that justice doesn't matter, or that it only matters when someone says that it does. If you start thinking like that, you'll end up like Molloy – doing the bare minimum, and not even doing that properly."

Gemma wanted to take a sip of her coffee, but found herself rendered immobile by the ferocity of Lindsey's look.

"Justice matters, Gemma. It always matters – even when people think it doesn't. *Especially* when people think it doesn't. You've got to believe that if you want to be a decent copper, girl. It's not just about the figures. Something happens when people do bad stuff and get away with it – even if no one else notices. It changes things."

"God, yes. I get that. I really do. Sorry." Her admission seemed to release something in her nervous system and she quickly took a long gulp from her mug.

"I know you do. Just don't forget it."

The two officers chatted on, initially about the case, but then more generally about Molloy and how utterly useless he was.

"He must have been in nearly every LPU on the force. They keep moving him around, but he just creates a new mess everywhere he goes," Lindsey said.

"Did you ever work with him?"

“Oh God, yes”, Lindsey replied, shuddering at the memory. “We were at Brierley Hill together, years ago now. What a laugh that was. Molloy was responsible for the best call-out I’ve ever heard about.”

And Lindsey proceeded to tell the story of the time Molloy had been sent out to deal with a man trying to smuggle a pet horse into his council flat in a multistorey block in Dudley.

“So, anyway,” she concluded, “Molloy says to the guy, ‘Why are you taking that horse up the stairs?’ And the bloke replies straight off – without a word of lie – ‘Because he won’t fit in the lift, will he?’”

There was a momentary pause whilst the punchline sank in and then both Gemma and Lindsey collapsed into full-throated laughter. Gemma became aware, as the laughter rolled on, that she felt – and she couldn’t think of a better way to put it – completely herself, as though her laughter came truly from within herself and was not prompted by the need to appear polite or to win Lindsey’s approval.

“Having fun are we, ladies?”

It appeared that their merriment had provoked a reaction. They were sitting in a quiet corner, specifically to try to avoid noise from the other customers, but next to them was a raised bench with bar stools where business customers could work on their laptops. However, one such customer had decided to spin round and interpose himself in Gemma and Lindsey’s conversation.

Lindsey shot Gemma a glance that said, “I’ll deal with this.”

“We’re good, thanks.”

“Is that a fact?”

"Aye up, here we go," Lindsey said. "Not today, sunshine."

He was tall, thin and muscular, in a smart suit and open-necked shirt. He looked older than Gemma, but younger than Lindsey. Probably early thirties. He was, all things considered, pretty good looking. But, despite that, Gemma was annoyed at his intervention. It wasn't that she didn't find him attractive – she did. It was the presumption that bothered her; the fact that he somehow felt entitled to join in their conversation – as though two women weren't allowed to enjoy themselves without a male being present.

"Can I at least get you two ladies a coffee?" he asked.

"No thanks. We've got to get back to work," Lindsey said, gathering her handbag from under the table.

Gemma couldn't believe it. She was so annoyed.

"Work? Look, I've got a Jag outside – racing green – if you fancy a spin. We could have some fun. Forget about work for a bit."

"Look, pal," said Lindsey, finally adopting a firm line, "we're not interested, OK? We don't want a spin in your Jag; we just want to be left alone."

His face fell. But not into a look of humiliated despair. Rather it fell into a look of grim-faced contempt. He turned back toward his laptop, but as he did so he let his frustrations slip out under his breath.

"Jeez… Dykes."

"What did you say?" Gemma asked accusingly, standing up and facing him.

"Nothing," he replied, gathering his things together.

"Yes you did. I heard you."

"Leave it, Gemma. It's not worth it."

"You said we were dykes. I heard you."

"Look, I'm going, OK? Is that good enough for you?"

She wanted to say no. She wanted to tell him that it wasn't good enough. It wasn't a surrender to the superior force of her argument; it was merely a tactical retreat that would enable him to regroup and try his luck somewhere else. But, against her better judgement, she was going to let it slide. People were staring, and her police training had taught her that you should never humiliate someone in public; it only made the situation worse. But, as he made to go, he couldn't resist one last dig.

"You and your girlfriend can stay here if you want."

Gemma's right hand instinctively clenched into a fist.

"Just let it go, Gemma," Lindsey said.

There was a moment when Gemma thought she was going to do it. But, looking at his stony-faced defiance, she knew that it was pointless. She wanted to punch some sense into him, but she knew that she couldn't. There was too much to be said – too much sense to be punched into him – so she worried that if she started punching she might not be able to stop. A punch was too much, and yet somehow still not enough. It wouldn't change anything for him, but it would change everything for her.

She unclenched her fist. He walked past and headed out of the door.

"We'd better get back," Lindsey said.

But it felt to Gemma as though she was already back; back in the world of Molloy and Inspector Davis. It was a world she had left behind for a few brief moments with Lindsey, but it was the world she had to live in.

TWENTY-SEVEN

It was now three weeks from the point at which Monument had issued their invoice to The SHYPP and so far no one in either organisation appeared to have noticed that anything was amiss. People, including those in the finance team, appeared more interested in who was going and who was staying as part of the VR trawl. There was a degree of concern amongst the remaining team members that they were going to be expected to carry out the same amount of work as previously, but with fewer members of staff. There had been much muttering about plates being spun and balls being dropped. It seemed typical of Monument – make a big announcement about cutting costs, but then, essentially, just engineer a situation where the same number of bricks would have to be produced with significantly less straw.

For once, however, Barry was quietly encouraged by Monument's apparent inability to properly judge the level of staffing that was required. It occurred to him that if the finance team was going to be under-resourced, the invoice to The SHYPP might be the ball that they would drop. Having received payment on time every quarter for fifteen years, perhaps no one would even bother to check that this quarter's invoice had been paid, especially as it was Saleema who had issued it and Saleema (as she delighted in telling everybody who came near her) would soon be gone.

Barry felt it wise to keep in regular contact with her in the run up to her departure, just to be sure that he was made aware if there were any concerns about the invoice to The SHYPP. This generally meant sitting through a fifteen-minute update report on Saleema's imminent departure every couple of days. Yet, despite the inevitable stresses of an international house move, Saleema dealt with it all without losing her cheery demeanour. This was partly because she had left her husband to do everything, and partly because she retained her absolutely unshakeable faith that the whole thing was God's will and so would somehow work itself out in the end, whatever problems the Devil might try to put in the way.

So Barry was more than a little surprised to go up to the finance team at the end of a particularly wearying day to find Saleema on the phone, apparently in tears. As she saw Barry approaching, she hung up.

"Everything OK, Saleema?"

"No, Barry, everything is not OK. Everything is not OK at all," she said, drawing her cardigan tightly around her in response to another of the comfort cooling system's apparently random bursts of activity.

Barry wondered if perhaps her father had died, but didn't like to ask directly. "Oh, I'm sorry to hear that." Beyond that, he didn't know quite what to say.

"It's all falling apart – everything!" Saleema cried, as if deciphering the question behind Barry's look. "I thought we'd got everything planned, but now I don't know what we're going to do." She tried to hold back her sobs, but it was no good.

Barry looked around. It was nearly 6pm and there was no one left on the finance desk islands apart from Saleema. Ruth was locked in her office, discussing something with Angela. He was tempted to phone downstairs to see if Jean was still at her desk, as she was generally the go-to person in situations like this, but, as he was standing not ten feet from Saleema, Barry reluctantly concluded that this meant that he should probably offer some pastoral support himself.

He edged toward Saleema and awkwardly placed a hand on her shoulder. Barry wasn't a man comfortable with physical contact with work colleagues, particularly colleagues of the opposite sex. Having placed his hand on her shoulder and this having failed to stem the flow of tears, Barry didn't really know what else to do. He looked around the office desperately for any obvious sources of support and advice, but there was none within calling distance.

"There, there," he said, patting Saleema's shoulder as though it were a ball being bounced. "I'm sure it's not that bad."

"It is, Barry. It really is."

There was nothing for it but to ask.

"Why don't you tell me all about it?"

"Oh, Barry. You're such a good man. I know you want to help, but I just don't think you'd understand. It's complicated – and a bit embarrassing."

Barry worried that this meant it might be a 'Woman's Problem'. For that reason, he thought there was a very real possibility that he *wouldn't* understand. He felt the need to show willing, however. "Why don't you try me?"

"It's to do with our move to Peshawar."

Barry sighed with relief.

"I'm sorry, Barry. I don't want to burden you."

"Oh, no, no, no. Sorry. No, I'm happy to listen – honestly."

This was all the invitation Saleema needed. "Well, you know we've been looking to go back to Pakistan to look after my father. We need to get over there soon – he's very frail now and he needs me. The hospital is chasing payment for his bill and he has no money to pay, so we were going to use my redundancy payment to clear his bill."

"Is there a problem?"

"Not with that, no. But he needs ongoing treatment and specialist care. You don't get those things for free in Pakistan. You have to pay, and he only has a small pension. It's barely enough to keep the roof over his head. We've been trying to get the money from my mother-in-law's estate released – it's quite a lot of money and we've been waiting over two years already. That would give us more than enough to pay his bills and leave us something to live on while we're out there. It all seemed to be working out exactly as we'd hoped."

Indeed it did. Barry was struggling to see what the problem could be.

"We thought everything was ready. They said they could release the money as soon as we got out there – Samuel has even booked the flights. The timing was perfect; providential. But now..." Saleema tailed off in despair.

"What?"

"Now the lawyers are saying they can't release my mother-in-law's money until we've paid the necessary 'taxes and administrative fees' – that's ten per cent of the estate! There's no way we can find that sort of money."

"Well, can't you just get them to deduct the ten per cent off the amount that they pay you?"

"Oh Barry," she said as though he were a small child to whom she was having to explain that not everyone in the world was a nice person. "They're not really taxes and administrative fees."

"Aren't they?"

"No! They're bribes: backhanders."

"Oh."

"And they can't just take ten per cent off the payment they make to us because that will show what they've done, and they obviously don't want to show that. That's why they're insisting that we have to pay them in cash – up front – before they'll release the money."

"Have you been to the police? Surely that's against the law."

"Oh Barry. This is Pakistan. We're Christians. No one cares. The police probably wouldn't even investigate, or if they did they'd ask us for an even bigger bribe to do anything about it. It's the way things are done."

"So what are you going to do?"

"That's just it. We don't know what to do. We can go out there, but without the money there's no way we can pay for my father's treatment. And without that..." The silence she left spoke for itself.

"But it's your money," said Barry, feeling affronted at the iniquity of it all. "Surely they've got to let you have it at some point?"

"We could go to the courts, but there's no Legal Aid. It would cost us a small fortune in legal fees and take years – and we still might not win. But, even if we did, my father hasn't got years. He needs the treatment to start now. Somehow, we've just got to find that ten per cent."

"Can't you try to negotiate them down a bit?"

"That's what we've been trying to do for the past year. We thought we'd got them to see sense, but ten per cent is as low as they'll go. It's normally twenty per cent for Christians!"

"Have you thought of taking out a loan? I mean it would only be for a few weeks, wouldn't it?"

"That's what my husband has been trying to do, but none of the English banks will loan us any money once he tells them we're going to Pakistan indefinitely. And none of the Pakistani banks seem interested in loaning money to Christians so that they can pay a bribe."

Barry could see their point, to be fair. "Family?"

"We've tried that and we've managed to raise something, but it's nowhere near enough. The estate's quite big because of my late father-in-law's business – about 80 million rupees – so ten per cent is a lot of money to find."

Barry wasn't fully conversant with the exchange rate of the Pakistani rupee, but 80 million of them sounded like a lot.

"Gosh," he said, conscious that he had nothing else to suggest. "You are in a pickle. Sorry."

"I know, and I was so sure that this was all God's doing," said Saleema with real conviction. "But unless we can find someone to lend us £40,000 then it looks like everything is going to fall apart, and my poor father…" She descended into tears again.

Barry, however, was no longer concerned about Saleema's welfare because he was experiencing something that felt like an epiphany.

"I'm sorry, but how much did you say you needed?"

"Forty thousand pounds," Saleema replied through her tears. "We need to find 8 million rupees in total – about £60,000. We think that between the three children we can probably raise £20,000, but that leaves us £40,000 short."

"You need £40,000? But you can pay it all back within a couple of weeks?" He wanted to be absolutely sure that he'd heard her correctly.

"Yes. Why? You don't happen to know someone who's got £40,000 to spare, do you?" Saleema asked with uncharacteristic sarcasm.

"As a matter of fact, Saleema," Barry said, his heart racing, "I think I just might."

TWENTY-EIGHT

The moment Barry got home, he raced upstairs to the home office and shut the door. On his way out of Monument's offices, he had quickly slipped Chris Malford's tenancy file under his arm. There were plenty of examples of Chris' signature on the file. This meant that all Barry had to do was practise copying it until he was confident that it would fool whoever was tasked with checking it at the bank.

His plan was simple: Saleema would check with Samuel, her husband, the precise amount of money they needed. She would then calculate the transaction fees that would have to be paid to convert that money into Pakistani rupees and transfer it to their Pakistani bank account. Barry would write a cheque for that amount from Chris Malford's account and give it to them. Once the solicitor released the estate, Samuel and Saleema could repay the money.

Barry spent much of the rest of the evening perfecting his impression of Chris Malford's signature. It took several attempts before he was able to get something anywhere near, but his art-school training was put to good use, and, after a while, he found himself able to produce a passable signature. He couldn't believe that a bank teller would be able to detect that any of his later attempts was a forgery.

All that he needed now was a text from Saleema confirming the amount of the cheque. Eventually, Barry's phone pinged.

"Thank u so much Barry. If Mr Malford is still willing/able to loan us the money, we need exactly £41,845. I hope that is OK? Thank u 4 sorting. God bless, S."

Barry texted back to say that, indeed, it was OK. He inserted the figure into the appropriate places in the cheque and went downstairs. He now had a reasonable chance of laundering nearly £42,000 of the money currently sitting in Chris Malford's account. Assuming he kept withdrawing £250 per day in cash from various cashpoints, the £6,746 that wasn't being paid to the Bhattis could be withdrawn before Monument were likely to notice that the money was missing and, crucially, before anyone was likely to discover the existence of Chris Malford's bank account and have it frozen.

That night, his sleep was filled with dreams of being pursued. Wide, open boulevards became narrower streets, became slender lanes, became threadlike alleys, which culminated in dead-ends. In his dream, he felt the darkening presence of his pursuer fall across his shoulder, but, as he turned to face him, Barry woke up. He tried to think of something else, something other than the money, but, every time he slipped back into sleep, the dream was always the same. He never saw his pursuer, but Barry knew exactly what he wanted.

The consequence was that, when he arrived at Monument's offices the next morning, Barry already felt as tired as he normally did after a full day's work. He had barely sat down and booted up his computer when his phone rang. It was Saleema's cheery voice that greeted him.

"Good morning, Barry. I saw your car pulling up on the car park, so I thought I'd just give you a quick ring."

"Ah, yes. Errr… Good morning, Saleema; obviously, yes. Uh… sorry," Barry replied, somewhat flustered. It was early enough, and he was tired enough, to still be occupying that awkward, pre-coffee hinterland between the world of wake and the world of sleep. Whilst his body had familiarised itself with the sensory world around him, his mind was still distracted by the shadowy presence of his dreams; the one that lurked just behind him and whispered of menace.

"I just wondered if everything was still OK? With Mr Malford." There was a pause whilst Saleema waited for Barry to respond. "The cheque?" she asked.

"Oh yes, the cheque. Yes, sorry… Yes, everything's fine. I've got it with me here. Do you want it now? I kind of assumed—"

"Oh, yes, please, Barry! That would be wonderful. I've arranged for my husband to come in with me so that he can pick it up and pay it in immediately," Saleema said, before adding in a whisper, "I don't really want him hanging around here, if I'm honest. People might start asking questions."

"Oh, right. Yes, of course. We don't want that. OK… I'll just pop up now then. Sorry."

"There's no need to apologise. I'll see you in a minute. Bye!"

A few moments later, Barry arrived at Saleema's desk. He was relieved to see that none of her colleagues were at their desks, although other staff were starting to arrive.

"Well, here it is. As requested." He proffered the cheque to Saleema in a plain white envelope in order not to draw too much attention to exactly what he was doing. He felt uncomfortably warm, but wondered if that was just because Saleema had adjusted the comfort cooling system.

She opened the envelope and took a surreptitious look at the cheque, wary of anyone else seeing. Her hand went up to her mouth and her eyes began to water. She couldn't say anything; she looked too emotional. Instead, she handed the envelope to her husband. Samuel Bhatti was a short, portly man with swept-back, greying hair and a toothbrush moustache. Despite retirement, he still wore a blazer and tie, like an off-duty army major. He took the envelope impassively and also quickly scanned the cheque. His face didn't register so much as a flicker.

"Thank you, Mr Todd," he said. "And you're sure the cheque is good?"

"Samuel!" Saleema slapped her husband's arm.

"Oh, absolutely. I've seen proof of funds." Barry was conscious of talking in a barely audible whisper.

"Wonderful! Thank you so much, Barry," said Saleema.

"Yes, I don't know if my wife explained to you, but it may take a few weeks for us to release the money," Samuel whispered. "We need to pay the cheque into our account here and then transfer the money over to our account in Pakistan. We fly out to Peshawar at the end of next week;

hopefully, by the time we get there the money will be waiting for us. Then we've got to arrange to withdraw it in cash and take it to the solicitors. They should release our money immediately, but it might take a few days to clear. We can wire the money back to Mr Malford's account as soon as it does. I assume the details on the cheque are the ones that we use?"

"Ah, yes... about that. It's not quite as simple as that, I'm afraid."

"Really?" Barry sensed Samuel Bhatti's antennae begin to rise. The fact was, Barry needed the Bhattis to repay the cash into his own account. If they simply repaid it directly to Christian Malford, then Barry would be no better off. But he needed to come up with a plausible reason as to why it would be necessary to pay the money to him. He could sense that Samuel Bhatti was considerably less trusting than his wife and knew that his carefully worked-out plan could all fall apart if what he said next wasn't perfectly chosen.

"No. The thing is... the money needs to go into a... different... account," said Barry, sensing, even as he did so, two sweat patches beginning to spread underneath his arms. "It's a business account or something... I'm not sure."

"Well, that's not a problem," said Saleema matter-of-factly. "Just give us the sort code and account number, and we can pay it into that, if that's what Mr Malford wants."

"Great," said Barry. "But what about the account name? I assume you need that."

"Not really. With electronic payments they never check them – as long as the account number and sort code are legitimate ones, they just transfer the money across anyway," Saleema replied.

"Really?" said Barry, with slightly more enthusiasm than he felt he should have shown for what was basically an obscure technical detail.

"Really! It's incredible," Saleema replied. "I'll say the money is supposed to be going to Christian Malford, but the only thing they check is that the account details are linked to a real account."

Barry was so stunned by what he was hearing that he wanted to check that he'd heard it right. "But surely that's a massive risk. You could get people to pay money meant for someone else into your own account and the bank would just do it because you've given details for a real account."

"Why do you think mandate fraud is so common?" Samuel said.

Suddenly a number of things began to make sense. Barry had changed the bank account details on the invoice that Saleema has raised, but he hadn't changed the account name. However, if the bank didn't check the name of the intended payee, then it was an invitation for criminals to send false invoices to legitimate companies requesting electronic payment be made. And because it was such an invitation, there was no chance the police could possibly investigate all the crimes committed.

So, Barry didn't have to bother concocting some frankly implausible excuse for the money to be paid somewhere else because, as long as Samuel and Saleema thought they were paying the money back to Christian Malford, it didn't matter.

"Well, you learn something new every day," he said, still somewhat stunned.

"Absolutely," said Saleema "We will make sure Mr Malford gets it back as soon as possible. Just let us have the payment details as quickly as you can. And please make sure he understands how grateful we are. This really is appreciated, Barry."

"Oh, absolutely. I've made sure he knows that."

It occurred to Barry that he could have just given Samuel his own bank account details there and then, but having the money in his bank account seemed a huge risk, despite what Alun had said. At the moment, there was still nothing to link Barry conclusively with the appropriation of Monument's money. Once it was sitting in Barry's account, though, the situation changed. Ideally, he needed to find a way to spend the money – or at least some of it – without it actually appearing in his bank account at all. It seemed a bit of a stretch, but the information that Saleema had just told him made it seem less implausible than it had done just a few moments ago.

"What I can't understand though," Samuel said in measured tones, "is why Mr Malford would do this for us. Why would a complete stranger help us out in this way? He's taking a bit of a risk, isn't he?"

"Oh Samuel!" said Saleema. "It's because he's a Christian. I'm sure the Lord has laid it upon his heart. Isn't that the case, Barry?"

Barry hadn't really thought about this before. He'd been so eager to snap up the opportunity of getting the money offshore that he hadn't thought about trying to explain why someone would go to such extraordinary lengths and take such extraordinary risks in order to help someone they'd never met.

Barry didn't really know a lot about Christians. He remembered Neville, who would do anything to help anyone. And, of course, there was Jean, who seemed to be someone who took the whole thing very seriously indeed; there was Sally, who was driven by a ferocious desire to champion the underdog; and then there was Saleema, who seemed simply incorruptible.

None of those people appeared to Barry to have much in common, except perhaps that they persisted in the belief that bad things happened to people who did bad things, long after everyone else had given up the idea as charmingly misguided. But, given that Saleema knew more about Christians than him and she clearly thought that this was the most obvious explanation for Chris Malford's largesse, it seemed simplest just to go along with that.

"Yes, that's it. Christian by name, Christian by nature," Barry said, before realising that it sounded awfully lame. "Sorry."

"Anyway," said Samuel, "I'd better be off. I'll pay this in today. And please let Mr Malford know that we'll be praying for him."

"I'll definitely make sure he knows."

"Oh... and I hope it goes without saying," Samuel added in a conspiratorial whisper, "we'd rather you didn't mention anything about this to anyone else. We wouldn't want anyone to get the wrong idea."

"Oh, absolutely not," Barry assured him. "I understand. Your secret's safe with me. And Mr Malford has asked for similar discretion from you. He doesn't want everyone knowing what he's done."

"Of course not. 'Do not let your left hand know what your right hand is doing, so that your giving may be in secret.' Matthew chapter six, verses three and four. We understand," Samuel replied. "Not a word, ever. We promise."

As Samuel left, Barry saw that Blessing, one of the other finance officers, had arrived. She seemed intrigued as to why Saleema's husband had turned up to the office and why he was in conversation with Barry, so Barry quickly made his excuses and returned to his desk.

In his head he knew he could relax now. Most of the money would be gone from Chris Malford's account within a few days and would be available for Barry to spend somehow a couple of weeks later. He would have finished withdrawing the rest in cash by the time the payment was noticed to be missing.

He was in the clear.

TWENTY-NINE

Langley appeared to be agitated. He'd taken to hovering round Barry's desk and asking for almost daily updates on voids and arrears. Whenever Barry left his desk, even for a moment, he would return to find a scribbled note left on his keyboard or another email query in his inbox. Langley's eyes, those small, blackened coals, seemed anxious and wary. Improving performance was obviously not proving as simple as he'd hoped, and his glances seemed to be nervously scouring the landscape for a potential sacrificial lamb. But Barry didn't care anymore because he knew that if everything went to plan, he would shortly have an insurance policy to fall back on.

At about 11am one morning, Barry sauntered into the staff kitchen and made himself a coffee. He knew he ought to have taken it back to his desk and kept working, but, to be honest, he couldn't be bothered. As it was mid-morning and everyone else at Monument knew better than to stay away from their desk for any longer than was strictly necessary, Barry found himself alone. He decided to grab five minutes in the breakout space, where there were some comfy seats and out-of-date magazines strewn across a coffee table, and a large window inviting Barry to enjoy the view over Kingsbury Water Park, where some Canada geese were skidding across the water. He had probably been away from his desk for no more than five minutes when he heard the door open behind him.

"Oh, you are here. I didn't think you would be."

Barry's heart sank. He had just wanted to get away for a few moments, so as to not be constantly bombarded with Langley's questions, but even hoping for five minutes alone with a cup of coffee now appeared an unreasonable expectation. Barry was pretty sure he wasn't imagining it – things really had been different when Neville had been in charge. But that, of course, was why he'd had to go. In the twentieth century being a 'modern' employer meant treating your staff well, and driving up their terms and conditions in order to attract the best people, whereas in the twenty-first century it meant exactly the opposite.

He turned around and was relieved to see that it was Jean. She had a sheaf of papers with her which she had clearly intended to discuss, but, seeing the expression on Barry's face, she put them to one side.

"Are you OK?" Jean asked.

"Uh, yes. I think so…"

"It's just that… you don't seem yourself lately," she said, taking a seat next to him.

Barry didn't know how to respond because he wasn't sure who 'himself' was anymore. For forty-eight years, he'd lived his life based on one set of assumptions, none of which seemed to hold true anymore. All of the things his grandmother had told him – that goodness was its own reward; that you could be sure your sins would find you out – all seemed self-evident nonsense now that it was clear that you could break the rules and no one cared.

So, in a sense, Barry could see that he hadn't been himself lately. He'd been someone else: someone who believed that if you wanted something then you had to go out and get it rather than waiting politely in a line. He'd wasted forty-eight years waiting politely in the belief that it was only by doing so that he would be rewarded. That was what Jean meant by Barry being 'himself'. But now he was going to grab what he wanted, because he knew that no one would stop him. He also knew with a bitter, unshakeable certainty that following the rules didn't stop bad things happening either. So it was a new 'himself' and, if he was being honest, he was still getting used to it. For the moment, it still felt like he was wearing his shoes on the wrong feet.

But Barry knew that he couldn't explain all that to Jean and so he dissembled to her. "Things are just very busy, Jean. And Langley has very clear expectations about where we need to be."

"It feels like it's more than that, Barry. You've had a lot happen – lots of knocks – I'm just worried it's taking its toll."

"I'll be fine." He hated lying, especially to Jean, but he couldn't see another way.

"Did you have that conversation with your wife?"

Barry sighed and took a swig of his coffee. "I tried, but, to be honest, it didn't go well. Our daughter went off to university a few weeks ago and I think that's her main focus at the moment."

"Oh. And how are you finding that? It must be difficult, after what happened with your son."

"It's not too bad, really. It's just that I thought we'd find more time for each other and that's not quite happened yet. I tried taking her out and talking to her, but… I don't know, somehow the conversation didn't quite happen."

"You ended up talking about something else?"

"Not really. I talked to her about stuff. It's just that…" Barry toyed with a shoelace whilst he tried to find the right words. "She didn't seem that interested."

He knew the moment that he'd said it that it sounded harsh, but he couldn't think of any other way to put it. He expected Jean to reprimand him, but she just looked at him like her heart was going to break.

"Oh Barry, I'm sorry," was all she could bring herself to say, and the silence that she left was filled with a compassion that washed over Barry like a tide.

"It's not your fault," he said.

"I know, but it's so disappointing, isn't it, when you want someone's heart to echo your own and they just stare at you blankly?"

It was indeed. That was exactly how Barry felt, but he hadn't realised until Jean had told him. It released him from the need to pretend.

"I don't know what to do," he said.

"The thing is, Barry, the more intimately we know someone, the more likely they are to disappoint us. It's just the way it is. We're all deeply flawed creatures. We don't like to admit it, but we are. We just hope nobody notices. And most of the time they don't. But the people we're closest to see it – and it disappoints them. But they can't say because they know that they're flawed too.

"Oh, when we first meet someone, we think that they're wonderful and perfect, and so much better than us – that they can make up for all of our flaws. But they're not. Nobody is. They're just another lost soul looking for someone to hold on to. We all are."

"You don't seem to need anyone."

Jean fixed Barry with a hard stare. "Let me tell you this, Barry: we're all just beggars scavenging for love. All of us."

And the way that she said it, Barry believed that she really understood.

"Do you have a family, Jean?" he asked.

"Oh yes. I'm one of three sisters – the Adam Girls. I was the youngest. 'The Last Adam' my father used to call me – I think to try and emphasise to my mother that he really didn't want any more, rather than to suggest I was the Messiah!"

She laughed again at the memory of it.

But Barry wasn't laughing. "I don't feel like she loves me anymore, if I'm honest. If she ever did, really."

"Oh Barry, people get themselves in all of a mess because they confuse that tingly feeling in the pit of their stomach with love. Love isn't a feeling we have; it's a choice we make. Love is choosing to serve another human being, knowing that they're going to disappoint us. Love, as St Paul said, is choosing to be patient when we want to scream in frustration; it's choosing to be kind when we burn with the urge to be cruel; and it's biting our tongue when we're desperate to point out someone's failings to them. Love is looking into the filthy, black heart of another human being and defying the urge to jump ship – and hoping to God that they're looking at us and doing the same. Love, as St Paul *didn't* say, is bloody hard work."

"I guess so. It just seems very sad. The best feeling in the world is knowing that you actually mean something to someone else. That's what I think about when I think about love. It seems a bit depressing to think of people only staying together out of a grim determination."

"That's not what I said – or, at least, it's not what I meant. I understand we need someone to believe in us. It's just that, in reality, sometimes it takes an effort of will to keep believing. It's a tough time for your wife, after everything that happened with your son and now your daughter moving out… You just need to keep going. I'm sure it'll be all right."

It was the first time Barry felt a sense of disappointment with Jean. That was her advice? Barry had been "keeping going" for three years since they'd lost Christopher, but it still wasn't "all right" yet. He had no reason to believe it would suddenly change now. Even the money couldn't change that.

The door to the kitchen opened and there stood the angular frame of Langley. He seemed slightly surprised to see Barry there, despite the fact that someone had clearly told him that's where he was.

"Ah, Barry! You *are* here. Taking a break?" he asked, pointedly. "Anyway, message from the police. They've released that flat at Neville Thompson House. Given how long it's been empty now, can you get Lee on to it straight away?"

Without waiting for an answer, he turned on his heels and was gone. Barry would, of course, get Lee on to it straight away, but there was a lot to do before a new tenant could move in. The whole flat would need deep cleaning and the stain on the floor where Chris Malford's body had lain would need particular attention. They would need to clear out all of his belongings and then probably redecorate, at least in the living room, to try to get rid of the stubborn stench of death.

But after all that, some poor, desperate soul would be offered a tenancy there. Maybe people would mention to him or her what had happened, but they would bring in their own furniture, perhaps redecorate the other rooms, hang up a few pictures, and Chris Malford would be forgotten about. Just as he was for those two weeks when his body had lain undisturbed. There would be no blue plaque outside the door; no memorial within. There would be no permanent record that he had ever existed.

"I wonder if people would miss me if I was gone," said Barry.

"What a ridiculous thing to say," said Jean. "Of course we would."

"It makes you think though, doesn't it? This whole Chris Malford thing? Everything just moving on like he never existed."

"It's all terribly sad."

Barry knew that it really was terribly sad. Not just the fact that Chris had died, but the fact that no one had noticed and no one seemed to care. It could have happened to him – an accident, a heart attack, an irate tenant attacking him. And the fact was that he was less sure than Jean was that he would be missed. Oh, of course, everyone would make a big fuss for the first couple of weeks. But then they'd get a new area housing manager in and things would carry on as they had before. People would move on and all trace of Barry Todd ever having served at Monument would be lost. It re-emphasised to him the necessity of following through with the plan he'd embarked upon, whatever misgivings may have been lurking unacknowledged in the shadows of his heart.

THIRTY

The following Thursday was an unusual day. It was both Saleema's last day at Monument (and thus a cause for modest celebration) and also Chris Malford's funeral. Under Section 46 of the Public Health (Control of Diseases) Act 1984, it was the duty of the local authority where a body was lying to fund a funeral if there was no next of kin and the deceased had insufficient funds to pay for the funeral out of their estate. It was, Barry felt as he drove through the gates of Woodlands Cemetery and Crematorium, indicative of a certain *esprit de l'age* that the reason the poor and unloved of Britain were guaranteed a funeral at the taxpayers' expense was not, as one might have supposed, because of a Christian desire on behalf of the state to ensure that all its citizens, no matter how apparently insignificant, were allowed to depart this life with due dignity and decorum. Instead, the statute under which the local authority was required to act suggested a rather grudging acknowledgement that if the state didn't pay for the proper disposal of a deceased person's body it would, in due course, become a public health hazard. The difference between these two positions could be summed up in the architecture of Solihull's two main cemeteries.

Robin Hood Cemetery and Crematorium, built in 1931, had been designed in a Romanesque style to look rather like a medieval Franciscan monastery. The myriad of small, arched windows, each separated from the other by its own colonette, could hardly be described as the lowest-cost design option if the building's primary purpose was to prevent the spread of disease. If, however, the purpose of the building was somewhat larger – if it was, for instance, to surround the ugliness of death with beauty, in faith that human life did not fully end with death, but somehow maintained a relationship with all eternity – then putting an apse with colonetted blind-windows at the east end of the building made perfect sense. Which is presumably why the architect had done precisely that.

If, however, you were part of a culture that could no longer bring itself to believe that beauty had any purpose other than to hide the underlying meaninglessness of life, then you would fail to see the point of such architectural niceties and would probably produce a building of unadorned functionality, which is exactly what the architect of Woodlands Cemetery and Crematorium had done. Built in 1984, the building paid a surely unintentional *homage* to the ideology of human body disposal encapsulated in the Public Health Act of that same year. Rather than suggesting that 'death was not the end', it suggested, rather apologetically, that death was very much the end, so there wasn't a huge amount of point in investing much effort in varnishing the truth. In contrast to its older sibling, Woodlands echoed not so much the glories of Assisi as the rather more limited charms of Tibshelf Services. It wasn't ugly, nor could one honestly say it was badly designed, if one understood its function as being to ensure the protection of mourners, not only from the elements, but also from the idea that the deceased was just one of a long line of truncated lives stretching back from time immemorial and on into the future. If that was what Woodlands was for, then it fulfilled its brief better than most. It was all just rather… banal.

Barry had always been slightly disappointed by contemporary architecture – just as, at college, he'd always been disappointed by contemporary art – without quite being able to put his finger on why (or, at least, not in a way that seemed to satisfy his tutors). As he pulled up outside and took in the building before him, however, he finally understood his disappointment: it was that contemporary art and architecture refused to pretend. All this time, Barry had acted as though the rules mattered in some fundamental sense that was written into the structure of the universe, and he'd struggled to understand why life didn't seem to work out the way he thought it should. The answer had been – quite literally – right in front of him, in the buildings and works of art of the post-modern age. "None of this matters," they said. "You're on your own. Get on with it." Which was exactly what Barry now intended to do.

But, first, of course, there was the small matter of the funeral service itself. Barry was accompanied on his journey by Jean, who, when she found out about Chris' funeral, had insisted that she join him.

There weren't many people gathered to await the arrival of the coffin, but the few who were, all huddled under the canopy to protect themselves from the mournful November drizzle. The chief mourner was the relevant employee from social services, who had the look of a woman whose work wardrobe consisted entirely of outfits in black. It looked to Barry as though she'd been given the job largely because of her ability to adopt the look of someone whose face was hewn from granite. She was joined by an older, bearded man in a rather unfortunate faux-leather jacket, whose lanyard indicated that he came from the National Offender Management Service, so Barry assumed he was Chris' probation officer. There was another woman whom Barry couldn't identify, but who was talking to a police officer whom Barry recognised as PC Rathbone.

And, of course, there was the minister. Chris Malford had never been baptised, let alone confirmed, and had not, as far as anyone was aware, ever attended his local parish church. But, for the purposes of the day, he would be buried as a loyal Anglican. This was not because of any belief on the part of social services that all paupers should be granted in death the dignity that had been denied them in life and that could only be found in a Christian funeral conducted with due ceremony by the Established Church. Frankly, they'd have much rather had a default position of everyone being given a secular funeral. But the problem was that secular officiants all required paying. The Church of England was the only institution that was prepared to provide social services with officiants for free, and, in a time of public-sector austerity, that meant that it won hands down over the competition. It also meant that the Church got to choose the rite that was used. This meant, as far as social services were concerned, the tooth-grindingly awful prospect of twenty minutes of unexpurgated Christianity.

The minister was an older man – Barry guessed in his late fifties – with a balding pate and an angular poise. A greying beard and moustache neatly dressed his chin and upper lip. He wore a cassock and surplice with a black preaching scarf. And he had the shiniest black shoes Barry had seen in a long while, as if he'd polished them especially for the occasion. He looked suitably sombre, which impressed Barry for some reason. The probation officer was taking the opportunity to smoke a cigarette, rather emphasising the fact that he was only there out of professional obligation. The minister, however, stood tall and straight, looking ahead with an intensity and seriousness of gaze that belied the fact that there were only six people there preparing for the funeral of a man they didn't really know.

Jean went over to have a chat with the minister. Barry wondered why, but, before he had a chance to ask, the hearse arrived and everyone went inside. There was a generic service book provided for the occasion, without any personalisation. Barry wondered why he felt slightly unsettled and then realised that there was no organist, so the chapel was held in a rather eerie silence that spread its tentacles across the room and had begun to wrap them around Barry's heart when a voice came from behind him.

"Please stand." It was clearly an instruction, but it was said with such warmth and yet such seriousness of purpose that Barry wanted to comply anyway. The mourners all stood.

"'I am the resurrection and the life,' says the Lord," intoned the minister as he led the coffin down the aisle toward the front of the chapel. "'Those who believe in me, even though they die, will live, and everyone who lives and believes in me will never die.'"

This had always struck Barry as quite a strange claim for the Church to make, particularly given the fact that everyone was gathered around a coffin. Further verses of scripture followed, some of which seemed fairly brutal in their assessment of the situation ("We brought nothing into the world, and we take nothing out. The Lord gave, and the Lord has taken away; blessed be the name of the Lord.") and others of which attempted – none too successfully in Barry's view – to offer some comfort ("The steadfast love of the Lord never ceases, his mercies never come to an end; they are new every morning. Great is his faithfulness."). But none of them seemed self-evidently true, particularly under the circumstances. Barry felt as though he at least understood why the woman from social services was so granite-faced – if she had to sit through this kind of stuff all the time, he could imagine it would get a little wearing. All this talk of God and His goodness toward humanity, our obligation to think well of Him, and of resurrection and not dying, seemed to be in wilful defiance of reality. And of his own raw pain.

Eventually, the coffin reached the front of the chapel. The funeral directors bowed to the minister, turned on their heels and walked out. Clearly their fee didn't extend to actually having to sit through the service.

The minister stood at the lectern and looked out over the few hardy souls who remained. "We meet in the name of Jesus Christ," he began.

That seemed somewhat of a presumption from Barry's perspective, and Granite-faced Woman certainly didn't look impressed, but he said it as though it were the most obvious thing in the world.

"We come here today," the minister continued, "to remember before God our brother, Christian; to give thanks for his life; to commend him to God, our merciful redeemer and judge; to commit his body to be cremated; and to comfort one another in our grief."

It all felt a long way away from Section 46 of the Public Health (Control of Diseases) Act 1984.

The minister said a prayer, then, much to Barry's surprise, he said, "I'd now like to call upon Jean Adam, from Monument Housing Association, to deliver a brief tribute."

Granite-faced Woman suddenly looked up in alarm – this was clearly not on her agenda and had not been agreed. Jean simply glided past her, oblivious, and headed toward the front of the chapel. Barry looked at his service book for some clue as to what she might be expected to say.

According to the brief note he found at the back, it appeared that Jean was supposed to *"proclaim the gospel in the context of the death of this particular person"*. Under the circumstances, it felt like quite a challenge, even for someone of Jean's undoubted rhetorical skills. But, as she took her place at lectern, she didn't appear in the least bit fazed.

"The first thing to say is that I am neither a friend nor a relative of Christian, so I can't recount stories about his excitement at Christmas as a child or of some private act of kindness that I'll never forget. I'm just a housing assistant at Monument, and part of my job is to go through the tenancy agreement with prospective tenants and make sure that they understand what they're signing. It's not a particularly thrilling job, but it sets the foundations of the relationship between the landlord and our tenant. It also gives me the opportunity to talk through other things too – issues or problems that I might pick up on, or which they might disclose – and to let them know that those things matter too; that we care about more than just their rent money."

Barry couldn't help wondering what Langley would think if he found out about this.

"So, it feels like one of the most important things we do – so important, in fact, that I can't quite believe that they let someone on my lowly grade do it."

Of course, Monument always said that going through the tenancy agreement was one of the most important things that they did, but Barry had always assumed that no one actually believed it. They just said it to make the housing assistants feel important, when what they were actually doing was a job that the housing officers didn't want to do. Bizarrely, however, Jean didn't see it as an imposition at all, but as an honour.

"I first met Christian nearly five years ago, when he signed up for his flat at Neville Thompson House," she continued. "He'd lived with us before, as a young man, so he knew the drill and wasn't particularly interested, if I'm being honest. In those situations, the thing you have to do is to make sure that you listen to them before you expect them to listen to you."

Barry felt this was a tip Jean ought to pass on to Taneesha.

"When you looked at his application form, it was clear that he'd had a tough life. He'd been in care, then a young offenders' institution and then in one of our specialist housing schemes, The SHYPP in Chelmsley Wood. There'd been addiction problems and more run-ins with the criminal justice system. When he came to Neville Thompson House, he'd just been released from prison again. But the thing that struck me was that he didn't have a family. Oh, there were plenty of professional agencies involved in his life (some of whom are represented here today), but there was no one who loved him or cared about him in a purely personal sense. It seemed so sad; genuinely a tragedy. He was fully grown up physically, and yet, sitting there in front of me, he was still, in an emotional sense, a child. He so desperately wanted to be loved and yet he didn't know how. The world of love seemed closed to him. And so, sadly, he had closed himself to it."

This had clearly been a tenancy sign-up meeting unlike any that Barry had ever attended.

"So often we say of people like Christian, 'The problem with him is he's into drugs' or 'into crime'. We look at their lives through the professional lenses that we approach them with, not through the loving eyes that a mother or a friend might. But Christian was not a drug addict or a criminal – although these things played a part in his life, they were not the totality of who he was. At root, as today's service reminds us, he was a lost soul looking for love. In that sense, he was not so very different from all the rest of us. His issue was that he never found it; he never knew that he was lovable because none of us were able to tell him. He never found himself in love.

"As we went through his form I came to the bit where we record someone's religion or belief. 'Do you have a religion?' I asked him. 'I don't believe in nuffink,' came the rather terse reply. I was disappointed, but not surprised. 'Do you want me to tick "atheist"?' I asked. 'No,' he said. 'I don't believe in that neither.'"

The minister chuckled. Granite-faced Woman cast a surreptitious glance down at her watch.

"It struck me as a beautifully naïve answer, but also one that contained an unintentional germ of truth. Christian was not anybody's idea of a religious person, but he couldn't quite bring himself to entirely abandon hope. He, quite literally, couldn't believe in nothing. So, in a rather animistic sense, he did have a kind of faith. It was the faith of the psalmist who rails against the inscrutability of God, whilst hoping for a change in fortune; and the faith of Job, who stands there wanting to know why God has allowed him to be afflicted, and hoping for an answer. And maybe it was the faith of Christ himself, demanding to know why God had abandoned him on the cross, whilst hoping for a resurrection.

"And who wouldn't forgive him for that? Christian's life contained no great successes, no brilliant triumphs against the odds. According to any worldly measure, his life was an abject failure. Even his victory over drugs was cruelly snatched away from him at the last. Simply surviving for thirty-three years was about as much as he could claim. But today, we honour him in all his failure because – as all those of us who came into contact with him can attest – he was a person of intrinsic value. His worth came, not from success, but simply from the fact that he was human. So often we would have battles with Christian – as I'm sure some of you did too. People would complain about him or his visitors; there were sometimes problems with his rent. But he would always come back to us and demand – sometimes very bluntly – to be treated fairly because he knew, deep down, that he was of equal value to everyone else and he wanted people to recognise that. He had faith that something, somewhere, gave him that value, no matter what people said or how they treated him.

"It was an angry faith, certainly. And it was the faith of someone who believed in God, not so that he could love Him, but so that he could hate Him – for His silence and His apparent passivity in the face of Christian's many travails. But it was, nevertheless, a faith that I believe will be honoured by God. So it is my faith that the resurrection he never experienced in life will be God's gift to him in death."

With that, she was finished. Suddenly the world of faith seemed tantalisingly close. Like the glass walls of the exec team's offices, Barry could see glimpses of it through the frosting. But he couldn't quite touch it, although he could see that it was just millimetres away. And, because he couldn't touch it, he knew he had to shut his eyes and pretend it wasn't there.

The money – that was real. He could feel it in his pocket. That was the truth he had to follow. He'd felt the truth of Jean's words for a moment, but then it was gone. He wanted to grasp it, but when he looked at his hand he saw that it was empty.

The probation officer leant over from behind and put a hand on Jean's shoulder before mouthing, "Thank you."

Granite-faced Woman seemed less impressed. She looked at Jean as though she'd committed some terrible act of betrayal – introducing God into the equation was not what social services were paying for; it was bad enough that the minister got to do it, without anyone else joining in.

The service continued with the kindly minister gently leading the congregation through the prayers. Eventually, they reached the Lord's Prayer. Barry had not had to recite that since he'd been at school, and it appeared that, at some point in the intervening thirty years, someone had changed the words, which caused him some anxiety. He was pretty sure it was only our trespasses we needed forgivness for when he was child, but now it seemed that it was our sins. That felt a lot more serious – it seemed to cover a much broader range of infractions.

Barry looked over his shoulder, but there was no one there.

None of it seemed to throw Granite-faced Woman, though, who merely continued to stare ahead silently.

It didn't seem long before they reached the end, and the kindly minister stood by the coffin and prepared to send it into the flames. Even as he did so, he spoke like someone for whom Christian Malford's sad and lonely life actually mattered; as though the service mattered in and of itself, and wasn't just a nice way to dispose of a body.

"We have entrusted our brother Christian to God's mercy and we now commit his body to be cremated; earth to earth, ashes to ashes, dust to dust," he said, before discretely pressing a button, whereupon curtains began to close around the coffin.

Suddenly, Barry was transported back three years. No longer was it the light-oak coffin of Chris Malford heading toward cremation. Instead, it was a white coffin disappearing into the flames, while his wife crumpled into him and sobbed uncontrollably.

He hadn't cried at the time; he couldn't. It had all happened so quickly that he hadn't had time to take it all in. And everyone had kept telling him how he had to "stay strong" for Lauren and his wife. But he cried now. Barry didn't know why, but all of a sudden he couldn't stop himself. Big, loud, full-throated sobs were emanating from somewhere deep inside of him, such that he could feel every spare ounce of fat on his gelatinous frame wobbling in sympathy.

"Oh Chris… Chris," Barry cried through his tears. "I'm sorry I let you down, son. I'm sorry; I'm so sorry."

The minister looked up in slight alarm. He certainly didn't appear to have expected tears. Jean however, quickly intervened. She sat down next to Barry and held him softly, whilst he continued to cry.

THIRTY-ONE

Jean had suggested they go for a coffee and a chat, but Barry wasn't in the mood. Or, rather, he would have very much valued a chat with Jean, but he didn't know what to say. It had all been terrible, but it had happened three years ago, and it seemed pointless picking at the whole thing again like a scabrous wound.

But, more than that, he also recognised that there was a whole area of his life that he couldn't now discuss with Jean. How could he talk about how he felt without also talking about what he'd done? And talking about what he'd done didn't seem like a good idea at all. There was only one solution, and that was to deal with the situation alone. Jean had been surprisingly amenable to this suggestion. She agreed to get a cab back to the office, and let Angela and Langley know that Barry needed some 'time out'.

The minister offered to take him to a side chapel if he wanted to be alone there.

"Thanks for the offer," Barry said, "but to be honest, I think I'm going to go to the museum and art gallery."

"Oh, do you like art?"

"Love it. Even went to art college."

"That's great. It can help at times like this – being a spiritual person."

"Well, I'm not sure that I am really. It's art I like."

"Yes, but art is just spirituality in drag, isn't it?"

Barry looked at the minister quizzically.

"It fools you into having a spiritual moment," the minister explained. "You think you're looking at one thing, but then you suddenly find you're looking at something else. And then you start to think about the things that matter to you and how you make sense of it all. Or at least, you do if it's any good."

Barry felt relieved. He had never thought about it like that before. He'd always thought of spirituality as being the preserve of churches and chapels, so he was delighted to discover that he could, apparently, still have a spiritual moment whilst doing something he actually enjoyed.

And so it was that he found himself wandering through a gallery of 'Seventeenth-Century Art in the Dutch Republic and Flanders'.

Nicolaes Pickenoy had been Amsterdam's leading portrait painter until he had the misfortune to be eclipsed by Rembrandt. He carried on for much of the 1630s, turning out some striking portraits, with their sharply penetrating light accentuating the features of the sitter in a way that seemed to illuminate not only their skin but also something of their soul. But by 1637 even he seemed to have acknowledged that he was up against one of the great portrayers of the human condition, and he pretty much stopped painting after that. However, before he did, he managed to turn out *Portrait of a Woman*, and Barry had always been rather grateful that he had.

As Dr Potter had once noted, the history of Western art was, at least in part, the history of men looking at women. Even when the subject was ostensibly something else, or women only formed part of a larger whole, Barry had to agree with his erstwhile tutor that underneath it all there was a pretty clear subtext, which told you a lot about how men looked at women and what they thought women were for. The worst of French and Italian art seemed to view them as little more than titillating decoration.

But the Dutch seemed to have no truck with such fripperies. Maybe it was, as Dr Potter had suggested, their puritanical Reformation instincts, but the women of Protestant art seemed more inclined to fix you with their stare and demand that you view them on their own terms, rather than invite you to see them as a means of achieving your own sexual fulfilment, as their Catholic counterparts did.

Or so it seemed with Pickenoy's unnamed sitter, at least. She was clearly a wealthy young woman, dressed as she was in a fine, black *tabbaard*, with gold-embroidered sleeves and an elaborate ruff. She wore gold jewellery and held an expensive, folding fan, all of which was painted beautifully. But the thing that really held Barry's attention was her face.

There were no 'come hither' eyes inviting you to cast your eyes upon her ample charms; no visual surrender to a rapacious male gaze. Instead, there was a stare that was at once both determined and yet also somehow brittle. She was undoubtedly attractive and she was clearly confident in her social position, but the fragility of her half-smile made her also appear vulnerable in a way that humanised her rather than making her seem weak. Pickenoy had captured perfectly that dichotomy in a way that reached across the centuries and made this woman speak in a register that Barry could still recognise.

The thing he liked most though, was the fact that she reminded him of Lauren. It wasn't just the slightly ruddy cheeks and dark brown eyes that both women shared. Lauren could look at her father with burning defiance, and yet there was also something in his daughter's look that, despite her best endeavours, betrayed a fragility in her self-esteem.

Of course, Pickenoy's portrait was a pendant to another portrait, almost certainly of the woman's husband. That, it seemed, had been lost, and so she hung on the wall on her own. But understanding that there was an unseen figure looming over her, and that that figure was male changed Barry's sense of why she might have looked as she did. It wasn't the fact that she was alone that intimidated her; it was the fact that she wasn't. The space she inhabited wasn't her own, but shared with a protector – her husband – who was the source of her wealth and status. It wasn't the viewer she needed to appease, but him. And, Barry thought (considering the fact that her black dress betrayed a certain Protestant mind-set), maybe even Him.

In either event, Barry reflected, it was what he couldn't see that made sense of what he could. Which alerted him to a rather striking thought about his daughter. She, too, was a pendant to a portrait that had now been lost. She, too, now stood alone when, actually, she was really one of a pair. Perhaps it was the unseen portrait that explained her too. Perhaps it was not a presence, but an absence that made sense of her apparent inscrutability.

At which point, Barry realised that the minister had been right. Pickenoy had tricked him into having a spiritual moment. He thought he'd been looking at a picture of a young, attractive, seventeenth-century Dutch woman, and then he'd discovered himself looking at something altogether different; something that wasn't even there.

He decided that, whatever it was, it called for a cup of tea and a cake. So off he headed to the Edwardian Tea Rooms.

The Edwardian Tea Rooms were, as far as Barry was concerned, the museum and art gallery's crowning glory, for not only did they contain examples of great art in a stunning architectural setting, they also contained examples of great cake.

The comforting smell of roasting coffee and baked treats perfumed the air as he entered, whilst the deep-red walls and mosaic-tiled floor gently suggested to Barry an earlier, simpler age, when God was in His heaven and all was right in the world. But he also became aware of the huge roof lantern, which ran the entire length of the galleried hall and threw daylight into even its most recessed corner. Even on an overcast late-November day, something made it feel uncomfortably bright.

As he sat down with a coffee and a generously proportioned chocolate muffin, he felt his pocket vibrate. It was a text from Saleema.

"So sorry u can't be here bt Jean has explained. Wanted to say goodbye properly & thank u. Just 2 let u no the money has arrived safely in Pak. We fly out tomorrow. Hope 2 b able to repay money next week. Just let us no where u want it sent. Thx & God bless u, Saleema."

Having dismissed the text message, Barry saw something else on his phone screen, but this message confused him: "*Lauren Todd mentioned you in a comment.*"

Barry was not much given to using social media, but Lauren had insisted on setting up a profile for him before she'd gone away, so she could keep in touch. He wasn't quite sure what he was supposed to do, but he swiped across the message anyway and, sure enough, his social media feed appeared before him. It featured a picture of a large blue whale – the cover image of a David Attenborough DVD box set. It had been posted, not by Lauren, but by his wife. Above it she had written just one word: *"Beautiful"*. Below it, Lauren had posted "*Looks like that's Mum's Christmas present sorted then* ***Barry Todd.***"

It hadn't occurred to Barry that Christmas was that close, but looking at the date he realised it was less than a month away. He felt a slight twinge of regret that his wife felt compelled to tell the world that she found a blue whale beautiful, but seemed singularly ill-disposed toward telling her husband what she thought about him.

As he assailed the phone with a wounded stare, it suddenly began vibrating in his hand and Lucy's name came up.

"Sorry to bother you, Barry, but I just need to give you a heads-up."

"What's the problem, Luce?"

"I've just got off the phone to Iulia Nicolescu. She's missed her rent payment this week."

Barry let out a weary sigh. "And?"

"Well, she was very upset. I couldn't quite work out all that she said to be honest. But we aren't going to get our money."

"Is that just this week or is that ever?"

"Difficult to say. She was going on about not being able to work at the moment because the police had been round. Although I don't understand that, because she's an EU national – she's got a legal right to live and work here; it's just claiming benefits that she can't do."

Barry didn't want to crush Lucy's youthful naïveté, but it appeared that his suspicions about Iulia's source of income were confirmed.

"Don't worry," said Barry. "I'll pop down this afternoon and have a chat."

"I've told her she's got until close of play tomorrow to get back up to date with her agreement or we'll have to request the eviction. Is that OK?"

"Absolutely. I'll make sure she understands she's running out of options."

Indeed, she was. But so was Barry. If Iulia backed out of the agreement now, he realised that Langley would be asking some very awkward questions as to why Iulia's eviction had not been requested the moment she had first breached the court order.

Barry finished his coffee and muffin, and headed back to his car, stopping as he did so to make his daily withdrawal of £250 from a nearby cashpoint.

He knew it wasn't Iulia's fault, but it annoyed him nonetheless that his attempt to do the right thing might backfire. *Why do I even bother?* He asked himself in frustration. And, no matter how long and hard he thought about it as he drove over to Coleshill, he still couldn't think of a convincing answer.

THIRTY-TWO

The scent of bleach rose up through the stairwell, but failed to conceal the unmistakable aroma of urine that lurked in its shadowed corners. A handmade sign at the foot of the stairs read *"Polite notice – Late night 'Gentleman Callers' are not welcome in* any *of these flats. We will report you to the police!"* Barry sighed as he ripped it off the wall. This was clearly not going to be an easy conversation. The stairs spiralled up, passing a window at each turn before continuing on their weary way. Barry followed them up to the very top, all the time hoping for some miraculous deliverance from the cup that Lucy had passed him.

"Miss Nicolescu? It's Mr Todd, from the housing association. Can I come in?"

The spyhole was checked. Chains were unchained, bolts were unbolted and, finally, a lock was unlocked. Barry was invited in and offered a seat on a second-hand easy chair, somehow made presentable by the addition of a throw. The room was tidy but sparsely furnished, yet its cleanness and the precision with which photos were arranged on the mantelpiece spoke of it being a home that was loved.

Barry took his seat at right angles to Iulia on the sofa. She looked drained, as if the act of simply living was beyond her now. Her eyes were shadowed and her skin was sallow, but she was still shapely and trim. The fog from her cigarette hung in the air like a cloud presaging a warning.

"I understand you're not able to keep to our agreement, Miss Nicolescu. About your rent and arrears."

"I have make payments, Meester Todd," she said, sucking disconsolately on her cigarette. "But I cannot make payments now."

"I know, but we have a suspended possession order against you, Miss Nicolescu. If you miss a payment – even one – we have to take possession of the flat. Do you understand that?"

"I know. Meess Hampton explain."

"I know things aren't easy for you, but you have to appreciate that I can't allow you to live here rent free. My boss will expect me to act."

"I understand Meester Todd, but I try everything. Everything. I get some money before, but…" There was a pause as she sought to explain the delicacy of the situation. "It not so easy now. The neighbours – they watch who come to flat."

"Yes. Miss Hampton explained that the police have been round."

There was an awkward silence whilst they both developed a sudden fascination with the floor.

"Are you looking for work at the moment?" Barry immediately felt the need to clarify. "I mean, a proper job."

Iulia glowered at him, a hurt look in her eyes. "I am trying, but no one is employing me. Everyone insist on 'references', on 'full employment history', and when I explain what happen to me…" Her sentence petered out in despair. "It so unfair!"

Iulia threw out a blanket of smoke from her cigarette and watched as it settled heavily over the room like a duvet. She looked desperate; her eyes sunken and the light from them gone. Barry felt genuinely sorry for her. This wasn't what he'd come into social housing to do.

"Is there anywhere you could go – if you couldn't stay here? A friend perhaps? Or maybe a relative?"

"There is nowhere. The friends I come with – they all go back now. I have no family here." Her eyes glassed with the suggestion of a tear. "Shakira – next door – she my only friend here. But she have baby now and her flat is small too. Meess Hampton say I not able to stay there."

"Yes, that's right, I'm afraid. Ms Jackson-Lewis would be in breach of her tenancy if she took you in. I'm sorry, but I was just trying to understand what your options are."

"Options? There are no options. I have no money, no job, no family or friends here. I will have to go back to Romania… and they will kill me." She coughed a forlorn, bronchial rasp. It sounded as though her heart had been broken into a thousand pieces, which were now rattling around inside her chest.

"Well, as Miss Hampton explained, we've been contacted by the Romanian Migrants Welfare Association—"

"They are not welfare association. They are criminal. They look for me – to kill me!"

Barry hadn't discussed with Costel exactly what his intentions were, but it seemed a not-unreasonable assessment of the situation.

"You're sure there's no one else who can help you?"

"Absolute," Iulia replied. "This is the best place for me; the safest place. I sure I can get job sometime. But for now…" She stubbed her cigarette out, despondently.

It seemed they had reached the end of the road. Barry had nothing else to suggest. "I'm obviously very touched by your story, Miss Nicolescu, but, I'm sorry, there's nothing I can do to help. My hands are tied, I'm afraid."

Iulia's head snapped up sharply and she fixed Barry with an accusing stare. "Then you kill me! If you evict me, you slit my throat!" She threw the words at him like a knife.

"I appreciate how difficult this is for you, but I don't know what to suggest." He really didn't. But he did know that if there was anything he could have done in that moment to avoid the inevitable then he would have done it.

Iulia's face crumpled into a tearful grimace. Barry grabbed a tissue from his jacket pocket and leant forward to proffer it to her. As he did so, his most recent cash withdrawal fell out of his jacket pocket and deposited itself across Iulia's carpet. Barry quickly knelt on the carpet to retrieve it. A moment later he was joined by Iulia.

"You have money?" she asked, picking up some stray notes. There was something different about her voice. It still sounded like Iulia, but something about its timbre had changed.

"Well, yes, I suppose I do... Sort of. But it's not quite as simple as that," said Barry as he scrabbled round trying to recover the last of his money.

He felt himself becoming flustered. His shirt removed itself from the back of his trousers as he reached forward under the coffee table, and he felt all the blood in his body rush toward his face as he sensed his upper buttocks being exposed. Yet, when he straightened up, Iulia did not appear repulsed or embarrassed, as he imagined she would. She was kneeling calmly before him with a strange look in her eye. Only moments previously she had looked like a woman slowly marching toward her death, but now she looked alive. And that transformed her.

"You have money," she said again. This was only partly true. Barry did indeed have some of his money, but the rest remained in Iulia's hands and she showed little sign of intending to hand it back to him. Given that, for obvious reasons, Barry could produce no evidence that the money was legitimately his, he recognised that he would need to stifle his immediate response, which was to threaten to go to the police if she didn't return the money forthwith.

"That's my money, Miss Nicolescu. Thank you," he said sternly, reaching out his hand.

She flicked an eyebrow casually. "You want money; I give you money. No problem."

Iulia dangled the money invitingly in front of his empty hand. Barry went to grab it, at which point she snatched it away.

"But think, Meester Todd. You say yourself, you not want to evict me. Why you not help me?"

"You've got a debt of nearly £2,500. A couple of hundred quid off me is not going to help you for long."

"But maybe you have *more* money."

Barry paused. He did indeed have more money, but he couldn't quite see why Iulia suddenly seemed to expect that he would be prepared to give it to her in order to forestall her eviction.

"Even if that were the case, it's against the rules."

She spoke to him as though she were a child. "You good man, Meester Todd. You want to help me. I see that." She tilted her head to one side, then bowed it forward and looked up at Barry, opening her eyes fully as she did so. The look she gave him, and the voice, provoked the first stirrings of desire in Barry. But he knew it was an impossible desire. She was far too young and far too pretty. And that fact broke his heart.

The Todds could not be said to have enjoyed a particularly active sex life since Christopher's death. Barry had hoped that, once Lauren had moved out, things might have improved. But, in the two months since Lauren's departure, his wife's demeanour had not suggested that it was likely to be on the agenda for the foreseeable future. And he now realised that that fact broke his heart too. Of course, Iulia could not possibly have known that, but Barry wondered for a moment if somehow her look had penetrated his heart and now sought to reunite its broken pieces.

"If I was to 'help' you, as you put it, I could lose my job. You do understand that? We're not allowed to help our tenants – well, not in that way – so I'd be putting you in a position where you could get me fired."

"But I never do that, Meester Todd. If you help me to stay here I never betray you, never!" She moved closer to Barry. He wanted to back away, but his chair was behind him.

"Obviously, I'd love to help you if I could. And, yes, I do have a little bit of money – not much, you understand – but enough potentially to get you through this. Over time. Like I said, I don't want to evict you. But it's the risk, you see. It can't all be down to me. I'd need you to do something too. For me."

"Of course!" said Iulia. She was now so close he could taste the smoke on her breath. "I not expect you to help me for nothing. I help you too."

"But you couldn't pay me back."

"Not with money, no. But maybe something else. You have something I need. Maybe I have something you like?" she asked, flicking open the button on her jeans. "Maybe we swap? I do whatever you want, Meester Todd."

She said it with such compassion that Barry wanted to believe, more than anything in the world, that it was true. He fixed her with a penetrating stare, his heart beating hard through his chest. "Really?"

"I will do anything to stay here – in this country – Meester Todd," she replied, deftly unbuckling Barry's trouser belt with her free hand. "Anything."

"Right," Barry squeaked, feeling Iulia's hand slip effortless inside his Y-fronts. "But when you say 'anything'…"

She gently lactated him for a few moments, then suddenly snapped her hold into a vice-like grip.

"You help me to stay here?" she asked, meeting Barry's agonised stare full-on. "My rent? The money I owe? You pay me, so I can pay these things?"

Under the circumstances, Barry didn't feel he had any option but to agree. "Yes, yes!"

"Not just one week?"

"Of course not! For as long as you need." In truth, it didn't feel like it would be much of a hardship. "As long as you can promise me you won't say anything to anyone about our… arrangement."

"Then we have deal." And instantly her eyes melted into pools of tenderness in which Barry allowed himself to wallow.

THIRTY-THREE

"Barry, could you come in and see me, please?"

It wasn't what Barry wanted to hear first thing on a Monday morning, particularly when the person doing the beckoning was Langley. It brought him back to reality – or, at least, it brought him back into the public world – and reminded him that it was the world that he still had to occupy, at least for some of the time. But something had changed the previous Thursday: something that had opened up a door to a different reality, a very private one. And it was this world that Barry had found occupying his mind since his encounter with Iulia.

After Christopher, it was as though he had become suspended in his grief, like a ship trapped in the winter ice. He hadn't known how to proceed safely in a world that seemed so uncomprehending of his pain. But after his encounter with Iulia he now knew that there was another man lurking inside of him. And Barry knew that it was this man whom he now had to invite to the forefront of his person. The money, Iulia, everything – this would be the axe that he would take to the frozen sea in which this new Barry was trapped. He would be careful to keep his old self for public display, of course. But he had decided that, in his private moments, it would be this new man who would drive him. Now, however, Langley's sudden hailing of him brought Barry back into the public world in which he still, for the moment at least, had to live.

Upon entering Langley's office, Barry saw that Angela was waiting for him too. Her involvement in a meeting was never a positive sign. He saw that she was rotating her pen nervously in her fingers. She looked up briefly to welcome him into the room, but then her eyes began to flicker, seemingly anxious to look everywhere except at Barry's pleading face. He felt a tide of nausea spread through his stomach.

"Barry, come in and take a seat. Thanks for taking the time to meet with us," she said. "I'm sorry it's taken us a while to get back to you, but we wanted to give proper consideration to your counterproposal before reaching a formal decision about the proposed removal of your company car."

The tide ebbed away as suddenly as it had risen. "Oh, that. Right. Not a problem. I thought it was something else… sorry."

"Well, we've had a lot of information to consider and a number of competing priorities to balance so, as you can imagine, we've had to make some very difficult judgements."

Barry sighed. *Just give me the letter and let's get this over with,* he thought to himself. But he didn't say anything, as usual. He felt certain it would only prolong the agony.

He had, of course, been expecting it, so it wasn't really that much of a surprise. And for a moment he had feared that things could have been a lot worse. But Barry was still disappointed as he returned to his desk. Angela had brought in lots of calculations that showed him he really wouldn't be much worse off at all, once the tax and enhanced mileage rate were taken into account. But if that were the case, why were they bothering to take it away? No, it wasn't the financial impact that annoyed Barry (after all, he hardly needed to worry about that now), it was the fact that they had swatted him aside so effortlessly; that his needs clearly mattered so little to them.

He was still ruminating on it all when he felt the mobile phone in his pocket vibrate. It was a text from Saleema.

"Arrived safely. All good. Funds now in our account – praise God! Just let us no where CM wants us 2 send his money & it shd b with him in 24 hrs. Will top up repayment to £42k as a thank u. Many thx once again. God bless, S x"

Barry took a deep breath and exhaled. It was as if some divine force had decided to redouble his resolve at his moment of greatest weakness. All he had to do now was think of a way to spend the money without it actually passing through his account. But, even without it, Barry still had the £6,740 that he had already withdrawn. The previous day Barry had withdrawn the final £240 from Chris Malford's account, so even if Monument did now spot that their money was missing, and even if the bank did track the stray payment down to Chris Malford, when they came to recoup it they would soon discover that there was just £4.77 left in his account.

Barry had done what he'd set out do.

But somehow he wasn't yet feeling what he'd set out to feel.

THIRTY-FOUR

Sally Hedges looked at the reminder notice that had arrived in the post and sighed. This was not the start to the day she had wanted.

"Marilyn!" she called across the office.

"Yes, Sally?"

"Last quarter's payment to Monument – we paid that, didn't we?"

"Oh yes, we definitely paid it. I distinctly remember because we had all that kerfuffle about the changing bank details and the deadline we had to pay by. We paid by CHAPS – do you remember?"

Indeed Sally did remember. In light of that, it was all the more incredible that Monument were chasing them for late payment. But Sally was nothing if not thorough.

"Can you log on and check that the payment definitely went – and that it went to the right place? I want to be absolutely sure before I phone them up."

Marilyn did as Sally instructed. Sure enough, the payment had gone out to Monument on Monday 2nd November. Both the payment amount and the recipient account details were consistent with the invoice and the CHAPS authorisation.

"Well, according to this, they've definitely had their money. It went exactly where they asked for it to go," Marilyn reassured her boss, unaware that the first of these sentences was not as automatically consistent with the second as she supposed.

"Well, they've sent us a reminder notice," said Sally.

"That's ridiculous."

Sally looked at the reminder notice. Attached to it was a copy invoice. Apart from the name of the issuing officer, all the details seemed consistent between it and the reminder.

"Get the original, would you?" Sally asked. Marilyn dutifully did so, and Sally took the copy invoice and put it next to the original. That was when she first noticed it – the payment details were different between the copy invoice and the original. The reminder notice contained the same bank details as the copy invoice, but they were different to those on the original invoice they'd received.

"Would you believe it?" Sally said, showing Marilyn the discrepancy. "Look – someone at Monument is trying to pull a fast one on us. What do you think?"

"Well, I wouldn't like to say. But there's definitely something not right. And I'm pretty sure the problem's not at our end," Marilyn replied, before venturing a further thought. "Of course, the original came from Saleema Bhatti. That's the woman who got the last invoice wrong. I hear she left Monument last week – which seems very sudden. Gone abroad, apparently…" She left the sentence dangling behind her tantalisingly, like a fox-fur stole.

"Agreed. Look, I need to make a couple of calls. Do you mind waiting outside for a bit? It's obviously going to be a little sensitive. Make yourself a cup of tea. In fact, do me a favour and make me one too, would you?"

Marilyn dutifully headed off to the kitchenette. Fifteen minutes later she had been to the shop to get some fresh milk and was heading back to the office with two cups of tea in her hands when Sally emerged, red-faced and looking decidedly unhappy.

"Marilyn!" she called across the reception area. "I think you'd better come in and sit down."

Over at Monument's offices, Langley had been called in to Ruth's office to be debriefed on her recent call with Sally. "But they phoned up and told us they'd paid it. It's even showing in our management accounts. If I'd known we'd not received it, then I'd have cancelled the agreement weeks ago."

"It's called an accrual, Langley," Ruth explained, peering at him imperiously from underneath a helmet of red hair. "We assume the money's going to come in because we've invoiced for it, and it always has in the past. On this occasion, however, it seems it didn't actually arrive in our bank account."

"So they've paid us, but we haven't received it?"

"No. They *think* that they've paid us, but they've actually paid someone else."

"How is that even possible? I mean, the payment details are on the invoice – all they have to do is send the payment there. They've been doing it for fifteen years, for God's sake!"

"It's a fraud, Langley. Not a mistake – a fraud."

"A fraud?" He greeted the word like a stranger. "But don't we have controls in place to prevent that sort of thing?"

"Yes, *we* do. But, evidently, The SHYPP don't."

Blessing had been standing quietly by Ruth's desk, having delivered a summary of her findings. "With respect, madam," she interjected, "things may not be that simple. I think someone has taken advantage of the confusion caused by the changes to our bank accounts."

Ruth shifted uncomfortably in her seat, then drew her ample frame up to its full height. "I don't think there was any confusion," she said, calmly. "We sent out a letter saying our bank details were changing and then we sent out an invoice with the new details. If they had any doubts about it, all they had to do was phone up and check."

"Exactly," said Langley. "If we haven't got the money, it's their problem. I'm sorry, but that puts them in breach of the agreement. I'm entitled to give them notice now."

"With respect, Mr Burrell, sir, I don't think you are."

Ruth's eyes narrowed, and she leant forward intently to address her finance officer. "And why not?"

"Because I think the invoice may have been amended by someone here."

"So did you actually ring up and check that the new payment details were correct?"

"Yes, yes," said Marilyn, her voice rising shrilly. "I phoned up Barry, just like we agreed."

"And he confirmed the details on this invoice were correct?"

"Yes! Yes! Well, not exactly."

"Marilyn! What do you mean, 'not exactly'?"

"Well, when I spoke to Barry, he didn't have the new account details to hand," she said, before adding, "but he did confirm that the bank account details had changed, that we'd been sent a letter about it, and that Saleema and Langley were authorised employees."

"But you didn't actually check the account details with anyone at Monument?"

"Well, no. Everything seemed to check out. I couldn't believe that someone trying to defraud us would do it in the exact same week that Monument's bank account was changing. It just seemed too much of a coincidence."

Sally fixed her with a beady stare. "Unless, of course, they chose to do it in the exact same week because they *knew* that Monument's bank details were changing."

"Oh. I hadn't thought of that."

There was a long pause whilst Sally's jaw locked and her hands clenched into fists. Silence blanketed the room before it was disturbed by the phone ringing. Sally answered it swiftly.

"Hello, Mrs Hedges? It's Promilla, from the bank. I'm just getting back to you about your missing payment. I've had a look, and it was paid fully in accordance with the instructions on your CHAPS authorisation letter. But we've checked the name of that account holder now and confirmed that the account name is not Monument Housing Association."

Sally was going to query whether paying into an account that was not in the name of Monument Housing

Association could be described as being 'fully' in accordance with her instructions, but she thought better of it. At that moment, all she needed was confirmation of whose account the money had gone into.

"And who was the recipient?" she asked.

"Christian Malford. Does that name mean anything to you?"

"Nothing immediately springs to mind. We'll check our records and see if it turns anything up. But can I ask – is the money still in the account? Can you get it back to us?"

"I'm afraid not. There have been a number of cash withdrawals over the past month and then a major withdrawal by cheque last week."

"And where did that go to?" asked Sally, hoping that somehow it wasn't too late for her to rescue the situation.

"Umm… I'm afraid I can't tell you that. I can only give that level of information to the police."

"But it's our money!"

"Only until it arrived in Mr Malford's account. Then – technically – it became his money. It is one of our accounts, but I'm afraid I can't divulge details of what happened to it. Data protection and all that. To be honest, I shouldn't even have told you as much as I have."

"I understand all that," Sally said, as calmly as she could manage. "But I don't suppose you could tell me – this cheque withdrawal – it didn't happen to go to a Saleema Bhatti, did it?"

There was a pause on the other end of the phone. It was so long that, for a moment, Sally wondered if Promilla had ended the call.

But eventually she responded. "I'm sorry, but I can't give out that level of information. I'm not even supposed to know it."

"I understand the sensitivities, Promilla, but we're a charity. This is charity money. We can't afford to lose it. We work with homeless young people—"

"I understand all that Mrs Hedges, but—"

"So you'll also understand that we need to do everything we can to get our money back," Sally said, desperately. "If we knew that the money went to Saleema Bhatti, then it might not be too late to do something about it."

There was another long pause during which Promilla assessed her options before answering very deliberately. "I'm sorry Mrs Hedges, but I'm not allowed to *confirm* that information. I hope you understand."

"Perfectly. Thank you for your help."

Blessing had been subject to enough jokes about Nigerians working in finance to worry about where everybody would start laying the blame. Therefore, she decided it was in her own interests to solve the crime herself and present her findings to Ruth.

"I'm sorry to disturb you again, madam," she said upon entering Ruth's office for the second time that morning, "but I've had another phone call from Mrs Hedges."

"Good news or bad news?"

Blessing didn't want to commit herself. She was now absolutely confident that she could prove her own innocence, which felt like good news. But she also recognised that the money Monument was owed was probably gone for good, along with the employee who had purloined it, so she could understand that Ruth might view things rather less positively.

"Well, they've identified where the money was sent to, but I'm afraid it's not there now. Some was withdrawn in cash, but most of it has been moved on."

"Do we know where?"

"I'm afraid not. They wouldn't say officially," Blessing replied, before adding invitingly, "although we have our suspicions."

"Do we?"

"Well, obviously, madam, we can't jump to conclusions," said Blessing as a precursor to doing precisely that. "But at the moment everything seems to be pointing in one direction."

"Here we go. It was tea with one, wasn't it?" Lucy said, handing Barry his *"Is it Friday yet?"* mug.

"Yes, that's right. Thanks."

He was relieved to see from the latest report that arrears in his two teams had finally started to go down. He was in the mood for celebrating and he knew just how he intended to do it. He added an appointment to his diary for that afternoon. But, before leaving for it, there was just one thing he needed to check.

"Did you get that payment from Iulia Nicolescu last week, Luce?"

"Oh yes. Sorry, I forgot to tell you. I don't know how she's managed it, but she's brought herself up to date with the court order."

"I think she's managed to get some casual work," Barry said.

"Good. Nothing's come in this week yet, though."

Of course it hasn't, thought Barry. And if it didn't come in by the end of the week then she would be in breach of her court order again and back to facing eviction, which would obviously be a terrible thing. What Iulia needed was another injection of cash – and quickly – if she was to retain her home. Her safety, and possibly even her life, depended on it.

"Give her till Thursday again, then ring her up," said Barry, "but I'm pretty sure she's intending to pay. Probably just waiting to get paid."

"OK, but I've still got two other eviction reports I need you to sign off. Are you about this afternoon?"

"Umm… well, I have got a long lunch planned; it's in my diary."

"Is it? I didn't see anything when I looked."

She quickly looked again at Barry's electronic diary. Sure enough, there were two-and-a-half hours blocked out. "Oh, so it is," she said, surprised. "Good for you. Giving blood – what a public-spirited thing to do."

"Oh, I don't know. If I've got some spare and somebody needs it, it just seems selfish to keep it all for myself." And when he thought about it like that, it really did. He finished responding to his emails, stood up and grabbed the coat off the back of his chair.

"Oh well," said Barry to no one in particular, "I'm off to perform my civic duty."

And, in a strange way, it didn't feel like lying.

THIRTY-FIVE

As Barry handed over his £200 to Iulia later that afternoon, he felt a good deal less confident about his civic-mindedness than he had done a couple of hours earlier. Considering she'd just been given a lifeline, Iulia hadn't seemed grateful at all.

And, despite her undoubted professional skills, he had, to be honest, been more than a little disappointed with the whole experience. Sex, it appeared, was one of the few areas of life where professionalism was not a virtue. For all their physical intimacy, Iulia's look was one of emotional detachment. That wasn't what he wanted – quite the reverse – and he needed her to understand that.

"I don't do this normally," he said, sitting back down, half-dressed, on the unmade bed. "You're my first. Well, obviously you're not my first – I'm married. But the first I've had this kind of arrangement with."

She sat in the corner of the room on an easy chair, in her pants and a T-shirt, staring out of the window. She said nothing, but exhaled the smoke from her cigarette like a sigh. It wandered lazily between them before curling up toward the ceiling. Barry stared ahead at the small television in the corner, not daring to make eye contact with Iulia.

"It's just that my wife... Well, things aren't easy at the moment. We lost our son a few years ago, you see. He died. It was all totally unexpected: overdose. In his own bedroom. Only seventeen. We were away for the weekend – which had been my idea. There'd never been a hint of problems..."

Barry felt different to Costel and all the other men whose needs Iulia had been forced to service. He was in need of her grace and he wanted her to see that he knew that. Because that would surely melt her heart.

"She blames herself. My wife. That she didn't see the signs. But it's difficult with teenagers. I've told her that. But she won't forgive herself, I suppose. Or me. For making her go away that weekend. And that makes things... difficult... between the two of us.

"But obviously, I'm upset too, and I don't think she gets that. I need to talk. I need to feel that someone understands. But I just feel lonely at the moment. Very lonely. My daughter's gone off to university now too, which doesn't help. There's no one to talk to. And then I missed out on a job I really should have got—"

"You have job. Good job. With good company."

"I don't know about that. The pay's not what it should be – I've not had a pay rise for three years. And Monument's not like it was when I joined. They'd chuck you out on the street now – if it wasn't for what I'm doing. All this, it shouldn't be necessary. If it was down to me, it wouldn't be. But it's them. They've forced us both into this situation, really."

A punch of smoke hit the air as Iulia choked, incredulous. "You give me your money because of them? You expect me to believe this?"

Barry finally turned to face her. "It's true, honestly. I want to help you – because of Neville. Because of what it used to be like. He'd never have let you be evicted… Besides, I can afford it."

"How you afford it? If they pay you so bad?"

"It's all rather complicated, really," Barry said, sensing a shift in her demeanour. "Technically, I'm using their money to pay you. But you're paying it straight on to them anyway, so it's not really theft. It still gets to them in the end. It felt like the right thing to do."

She coughed a hollow laugh, which gave way to an accusing silence. Eventually, Iulia turned her gaze from the window and fixed Barry with a look that was so piercing, so wounded, that he immediately fell silent.

"You go now," she said, tossing Barry's trousers toward him. "I take shower."

It was as if there were a hole at the heart of their encounter. Barry wondered if a muffin could fill it. He knew there was a service station on his route back to the office, so he decided to find out.

The service station was an uncomfortable mix of bright lights and aching loneliness. Barry had the misfortune of making his stop at the same time as a coach-load of schoolchildren.

He bought himself a coffee and the largest muffin he could find, and looked for a seat as far away from the ebullient ten year-olds as possible. There didn't seem to be many options, but then he noticed a single seat free next to a youngish woman who appeared to be wholly entertained by writing something. Barry apologised for having to ask if the seat was free, and then apologised again for sitting in it when she said that it was.

He didn't mean to pry, but he couldn't help noticing what she was writing. It was a simple thank-you note, but it looked for all the world like a touching act of kindness by a person whose thoughtfulness in feeling it necessary to write one set her apart as good.

Dear Harry and Liz,

Thank you so much for a great few days. Everything's been so horrible, but it was wonderful to get away – and very much appreciated. I didn't realise how much I needed it until I was with you, but driving back now I'm missing you both already, so I just wanted to say thanks for all you've done. It was very thoughtful of you.

I hope the kids didn't mind having me around. (They're great by the way – a real credit to both of you.)

You really are the most wonderful friends. Thank you so much – I promise I'll return the favour one day if either of you ever need it!

Love and best wishes to you both,

She looked up and smiled awkwardly as she noticed Barry staring at her, and he was suddenly filled with a sense of unbearable longing. What he hungered after, he realised, was not her beauty, but the innate goodness that seemed to make her beautiful.

And what Barry also realised was that maybe the opposite was true for him. Maybe he wasn't ugly because of his physical and aesthetic deficiencies, but because of an innate moral deficiency that somehow soaked into his skin and disfigured him.

It made perfect sense; if people were hungry for goodness, the opposite was also true – malevolence invariably made them want to throw up. And Barry knew from the look Iulia had given him as he'd removed his clothing that lunchtime that he made women want to throw up.

He'd thought he wanted sex because of what happened at the end, but now he realised that he actually wanted it because of what happened at the beginning. And that, it transpired, was something that money couldn't buy.

Barry pushed his half-eaten muffin to one side. A horrible thought occurred to him: maybe the money wasn't going to change anything, not fundamentally. Maybe it wasn't enough – or, rather, maybe it was too much, but too much of the wrong thing. Maybe it wouldn't make things better after all. Maybe it might even make them worse.

THIRTY-SIX

"Ruth, you wanted to see me?"

"Yes, Barry, please come in."

"Sorry," Barry replied, entering the room. It was neat and tidy, but seemed to strain ever-so-slightly at the seams trying to contain all of Ruth's various accoutrements – which, Barry thought, was not unlike the trouser suit she was wearing.

"Take a seat," she said. "Obviously, you know Langley…"

"Morning, Barry."

A bolus of unease sat, firm and immovable, in the pit of Barry's stomach. He had arrived at work that morning to find an email and a phone message from Ruth calling him to an urgent meeting at 9.30am. Ruth never called him into a meeting – there was no need for her to; she was, after all, the director of finance, not housing. If Ruth was calling him into a meeting, then it could only mean one thing.

"And this is one of our auditors, Hope Mansell."

Hope was an intimidatingly young Anglo-Jamaican woman with a commanding demeanour and jet-black hair swept back into a bun. "Pleased to meet you, Barry," she said unsmilingly, whilst proffering her hand.

"Auditors? I hope there's nothing wrong," Barry said, as innocently as he could manage. But his unease quickly spread from the pit of his stomach to every part of his being.

"It's OK. There's nothing for you to worry about," Ruth said.

But Barry knew that there was everything for him to worry about, so he concentrated his efforts into twisting and untwisting his tie around his fingers like thread around a bobbin.

"It appears that Monument may have been the victim of a fraud," Hope said. "The quarterly payment from The SHYPP has been… misdirected."

"Misdirected?"

"Yes. The quarterly invoice has been paid, but not into our account," Ruth explained.

"Which means that we don't have the money!" Langley said.

"But how can that have happened?" Barry asked.

"Well, that's why we wanted to talk to you," Hope replied, the effect of her caramelly voice somewhat undercut by the coldness of her eyes. "We were hoping that you would answer a few questions that might help us find all that out."

Despite the December chill outside, Barry felt heat burning through his face and sweat patches beginning to form in the palms of his hands, which began to soak into the fabric of his tie.

"Errr… OK… Is it me or is it awfully hot in here?"

Ruth obligingly adjusted the temperature of the comfort cooling system on the control panel.

Hope peered at Barry authoritatively over the reading glasses perched on her nose. "Me and my team have been investigating this since your internal people discovered the problem yesterday and it looks to us like a fairly traditional mandate fraud."

"Mandate fraud?"

"Someone has amended the payment details on your invoice."

"So the money's gone to them instead of us?" Barry asked.

"It would appear so," replied Hope, looking even more sombre than the occasion required, in Barry's opinion.

"But the good news is we think we know who did it!" Langley said.

The colour slowly leaked from Barry's face until all that was left was a sallow, variegated white. He felt as if he were about to be sick and then as if he might suddenly defecate. How had they worked it out so quickly? He had been so sure that nothing could be traced back to him, but they'd obviously been watching him all this time. And as for Alun's reassurances that such crimes were almost never investigated, how could he have been so stupid as to take at face value the inebriated rantings of someone who had such an obvious axe to grind?

"To be fair," said Ruth, glaring at Langley through the solid frames of her glasses, "we can't say with any degree of confidence yet that we know who was involved. But there are a couple things that seem to be pointing us in a certain direction. Which is why we wanted to speak to you."

Barry was torn. Should he just fold and confess all now in the hope of a lesser sentence? Or could he try to bluff his way out of it? Twin emotions rose up in him, vying for supremacy. He suddenly found that he had no idea how to hold himself together anymore, how to sit or even how to breathe. And certainly not what to say. In view of this, he decided to play for time while he found out how much they knew.

"And how do you think I can help?" he asked, clenching his buttocks determinedly as if trying to stop the truth leaking out.

"Well, there are obviously a couple of people who could have been involved here and at The SHYPP," said Hope.

"And we need to work out if any of them have been lying," said Langley.

"We need to try to eliminate as many people as we can," Hope clarified, shooting Langley a glance as she did so. "May I just ask, Barry, have you had any problems with The SHYPP's payments before?"

"Oh, no. Never. The SHYPP's been open fifteen years and I've been involved right from the beginning. They've been a bit slow to pay sometimes, but I'm positive we've never had a payment go missing before. Absolutely positive."

"OK. So tell me Barry, what was your understanding of the process for producing the invoice?" Hope asked.

"Well, it was down to Saleema really. She was supposed to get the figure for the rent that was due from the rent accounting system and then get the figure for repairs from Bob."

Hope looked up from her tablet and lifted an eyebrow in gentle enquiry. "Supposed to?"

"Well, Saleema hadn't been doing it long, and I think it's fair to say the first invoice she'd done hadn't been a hundred per cent accurate. So she liked to run them past me first. Of course, I just told her what to do with the rent due figure. I didn't check anything else."

"Obviously. And did she check this invoice with you too?"

"Well, yes. I talked her through the calculation she needed to do. She did it and then sent me through a PDF of the draft invoice."

"And did you notice anything about the draft invoice?"

"Not really. Just that, as far as I could tell, it was correct. So I told her to issue it – Langley was chasing payment and wanted to get the money in, so I didn't want it delayed anymore."

"And did she issue it by email at all?"

"No. Definitely by post. Sally's a bit old school about things like that. I think she gets loads of fake ones via email – like the rest of us. Anyway, she insists on getting a letter in an envelope through the post before she pays anything. I made a point of telling Saleema that."

"I see," said Hope flicking an eyebrow up at Barry, then typing some notes into her tablet. "Now I want to move on, if I can. I understand that you had a phone conversation with Marilyn from The SHYPP about the invoice before she paid it."

"Yes, that's right." If Marilyn had told them about the call, it seemed pointless to deny that it had happened.

"And what did she ask you?"

"Well, she said they'd had an invoice, but it had different payment details to usual. They just wanted to check whether ours had changed."

"And what did you tell her?"

"Well, I said that, as far as I'd been told, they had. There'd been a letter about it."

"And did you actually confirm what the new details were?"

"Well, no, I couldn't. I don't know our bank account details," Barry replied, entirely truthfully. "But I knew that they were changing because Saleema had told me."

Langley's eyes narrowed. "So Saleema knew Sally would only pay against a paper invoice, and she was aware that the bank details were changing before she sent the invoice out?"

"Oh yes," Barry said.

Meaningful looks were exchanged between the other three.

"And can I ask, did anyone else at Monument know that the invoice was being issued to The SHYPP that week?" Ruth asked.

"Well, no. Not as far as I'm aware. It was quite unusual for us to issue the invoice that early, to be honest. We were only issuing it when we did because Langley was pressing for payment. Normally, it would have gone out later."

Hope looked up sharply from her tablet. "It would normally have gone out later? What do you mean?"

"Well, normally, we'd wait until Bob had sent through the list of repairs and their costs. That could take weeks from quarter end. But Langley said he wanted the invoice out sooner, so we chased Bob up."

"Only so we'd get our money sooner!" Langley said. "Actually, only so we'd get our money when it was due, rather than seven weeks late!"

Hope noted all this down. "That's fine. Did anyone phone you up at all, before the invoice was sent out, asking about it?"

"Errr… No. I'm sure I'd have remembered that. But, no, no one phoned me about the invoice – not before Marilyn did. Sorry."

"So only Saleema was aware the invoice had been issued?" asked Langley.

"Well, only Saleema and me. And you of course, Langley."

"Yes, well I hope you can discount me from your enquiries, Hope!" Langley said, laughing blithely.

Hope remained impassive and didn't respond. She tapped a few more thoughts into her tablet. "Barry, does the name Christian Malford mean anything to you?"

"Chris Malford? Yeah. He was one of our tenants."

"One of our tenants?" Langley said, suddenly sitting up.

"He was. Died a few weeks ago. Very sad."

"He's dead?" asked Hope, her look of grim-faced professionalism slipping for a moment.

"Yes. Drug overdose. The police are investigating though. They seem to think it may not be as simple as that. They came round asking for CCTV footage. They think someone else might have been involved – that it was deliberate – after what happened with poor Shana Backley at The SHYPP. I sent them the CCTV, but I've not heard anything more since."

Hope's face betrayed her mounting concern. "And did Mr Malford die before or after the invoice was issued? This really is very important."

"Oh, just before," Barry replied. "Lee discovered his body on the Thursday, and I remember coming into work the next morning and having a conversation with Langley and Saleema about the invoice then. But he'd been dead for a couple of weeks before that, according to the CCTV."

"And did Saleema know?" asked Ruth.

Barry paused. He wanted to get his answer right, and the right answer was "almost certainly not". Monument had over 7,000 tenants and no one in the finance team was likely to know the names of any of them. Of course, the people in area housing team B would have heard Barry and Lee talking about Chris Malford. But such news was unlikely ever to reach the dizzy heights of the central services floor. Barry had certainly never mentioned anything to anyone.

But the cogs in Barry's mind were beginning to whir and tick their way into new positions. He now realised that, having investigated this as any good auditor would, Hope would have discovered that the apparent beneficiary of the fraud was not Barry Todd, but Saleema Bhatti. There was, therefore, a potential advantage to Barry in ensuring that the suspicions she was floating before him were not dismissed too easily. So what he actually said was, "Well, I guess it's possible." Which it was. Theoretically.

A silence descended on the room. There were more looks exchanged between Ruth, Langley and Hope.

"May I just check, Barry," Hope asked, "did Saleema ever suggest to you that she had any money troubles?"

"Money troubles? Well…"

"Oh, for goodness' sake!" Langley said impatiently. "Blessing says she heard Saleema having several phone conversations with her husband that seemed to be about money, and she saw you speaking to Saleema after one of those. She says when she came in the other day, she saw

Saleema and her husband in conversation with you. Were they talking to you about money?"

"Well, yes, I did chat with Saleema. Her father was very ill, y'know. I guess I wanted to be supportive…" Barry petered out whilst three sombre faces looked at him expectantly.

"They told you not to say anything, didn't they?" Ruth said.

"I'd rather not answer that question," Barry said. Which was, of course, an answer in itself.

"I know you got on with Saleema, Barry," Ruth continued, "but you've got to realise that nearly £50,000 of our money has been misdirected, and we need to find out where it's gone."

Barry felt bad. He didn't want to lie – that would be wrong – but surely it couldn't be wrong if he just told the truth?

"Her father was ill. In Pakistan. Obviously, they don't have an NHS over there so she'd had to pay for his operation herself."

"Did she ever ask you for money?" asked Hope. "To pay for his operation, perhaps?"

"Oh no. She had her redundancy money to pay for that. But there was other stuff – chemotherapy and stuff – that he needed going forward, and she still had to pay for that."

"And she needed money for that?" asked Hope.

"Well, it was more complicated than that. It was all a bit of a mess, to be honest. She thought she'd got the money, but then it turned out that she hadn't."

"So she did need some money? She actually said that to you?" Ruth pressed.

Barry paused for a moment before continuing, but he'd already said so much it seemed implausible to deny the obvious fact now. And, besides, it was the truth.

"Yes, she said she needed some money."

"Did she say how much?" Hope asked.

Barry paused again. Three pairs of eyes stared at him intently. "About £42,000."

Langley slammed his pen down on the desk and pushed his chair back. Ruth slumped slightly forward in her seat and buried her head in her hands. If he hadn't known her better, Barry could have sworn he'd heard her mutter, "Oh shit," under her breath. Only Hope remained impassive.

"Thank you for being so honest, Barry. I know it isn't easy to betray confidences, but you've done the right thing," she said. "That really has been incredibly useful in helping me to understand what's happened here."

Barry blinked. Was that it? An awkward silence descended on the room. Finally, Langley spoke.

"Well, that's just brilliant! Our own staff member has nicked our money – and we've paid them for the privilege!"

Barry wanted to say, "I am here, you know." It was perhaps all he'd ever really wanted to say.

But before he could do so, Ruth snapped at Langley. "Langley!" She said, shooting her colleague a ferocious stare and then indicated toward Barry with a glare. "Now is not the appropriate time."

Langley was duly admonished. "Sorry, Barry. Just forget that I said that."

"Right," said Ruth, trying to regain her composure. "Thank you for your cooperation, Barry. It's been very helpful. I think we've managed to fill in a few of the blanks."

"Absolutely," Hope agreed. "I'm going to be writing a report for the chair of the audit committee to detail what I've found and what seems to have gone wrong. Is there anything else you'd like to tell us?"

"Errr… Not really, if I'm honest," Barry replied. He felt as though he'd said enough.

"Well, thanks for your time," Hope concluded. "I'll come back to you if I need anything else."

And without further ado, Barry was ushered from the room.

He didn't understand it. They hadn't mentioned the cash machine withdrawals – or the bank details Barry had nefariously removed from Chris Malford's flat. They weren't questioning him about his involvement in the amendment of the invoice or even its transit route from Saleema's desk to Sally's. All their attention seemed focused on Saleema. The possibility of Barry being involved – even if only as Saleema's accomplice – genuinely didn't appear to have occurred to them.

Back in Ruth's office conclusions were being drawn – and nothing could have been further from anyone's mind than the fate of Barry Todd.

"So, given what we know now, where does that leave us?" Ruth asked.

"I'm not going to kid you, from our perspective things aren't looking good," Hope replied. "Everything points toward this being a fairly standard mandate fraud. The police very rarely investigate frauds like that for amounts like this. But I think we're beginning to build up a pretty clear picture of where the money's most probably ended up. Unfortunately, if, as Mrs Hedges claims, it's the Bhattis' account in Pakistan then our options are… limited, I'm afraid."

"Is there anything we can do?" Ruth asked.

"Well, I'm interested in this Christian Malford link. That's probably your best chance of getting the police to do something. These frauds generally work because there's a sap at the end of the line whose bank account is the one that gets used. They get paid a couple of grand for their trouble, and the mastermind keeps the rest."

"And Malford was set up to be that sap?"

"Looks like it, but maybe he got nervous and threatened to go to the police. At any rate, you need to pass this information on to them. It may help them with their other investigation, which might help them to track down anyone involved. Unfortunately, if they're out of the country – particularly if it's Pakistan – they'll generally end matters there. But at least we'll know."

"So that's it? We just have to write the money off?" asked Langley, barely concealing his annoyance.

"Well, obviously, I'm not suggesting you can't get your money back."

"Glad to hear it."

"The fact is, you've asked The SHYPP for money and you haven't received it. It's their job to take all reasonable care to make sure you get the money they owe you. But they have admitted – and Barry has just confirmed – that they didn't actually check the payment details properly with you. They assumed that the fact the details had changed meant they'd changed to the ones on the invoice. Their systems have failed too, so a degree of fault lies with them."

"So we can still demand payment from The SHYPP?" asked Langley. "And then start cancelling the management agreement when they can't pay?"

"Well, you can, but that's not without its risks. If The SHYPP can prove that there was some involvement from someone here, then that does weaken your case. And the evidence so far does seem to be pointing in that direction. Of course, it could be that Mrs Hedges is bluffing and the money's ended up with someone connected to The SHYPP, which would obviously strengthen your case. Ultimately, it all depends on where the bank says the money's ended up."

"I see," said Ruth. "And how do we find that out? Clearly, that's what's going to show who's stolen it."

"I can't help you with that, I'm afraid," Hope replied. "The bank isn't allowed to divulge that information. They certainly won't tell me. Once the money hit Malford's account it became his, and the bank can't tell anyone except him where it's gone from there."

Langley could hardly contain his rage. "But he's dead! How are we supposed to find out where our money's gone if they won't tell anyone? Hold a *séance*?"

Hope remained calm. "Well, obviously, they can tell the police as well, but only if they believe that money comes from the proceeds of a crime. And, even then, the police will need to go to court and convince a judge. Of course, given the sums involved they may not bother. But if it is linked to a murder investigation, I suspect they'll at least try to find out what's gone on. My point is that their priority will be the murder investigation, not getting your money back. You just need to understand that."

"For goodness' sake!" Langley said, slamming his pen down again.

"What I suggest you do now is report the fraud to the police and make them aware of the potential link with their Malford investigation."

"Shouldn't The SHYPP be reporting the crime? After all, it's their payment that's gone missing," Ruth asked.

"Normally, yes, but, the fact is, the police only have a duty to update the organisation that reported the crime. The other party will have no knowledge of how things are progressing or the leads that are being followed, so it's in your interests to make sure the organisation being updated is you and not The SHYPP – particularly given the circumstances."

"Understood. I'll phone the police right away," Ruth said.

"OK. Are you done with me?" asked Langley.

"Yes. Thanks," Ruth replied.

Langley left the two women and returned to his office. Hope began packing up her tablet before turning to Ruth. "I hate to ask this, but…"

"Yes?"

"Well, it's just a thought, but Barry said that only he, Langley and Saleema knew when the invoice was being issued. I just wondered if you thought it was possible that maybe… Langley was involved in some way? Have you had any suspicions?"

Ruth narrowed her eyes and looked at Hope intently. "And why would you say that?"

"Well, he was the one who started the whole invoicing process off, wasn't he? By his own admission, he brought the usual invoicing timescale forward, and that meant it clashed with the exact week that you were changing your accounts – which was, of course, the week of maximum confusion. And then he was apparently phoning Marilyn chasing the payment only a couple of days after the invoice had been issued. It just seems a bit… odd."

Ruth paused for a moment. "He also invited himself along to our meeting just now."

"I wondered about that. I didn't like to say anything when he turned up, but I wasn't expecting him. And, I have to admit, there were one or two questions I wanted to ask Barry about Langley's involvement in the whole process, but I felt a bit uncomfortable asking them with Langley sitting there next to me. And you could tell that Barry was uncomfortable having him there too."

"And – I'm sure it's nothing – but I thought Langley seemed awfully keen to make sure all the attention was diverted on to Saleema," Ruth said.

"Yes, it was quite embarrassing at one point… But, as you say, I'm sure it's nothing."

"Yes, I'm sure it is."

"Of course, I also ought to ask you about this guy," Hope said, indicating the seat where Barry had been sitting. "Any suspicions about him?"

Ruth let out a hollow laugh. "Barry? Are you joking? Worked with us over twenty years. Lovely guy, but not the sharpest tool in the box. Wouldn't know how to steal fifty quid, never mind fifty grand."

"No, I thought not," Hope smiled. "He did seem rather bemused by the whole thing. I just didn't want you to think I was ignoring anyone."

"No, no, I understand. You're just doing your job. But it doesn't seem very likely. Like he said, in the fifteen years he's been involved, we've never had a problem with The SHYPP's payments before."

"But then you suddenly get one in Langley's first month in post. Coincidence?"

"I guess we'll find that out when the police trace where the money went to."

"It's the first rule of auditing: follow the money."

THIRTY-SEVEN

The next day, following a call from Ruth, Lindsey Norton appeared at Monument's offices – where there was much speculation as to the precise reason for her long interview with the finance director. Langley hovered by her office all afternoon, desperate – Barry suspected – to find out whether he was any closer to being able to terminate the management agreement with The SHYPP. Barry, in contrast, waited to be called in for an interview, but the invitation never came, so he felt no particular guilt in deciding at 5pm that he might as well go home.

As attention still seemed to be focused squarely on Saleema, there seemed no reason for him to panic yet. It was, rather, the issue of how to purchase a car using Monument's money without creating a clear trail back to himself that was vexing Barry as he arrived home that evening. Given that the police were now involved, just transferring the money into his own account seemed fraught with risk.

He had been used to quickly shooting upstairs as soon as he entered the house to hide his latest cash withdrawal. Tonight, however, his wife was waiting for him and the moment she heard him come through the front door she leapt from the sofa to accost him.

"Barry! Why haven't you been answering your phone? I've been trying to call you!" She fixed him with an accusing stare.

"Oh, I've been in meetings. Sorry."

"Have you heard about Lauren?"

"No. What's the matter?"

"It's all over social media – haven't you seen?" She held her tablet up to Barry's face.

"What is? I've not seen anything."

"She's got a boyfriend! Look!"

Barry stared at the social media feed in front of him. *"Lauren Todd changed her relationship status"* it read, before going on to say *"Lauren is now in a relationship"*. And there was a photo of Lauren looking exuberantly happy – happier than Barry could remember seeing her looking at any point since her brother's death – next to a very handsome young man with his arm around her. He looked pretty pleased with himself too.

"Is that it?" asked Barry, incredulously. "Is that all you're worried about? She's at university, love; it happens."

"But why didn't she tell us? What's she trying to hide?"

"She's hardly trying to hide anything; it's all over Facebook."

"Why didn't she tell me, at least? Why do I only find out at the same time as everyone else?"

"Well, maybe she knew how you'd react."

"It feels like a knife in the heart," she said, collapsing on the sofa. "It's like she's abandoning us – abandoning me!"

"She's at university, love. She's growing up – moving on with her life. She's not our little baby anymore."

Out of the very long list of bad things that he could have said at that point, it transpired that that was just about the worst thing for Barry to say. She looked at Barry as though he was the most cruel and heartless husband any woman could have, before burying her head in her hands and beginning to sob.

Barry didn't know quite what to do. It seemed something of an overreaction – Lauren had, after all, had boyfriends before, when she was at school. His wife hadn't got upset – or at least, not this upset – about any of them. Having utterly failed to offer appropriate comfort to her with his last utterance, Barry didn't know what else he could say.

"If you're that upset about it, why don't you give her a ring? But I'm sure there's nothing to worry about… I'm not worried about it."

"If you're going to be like that you might as well go!" she said before grabbing the phone. In light of her instruction, Barry decided to go upstairs and paint until tea was ready.

He had set up his easel in the home office and, for the past few weeks, had been trying to get back into the discipline of painting. Recognising that it had been nearly twenty years since he'd last painted regularly, Barry had deliberately set his initial goals quite low and decided to start by copying other people's works – just to get his hand (and, indeed, his eye) back in the knack.

The first work he had taken it upon himself to copy was *Never Morning Wore to Evening but Some Heart Did Break* (Walter Langley, 1894). Barry wished he could come up with some profound reason for choosing that painting to copy, but the reality was that, even when he'd been a regular painter, he'd always struggled with faces, and Walter Langley's picture had the advantage from that perspective of featuring a woman whose face was not in view.

The woman had just been told that her fisherman husband would not be coming back. In despair, she sits on the shore, her face buried in her hands. What Barry liked was that the artist had managed to convey the full depth of her emotion without disclosing any of her features (although Barry knew from Walter Langley's other works that this wasn't because he 'couldn't do' faces). It was a really difficult trick to pull off and it was one that Barry wanted to emulate, so, as he copied the print on the table in front of him, he tried to see how his illustrious predecessor had done it.

The more he studied it, however, the more Barry wondered if there was a deeper reason why he felt so strangely attracted to the picture. There was something that moved him about the fact that the young woman was so obviously distraught at the death of her husband. It would, he felt sure, have been a comfort to the fisherman to see how much his death had distressed his wife. Yes, as the painting's title acknowledged, these personal tragedies happened every day, but that didn't mean that the suffering was any less keenly felt.

Barry couldn't help wondering, as he tried to capture the doleful slope of the young widow's shoulder, whether his wife would be as distraught if he didn't come back from work one day. Judging by her recent parting shot, Barry suspected not and he rather regretted that fact. He wanted to be able to provoke that strength of emotion in someone; to know that his absence would reduce his wife, at least, to despair. But somehow, if he had ever had that knack, he certainly appeared to have lost it. Now Barry felt exhausted from all the effort it required to simply not annoy her.

He seemed to be part of the wallpaper of so many people's lives, but not part of the architecture. He didn't hold anything up. He wondered if that was how the young widow had felt about her husband before he died. Maybe they'd rowed and bickered, just like Barry and his wife did. Maybe it had taken his death to make her realise what she'd lost. It made Barry think.

His thoughts were interrupted by the sound of a raised voice coming from downstairs. He took this to mean that the telephone conversation between Lauren and her mum was not going well. He decided that the simplest thing to do was to stay out of the way until things had died down. Ten minutes later, it seemed that the call had ended, but Barry waited a further fifteen minutes before venturing downstairs.

The first thing he noticed upon returning to the ground floor was that his tea wasn't ready. The second thing he noticed was that his wife was still sitting on the sofa, rather than in the kitchen preparing their meal. For once, she didn't have her tablet in her hand, nor was she watching David Attenborough. In fact, she didn't appear to be doing anything – just sitting, staring silently into space. Barry realised that now would be a spectacularly bad time to ask her when tea was going to be ready.

"What do you want for tea?" he asked, in a vain attempt to suggest that he was not expecting her to make it.

"I'm not hungry."

Barry's pupils dilated in astonishment. Not hungry? This was uncharted conversational territory. Food and the Todds' ability to consume it in substantial quantities whatever the situation, had been the one constant in their relationship. If even that anchor point was now gone, then Barry truly had been cast adrift in a dinghy on the great ocean of life.

It took a while for him to assess his options. It was only once he had mentally exhausted every other option that he reluctantly came to the conclusion that he would have to ask the question that he generally sought to avoid asking at all costs.

"What's the matter?"

"She says she's not coming back for Christmas. Lauren. She says she'd rather spend it with her boyfriend's family than with me." At which point she dissolved into tears.

Barry now had nowhere left to go. He wanted to tell her that everything would be all right – that he would explain to Lauren that he'd managed to steal nearly £50,000 from work and he would treat her to whatever she wanted if she just agreed to come home over the festive period. But he knew that wouldn't be a good idea.

The fact was, Barry now realised, that money couldn't solve this kind of problem. Not really. He could buy sex, he could buy a new car, he could possibly even buy Lauren's physical presence in their lounge for a few hours on Christmas Day, but somehow none of that was enough.

Barry looked at his wife. Then he turned round and looked into the empty kitchen. He didn't know where to begin. He'd travelled so far down the road he was on, he didn't know the way back now. He was hungry, but he knew he was hungry for the wrong thing. Somehow though, he just couldn't stop himself.

"It's all right, love. I'll phone for a pizza."

THIRTY-EIGHT

The argument had hung in the air for the rest of the evening like the lingering smell of Barry's garlic bread; stultifying and pungent. She had said nothing more to him, but instead had taken out her frustrations on cupboard doors and a few hapless pieces of crockery, whilst shooting the occasional loud stare in Barry's direction. He didn't know what to say. It wasn't as if she were making an accusation to which he could respond, but he felt accused nonetheless. Not of doing something – or even of not doing something – but of something altogether more elusive. Where once he had been the shiver in her spine, now Barry sensed that he had become the darkness behind her glower. He didn't know quite how it had happened, but he could sense that it had.

But he tried to put all that out of his mind as he arrived at work the following morning. He had his fortnightly supervision session with Langley to contend with, which was an altogether less-ambiguous proposition. As he approached Langley's office, however, he could hear that his boss was on the phone.

"But why would I want to carry on paying for a Subaru when I've got a Jaguar for free?"

Barry hovered by the door. It felt like a bad time to enter.

"Yes, I know I signed an agreement, but that was twelve months ago – I needed a car then. I don't need one now... Well, can't I just cancel the agreement? I can drop the keys round whenever... Settle it in full? And how much would it cost me to do that?"

It appeared that there was at least one downside to getting a company car – you still had to pay for your own car if you'd signed a forty-two-month personal contract plan to that effect barely twelve months previously.

"How much? There's no way I can afford to pay that! I haven't got that kind of money... Yes, but I can't afford to carry on paying for this car and getting taxed for my new company car as well. I have bills to pay. Surely there's got to be another way round this?"

It appeared that there wasn't.

"Well, I'll just sell it then," said Langley, defiantly. "I can settle up with you when I've done that... But how can you stop me doing that? It's *my* car! OK, so I don't technically own it fully yet, but—"

As he listened, Barry felt a certain sense of satisfaction. Langley had taken great pleasure in ensuring everyone knew when he had bought his flame red Subaru BRZ SE Lux sports car twelve months previously. He'd even made repeated, none-too-subtle reference, to how much he'd paid. Now, however, it appeared that it was something of a burden, and one that he was desperate to be relieved of.

"Well, can't you sell it for me then?… What? And how much do you think that shortfall might be?… And I'd have to pay that? But that's ridiculous; the car's immaculate – and barely a year old!

"Look, Phil, I'm desperate. I need to resolve the situation soon. I've got another payment next week and I just can't afford it. I've got my mother to look after, and with Christmas coming as well…"

Finally, Langley noticed Barry standing outside his office through a gap in the patterned frosting.

"Look, I've got someone waiting for a meeting with me, but I'm sorry, this is just not acceptable. I entered into that agreement in good faith. You can't insist I keep paying for a car I don't need, then stop me from selling it myself, and then penalise me if you sell it for me. I shall be speaking to Nigel about this. I'm very disappointed!"

As Langley hung up, a thought occurred to Barry. What Langley needed in order to get himself out this unfortunate position was someone in desperate need of a flame red, mid-range sports car, who knew him and who would, therefore, trust him enough to buy the car off him without feeling the need to check whether or not he actually owned it. The purchaser would also need to be prepared to pay slightly over the odds for the car in order to minimise (and ideally eliminate) the shortfall between the settlement figure on the agreement and the value of the car. And he would have to be prepared to wait a couple of days after paying – in full – for the car whilst Langley paid off his contract and could therefore safely notify the DVLA of the change of ownership without the dealership picking up on what he'd done.

It seemed, at best, a tall order. But the idea occurred to Barry that, now he was in want of a replacement vehicle, it wouldn't be unreasonable to assume that he might be in the market for something like a... Subaru BRZ SE Lux, for instance.

"Problem with the car, Langley?" he asked as he entered the office.

"Not a problem, exactly. More of a challenge, Barry. A challenge waiting to be risen to."

"I haven't had a chance to sort myself out yet, as it happens. You haven't got one going spare have you?"

Langley's eyes sparked into life. "Well, as a matter of fact I have, Barry; as a matter of fact, I have. You wouldn't be interested in a nearly new Subaru BRZ would you? SE Lux. Barely twelve months old, only 12,000 on the clock. Nearly a full year's tax on it and no MOT due for two years. Top of the range, all the whistles and bells."

Barry had never thought of buying a sports car before. But the more Langley went on about the twin-tail muffler cutter and keyless access system, the more it confirmed in Barry's mind the idea that Langley might unwittingly be presenting him with the perfect opportunity to spend a large amount of the money currently waiting for him in the Bhattis' bank account without any of it passing through his own.

"How much?" he asked.

Langley stopped speaking and blinked. He hadn't yet extolled the virtues of the four-sensor/four-channel ABS system and yet it appeared that Barry was already sold. There was, however, the small matter of the bill.

"Well, this is a twenty-six/twenty-seven grand car, Barry," Langley said, carefully quoting (and slightly exaggerating) the new-car price that he had paid twelve months previously, rather than the more meaningful nearly new price for a car that was now a year old. "But, obviously, as a colleague, I wouldn't dream of charging you anything like that, even with all the optional extras I paid for. I'll just have to take a hit on those, I suppose."

"That'd be very generous of you. Thanks."

"The thing is though, there's only so far I can go. I could sell it on eBay and get a lot more than I would charge you. But I really appreciate what you're doing – filling in on Maxine's old patch and all that – so I guess I could let it go for… twenty-two-and-a-half."

"Sorry?" Barry was incredulous. Given that Langley had made no secret of how much he'd paid for the car, Barry could calculate that that was a good £2,000 more than the car's actual resale value.

"Twenty-two and a half," repeated Langley, unapologetically. "I appreciate it may be a lot less than you expected, but – for you – I'm prepared to do it for that price. Cash – in advance."

Barry's initial instinct was to politely decline. But then he reminded himself that, as it wasn't actually his money he would be paying with, he could hardly complain that he was being robbed. The fact that he would be paying Langley with money that he had stolen from under his nose added a certain *schadenfreude* to the whole transaction that couldn't be gained elsewhere and that, Barry concluded, was worth the small extra cost. Nevertheless, he felt the need to make at least some attempt to protect himself from Langley's naked profiteering and show his boss that he wasn't a complete fool.

"Twenty-one and half."

"Twenty-two."

"Done."

And you certainly have been, thought both men simultaneously.

THIRTY-NINE

Having just overcharged him £1,500 for a car, Langley appeared less willing than usual to give Barry a hard time over his teams' performance. He was also under strict instructions from Ruth not to raise the issue of the missing payment from The SHYPP; this was now being investigated by the police, so it would be inappropriate to speculate on who might be to blame, or for The SHYPP to be put under any pressure by Monument staff, Langley had been told. This meant that Barry's supervision session went much better than he had been anticipating; so well, in fact, that by the end of it he felt emboldened to ask Langley the question that had been playing on his mind for the last few weeks since Maxine's sudden departure.

"I was wondering if there was any decision yet – about the future. It's just that, when I got asked about taking over Maxine's team, you said it would only be a temporary thing for a couple of weeks. Well, it's been quite a bit longer than that now, and – as you can tell – I'm finding it all pretty tough, running two teams and everything. So, I was just wondering if there'd been any decisions yet. Sorry."

Langley exhaled slowly. "I believe there are still a couple of things to finalise, but we're nearly there."

"And?"

"An announcement will be made when it's all sorted."

"Which will be when?"

"I think the plan is to make it before Christmas, as long as everything is sorted."

That was as much as he would say. But, when he finally got Barry out of his office, Langley went straight in to see Angela. The upshot was that late that afternoon an email came round from Andrew advising all managers not to allow any leave or book any appointments for the following Wednesday afternoon. Any existing appointments should be rearranged. There would be a staff update given to all staff then, and attendance would be mandatory. Team members were to be advised accordingly.

The moment Barry left his supervision meeting he immediately texted Saleema with the bank details that Langley had given him, and asked her to arrange for £22,000 to be sent to that account. He had omitted to mention that the account holder was Langley, but – as Saleema had assured him banks didn't check the names, only the account number and sort code – it didn't seem to matter. Saleema texted back straight away and said that they would arrange an international money transfer immediately; Mr Malford should have his money within twenty-four hours. Barry thought it churlish to correct her. Instead he told Langley that he had arranged a transfer of funds and that his boss should keep an eye out for the money arriving in his account the next day.

Sure enough, by lunchtime the following day, Langley saw that the money had arrived in his account. He immediately phoned up his car finance company and arranged to make the settlement payment on his contract. That would take three working days to clear, then Langley could send the V5 through to the DVLA and Barry could have his car.

For a man who had been assured that he had nothing to worry about, Barry still found himself spending an inordinate amount of time being worried. Wherever he went, his worry seemed to follow. Like the smell of Iulia's cigarettes, it clung to him, working its way into the weave of his clothing, refusing to be forgotten. And nothing he could do seemed able to wash it out.

He had agreed with Langley that neither of them would mention their agreement or its terms to anyone else. But, as Barry waited the apparently interminable three working days for Langley's payment to clear, he found his mind continually circling the issue of what could go wrong. As he did so, the thought occurred to him that if it was clear that it was he who had caused the money to be placed in Langley's account, it didn't much matter that the money hadn't actually gone through his own account first. It would be obvious, surely, to any half-decent investigator what had happened. What he needed to do, therefore, was pre-emptively spike Langley's guns, so that if his boss attempted to suggest at any point in future that Barry had had anything to do with the £22,000 appearing in Langley's account, he could rely on the cover story he had already created.

Barry's brain ached as he thought about it, but, after a couple of sleepless nights, he decided to go and see Angela.

"Oh, hi Barry. How can I help?"

"Well, there's two things, really. I know you've given me till Christmas to hand the car back, but it looks like I've got myself sorted with a new one, so I can probably hand it back this week – if that's OK? One less thing to worry about, with Christmas and all that."

"Well, if you're sure. How did you get yourself sorted out so quickly?"

"Well, that's the other thing I wanted to talk to you about. Can I talk to you confidentially?"

Angela leant forward and slipped effortlessly into 'tilty head' mode. "Of course."

"It's just that… well, Langley has offered me his car."

"Not his company car?"

"No, no, not his Jag. His old car: the Subaru."

"Oh, very nice! So what's the problem?"

"Well, the thing is…" Barry paused for a moment and sighed for dramatic effect. "I just wondered if there were any rules about that kind of thing."

"Oh good grief, no. That's entirely a private matter between you and Langley. If he wants to sell you his old car and you're happy to buy it—"

"Well, that's just it. He doesn't want to sell me the car. He wants to give it to me – for free."

"*Give* it to you?" Angela said, dropping the pen that she'd been idly twisting between her fingers.

"Yes. He says he doesn't need it anymore – not now he's got the company Jag – so he thought I may as well have it. It's just sitting on his drive otherwise, he says..." Barry tapered off, not sure what else he could say.

Angela appeared somewhat taken aback. She picked up the pen and began scribbling furiously. "Well, that really is very generous. Did he say why?"

"Not really. I think he feels a bit bad about taking my company car off me. And for not being able to pay me for covering the extra team, which has dragged on longer than he thought. And, of course, he had to block my VR application too. It doesn't look good; he can see that, I guess."

Angela didn't appear to know quite what to say. "Has he asked you for anything in return? Not money necessarily, but maybe something else – to do something for him, perhaps?"

"Well, no... not yet, at any rate. He just said I'd be doing him a favour. Said he needed to get shot of it quickly. Urgently, in fact. I don't quite know why."

Angela's brow steepled into a concerned frown. "Do you want me to have a word with him about it?"

"Oh God, no!" Barry said, with what he immediately realised was perhaps slightly too much alarm. "I mean, he's sensitive about it. He doesn't want people to know what he's done. And to be honest, neither do I. As far as everyone else knows, I'll have paid him for the car. It's a bit embarrassing for me – to take someone else's charity like that. I just didn't want you to think that I was taking advantage of him."

"Thanks for making me aware of this, Barry," she said, a slightly awkward, fixed smile appearing on her face. "I obviously won't say anything to anyone about this—"

"That'd be great. Thanks."

"But I do want to make a note about our conversation – if that's OK with you?" she asked, looking at Barry in a way that suggested it wasn't really a question.

"A note?"

"Yes. It's to protect you really. To show that you did the right thing… if, for any reason, anybody tries to say later on that you didn't."

"But you won't mention anything to anyone, will you? I promised that I'd keep things between the two of us. I wouldn't want him to think I've gone behind his back."

"Oh, absolutely not. I understand that, Barry. Not a word. To anyone. I promise." Then she put her pen down on the table with a deliberation that seemed to suggest an unwritten agreement was also being entered into. "But you must promise me, if you're asked to do anything because you got the car that makes you feel uncomfortable in any way, you must come to me immediately. Can you promise me that?"

"Absolutely," agreed Barry, with a smile.

"Great," she said. Then she fixed him with a firm stare, as though she were trying to bore her words into Barry's soul. "You've done the right thing, Barry. I hope that you know that. And I know that you would never try to take advantage of someone. So don't worry, you won't get in trouble for any of this, I promise – because we'll have the note."

As Barry left Angela's office he expected to feel relieved. After all, she had just told him that he'd done the right thing and promised him that he wouldn't get into any trouble. But he also felt like a fraud. In fact, he didn't feel *like* a fraud; he felt that he *was* a fraud. It was as if his crime had somehow crept inside of him when he wasn't looking and taken him over.

When he got back to his desk, there was an email from Langley waiting for him. *"Good news! My finance company have just confirmed receipt of your money. You can pick up the Subaru tomorrow, if you'd like. L."*

"Well, I'll be damned," said Barry to himself. And, in that moment, he felt for the first time that he just might be.

PART 4

"We live by encouragement and die without it – slowly, sadly, and angrily."

Celeste Holm

NIGHT WITH HER TRAIN OF STARS AND HER GREAT GIFT OF SLEEP

9th December 2015 –

19th January 2016

FORTY

The next day Barry came to work in his company car for the last time. He dropped the keys off with Angela, and then Langley took Barry to his house, where the gleaming Subaru was waiting for him. He'd even gone to the trouble of having it valeted.

Upon being invited to try out his new car, Barry noticed, for the first time, exactly how low slung it was. For a man of Langley's youthful years and trim frame this wasn't necessarily a problem. For the fuller figure of Barry Todd, however, getting into and out of his new car was clearly going to be something of a challenge. Once he'd managed to squeeze himself in, he realised that the steering wheel rubbed against his stomach.

"You can move the seat back a couple more inches, if you need to," suggested Langley.

The car was so small, and Barry was so large, he felt like a hippo trying to fit into one of those toy cars that his father had paid 10p for him to sit in for three minutes when he was on holiday as a child. Moving the seat back wasn't the issue. Nevertheless, he tried to stay positive – it was just the incentive he needed to shed some of his excess pounds, he decided.

He could feel the comforting softness of the leather steering wheel in his hands. And he could savour that new-car smell rising in his nostrils – the unmistakable scent of polished leather and Scandinavian-pine air freshener – which had always so excited him as a child when he'd first got into his dad's new cars.

But even as Langley waxed lyrical about the "throaty roar" of the engine and its "bottom-end grunt", Barry felt strangely empty. He'd often thought he'd like a bright-red sports car without being able to specify exactly why. But now, as he actually sat in the driving seat of one for the first time, it struck him. When he saw the picture in his head of what it would be like owning a sports car, it wasn't the curve of the roofline or the smell of the leather that most struck him, rather it was how it made him feel. Yet he now realised, with a sense of disappointment, that what he wanted to experience was an emotion that a piece of Japanese engineering – however fastidiously assembled – just couldn't deliver. The exhilaration Langley promised him wasn't just about the car's acceleration, it was about knowing that other people were looking at the driver and feeling that they wanted to emulate him.

The problem was that the driver was still Barry Todd. He may have changed his car, but he hadn't changed who he was.

Both Langley and Barry needed to get to mid-morning meetings, but Barry was cautious driving his new car for the first time. He felt oddly similar to how he'd felt when he'd walked away from the mini-market with the first £250 withdrawal in his pocket – as though he expected to suddenly lose his good fortune at any moment. And as though he was being watched.

In Barry's case, his next appointment was one of his now-regular visits to Iulia. With Christmas fast approaching, Barry felt it was important that there was no need for Iulia to worry about losing her home. Whatever his personal misgivings about the unsatisfactory nature of their sessions, therefore, he was prepared to persevere in order to ensure that Monument's roof remained over her head – it was, after all, the season of goodwill.

As he drove cautiously toward Coleshill, the sound of Slade and Roy Wood blasting out their festive cheer on the car's eight-speaker sound system, his musings were interrupted by a phone call. Fortunately, before driving off, Langley had shown Barry how to connect his mobile phone to the car's Bluetooth system so he could answer the call hands-free.

"Meester Todd. It is Meess Nicolescu."

"Oh, hullo. I'm just on my way to you now. Sorry I'm a bit late – I've just been picking up my new car. I think you'll be impressed—"

"That is why I phone. You not need to come. I have job now," she said, before adding pointedly, "Real job."

Barry's heart sank. In all his considerations of things that could go wrong, Iulia getting a job was the one possibility that simply hadn't occurred to him. Her career history seemed too debased for any legitimate employer to take a chance on her – she'd even suggested as much herself. And his wife had had no luck in securing paid employment several months after having been made redundant by Langley, despite facing none of the apparently insuperable obstacles that confronted Iulia. He had, however, reckoned without the indomitable spirit and indefatigable work ethic of the Romanian people. A people that had survived, and indeed defeated, the might of the Soviet Bloc and its dictatorship would not regard any obstacle as insuperable. The prospect of having to find a job in the fastest-growing economy in Europe would not phase them.

"Well congratulations. But I can still come down. It's no problem. I'm happy to pay," Barry said. "I'm sure the money would come in useful. It is Christmas."

He had hoped for a momentary pause whilst she considered his offer. He felt that it was an attractive one; one that might tempt her to 'keep her hand in' as it were, to supplement her no-doubt meagre wages. He was to be sadly disappointed.

"No," she said instantly. "I not want to see you again. I start work Monday. At hotel. It is good job – permanent job, not just Christmas."

"Yes, but surely you won't get paid for four weeks. I can help you out in the short term."

"I pay rent from my wages," she said, before adding ominously, "maybe. You try to evict me, I tell Meess Hampton what you do. Where my rent money come from. It will be very bad for you."

Barry felt his heart suddenly cease pounding in his chest, as though suspended in time. And then he felt a large, and potentially very disruptive, penny drop. Whereas previously, Iulia had had every reason to keep quiet about their arrangement and could only rely on Barry's goodwill to keep her in her flat, the boot was now firmly on the other foot. Now that she had her own income, she had no need of Barry's largesse – and therefore every reason to exploit his vulnerability.

"But we agreed – not a word to anyone. You promised." The betrayal felt total. "You can't just not pay your rent. We'll have to do something. It's not my decision. It's Miss Hampton. She'll have to execute the court order. She'll just go to my boss if I won't do it."

"You better make sure my rent is paid then." And with that the phone went dead.

Barry pulled over and clasped his steering wheel hard whilst hyperventilating. His cheeks flushed red and he felt a thin film of sweat bleed through his skin, as the twin urges to vomit and to defecate fought for supremacy within him. He could see the remains of the money he had stolen from Monument being spent, not on art materials, Lauren's living costs and clearing his mortgage, but on buying Iulia's silence. And perhaps even that amount would not be enough.

He scoured the situation desperately for a straw that he could clutch at. And when he found one he clung on to it determinedly. She had no proof. He had given her no evidence to back up his claim about using Monument's money, and what he'd said had been sufficiently vague for there to be no reason for anyone to believe her. And, even if they did, well, when they looked at Barry's bank accounts they would find no evidence to support her accusation. Because, he reminded himself, there was no evidence. He exhaled slowly.

However, almost immediately, a photo message from Iulia arrived on his phone that brutally snatched away even that forlorn hope. It was slightly blurred and was taken from behind so you couldn't see the face of the naked figure in front of you. But the large frame and the windswept hair failing to quite cover a growing bald-spot would have looked disconcertingly familiar to anyone who knew Barry Todd. Given that the wallpaper and the print of Ghirlandaio's *Madonna and Child* that adorned it clearly identified the photo as having been taken in Iulia's flat, it would certainly be enough to warrant Barry's dismissal – regardless of the outcome of any investigation into where the money to pay Iulia's rent had come from.

The whole creaking edifice he had painstakingly built was in danger of crashing down on top of him. His job, his future employment prospects, the money, maybe even his marriage – they would all be gone if Iulia carried through with her threat. Barry knew that he couldn't let that happen, he just couldn't. Not after everything he'd been through. Not after the job, and Chris Malford, and the VR application, and the car. Not after Christopher. After Christopher, he deserved this, surely. He deserved this one puny consolation for the endless, incomprehensible, overwhelming pain that had been visited upon him. He began, therefore, to try to think of a way to neutralise the threat that Iulia now posed. But, as he did so, his mind was filled with thoughts that he didn't want to think, and his heart with feelings he was desperate not to feel.

In the end, he concluded, she had brought it on herself. He had been generous and – at great personal risk to himself – had done what was necessary to protect her. Yet now she was threatening to throw it all back in his face. In light of this, he felt perfectly justified fighting fire with fire. He picked up his phone and called Iulia back.

"I not want to speak to you, Meester Todd. There is nothing to say. I hang up now and I not expect to hear from you again."

But, before she could end the call, Barry blurted out, "I'll tell them where you are!"

There was a pause.

"What?"

"I'll tell them where you are. The Romanian Migrants Welfare Association – or whoever they are. They've been asking after you. They've even left a number for me to call them on. If I get fired by Monument, there's nothing to stop me going straight to them."

It was, he told himself, the only solution that made sense. She had to believe he was prepared to do it. That was the only way to protect himself – to make her believe that she still had something to lose too.

"You can't, Meester Todd. They will kill me. They will kill me!"

"Don't worry. I'll carry on paying your rent. I'm happy to help you. You'll be better off. Maybe even be able to save up for a deposit for a place of your own. But we carry on. With our… arrangement."

Barry thought he heard a sob at the other end of the line.

"I'll see you in twenty minutes," he said. "Sorry."

And he was, in a way. But not in the same way as he had been before. He wasn't despoiling her, as he'd supposed. *Her heart is as cold and black as everybody else's,* Barry reflected. *Maybe even mine.*

FORTY-ONE

An hour or so later, Barry drove back to Monument's offices with a heavy heart. It wasn't just the prospect of another one of Andrew's staff update presentations that sent his spirits lower; something had changed. In fact, everything had changed, even though he'd never made a decision to change everything. He'd just made a hundred little decisions that had piled up on top of one another like dirty plates. But now, he saw that he couldn't remove any one of those plates without the whole pile toppling over.

Upon arriving back at the office, he joined the rest of Monument's staff dutifully gathered in the top-floor conference room for the staff update. It would be wrong to say that everyone in the room was on tenterhooks, nor was there quite what you could describe as an air of expectation. It was more a sense of weary resignation. Anyone who'd been at Monument for any length of time had heard one of Andrew's staff briefings before, and they never involved announcing more resources and bumper pay increases for front-line staff.

The various members of the exec team were already at the front on a raised platform when Barry sidled into the room. They were the only ones who got seats. Because of the number of people to be accommodated, everybody else had to stand. Andrew made his way to the front of the stage. He had the trim-but-leathery look of an ageing matinée idol who still regarded himself as something of a 'catch'. He swirled his glass of water like it was a dry Martini, before tapping his lapel microphone to check that it was on. The rest of the exec broke out into polite applause, which failed to catch with the rest of the room.

"Thank you all for making the time to come here this afternoon," Andrew said, as though people had actually been given a choice over whether to attend or not. And then he smiled broadly, which Barry hated because it highlighted his perfect, whitened teeth. Fortunately, because he always started off these presentations with a recap of The Bad News, Barry knew that Andrew would adopt his sombre face soon. He was not to be disappointed.

"As you know, we've been facing many challenges as a business over the past few years and that is only going to accelerate in future. Cuts to social housing rents, the freezing of local housing allowance levels and more restrictions to housing benefit entitlement all affect our revenue streams going forward. On top of which, we also face increasing difficulties in accessing capital grants at rates that will make our future social housing developments viable. It's almost a perfect storm.

"Fortunately, because we've never shied away from taking difficult decisions, Monument is prepared for these challenges. But we cannot be complacent."

It was classic Andrew: paint a picture of impending calamity; reassure people that Monument would be OK because of its brilliant business strategy; then, just so that people don't feel too reassured, point out that it could all still go wrong if they're not careful.

"Financial projections show that the cuts to social rents alone will take £17.5 million out of the business plan over the next four years. This means that, by year four of the cuts programme, we'll be generating £7 million less income each year than we budgeted for – unless we take action now. Action to further improve efficiency and drive down costs."

Well, we could start by cutting your salary, Barry wanted to shout out. He realised, however, that it was probably not this that Andrew was about to announce.

"One way we could do this is by cutting back on staff and by freezing staff salaries. Maybe cutting the level of service that we give to our customers," said Andrew to a few audible groans from the floor.

"But don't worry, because that isn't the Monument way!" he went on, his broad smile suddenly returning. "The Monument way is to look to *grow* our way out of problems, to expand the business to give ourselves a larger income stream; to achieve efficiencies by leveraging additional business synergies from potential partners."

Barry wasn't quite sure what this meant, but at least it seemed to be steering away from the 'more bricks from less straw' business model that he'd feared.

"That's why I'm delighted to announce that we have reached an outline agreement for a new and exciting expansion of the business to take place next year. It will dramatically increase our stock and our sphere of operations. It will open up new markets and the possibility of new local-authority partnerships. And, crucially, it will secure both jobs and the service level to customers.

"Colleagues, I am delighted to announce our intention to merge with London-based Three Acts Housing Association."

Barry was stunned. Three Acts was a larger association – why would Andrew agree to what would effectively be a takeover?

As Andrew went on, the answer became apparent. Whilst Monument had taken the "tough decisions necessary" to prepare for the future, Three Acts had expanded rapidly over recent years and had perhaps over-extended themselves, so when government funding cuts had hit they had a far less comfortable cushion to fall back on.

Oh, and a surreptitious internet search on Barry's smartphone also revealed that their chief executive was sixty-two, so he was probably looking for a nice early retirement package.

Sure enough, a couple of minutes later Andrew announced that he would be taking up the role of chief executive designate of the newly merged association whilst Three Acts' current CEO would be, "pursuing new opportunities outside the association". This would probably involve lots of golf, if Barry's previous experience was anything to go by.

Of course, there was one genuine synergy between the two associations that Barry was aware of, but it didn't seem to be one that Andrew was particularly interested in leveraging. Back in the late 1960s, in the wake of *Cathy Come Home*, an earnest young curate from North London had taken it upon himself to set up what was then called Acts 3 Community Housing Association using a couple of surplus parsonages from the neighbouring parish. It had been called Acts 3 after the story of the curing of the crippled beggar in the third chapter of the Acts of the Apostles:

> *"When he saw Peter and John about to go into the temple he asked them for alms… And he fixed his attention on them expecting to receive something from them. But Peter said, 'I have no silver or gold, but what I have I give to you; in the name of Jesus Christ of Nazareth, stand up and walk.'"*

The point about Acts 3 CHA was that the housing was just the starting point of the journey that they wanted to take with people, one that would seek to meet their deeper needs – the ones that they thought would never be met. Later Acts 3's reputation was so strong that it had provided the inspiration to a small group of churches not far from Kingsbury that had gone on to set up the association that eventually became Monument. So, in a sense, Barry could see that the merger was a coming together of two associations with very similar roots.

But once Acts 3's original founders had moved on or retired, there was no one to hold on to the original motives that had inspired its founding. Its religious narrative came to be seen as an unnecessary complication – after all, as long as you were doing good, did it really matter what was going on in your heart? And so it became plain old Three Acts Housing Association to emphasise the three different things that the association did – provide social housing; deliver information, advice and guidance to the unemployed; and offer care services to the elderly and the infirm.

It seemed a subtle change at first; after all, they were still focused on providing *"More than just a home"* as their strapline proudly declared. But somehow, something more fundamental had changed without anyone actively deciding that it should. A hundred little plates had been piled on top of one another until they reached so high that everyone was scared to start removing them. It had been the same trajectory that Monument had travelled – one that had ultimately led to Neville's unceremonious defenestration.

"I know that many of you might be worried about what this might mean for your job," Andrew went on, "and I'm also aware that some of you have been worried about what's going to happen after the recent round of voluntary redundancies. Well, the good news is that – because we've both recently undertaken VR trawls focused on our central services, and we don't currently have any geographical overlap in service areas – we believe we can achieve this merger without any compulsory redundancies below director level."

The room – except for the directors sitting obediently behind Andrew – breathed a collective sigh of relief. So that had been his plan all along: clear out the dead wood now to make way for the merger. Once the two finance and HR teams were merged, there would no doubt be more than enough capacity to cope with the workload.

With that concern out of the way, there was only one question left.

"Of course," Andrew continued as if anticipating everyone's thought, "there is the vexed question of the name. Well, we've agreed that we will engage an agency to look at creating a new name for the merged association. We hope to be able to go live with that at the launch in April. But, for the moment, whilst we're still awaiting formal approval for the merger from our regulator, we've decided to use a composite name. So, in the short term, we'll be referring to the new entity as Acts & Monument Housing Group."

The explanations went on, the business-plan objectives were restated and the strength of the 'customer offer' was spelt out. It was all going to be wonderful, everyone was assured. And Barry was sure that some people would believe it. For those employees who had been around long enough to hear these merger announcements before, however, there was a certain world-weary cynicism.

Inevitably, the announcement became a topic of discussion around the office that afternoon. There were those who (despite Andrew's assurances) were worried about their jobs. And there were those who were worried about their boss' job – not because they cared about their boss, but because they cared who their boss was, and the idea that their boss might no longer be the clueless buffoon they had grown used to, but instead might be a different clueless buffoon, perhaps one based miles away, filled them with a certain dread.

And then there was the name.

"Actually, I quite like it," was Jean's view.

Barry was surprised. Acts & Monument seemed such an ungainly name – such an obvious compromise just to get the deal agreed – that Barry couldn't believe that anyone could possibly warm to it. And he had such high regard for Jean's opinion of things that he'd rather hoped that she would be able to articulate better than he could why the whole thing was a terrible idea, so that he could carry on feeling bitter and resentful whilst, at the same time, still claiming the moral high ground. Barry's face obviously couldn't quite mask his disappointment.

"Oh, I know it probably seems a bit silly," she said. "But actually, it says something rather profound – if you look for it."

"Acts & Monument – really?"

"Well, it's what we're all about isn't it?" she replied, matter-of-factly. "Acts and monuments."

"Are we?"

"Yes, of course we are. What was it Napoleon said?"

Barry didn't know. The only quote of Napoleon's that he knew was, "Not tonight, Josephine", but, in the context of their conversation, he was fairly confident this wasn't the one Jean was referring to. Thankfully, as if anticipating Barry's ignorance of France's Napoleonic-era history, she answered her own question.

"'Man is made great by the monuments he leaves behind.'"

"Oh, I see," said Barry, despite not seeing at all.

"Well, we create monuments, don't we? We build homes for people, and they're left long after we've all gone."

"Yeah, I suppose so, but they're not really monuments, are they? They're just buildings."

"Oh, but they are, Barry! They're monuments to our age – to the things we value; our priorities. We've made a point of building housing for people who can't afford to pay for it to be built themselves. That tells you something about us. Other generations haven't done that. And people in other places don't do that now. So that act creates a little monument to our age, doesn't it? Just as each of our acts as individuals creates a little monument to our lives."

Barry thought about it for a moment. It was an idea that made him uncomfortable, but he could feel the logic of Jean's position.

"Small stones make big ripples, I suppose," Barry said, by way of trying to agree with Jean. But he hoped it wasn't true.

FORTY-TWO

That evening, Barry pulled up on his drive and tooted his horn. He hoped this would be enough to bring his wife to the front door. He hadn't told her about his new car because he hadn't ever quite got round to telling her that he was losing his old car – it just seemed like one more indignity he didn't want to have to explain. By showing her his flashy, new car first, he reasoned, she would be so taken with it that he could draw a discreet veil over what had happened to his comparatively dull old car. Sadly, however, his vigorous tooting failed to stir any response from inside the house, so Barry switched off the engine, shoe-horned his way out of the car and stood on the drive calling into the house as the dampness of the cold December evening enveloped him.

"Hiya, love. Come out here a minute; I've got something to show you."

"What?"

"It's a surprise."

"A surprise? What is it?"

"Well, if I tell you that, it won't be a surprise! Just come here and have a look."

"I've got some lamb chops on the go and there's still the vegetables to prepare. Can't you just tell me? And you're letting a draught in."

She was in her slippers and it had been raining, so Barry could see that she was determined not to come out. Eventually, they agreed that the compromise position would be for her to stand at the front door and peer out into the inky blackness. Barry reached inside the house and turned the porch light on to illuminate the drive, then stepped back to stand proudly by his new car.

"Ta-dah!" Barry exclaimed.

"What's that?"

"My new car!"

She stood for a moment, her cardigan pulled tight against the first bite of the evening frost. At first she said nothing, she didn't even move, so that it felt as though everything was frozen, even the weather. But then a look of confusion slowly formed on her face. "What happened to the old one?"

This was not an issue that Barry particularly wanted to discuss, and particularly not as he could feel his bones rattling with the winter cold, which swirled through the fabric of his suit. But it was clear that his ingenious plan of introducing the new car first had failed to divert attention away from the obvious prior question.

"It's gone back. It was the end of the lease," Barry explained, which was indeed the truth (although not the whole truth). "I've got this now. What do you think?"

His wife stared at him as though he was a cat that had just dropped a dead mouse at her feet. And he knew in that instant that there was nothing he could say that would make her see the car in the way that he'd hoped she would.

"But where's Lauren going to sit?"

"There's two seats in the back," he answered lamely.

"With no legroom! And never mind the back – what about the front? How am I ever going to fit in there?"

It was, as Barry himself had discovered, a good point, and one to which he could devise no good response. Fortunately, before his inability to come up with an appropriate answer was exposed, his wife continued her observations.

"It's hardly a family car, is it?"

This was, Barry was forced to concede, also true. "Yeah, but we don't need a family car anymore," he said. "Not now there's just the two of us again."

At which point, his wife burst into tears and returned to her vegetables.

For her part, Lindsey Norton was feeling a sense of accomplishment. She was no expert in economic crime, but she'd managed to secure a production order from the court in double-quick time. This would compel the banks involved to divulge the destination of the missing money after it had left Chris Malford's account. But she had also sought production orders against Adam Furst and Shana Backley. This would reveal whether either of them had had any suspicious activity on their bank accounts around the time of, and subsequent to, Chris Malford's death. The banks had twenty-eight days to respond; the question was, what could Lindsey do whilst she was waiting?

She could see that there was a clear picture emerging that suggested that Adam Furst's disappearance at the same time as the money was more than just coincidence. It seemed obvious that this was where her investigations should focus. But she wasn't a fraud expert, so, in order to try to figure out the link, she contacted Rob Worrall from the economic crime unit to see if he could give her a steer on how best to proceed. Apart from being Gemma's boyfriend, Rob was also known as a good copper, although perhaps one who loved himself just a bit too much. He entered Lindsey's office with the confident demeanour of an opening batsman returning to the pavilion after knocking a quick-fire century. Lindsey couldn't see what Gemma saw in him, to be honest.

Sitting in the cramped office, Rob nonchalantly slapped the file back down on her desk and took a swig from his coffee. "The thing you've got to think about is, what kind of crime is this?"

"It's a fraud," Lindsey replied, somewhat nonplussed that Rob felt the need to ask the question.

"Yes, but what kind of crime is a fraud?"

This was everything that frustrated Lindsey about Rob, so she just decided to cut to the chase. "I dunno. What?"

"Well, it's a deception isn't it? A sleight of hand. And how do magicians get away with a sleight of hand?"

Lindsey thought about it for a moment. "They divert your attention."

"Exactly! They try and get you to focus all your attention on the place where nothing is going on, so that you don't notice what they're up to," Rob announced triumphantly, reaching over and pilfering a couple of Lindsey's Bourbon creams. "Fraudsters are the same. They'll create a complete mess in one place to get your attention there, then they'll get the money out somewhere else without you noticing."

"So you don't think it's all about Furst?"

"I'm not saying that. I'm just saying it might be that's what someone *wants* you to think, but actually it's nothing to do with him. It might be someone else entirely."

"Yeah, but the money went through Malford's account. Furst was there at the time Malford died. There's the missing paperwork and the gap on the dresser."

"Could be nothing."

"Honestly? You really think that, Rob?"

"Even if there was a gap in the dust – so what? It may be that nothing was removed at all. It could have just been that someone put a clipboard or a folder on the dressing table when they came in later – the funeral director or one of the housing guys – and that moved the dust. But, even if something was removed, it doesn't mean it was removed by Furst. Surely, if it had been, there'd have been at least some of the dust replaced in the two weeks since Furst had been there. It wouldn't be a totally clean gap," Rob said, gently swinging back and forth in his chair.

A look of growing disappointment spread across Lindsey's face. He was right, of course, although she hated to admit it. Everyone had been so keen to pin everything on Adam Furst, they'd forgotten the first rule of policing – follow the facts, not your prejudices.

"So you don't think any of this is anything to do with him?"

"I didn't say that. He's clearly linked to the two deaths, so you need to find him. It's just that I'm not sure you can assume he's linked to the fraud. But, ultimately, the only way to find out if he is involved is to see where the money's gone. Follow the money; whoever's account the money's ended up in is definitely involved in the fraud. You just need to find out then if they've got any links to Furst."

"So what do you suggest we do now?"

"If it was me – and obviously, this one hasn't come out to us from Action Fraud yet – but if it did, the first place I'd want to be looking is at all the people who had a hand in the whole invoicing shambles. I'd be asking for production orders against all of them."

"All of them?"

"If it was me. The thing is, you can see that the two women at The SHYPP could have made a couple of genuine errors. But it's not impossible that one or other of them has deliberately screwed up and tried to make it look like an innocent mistake."

"So the two from The SHYPP – I get that. What about Monument? There's Bhatti, obviously. What about Burrell?"

"Yeah, I'd want to have a look at him. He seems to have been very keen to get the invoice out and the payment in as quickly as possible. And it's all happened on his watch. Same for the finance director woman – she's the one who created the chaos in the first place by mucking about with the bank accounts. Again, might be nothing, but might be a handy excuse for her to slip the money out while everyone's looking the other way. And she took the decision to let Bhatti go. She could easily have implicated her, knowing that she wouldn't be around to answer questions when the balloon went up."

"Right. Five of them," said Lindsey, making a note of all the names.

"Six, actually."

"Six?" Lindsey said, her forehead creasing, anxiously.

"Yeah. Think about it. Who's the one person who connects them all? Knows all the Monument staff and all the staff at The SHYPP? And had direct connections to all the tenants at Monument and The SHYPP?"

Lindsey thought about it for a moment whilst Rob gave her a patronising stare.

"Barry Todd!"

"Bingo!" he said, snaffling a couple more biscuits. "You're getting the hang of this."

And, for the first time, Lindsey thought that perhaps she just might be.

FORTY-THREE

Barry hadn't expected DS Norton's phone call, and, when it came, he felt his chest tighten and a small ball of pressure push against the back of his throat. He loosened his tie and undid his top button, as she assured him that seeking a production order was standard procedure. It was being done for everyone connected to the case, she went on, and would simply allow the police to eliminate him from their enquiries. This last point felt rather moot to Barry, but DS Norton insisted that, as long as there was no connection financially between him and Adam Furst, there would be no reason for the police to take their interest in him any further. When put like that, Barry felt it would be unreasonable to object.

But the secret that had once seemed as light as a feather now felt like a Sisyphean burden, heavy and unrelenting. And, despite Alun's reassurances, there seemed no escape from its shadow. It wasn't always visible, but it was always there, prowling the liminal space at the threshold of his consciousness. Its constant presence felt wearying. Slowly, remorselessly, it was beating Barry down, reshaping him like the unremitting drip of water on a stone.

None of the six people identified by Rob Worrall objected to production orders being granted, and so they all were in short order. The banks, for their part, were given twenty-eight days to produce all the necessary information, so it would not be until the new year that Lindsey Norton would be able to sift through the documents.

Meanwhile, in the run up to Christmas, Barry noticed the frantic phone conversations between Lauren and her mum becoming increasingly short-tempered. Then there was a week or so of texts between them long into the night. But in the week leading up to Christmas there appeared to be nothing at all. By Christmas Eve, Barry had still heard nothing and so decided he needed to phone Lauren himself. After several unreturned calls, he finally managed to get through to her. She was with her boyfriend's family. They were, apparently, lovely – far lovelier it seemed than her own – and they were delighted to have her with them for the holidays (Barry was tempted to ask Lauren to pass the phone over to her putative mother-in-law just so he could check that fact, but ultimately thought better of it).

"What about coming over here for a bit? Your mum wants to see you… Obviously, I want to see you too, but your mum's really upset about it."

"I want to come home, Dad, but she won't let me."

"What do you mean? She's desperate to see you."

"But not Tyreece. She says she doesn't want me coming home with him. She wants it just to be family."

This information was new to Barry and he didn't know quite how to respond. Lauren could be awkward and stubborn, but she wasn't generally unreasonable. And it didn't seem unreasonable to Barry for her to want to bring her boyfriend home. He tried to think of a compromise that would make his wife's insistence look less capricious.

"Well, it'd be nice to spend Christmas Day together as a family – and I'm sure Tyreece's family want to see him on Christmas Day too. But, after that, I'm sure there'd be no problem—"

"There is, Dad! I suggested Tyreece came over for Boxing Day and she wouldn't have it. Said she wanted it to be just the three of us. You've got to sort her out, Dad – I swear to God, she's getting worse. She's being totally irrational about the whole thing."

Barry didn't know whose side to take. Lauren loved Christmas with the family and so he'd expected that, after the whole fuss had died down, she would make some sort of appearance. But his wife did indeed seem to be behaving totally irrationally. He tried raising the subject with her later that evening, but the topic was abruptly shut down. Christmas was a time for family; Tyreece was not family; *ergo* Christmas was not a time for Tyreece.

So when Christmas Day itself finally arrived, Lauren pointedly failed to. This was bad news, and not just because Barry missed his daughter. Barry's relationship with his father, Ron, was not an easy one and this tended to make Todd family gatherings particularly fraught. Lauren, being the youngest and most doted-on granddaughter, could argue back and generally had more success than Barry in taming her grandad's wildly inappropriate sense of humour. Ron rarely missed an opportunity to drop one of his infamous *bon mots* into the conversation at family gatherings, but generally Barry tried to let them slide. The one thing which Barry absolutely could not abide though, was his dad's reaction when people worked out that he and Barry's mum, Mary, were married. Ron and Mary had both worked at Dudley Council, but, with Todd being a fairly common surname, it was not immediately apparent that the two of them were related, particularly given that Ron never mentioned that he was married when Mary wasn't with him (and he complained about it endlessly when she was).

As was tradition, the Todds went out for a Boxing Day meal at a local pub, where Ron bumped into an old work colleague. Seeing Ron and Mary together provoked the obvious question.

"So are you two related then?"

And Ron replied exactly as he always did, "Only by marriage!" And then he hooted wildly with laughter.

Barry hated it. It wasn't just that it denigrated his mum. It was that it seemed to denigrate the whole marriage – which, of course, Barry was a product of. It suggested that marriage wasn't really like being related properly; it could be put on and off like a coat. So, Barry felt obliged to protest on his mother's behalf.

"Da-ad!"

But his father's defence was the same as always. "No need to get your hair off, son; it's only a joke!"

And his mother concurred, "Yes, Barry – it's only a joke. Your dad's just having a bit of fun!"

If even his mother wasn't offended, it seemed churlish of Barry to complain. After all, it was only a joke. Yet it was one with a subtle intimation that Ron never made fully visible. Barry felt that about a lot of his dad's jokes. The thing you didn't notice was often the thing that shouldn't have been ignored: an undercurrent that could not be seen, but which pulled at things under the surface to make them appear other than they truly were.

So as Barry pulled his cracker and put on his party hat, he was particularly ill-disposed toward the idea of festive cheer. Christmas without Lauren didn't feel like Christmas. It hadn't felt like Christmas since they'd lost Christopher, but, without Lauren too, there was no mediating presence to shield him from the full force of his father's jocularity. Or his wife's carefully crafted annoyance.

He crept over to the bar and ordered himself the first of what, he decided, would be many beers that would be drunk over the holiday week.

FORTY-FOUR

Alun hadn't been wrong when he'd told Barry that it took typically five or six months for Action Fraud to pass the case on to the National Fraud Intelligence Bureau and for them to then decide what to do with it. But he had reckoned without Sally Hedges' considerable powers of persuasion. She had taken it upon herself to phone the NFIB every working day from the moment she was aware that the case had been passed on to them, asking them when the case would be passed back to the local police. Then she used her connections with the local police to get a meeting with the assistant chief constable, and got him to give her his personal assurance that, when the case arrived with them, there would be a full and proper investigation.

The fact was, Sally was worried – and not just about the survival of The SHYPP Trust, which would reluctantly have to hand the keys to the scheme back to Monument if they were found to be liable for the missing money. No, she was also worried for herself. Her own board – and particularly the new treasurer – were starting to ask questions about how such a mix up could possibly have occurred. At the last trustee meeting it had been suggested that The SHYPP might need to consider setting up an audit committee. Sally shuddered at the very thought.

The spotlight that she had hoped to keep firmly focused on Monument was gradually being shifted onto her. Even when Sally took the draconian step of suspending Marilyn for failing to observe proper protocols, the trustees said that they felt that an independent pair of eyes was needed to investigate matters, and it was pretty clear who those eyes were supposed to be independent of.

She sensed that her authority – that most intangible of assets – was starting to drain away. It was imperative, therefore, that she established her credibility in the eyes of the board. It was starting to feel like her career may depend on it.

But her efforts had the desired effect. When Rob Worrall returned to work at the economic crime unit after his Christmas break, there was a file on his desk marked *"Monument Housing Association"*. His first phone call was from Sally, asking for an update on his investigations so far. Given that he had barely had time to make a cup of tea, let alone study the file, he had no progress to report. But he adroitly avoided admitting as much by politely pointing out to Sally that, as it was Monument that had reported the crime, he could only update them on the investigation's progress.

His second phone call was from Lindsey Norton.

"How's Gemma?" she asked after the usual pleasantries had been exchanged.

"Still stuck on traffic. Pretty pee'd off, if I'm honest – as much because she's got stuck with Molloy as anything else. She just wants it all to be over, but Backley's family are all over Davis like a rash. Nightmare solicitor too. I'll be honest, I think we need to find Furst and pin the whole thing on him before Davis'll feel comfortable letting her back in."

"Yeah, well, I got the results of those production orders back this morning," Lindsey said. "Nothing on Furst yet, but I've got some stuff that might give you a bit of a head start. You interested?"

Indeed he was.

"Both the women at The SHYPP seem clear. Nothing to report there. The finance director at Monument is the same. The housing guy – Todd – looks OK too. His finances are a bit tight, but there's nothing suspicious on any of his accounts. Backley's the same. Nothing going in or out except benefit payments."

"So you've got nothing for me?" Rob said, sitting back in his chair and putting his feet on his desk.

"Oh, I wouldn't say that. I definitely wouldn't say that. Firstly, there's Bhatti. She received a cheque for nearly forty-two grand from Malford's account, just before she left the country."

Rob sat up sharply. "So, after he died?"

"Exactly. And there were cash withdrawals of £250 made every day from Malford's account from various cashpoints after he'd died too."

"Furst, do you think?" he asked, taking the final gulp from his mug of tea.

"Possibly, but they were all made more than twenty-eight days ago, so there's no CCTV to confirm."

"And the money in the Bhattis' account has gone with them, I take it?"

"Transferred it straight on – lock, stock and barrel – to an account in their name in Pakistan."

"Bollocks." He slammed his empty mug down on his desk and slouched back in his chair. Because Pakistani accounts were beyond the jurisdiction of British courts, Lindsey hadn't been able to trace what had happened to the money thereafter, but she didn't really need to in order for Rob to make an educated guess. "So it's all gone for good?"

"You'd think so, wouldn't you? But – get this – there's then a transfer of twenty-two grand from an international money-transfer service into Burrell's account. And the reference on the payment was 'Repayment (SB)'."

"Saleema Bhatti, do you think?" Rob said, sitting up again.

"Could be. Or Samuel; he's her husband."

Rob sighed.

"You don't seem very happy about it," said Lindsey.

"Well, they're both abroad, which means the chances of getting a conviction are virtually nil. For less than fifty grand, it simply ain't worth the effort to pursue them."

"I guess not, but at least the housing people can afford it. Revenues of £49 million and an operating surplus of £7 million last year, according to their accounts."

"Yep. Low degree of harm. They've let their staff steal the money; they'll just have to bear the cost."

"But what about the payment to Burrell?" asked Lindsey. "Don't you think that gives us something to go on?"

"It's possible," said Rob, unenthusiastically. "But there's no crime in receiving twenty-two grand from a money-transfer service. We don't know it's linked to the fraud. It could be legit."

"It could be, but maybe it is linked. I know the Bhattis have gone, but maybe we can get a lead on Furst through this guy."

Rob thought about it for a minute. "Commercial fraud, small amount, little prospect of a conviction? Sounds like one for my 'do not bother' pile."

"But there's the link with Adam Furst," Lindsey pointed out. "Finding him might be the only way of getting Gemma off traffic and back into proper policing. And this payment on Burrell's account is the only lead we've got to follow at the moment."

When put like that, Rob felt that having a chat with Langley Burrell was the least he should do.

FORTY-FIVE

Arriving at Monument's offices, Rob and Lindsey were taken through to Langley's office where Barry was being ushered out after his fortnightly supervision meeting.

The moment she saw Langley, Lindsey knew that she recognised him, but she couldn't for the life of her think where from. She decided to let Rob take a lead on the questioning, whilst she tried to recall. Rob did the introductions and then explained what they'd found as a result of the production order.

"Obviously, we're not suggesting anything criminal here," he said. "We just need to understand what that money transfer payment on your account is, so we can eliminate it from our enquiries."

"Not a problem. I'm only too happy to help," Langley replied. "As you say, there's nothing suspicious about it, it's just that I sold my car. That was the payment for it.

Obviously, I had to pass it on to the car finance company to settle up with them."

"Oh, that's fine, then," said Rob. "But I don't see any payment going out for another car? Are you not driving at the moment?"

"Well, yes, I am actually. It's just that I got given a company car – with my promotion – so I didn't need my own car anymore."

"Right, and you've got that now have you?"

"Yes. It's a Jaguar XF – the racing-green one in the car park."

At which point, it suddenly hit Lindsey where she recognised Langley from. It was the idiot from the coffee shop! Him and his bloody stupid racing-green Jag. And what was worse, he obviously hadn't even remembered, which meant he probably did that kind of thing all the time. There was nothing Lindsey wanted more at that moment than to be able to pin something on that stuck-up, sexist, arrogant, little git.

"May I just ask you, Mr Burrell," she interjected, "who did you sell the car to?"

"Of course. It was the guy who just walked out, actually. Barry – Barry Todd."

"And he'll confirm that, will he?" Lindsey asked.

"I assume so. I mean, the car's in the car park and he has the keys, so he can hardly deny it."

"Right. So do you mind me asking why he paid you by international money transfer?"

"Well, I don't really know. I think you'll have to ask him that," Langley replied, shifting awkwardly in his seat for the first time. "I just told him how much I wanted and gave him my bank details, so he could pay. I didn't really discuss with him where the money was coming from."

"I'm just intrigued that it's described as a 'repayment'," Lindsey said.

"Yes, well, that's obviously a mistake. It should have said 'prepayment', but I just assumed it was a slip of his finger on the keyboard."

"And the initials – 'SB'. Those are Saleema Bhatti's initials, aren't they?"

"Oh, yes, I suppose so, but that's not what it meant. It refers to the car – or at least, that's what I assumed. It's a Subaru BRZ," Langley replied. But the flicker in his eye suggested the first stirrings of doubt in his mind.

"So you're not in contact with Saleema Bhatti?" Lindsey asked, noticing Langley's rising discomfort.

"No. Not at all."

"And if we were to check that – which obviously we can do – we definitely wouldn't find that this money had come from her?" asked Rob, also sensing that there was more to this than he had initially expected.

"Absolutely not."

"And what about Adam Furst? You wouldn't happen to have any knowledge of his whereabouts would you?" Lindsey asked.

"No. I don't even know who that is. I'm positive I don't know anything about him."

"Great. Well, we'll just check this car thing out with Mr Todd, and then we should be able to leave you in peace," Rob said, attempting to gauge Langley's reaction. Then he and Lindsey took their leave.

Barry's immediate reaction to being asked to come into an interview room to be asked a few questions by the police was to panic, but he kept reminding himself that there was still no conclusive evidence linking him with the missing money. He was further reassured when the two officers made it very clear that they just wanted to "check over a few facts" with him.

"We just wanted to ask, Mr Todd – have you recently bought a car from Langley Burrell?" asked Rob.

"Well..."

Barry was caught on the horns of a dilemma. It was clear that there was no way he could answer PC Worrall's question truthfully without ultimately incriminating himself. But, up until that point, it felt as though he hadn't really been actively deceiving anyone, they'd just asked the wrong questions and Barry hadn't volunteered the right answers. Somehow, that still felt all right, as though he was still on the right side of whatever moral boundary there was in his head. Now however, he was going to have to lie. It felt as though he was crossing a boundary and there was no way he could put any kind of gloss on it.

"I *own* Langley's old car. I've got the V5 and everything, but I didn't actually buy it. No, I couldn't say that. Sorry."

There was a momentary pause whilst Rob and Lindsey exchanged glances. "Will you just explain that for me, please?" asked Rob, finally.

"Well – and I realise this is going to sound ridiculous – he gave it to me. It was a gift."

"He *gave* you a twenty-grand car?" Lindsey asked, suddenly straightening up in her chair and opening her notebook.

"I know. I know what you're thinking. But, really, he did." There was a pause whilst he allowed this to sink in before he continued. "I mean, I couldn't believe it either."

"And just as a matter of interest, Mr Todd," Rob said, "why do you think Mr Burrell would agree to give you a car? It's a bit generous, isn't it?"

"Yeah, I suppose so. The thing is, he'd just taken my company car off me, so he said he felt a bit guilty about that. 'Specially as he got a new Jag an' all."

"So he didn't need it anymore?" suggested Lindsey.

"I guess not. And then, one day – it was just after you'd come in to talk to Ruth, actually, DS Norton – he said he needed to get rid of the car urgently, so did I want it as I was having to hand my car back. I mean, I said I couldn't afford to buy a car like that, but, in the end, he said I could have it for free, 'cause he was so desperate to get rid of it."

Lindsey and Rob's eyes met in a moment of shared awakening. "So do you have proof that he gave you the car?" Lindsey asked.

"Well, I'm not sure that I could call it proof – I mean, how can you prove that you haven't paid for something? But I was a bit surprised, so before I accepted it I spoke to Angela – she's the head of people investment – and she made a note. It's on my file, apparently."

Rob and Lindsey looked at each other again.

"Have you ever used an international money-transfer service, Mr Todd?" asked Rob.

"Never in my life," Barry said, placing his hand over his heart. "You can check my accounts – well, you have done, haven't you? So you can see for yourself."

"Have you had any contact with Saleema Bhatti?" Rob asked.

"I've not spoken to her since she left. Not a word." Barry felt a bead of sweat crawl from beneath his hairline and slide down his temple.

"And you're not aware of any contact between her and... anyone else here at Monument? Since she left."

"Oh no. I mean she's in Pakistan now, apparently," Barry replied, before adding, "You're not suggesting...?"

Rob quickly brought the meeting to a conclusion. "Well, thank you very much for your time, Mr Todd. We'll look into this and get back to you if we need anything else."

It was a relatively simple matter for the two officers to confirm the existence of the note on Barry's file and the contents of his conversation with Angela, which they duly did. It would be harder work, but still possible if necessary, for them to prove that the £22,000 had come to Langley via an international money transfer from an account controlled by one or both of the Bhattis, and not from one controlled by Barry Todd. And if they could do that, it seemed to the two officers that they would have caught Langley Burrell in a flat lie.

"He panicked, didn't he?" said Lindsey to her colleague as they reviewed the case together on the way back to the station. "After I came round and started asking questions."

"Looks like it. Not done this kind of thing before. Knows there's twenty-two grand heading toward his account so he quickly dumps the car on that sap to try and create a cover story for where it's come from."

"And thinks we'd be too thick to ask any questions. Amateur."

Lindsey tried to remain dispassionate, but she felt there would be a certain justice in an otherwise unjust world if poor old Gemma could get her proper job back in the process of sending that dreadful man down. And even if the CPS declined to prosecute or the jury failed to convict, the reality was that Langley Burrell would lose his job at the very least.

In a world that no longer believed in a perfect justice awaiting beyond the grave, it seemed all the more necessary for an imperfect justice to be administered in the here and now. So, whilst it certainly wouldn't be easy to confirm the origin of the money-transfer service's payment to Langley, Lindsey felt it was important that Rob understood that doing so might be of benefit to him and, more specifically, Gemma, even if he didn't seem to care that much about restoring people's battered faith in the police's ability to supplant divine judgement.

FORTY-SIX

"I hear everything you say, Sally, but the fact is no one is questioning that you have to pay us for The SHYPP and that it's your responsibility to make sure that we receive our payment. Nothing you've said changes those two basic facts."

Sally had demanded a meeting with Langley to discuss 'the situation'. In the event, however, Langley was unavailable, so the meeting was being chaired by Ruth who, Sally was informed, was now leading on the matter for Monument. Monument's ursine area housing manager (aka Barry Todd) was there too, presumably for some kind of moral support. Not that he seemed that keen to say anything.

"But we acted on your instructions!" Sally protested.

Ruth immediately corrected her. "No, you didn't. You acted on what you *thought* were our instructions, but you didn't check them properly."

"Yes we did!"

"With respect, you clearly didn't," Ruth replied calmly, "because if you had, you would have found out that the invoice you had wasn't the correct one. It's the fact that you didn't do that which has put us in this situation."

There was a pause. Both women knew that their respective legal positions were defensible, but hardly watertight. Sally could see that Ruth's strategy was to try to push her as hard as she could in the hope that Sally would make a settlement offer.

That was not, however, an option that Sally was prepared to countenance. Instead, she was trying to establish whether there was any way to avoid taking the 'nuclear' option. Sadly, it appeared that there wasn't, so Sally cleared her throat and prepared to settle matters once and for all.

"Can I ask, have you mentioned this to the HCA?"

Ruth froze. Barry suddenly sprang up in his seat. Sally had their attention. To invoke the name of the social housing regulator, The Homes & Communities Agency, was a crime so heinous in social housing circles that it could bring any meeting to a grinding halt immediately. It was the equivalent of a low punch in boxing, and therefore could only be employed as the absolute last resort. But it immediately had the desired effect; for the first time, Ruth became flustered.

"Well, I don't think there's any need for us to do that. I mean, this doesn't have a material effect on our accounts—"

As the regulator for social housing organisations, the HCA had to be kept informed of any frauds that were discovered within housing providers registered with them. But this was only the case if the fraud had a material effect on the organisation's accounts.

"Yes," Sally went on, "but it's only been a couple of years since your financial controller got fired. That was for fraud, wasn't it?"

"There was a thorough investigation by the HCA after that, and we've had a complete root-and-branch review of our operating procedures since then—"

"Which created complete chaos!"

"Which rationalised and streamlined everything, and introduced a range of new anti-fraud controls!"

"So it would be pretty embarrassing if any of your staff were found to have profited from this fraud, wouldn't it?"

Indeed it would. Ruth didn't seem quite sure how to respond.

"The fact is, Ruth," Sally continued, "less than 50,000 out of revenues of over £49 million is well below the materiality threshold. Monument would barely notice it was gone..."

"Surely you're not suggesting we just write it off? That's ridiculous!"

"But for us, well, 50,000 could shut us down. That counts as material in my book."

For fairly obvious reasons, if news of Monument's travails reached the ears of their regulator it would, as Sally had helpfully pointed out, make things... awkward. And so there was no intention on Monument's part to bring the whole sorry saga to their attention. Nor was there any need as, strictly speaking, the fraud was not 'material'. But The SHYPP Trust was also registered with the HCA, so the same obligation to report material frauds also rested on them. This had one very clear consequence, which Sally helpfully spelt out in case Ruth and Barry hadn't worked it out for themselves.

"If I leave this room knowing that you intend to pursue us for the money we've already paid you, you do understand, don't you, that I will be *obliged* to report this to the HCA?" Sally said, innocently. "Obviously, they would need to investigate things at our end, but I imagine they'd want to have a look at things here too – just to content themselves that everything was in order. Do you really want to force me to do that?"

On balance, Ruth decided that the answer to that was no.

"Good grief, Barry, was she serious?" said Ruth after Sally had been ushered unceremoniously from the room.

"She's never anything but. Sorry," Barry replied.

"So where do you think that leaves us?"

"Well, if she says she's going to report it, then she'll report it. You can assume from that she must be pretty confident of their case. Obviously, I've not been told anything about our side of the story, so it's just a matter of how comfortable you think we'd be with the HCA crawling all over our finance team."

Ruth left a long pause before deciding not to answer. "The thing is, Barry, this merger with Three Acts is dependent on HCA approval. We won't get that if we're under investigation – particularly if it's for financial mismanagement. Not after last time."

"I can't imagine Andrew would be very happy either, if it all fell through. Not now – not after he's announced it and everything."

Ruth hadn't thought of that, but she did now. Andrew would be forced to say goodbye to his bumper pay rise, and it would all be her fault. The consequences for her didn't bear thinking about.

"I mean," Barry went on, "if it looks like we can't manage £49 million, why would they let us manage twice as much?"

Why, indeed? However much it rankled, even Ruth could recognise that Monument had been caught in checkmate by the frightful Sally Hedges.

"You're right, Barry," she sighed. "Chasing fifty grand now will cost us more in the long run."

"So what are we going to do?"

"Keep our eyes on the prize, Barry. We'll just have to write it off. Like Sally said, fifty grand is basically a rounding error. We can hide it somewhere in the back of the accounts. No one'll notice."

"That sounds best," Barry said.

"I guess so. Ultimately, we don't want the HCA sniffing around, do we?"

"Oh, definitely not."

Of course, Sally's strategy hadn't been without risk. But when she received Ruth's email later that afternoon, confirming that Monument had agreed 'as a gesture of goodwill' that they wouldn't be pursuing their debt, she felt that she had saved The SHYPP Trust – and probably her job. There was just one more thing she needed to do to show the board that she was in control of the situation.

FORTY-SEVEN

The following day, Barry was called to a meeting with Andrew. Barry was never called to meetings with Andrew, so the news that he was required to attend a meeting with not only him but also Angela presaged a quickening of his heart rate and a moistening of his palms. After all, everyone had seen Langley being marched out of the building the previous day, escorted by police.

"How are you, Barry?" Angela asked. "You look tired."

He was tired. Not the grit-eyed tiredness of a disturbed night's sleep, but an existential weariness that made even breathing feel effortful. He'd seen it in the mirror that morning; his face looked knuckled and paunchy, like an old prizefighter.

"I'm fine. Just didn't get much sleep last night, that's all."

Nights were an endurance now. Their silence pressed in on him like the sea, dark and oppressive. Sleep was impossible. The secret, which once had nestled, small and timid, in the inner chambers of his heart, had grown. And it had mutated. It was a malignancy now, eating up the goodness in him from the inside. He could hear it gnawing through his stomach in the silence of the long winter nights. He seemed powerless to stop it. Despite all the assurances he had been given, he felt as though it would burst out at any moment.

But, he kept reminding himself, as far as his involvement in the whole saga was concerned, there was nothing for anyone to discover – no money in his account, no CCTV footage of the cash withdrawals, and no link between him and Chris Malford or Shana Backley. He couldn't be caught.

And yet, somehow, as he sat down in front of Andrew and Angela, none of that seemed to matter.

"Langley is going to be absent from the business for a little while," Angela said. "And obviously that means we'll be without a housing director at a crucial time."

"We're keen to maintain strategic focus as we prepare for the merger," Andrew added, "and we recognise that we need someone to assist with that – and with the day-to-day running of the department – who understands the business. Who knows Monument inside out."

"And we think that person is you, Barry," Angela continued, smiling and doing her 'tilty head' thing.

"I'm sorry?"

"We'd like you to be acting housing director," Andrew said with a wide grin.

"Me?"

"Yes," said Angela. "You've been here a long time and you understand Monument better than anyone else. You practically built our housing management system, so you can help with the integration of that with Three Acts' system. And you've got the respect and confidence of the staff, Barry. During a bit of… turbulence, we feel it's important we have someone who can provide some stability."

Barry was flabbergasted. This was not what he'd been expecting at all. They had seemed so keen to give the job to anyone except him only a few weeks previously.

"Obviously, this is only a temporary arrangement," said Andrew. "The precise structure of the new senior team will get sorted as part of the merger. But if things go well during the temporary period…"

Barry could fill in the silence for himself.

"That would be wonderful. Obviously, I've wanted the job since Karen left," Barry replied. "I was just wondering though…"

"About your salary?" Andrew asked, arching his eyebrow, playfully.

"Err… yes… Sorry."

"Well, we recognise that you've stepped in to help us at a crucial time. And that things haven't been easy because of… well, for a number of reasons," Angela said. "So we certainly think that additional remuneration would be appropriate."

"And now that we've lowered our headcount, we've got the space in the budget to be able to offer you something," continued Andrew.

"How does £500 a month extra sound?" Angela asked.

"Great. It sounds absolutely great. Thank you."

They needed him and now they finally recognised it. That was all he'd ever wanted. To get the recognition his hard work deserved. And he was getting it, Barry reminded himself, because he had seized the day and claimed what was rightfully his. What had happened to Langley was regrettable, of course, Barry recognised that. But he contented himself with the knowledge that Langley would be exonerated at some point. Probably. In the meantime, the universe was rewarding Barry for his initiative. All he had to do now was learn how to rid himself of the shadow that haunted his dreams, and then, perhaps, he could sleep again. If he could just do that, then Barry sensed that the possibilities for him were limitless.

He left the meeting with an uncharacteristic spring in his step and went back downstairs. But, instead of returning to his usual place on the desk island, he decided to take a detour – to the housing director's office.

"I'm sorry, but I'm afraid you can't go in there," one of the executive PAs called out anxiously.

"Oh, I think you'll find that I can," Barry replied, breezing past her. "Check with Andrew if you don't believe me," he added, watching her face drop into a look of open-mouthed astonishment. Barry had decided that he was going to enjoy this. Escaping the shadow of his secret seemed tantalisingly close. And if he could do that then maybe, just maybe, it would all have been worth it.

FORTY-EIGHT

After the weekend, Barry returned to work, not as area housing manager, but as acting housing director. There was the small matter of inducting the two temporary members of staff from the employment agency, who would be covering as area housing managers during Barry's temporary elevation. That took most of the morning, but after lunch Barry had been invited to attend his first appointment as a member of the exec team – a budget meeting with Ruth. Never before had Barry been so excited at the prospect of discussing budgets. Their meeting had barely started, however, when Blessing knocked on the door to disturb them.

"I am sorry to interrupt, madam," she said, "but there's a PC Worrall to see you. Do you want me to say that you're busy?"

"Oh, goodness me, no. Send him up."

"Do you need me to step out?" asked Barry.

"Not at all, Barry. You're part of the exec team now, and this is as much your problem as it is mine, so you might as well sit in. I take it you've worked out why Langley's not about at the moment?"

Barry reddened slightly. "Well, I saw him being taken out… by the police. You kind of put two and two together."

Rob Worrall appeared to be in a brusque mood when he entered the room. He had, it transpired, spent several hours interviewing Langley, but there was still no admission of guilt. And, despite a forensic examination of his computer and his mobile phone, there was absolutely no evidence of any contact between Langley and either of the Bhattis – or, indeed, Adam Furst. Barry was relieved to learn that PC Worrall's attention did not seem to be focused unduly on him.

"But, despite Mr Burrell's non-cooperation," Rob said, "we think we've worked out at least some of what happened after the money hit Malford's account. Firstly, someone has taken a few grand out in cash from various cashpoints around the West Midlands."

"Do we know who?" asked Ruth.

"'Fraid not. Whoever it was used Malford's card, but, as Malford was dead by that point, it clearly wasn't him. It might have been Furst – he was filmed walking off with Malford's wallet – but we don't honestly know. The rest of the money has gone into the Bhattis' account here. They've then moved it out to Pakistan. Because they'd already told their bank they were emigrating, no one picked that up as suspicious. It looks as though at least some of it has then been sent back to Burrell using an international money-transfer service. But he's refusing to admit anything."

"How can he possibly deny it?" asked Ruth.

"He's insistent the money came from Mr Todd, but we've checked all your accounts and there's nothing going in or out of any of them that's suspicious. And the money has clearly come from Peshawar – that's where the money transfer service was based and it's where the payment was made from."

"So it must have come from the Bhattis!" Ruth said.

"There's rather a lot of people living in Peshawar, not just the Bhattis. I'm afraid the CPS won't let us assume. But that does look like the most obvious explanation. Unfortunately, if we want to confirm for definite who the money came from, we'd have to go through the Pakistani courts to get the money transfer company to tell us."

"Can you do that?"

Rob shifted slightly in his seat and took a deep breath. "Well, we could. But, to be honest, the cost of doing that is not worth it for a fraud of this size. To send our officers out to Pakistan, to pay for a Pakistani QC – it all mounts up. And the judgements... Well, let's just say they can be a bit more hit-and-miss in Pakistan than we would normally expect here."

"What about the Bhattis? Can we track them down?" asked Ruth.

"Well, there again; they're in Pakistan now. We've got no contact details for them out there and they've got no family in this country who we could get to give us their contact details. Given the size of the fraud we're looking at, the costs involved in progressing this, well – I'm going to be honest – for a commercial fraud they're prohibitive."

Barry tried to stifle a sigh of relief. He felt the first stirrings of the knot in his stomach slowly beginning to untie itself. It appeared that everything Alun had told him was, broadly speaking, true. Ruth, however, had not quite given up yet.

"So what's the point at which it would be worth you pursuing this?"

"For a commercial fraud against an organisation of this size and with an offender overseas? Probably a million quid, if I'm being honest."

Barry wanted to laugh. He wanted to laugh more than at any point in the past three months. What had he ever been worried about? He'd been beating himself up at the potential consequences of stealing less than fifty grand. That feeling in the pit of his stomach, that voice in the back of his head; that sense of being watched – they were all trying to conspire to make him feel guilty. But he'd got a further £950,000 worth of moral headroom before the police would consider him as having done anything wrong – or, at least, wrong enough to warrant any kind of punishment (which, in the absence of a celestial CCTV system, was surely the only kind of 'wrong' that mattered).

"So what about Langley?" Ruth asked.

"I don't think the CPS will authorise charges unless he admits it, but his solicitor's probably told him that, so he'll just keep schtum. Of course, the burden of proof is higher in a criminal court. I'll send you my report when I've finished it and if you want to take civil action to recover your money – or at least some of it – well, your chances are better. And if you want to go down your own disciplinary processes, that's between you and him. But you'll have my report anyway."

"And what will that say?"

"Pretty much what I've just said: that we've worked out roughly what happened, but the amount of the fraud and the fact people have fled overseas means we can't really justify continuing the criminal investigation."

"So that's it?" Ruth asked.

"I'm afraid so. Obviously, if we can find this Adam Furst and establish some link to the fraud then it might get reopened. But, for various reasons, I'm not convinced personally."

"I thought he was key to it all," said Barry.

"I think that's what they wanted us to think. It's quite common with fraudsters," Rob explained. "They try to focus your attention on someone who's not important or only very peripheral, so that you're not looking at the people who seem unimportant but are actually central to the whole thing. It's how deception works. Like a sleight of hand. I must say, they've been very clever. But at the moment… well, like I say, there's nothing more we can do."

Barry had been told to expect this, but it didn't make it any less surprising to hear. Langley would be sacked, but it would cost a lot of money for Monument to try to reclaim the money from him through the civil courts and that was bound to attract the attention of the HCA. Frankly, Monument's finance team could do without the publicity at the moment, so they would probably just have to write the money off. It all felt extremely satisfactory indeed. There was just one thing he needed to check.

"Can I just ask? Does this mean that you're finished looking into the rest of us? We're 'free to go', to coin a phrase?"

"Oh, yes, Mr Todd. We're satisfied there's no evidence linking anyone else we looked into to any of this. The rest of you aren't under suspicion. My report will confirm that, so you can all rest easy. No more production orders, no more questions about your bank accounts or 'who-said-what-to-who-and-when'. That's all over."

"All over?"

Rob nodded.

"Well, that's a relief!"

Indeed, it was. It was all over – and nothing bad had happened. Except to Langley, who, frankly, deserved it. But even that was only a modest punishment – there would be no trial and no conviction. All that would happen is that he would lose a job that he should never have been appointed to in the first place. There was a certain justice in that, Barry felt.

But, as for everyone else, well, The SHYPP would be no worse off and Barry would be considerably better off. The Bhattis might have been rather unfairly apportioned some of the blame for the whole saga, but they'd never know. And they'd also been able to access 80 million Pakistani rupees which they wouldn't have been able to access without Barry's help – which in turn, was only made possible by Monument's (unwitting) help. Even Monument hadn't genuinely suffered – not really. All that would happen was that their surplus would be £6.95 million rather than £7 million. It was hardly enough to shift the world on its axis. There would be a brief note in the accounts (which no one would read) and things would carry on pretty much as before. But they would be spared the indignity of an HCA inspection – as, indeed, would The SHYPP. Andrew would even get approval for his beloved merger, which was, as Ruth had pointed out, the bigger prize in all of this.

So in the grand scheme of things, Barry concluded that small matters such as 'right' and 'wrong' were hardly worth worrying about. Even PC Worrall had suggested as much. If the small number of negative consequences were outweighed by the hugely more beneficial positive consequences, then in what sense was it even fair to describe his actions as 'wrong' at all? The world was now a better place overall, and it was all thanks to the actions of Barry Ronald Todd. When looked at like that, Barry couldn't help feeling that he deserved a medal.

Rob left Ruth and Barry to get on with their meeting, but by then Barry had other matters on his mind. Principally, the £20,000 that the Bhattis were still waiting to pay back to 'Christian Malford'. Given the ongoing police investigation, Barry had felt unable to issue any payment instructions to Saleema for fear of somehow creating a trail that could be traced back to him. However, now that he had received assurances that the police investigation was closed, it felt safe to finally respond to her request for payment details.

"I'm sorry Ruth, but I just need to send a quick text. Is that OK?" Barry asked. He took his bank card out of his wallet and texted the account number and sort code through to Saleema with a request that the outstanding funds be sent through to 'Mr Malford' at her earliest convenience.

As it was now the new year, the third quarter invoice for The SHYPP was due to be raised. It should, of course, have been raised before Christmas if Langley's instructions had been followed, but the ongoing police investigation had put a stop to that. However, now that Barry had confirmation that everything was concluded from the police's perspective, it felt important to get on to the matter of The SHYPP's quarterly invoice without further delay. If he wanted to land the housing director's job permanently, the first step would be expertly guiding The SHYPP's next payment into Monument's coffers without undue complications, and he intended to do precisely that. Barry was wise enough to know that his diversion of funds due to Monument was not a trick that could be repeated. His first phone call when he returned to his desk after his meeting with Ruth had ended, therefore, was to the offices of The SHYPP Trust.

"Oh, hi Sally. It's Barry… Barry Todd… From Monument."

"I know where you're from," replied Sally, acidly.

"Yes, sorry. We're just looking to raise the next invoice and – given our difficulties with the last one – I just wanted to make sure we got everything right this time. Is Marilyn about?"

There was a long pause.

"I'm sorry, but I'm afraid Marilyn doesn't work here anymore."

FORTY-NINE

The following day was Barry's first external appointment as acting housing director – a seminar for senior housing professionals on ways that housing associations could get around some of the government's new rent and housing benefit restrictions. Circumventing the clearly stated intention of government policy was what now passed as 'risk management' and 'prudent financial planning' amongst social housing professionals.

The seminar was to be held in central Birmingham, so Barry got a train into the city centre and then headed on foot toward the venue. Needles of rain pricked his skin like a conscience. But as he approached Chamberlain Square and the museum and art gallery on the way to his destination, he noticed a sight that brought him up short. The old Birmingham Central Library was being demolished and now stood with most of its interior exposed, like a rather pathetic, naked figure.

Barry felt a certain twinge of nostalgia. He'd spent many a happy hour in his teenage years studying in the central library. The huge inverted-ziggurat structure meant that it could accommodate far more works than anything anywhere else in the West Midlands, which meant that Barry had had unlimited access to the best art criticism in the world for free. And he could access it in a building that sought to echo the great Mesopotamian culture of the past. Just as it had been built on learning and knowledge, so a new great culture had been built in the industrial heartlands of Britain by a huge, democratising extension of access to information.

Barry had known that there was some plan somewhere to demolish the central library, but he couldn't quite believe that it would happen. It was, after all, probably the last, and certainly the finest, Brutalist monument left standing in the city. But now it was being consigned to history, after barely forty years. Brutalism was being expunged with a thoroughness that was, well… brutal.

The central library was not the museum and art gallery: it lacked the aesthetics. Its insides were all on the outside, like a body with no skin. *It isn't that it's 'wrong',* Barry thought, *it's just that it seems contrary to how people want to live – they want ornament, they want beauty.*

But, for all that, Barry couldn't help but feel that there was something admirable about the building that was being so unceremoniously demolished. It gave a glimpse of what kind of city a past generation thought Birmingham could be. It had created a place that valued knowledge and free access to it. All of which made Barry feel slightly uncomfortable. The central library that was being demolished didn't represent Birmingham's past; it represented a future that had once seemed inevitable, but that now seemed utterly implausible. Even in the supposedly philanthropic world of social housing, it was accepted that the vision embodied by buildings such as the central library had died when people like Neville retired or were 'forcibly exited' from the sector. *Maybe that's why it had to be demolished,* Barry thought.

And that thought made him sad. Because Barry didn't mind betraying people like Langley, but he did mind betraying Neville. He felt a certain twinge of regret that he couldn't quite shake as he reflected that the same fate as Neville had now befallen the unfortunate Marilyn, not as a result of the actions of some venal careerist, but because of him.

Barry had liked Marilyn. She'd always seemed like a decent person; one who, unlike so many others, didn't feel the need to trample on others to get what she wanted. And yet now it appeared that Barry had unwittingly trampled on her. As he walked on to his seminar, he wondered if his affection for yesterday's forgotten future really was based on something more substantial than nostalgia.

The seminar, of course, was utterly tedious, which gave Barry's mind a chance to wander. Firstly, he wondered if the final £20,000 that he had requested from Saleema the previous day had arrived in his account yet. She had promised to send it to him straight away. He decided, therefore, to duck out of his seminar at the first coffee break to check his bank balance.

When the paper statement from the cashpoint confirmed that the payment from Saleema had indeed arrived in his account, Barry breathed a sigh of relief. It was almost over. Within the next few days he could be mortgage free; Lauren's university maintenance would be taken care of, and he would also have his own car without having to depend on the none-too-reliable largesse of Monument Housing Association. He could decide in his own time whether he wanted to remain in their employment. But if he did, it would now be on his terms.

Part of him wanted to stay; to become the permanent housing director and run the department as he always felt it should have been run. How Neville would have wanted him to run it. Yet he wondered if he was capable of doing that anymore. Obviously, he was technically capable – he always had been – but there was a different kind of capability that Neville had always looked for in his team, which Barry felt he had somehow lost. And that made him sad too.

He wondered if his mood might be lifted by sampling the sultry charms of Iulia. There had been something of an uneasy truce between Barry and Iulia since their argument before Christmas. The festive break (and the inevitable frantic return to work afterwards) meant that it was now four weeks since Barry had been able to pay her a visit, and a fecund stirring in his loins was the inevitable result. He had heard nothing further from her and so he hoped that their little disagreement had been forgotten about.

He decided, therefore, that, rather than return for the session on 'Double Leaseback Agreements with Private Landlords as a Means of Avoiding Social Housing Rent Cuts', he would make a call to check if Iulia was available.

"Ah, Miss Nicolescu? It's Mr Todd here. From the housing association. Can you talk?"

"I not want to talk. I am at work for morning."

"Glad to hear it. I just wondered if you were free at all after lunch? For one of our… sessions."

"I am at work." She attempted to snap the conversation closed like a book.

"I understand that Miss Nicolescu, but we have an… arrangement. It's been four weeks now. I don't think it's unreasonable for me—"

"I start arrangement. Now I stop arrangement. That is my – how you say? – New Year Resolution."

Barry paused for a moment. "Well, I'm afraid I can't accept that, Miss Nicolescu. I was very clear, I hope, that our arrangement has to continue. It's not in your interests to end it."

"Do what you want!" Iulia snapped back. "I work now. I not need you anymore. It over, Meester Todd. Over."

"I don't think you've thought this through," said Barry, desperately. "There are… implications. The Romanian Migrants Welfare Association."

"You not dare contact them."

"I assure you, I very definitely would. I'd have to… to protect myself."

"Then I tell the housing people what you do!"

"Not if Costel gets to you first."

"I not stupid, Meester Todd. I protect myself. The photo – the photo of you. I keep copy – hard copy – in very safe place. Not in my flat. If anything happen to me, my friend send photo to housing people."

"And I'll lose my job. But, you… they'll know where you are. You've always said it yourself; they'll kill you if they know where you are."

"I rather die than have sex with you again!"

"But I'm only trying to help you!"

"You not help me. You say you help me, but you only think about yourself."

"Please don't make me do this."

"I not make you do anything. You do it yourself. If you want to, you not do it." There was a pause at the other end of the line before Iulia continued deliberately. "I promise you I not tell the housing people. I not tell the housing people if you don't tell where I am." She paused again.

"Look into your heart, Meester Todd. That is what I do. And that is why I stop now. There is goodness in my heart – just a leetle bit left. I not let you crush that."

"There's goodness in my heart too, but I can't just let this go. You could hold it over me – forever. I'd never be free. I'd always be worried about people finding out."

"And if they not find out? Everything is OK, then?"

"Well, yes… in a manner of speaking."

"Then there is no goodness in your heart. Not anymore. What you do – these are bad things. You know they are bad things, but still you do them. And now you threaten me if I do not carry on doing bad things. You are a bad man, Meester Todd. A very bad man!"

And with that, she hung up.

Barry stood for a moment in silence. She had, it seemed, thought of everything. Even if he now phoned the Romanian Migrants Welfare Association, he would not be safe. The incriminating photo had been printed off and lodged with a friend who had been told to hand it in to Monument if anything happened to Iulia. Whilst it remained in circulation, she held Barry in a rather awkward embrace, undergirded by the threat of mutually assured destruction. He needed to get that photo if he was ever to be free.

It seemed impossible, after all, she had given no indication of where it was, except to say that it wasn't in her flat. But then a half-remembered fragment of conversation floated to the forefront of his mind: "The friends I come with – they all go back now. I have no family here. Shakira, next door – she my only friend here."

It was hardly proof, but it was his only lead. He walked back to the train station and looked for the next train to Coleshill.

As he stood in the lobby and rang Shakira's doorbell, Barry noticed that the smell of urine finally seemed to have gone. That, at least, was some good news. He could hear the sound of a children's TV presenter booming through the door, advising him excitedly that, apparently, Old MacDonald had a farm. The baby within seemed unimpressed by this news. It occurred to Barry that the combined noise may have overwhelmed the rather puny efforts of the doorbell to announce his arrival, so he rapped his knuckles firmly against the door. This, eventually, seemed to provoke a response. The voluble presenter was faded out and the door was opened.

"Miss Jackson-Lewis? I'm here from the housing association. I'm sorry to bother you, but, I was just wondering, did Miss Nicolescu leave an envelope for us with you? She might have said it was very important."

Despite it being nearly midday, Shakira was still in her pyjamas. The floor behind her was covered by the accumulated cast-offs of a thousand failed attempts to stop her baby crying. She hugged the child to her shoulder, desperately bouncing him up and down to try to silence him. She looked like she hadn't slept at all during the three months that her son had been alive.

"Iulia? From next door? Yeah, she left me an envelope. But she said I had to hang on to it."

"And have you seen what's in it?"

"What? No. I just took it and hid it away like she said," Shakira shouted over the flensive wailing of her son. "Is she all right? Nothing's happened to her has it? I know they've been after her – the Romanian crew."

"Nothing's happened yet, but I'm afraid we have reason to believe she may be in real danger. I need to ask you for the envelope now."

"Oh God. I'd love to, but she said I should only pass it on to Miss Hampton in person."

The baby's screams continued.

"I understand that, but I'm afraid Miss Hampton's on leave at the moment. I'm her boss – Mr Todd." He flashed her his Monument ID badge. "I'll make sure this is passed on to her, but we need to see the contents of that envelope. Urgently. Every second we waste is another second we don't save her." He looked into her eyes desperately. "It really is a matter of life and death," he said.

Shakira looked at Barry with a mixture of panic and confusion in her eyes. Perhaps she wanted to phone Lucy and check if she really was on holiday. Maybe she wanted to phone Iulia to see if she really was in danger. But Barry could see that she definitely wanted to get back to silencing her baby's cries.

"Hang on a minute. It's just here." She reached behind some DVDs on the bookcase and withdrew an envelope that had been concealed there.

"Thank you so much, Miss Jackson-Lewis. And, I promise you, you've done the right thing."

"No worries. I just hope she's all right." Shakira closed the door and went back to Old MacDonald's animal husbandry inventory and to her crying son.

Barry opened the envelope and saw the all-too-familiar photo of him, just as he had anticipated. He swiftly ripped it up and deposited it in a bin on his way out. He had at least neutralised that threat. For now. But, he realised, he hadn't neutralised it for good. Shakira might phone up Iulia (when her son had finally stopped crying) to tell her what she'd done. And, even if she didn't, she would probably chat to her when Iulia returned from work; after all, they were friends. At which point, Iulia could simply print off another photo. She might give it to Shakira again, for use in future. But, given what had just happened, it seemed far more likely that she would just head straight over to Monument's offices and give it to Lucy herself (who, she would confirm, was not, in fact, on leave).

So, whilst the immediate threat may have been averted, in reality the threat posed by Iulia remained. And the possibility of her acting on her threat had, in fact, grown to a near-certainty. So further action was needed, and, as he walked back to Coleshill train station, it became all too apparent to Barry what that further action was. He'd hoped it wouldn't come to that. Yet the more he thought about it, the more he realised that he didn't have a choice. The choice was already made. But he still found himself shaking as he took a rather dishevelled business card from out of his wallet and dialled the number.

"Hullo, is that the Romanian Migrants Welfare Association?… Are you still looking for Iulia Nicolescu?… Yes, well I know where she's living, but if I give you her details you have to promise me that you'll act quickly."

Barry wondered if the fact that he felt bad about what he'd done meant that he could still describe himself as good. He decided, sadly, that it probably didn't. Frankly, however, he wasn't sure if it mattered anymore. After all, just a few miles away, one of the last monuments to moral certainty was being ruthlessly demolished.

But somehow he wished that it still did.

FIFTY

Barry faced a conundrum. He was supposed to be at a seminar, but his mind was somewhat distracted both by his recent exchange with Iulia and by the fact that he now had £20,000 of someone else's money in his bank account. He felt the urge to pay a visit to the museum and art gallery, which was advertising an exhibition of work by E.R. Hughes.

The alternative was to go back to work. This was less pleasurable than an afternoon in an art gallery, but did at least mean that he wouldn't have to explain where he'd been. He could just dismiss the seminar as rubbish and say that he'd felt his time would be better spent at the office. This had the advantage of making him appear diligent. Given that his promotion was not yet permanent, Barry felt that appearing to be diligent was probably the least he could do.

This was, however, to prove easier said than done. Monument's offices had been located in Kingsbury precisely because it was virtually inaccessible by public transport from anywhere where Monument's tenants might actually live. Barry had got a train into the city centre from home that morning and had bought a return ticket in the expectation that he would be at the seminar all day. He had arranged for his wife to drive him to Sutton Coldfield station that morning and to pick him up from there in the evening. But none of that would help him get to Kingsbury now. He decided that the best thing to do would be to head back toward Walmley and ask his wife to pick him up at the station. He could then drop her back home before heading on to Monument's office in the car.

He didn't anticipate any problems with his wife's availability. After all, her job hunting had taken something of a back seat since Christmas, largely, it seemed, because she insisted that she was too sick to look for a job. But Barry was well aware from their twenty-seven years together that his wife was not really sick – or at least not in the conventional sense. She may well have been 'worried sick', but that wasn't really the same thing. She clearly was worried about Lauren and her apparent unwillingness to communicate with her mother anymore, and this had somehow transformed itself into a series of headaches.

As their doctors' surgery was closed over Christmas, she had not had the opportunity to seek an expert medical opinion and so had sought comfort from the internet. This had convinced her that she had a brain tumour or, possibly, multiple sclerosis – she couldn't be quite sure. But what she could be sure of was that whatever she had was serious and possibly life-threatening.

When she eventually saw Dr Mughal, he assured her that this was unlikely to be the case. He had, however, agreed to refer her on for a CT scan, "Just to put your mind at rest, Mrs Todd." They were still awaiting an appointment to come through, but, in the meantime, his wife was convinced that she was too ill to look for a job.

But Barry didn't really feel that guilty about getting his wife to ferry him about, particularly as she was using the car that his industry and guile had provided in order to do so.

"Hiya love. It's me. Can you pick me up at the station in about forty minutes?"

"I thought you were in town all day?"

"Well, I was, but the seminar wasn't very good. I thought I'd come back and go into the office."

"The office? How are you going to get there?"

"Well, I was going to drop you off at home and then drive in."

"But I need the car."

"What do you mean, you need the car? You're supposed to be sick. Why do you need the car – *my* car?"

"I need to go down to Warwick to see Lauren."

"What for?"

"She's not spoken to me for weeks – I can't get her to answer her phone. She's unfriended me on Facebook! I need to speak to her, Barry."

"But why today? She's upset, I get that, but sooner or later she'll calm down."

"You don't know that."

"I know that her and this boy will probably break up – that's the way it is with youngsters – and when they do she'll want to talk to her mum. But don't go chasing around after her; it'll only annoy her more. Just come and pick me up. The next train's due in in about forty minutes."

There was a pause on the other end of the line.

"I can't do that, Barry. I'm already here."

"What?"

"Listen, Barry. Listen to me. I wanted to catch her before she went to her lectures, but she wasn't in. They said she'd stopped over at her boyfriend's. At her boyfriend's, Barry! Does that sound to you like they're about to break up?"

"I didn't say they were *about* to break up. I just said—"

"I've phoned and she doesn't answer. I need to talk to her – to explain about my headaches. I need to prepare her, in case the news is bad."

"Oh, for goodness' sake! There's nothing wrong with you! They're just headaches."

"You can't say that! You don't know what they're like."

Barry sensed that people around him were starting to stare. He took a deep breath and decided to try a calmer approach.

"So you're at the uni now?"

"Yes. I'm on campus. Apparently, she's due to come out of a lecture in a bit. I'm waiting outside to try to catch her. There's no way I can make it back to you in forty minutes."

Consequently, Barry found himself having to get a cab back to Kingsbury and he was not in a good mood, therefore, when he arrived back at his desk. The unfortunate fate that had befallen Marilyn, the 'situation' with Iulia, and the argument with his wife had all cast a shadow over his day that not even the arrival of £20,000 in his bank account seemed able to dislodge.

His first visitor was Angela. She was carrying a set of car keys.

"Barry, I saw you getting out of a cab a minute ago, and it made me think of these." She jangled the keys to Langley's Jaguar.

"Oh. What about them?"

"Goodness, you look miserable. Perhaps I can cheer you up."

Barry very much hoped that she could, but rather doubted it.

"Obviously, we've asked Langley to return all his company property whilst he's suspended, and that includes his company car. It's just sitting in the car park at the moment – which is hardly very safe – and we've been wondering what we could do with it. As it's officially the housing director's car, we wondered if you'd like to look after it for us? Temporarily, obviously – just while we get things… sorted out."

"That'd be great. Yes, thanks," Barry replied without much enthusiasm.

"It's a bit bigger than that little red sports car you've been going around in, and not quite as low slung. I thought it might suit you a bit better."

Even when she was giving him a free car, somehow Angela managed to make it sound like an insult.

He couldn't understand it. He'd been worried about his finances – and not getting the director's job – for so long that he had assumed that, once these issues were resolved, his life would be sorted. But here he was, with the job he'd always wanted and more money than he knew what to do with, yet his life seemed a bigger mess than ever.

He wanted to work his way through the thirty-six emails that had come in whilst he'd been out of the office, but before he had a chance to start, he had another visitor at his office door: Jean.

"I'm sorry to bother you, Barry, but we've just had a call from the police. They've been called to an incident at one of our flats. A 'Iulia Nicolescu'?" Jean said, reading the note stuck to her finger.

Barry started. "Oh yes. God, is she all right?"

"They don't know. They've not found her. A couple of guys kicked her front door in, apparently, just as she was returning from work. Bundled her into the back of a van and drove off. The police are saying we need to get someone round to secure the property, so Lucy's on the case now."

"Well, that sounds terrible. Let's just hope she's OK, eh?"

"Yes. The police are very concerned for her welfare. Lucy says you'll know what that's all about."

"Yes, yes. Terrible business."

Barry could feel himself redden, and the beginnings of a tear well up in his eyes. He was struggling to breathe and he felt a comber of sickness surge from the pit of his stomach toward his gullet.

"Are you all right, Barry? You don't look good. Not at all."

There was so much he wanted to say, but he realised that he couldn't. He wouldn't have known where to start, even if it was possible for him to say anything – which, of course, it wasn't. Not now.

The ocean between him and the rest of humanity could not be traversed anymore, and indeed was growing. The currents were taking him further and further away and he seemed powerless to stop them. Jean was standing not ten feet from him and yet she may as well have been on the moon.

"I'm fine, I'm fine," he said. "It's just very upsetting news. I knew there were people looking for her; that's why we moved her out to Coleshill in the first place. You just never imagine... Lovely girl."

"They always are, aren't they? At the beginning. Lovely girls. Just fell in with the wrong sort, I suppose."

A stabbing pain in his heart added itself to Barry's list of ailments. "Yes, that's it. That's it exactly. She fell in with the wrong sort."

The two of them fell into a gloomy silence before Jean asked, "Are you sure you're all right, Barry? You don't look well at all. Is something bothering you?"

Indeed there was, but it was not something he felt able to explain to her. "How do we get it back, Jean?" he asked instead. "Back to like it was before, when Neville was here."

"You mean before all this stuff with Langley?"

Barry didn't quite mean that at all, but it seemed a convenient entry point to the conversation he wanted to have. "They've told you, have they?" he asked.

"Well, not officially, but everyone's talking about it. Obviously, we know the money from The SHYPP is missing, and then the police came round and arrested him. It doesn't take a genius..."

"No. No, it doesn't," said Barry. Although, on this occasion, a genius might have been helpful.

"The thing is, Barry, housing associations haven't changed in isolation. *We've* changed – all of us. We seem to want a special caste of people to go around being good on our behalf, and then we express shock and horror when they behave exactly as the values of their age tell them they should!"

"What do you mean?"

"Post-modern people don't really believe in goodness anymore – or at least, they don't believe that goodness wins. People want to believe it, but they can't. And they often feel awful about that. But they're reassured by the fact that there are people who still seem to – people like Neville and, yes, even Sally. By giving money to charities, people feel as though they're believing in goodness, kind of by proxy. And that makes them feel better about themselves.

"But, actually, if goodness doesn't win, then why should we expect anyone to bother? How can we expect housing associations to value compassion and philanthropy when the rest of the world measures success only in terms of money?"

"Yeah. I guess so," said Barry. "Maybe that's what was different about Neville. He always said if you did the right thing then the money would take care of itself."

"Yes, he did, but it was more than that. He really believed that being good couldn't be based on what you got out of doing something. He felt – and maybe it sounds naïve, but I believe it too – that if we're only doing something because we're rewarded for doing it, then we're not really doing good. Even if we're helping the homeless or healing the sick. Goodness is about what's in our hearts."

Barry shifted uncomfortably in his seat.

"If we forget that, then morality just becomes a matter of what we think might make things better – or what we think we can get away with."

"Is that why people do it, do you think?" asked Barry. "Because they see everyone else get away with it?"

"I don't know, Barry. I'm sure everyone has their own story. I know Langley had to look after his mother, for instance, and that must have been a drain."

Barry started. "You what?"

"His mother. She had a stroke. That's why he gave up his job with Debenhams. To come up here so he was near her. He's round there practically every day. He's all she's got since her husband died. Left everything to his mistress. That's why Langley was so desperate to get the director's job – he said he needed the money to help pay for her care plan. But maybe it just wasn't enough… It's all terribly sad anyway."

Barry had clung on for so long to the belief that he was a good man who'd done a bad thing, because he believed that it mattered somehow – that it made him better than Langley. But now he realised you could be a bad man who did a good thing, and it amounted to pretty much the same.

"But what if it wasn't his fault?" he asked.

"At the end of the day, we all make our own choices, Barry. And when you're caught between the Devil and the deep, blue sea, there'll always be those who'll opt for the Devil. Which is such a shame, because everybody knows right from wrong. I really believe they do. We all do – in our hearts. It's just that we spend so long trying to silence that voice inside us because we've convinced ourselves that the voice is just a figment of our imagination. That we're silly for listening to our heart. But I don't think we are. I think that voice is real."

A rather awkward silence descended on the room. Barry's jaw locked shut as his face became redder and redder.

"I'm sorry, Barry. That turned into a bit of a rant. It wasn't meant to be." She changed the subject. "How are things at home? Your wife coping any better with your daughter being away?"

But Barry remained tight-lipped. "Well, you know. We're taking each day as it comes. It's pretty frustrating really," was as much as he would say.

"You've just got to keep on loving her, Barry," Jean said. "She's your wife – that's the deal. And the one thing we know from bitter experience is that love hurts. It's just the way it is sometimes."

Barry had spent forty-eight years on this earth biting his tongue, but now he rose from his seat and without further thought let those forty-eight years of frustration finally come tumbling out of his mouth.

"People always say 'love hurts', as though that's a proper answer, but it's not," he said, quaking with rage. "Loneliness hurts. Rejection hurts. Sitting in silence when your heart is bursting with things you can't say – that hurts. But that's not love. Love's supposed to cover all that up, isn't it? Love's what's supposed to make you feel wonderful. Love's the only thing in this godforsaken world that shouldn't bloody hurt!"

And without further ado, he grabbed his coat off the back of his chair and stormed out of the office, leaving Jean motionless, in a stunned silence.

It appeared that the E.R. Hughes exhibition would be receiving Barry's custom that day after all.

FIFTY-ONE

Edward Robert Hughes was a Pre-Raphaelite painter who wasn't particularly highly regarded when he was alive and whose reputation had suffered a precipitous decline in the first sixty years after his death. As a man ill-disposed toward the Pre-Raphaelites generally, it wasn't difficult for Barry to understand why, and the early sections of the exhibition merely confirmed his prejudices.

However, those sections were, in reality, only the *hors d'oeuvres* before the main course. The fact was that Hughes had been the subject of reappraisal by more recent critics, and was now the subject of his first one-man show more than a century after his death. And as far as Barry could tell, this was largely due to the enduring appeal of one of his last paintings, *Night with Her Train of Stars and Her Great Gift of Sleep* (1912).

Despite his general indifference to all things Pre-Raphaelite, even Barry had to concede that this painting was a masterpiece. He liked to think this was because it was, strictly speaking, more of a Symbolist painting than a Pre-Raphaelite one, so he still felt he could admire it without betraying his general principle that all Pre-Raphaelite art was rubbish.

Symbolist artists, as Dr Potter had elucidated to Barry and his largely uninterested classmates all those years ago, wanted to transcend the mere depiction of the material world. They set about creating works that were designed to provoke profound emotional, even spiritual, responses. And, being Symbolists, they did this by using the physical objects in their paintings as symbols that pointed to another world – a world that could be experienced in our day-to-day lives, but that was, perhaps, not fully seen. It was a deeper world, invisible to the naked eye, and one that thus could only be brought into view by the ministrations of art. It was a world of the soul, and, staring at Hughes' masterpiece, Barry became aware of something within him. It was something beyond a gnawing sense of guilt, but it spoke to him of guilt nonetheless.

The painting itself was set at twilight and showed a winged female figure, Night, flying through the sky, cradling a small baby in her arms. Behind her followed an army of tiny winged creatures – *putti* – some carrying glowing lights, others playing with Night's long robes. She had her finger on her lips to silence them.

Barry seemed to recall that it had once been his wife's favourite painting. She'd even put a print of it on the wall of Christopher's nursery. Many was the evening that Barry had held his screaming son in his arms and stared at that print, imploring Night to silence Christopher with the same effortless alacrity that she managed with the nameless baby in Hughes' painting.

And then, of course, she had. At which point, his wife had put the print in the loft. Barry had found it there when he'd gone up to get his painting kit before Christmas. He'd brought it down because it seemed a sad waste for such a beautiful picture.

Barry couldn't be sure, but it seemed that she'd got over her aversion to it. He'd even caught her staring at it that morning in what looked like an admiring way. It was what had prompted him to think about taking in the original.

One of the things that he liked about exhibitions was that the notes and displays gave you a chance to learn more about the artist and their work. For instance, he'd never much thought about it before, but the highly unusual title of the painting had not come from Hughes himself but from W.E. Henley's poem *'Margaritae Sorori'*. Barry read it for the first time from the large reproduction that accompanied the painting as part of the exhibition:

A late lark twitters from the quiet skies:
And from the west,
Where the sun, his day's work ended,
Lingers as in content,
There falls on the old, gray city
An influence luminous and serene,
A shining peace.
The smoke ascends
In a rosy-and-golden haze. The spires
Shine and are changed. In the valley
Shadows rise. The lark sings on. The sun,

Closing his benediction,
Sinks, and the darkening air
Thrills with a sense of the triumphing night
Night with her train of stars
And her great gift of sleep.
So be my passing!
My task accomplish'd and the long day done,
My wages taken, and in my heart
Some late lark singing,
Let me be gather'd to the quiet west,
The sundown splendid and serene,
Death.

Barry had looked at the picture so many times, yet it was only now that he read Henley's poem that he felt as though he truly saw it – as though he saw it for the first time as Hughes had intended. It suddenly hit him that it wasn't a picture about the innocent sleep of babes at all. The wings of Night were not the white wings of an angel, but the black wings of Death. The figure of Night bringing sleep was a symbol (of course it was!) of Death bringing oblivion. The child she cradled in her arms represented the departing soul. The dividing line between day and night in the picture actually symbolised the line between life and death.

Barry couldn't believe that he'd never seen it before, but suddenly all the other elements in the painting began to make sense. The *putti* clutching at Night's robe were not playing with her; they were trying to pull her back. The finger that Night placed on her lips was not merely an injunction to the playful *putti* to be quiet so they didn't wake a sleeping child. It was a bidding to let Death take its course because, as Henley had observed, death need not be sorrowful. It could be 'splendid and serene'. And there, beneath Night, a flock of birds were seen flying home to roost. It felt to Barry a particularly apposite metaphor.

He realised that he couldn't ever be truly free, not now. He knew he would never again be free to say the first thing that came into his head, and probably not even the second. He would forever be calibrating in his mind what it was safe to say. And he would do that because he had to stop people discovering the truth. The fact was that everything in his life was a lie now. It was all based on the lie that he'd made people believe, that Barry Todd was a good man. He wasn't, not anymore. Iulia had been right. He was a bad man, "a very bad man".

Barry looked back at Hughes' picture, at the sleeping child in Night's arms. Unlike the *putti,* frenetically chasing after Night and trying to pull her back, the sleeping child was at peace. He saw no need to fight his fate, to struggle free from Night's arms. His heart may indeed even have thrilled with a sense of 'triumphing night', as Henley had supposed. And Barry felt as if he finally understood – fully understood – the painting's title. This sleep, this deepest sleep, truly was a 'great gift'. Because the baby didn't have to worry anymore. It was all over; the struggles and travails that still wracked the *putti* were his no more. Death was not a grim reaper, but a protective, motherly figure who cradled you with true love.

And perhaps that, after all, was all he'd ever wanted.

FIFTY-TWO

The more he thought about it the more it made sense. He'd got the money put aside to pay for Lauren's maintenance whilst she was at university. It didn't need him to be physically present to pay it to her; he could just send it through in one payment. He'd bought a car, so his wife wouldn't be left without one, and she could exchange the Subaru for something more suitable if she wanted to. And there was twenty grand still left, which he could use to clear the mortgage. With the insurance money as well, she'd be all right. In fact, she'd probably be better off.

Besides, she didn't want him around, not really. Occasionally, she said that she did, but what Barry always suspected was that she wanted his help. She wanted a good home in a nice area, a decent car and, of course, she had wanted help looking after Lauren. But, Barry was reluctantly forced to conclude that she didn't want *him* – Barry Todd, specifically – to provide those things. Anyone would have done. It was just that she'd got stuck with him.

And then, as if to prove his point, his phone pinged with a text message from his wife advising him that she wouldn't be back home for dinner that evening. Yes, he knew that she was trying to speak to Lauren, and, yes, she'd apologised (*"I'm really really sorry"*). She even said she'd left him a note explaining "*everything*", which, on the basis of Barry's previous experience of her explanatory notes, he assumed meant explaining how he could actually cook his own tea for once. But all that was hardly the point. The fact was that – as her text message amply demonstrated – she'd rather be somewhere else, doing something else, with someone else. She didn't want to be around him. And, if he was being honest, he didn't want to be around her either, not anymore.

But, given his ample frame, thinning hair and potato-like face, it appeared almost inconceivably unlikely that he would be able to find another, more suitable, life-companion now. The sad fact was that he had just received proof positive that he couldn't even pay someone to have sex with him. For all his sudden wealth, it appeared it wasn't enough to give him the one thing he actually wanted. That, it seemed, was altogether more elusive.

"That's all right" he texted back, after pulling up on the drive at home. *"I'll sort myself something out. Love you x"*

It was a lie of course. Yet another one. It wasn't all right, and he probably wouldn't be able to sort himself something out, no matter how idiot-proof his wife's cooking instructions were. And he didn't love her; not if love meant being patient and kind and all that other stuff Jean had gone on about. But he couldn't face telling her that.

"Love is looking into the filthy, black heart of another human being and defying the urge to jump ship." That's what Jean had said. Well, Barry had looked into his own heart and he was done with defying. It was time to jump.

"When you're caught between the Devil and the deep, blue sea, there will always be some people who will choose the Devil." Well, Barry had tried that and was reluctantly forced to conclude that it hadn't worked out for him. In light of that, the deep, blue sea now looked a surprisingly attractive option.

The house breathed out its silence as Barry entered and hung up his coat in the hall. The fact that he was on his own was helpful; it would give him time to research online without having to worry about his wife getting suspicious. He checked the kitchen table, but couldn't see any note, so he pulled the Dial-a-Pizza leaflet off the noticeboard instead. He phoned through his order then went upstairs to get changed.

He'd barely got out of his work suit when the doorbell rang. Given that it had only been ten minutes since he'd placed his order, Barry was surprised. But, as he approached the front door, he saw that it wasn't the pizza-delivery man as he had supposed. Instead, through the frosted glass, he saw two blobs of fluorescent yellow, one large and round, one small and thin.

"PC Rathbone? PC Molloy!" This was not what he'd expected at all, but, judging by the look on their faces, seeing him was not what they had expected either.

"I thought you'd been taken off the Malford case. DS Norton told me..."

"Uh, we have been," said Gemma. "That's not what this is about."

A horrible thought entered Barry's mind and the colour drained from his cheeks. "This isn't about Iulia Nicolescu, is it? Because if it is—"

"Who?" asked Gemma. "No. No, it isn't. Look, can we come in, Mr Todd?"

"Umm. Yes, yes, of course. Come in," Barry replied, ushering them into the lounge.

He had come so far, and if they'd just left him alone, he would have brought matters to a conclusion himself soon enough anyway. But now it looked as if even that rather hollow consolation was to be denied him.

"So why are you here?"

"Of course," Gemma replied. "I'm sorry, Mr Todd, but I'm afraid there's been... an accident."

"An accident?"

"Well, an incident," Molloy corrected. "We're on traffic at the moment. Our colleagues from motorways have asked us to come and see you."

"I'm sorry, I don't understand..."

"A car belonging to you has been found abandoned," Gemma said.

"Belonging to me? But that's imposs— oh, hang on..."

"A Subaru BRZ?" Molloy asked. "SE Lux. Flame red."

"Yes. Yes, that's my car."

"We found it on a road near a bridge over the motorway. There was a note," said Gemma, reaching inside her folder and withdrawing a manila envelope on which was written *"To whom it may concern"* in beautifully crafted handwriting.

At which point, Barry realised that the note the earlier text message had been referring to was not, as he had supposed, his wife's instructions for how to cook her mother's chicken and leek pie.

"What's happened?" asked Barry, grabbing the envelope from Gemma and frantically removing its contents.

Barry's wife had been a secretary at Dudley Art College. She'd often talked of doing some of the courses on offer in her own time, but, in the event, the only one she'd ever done was calligraphy. So, whilst her painting skills were non-existent and her knowledge of art history was distinctly patchy, her handwriting was always beautiful – in marked contrast to Barry's spidery scrawl. He'd always rather admired that about her, if nothing else. And he admired the beauty of her note now. There was a goodness to it, somehow, that shone through, even before he'd had a chance to read what it actually said.

"I'm sorry, Mr Todd, but there are some questions we have to ask. It's for the paperwork," said Molloy.

But Barry's attention was wholly focused on the letter in front of him:

> *Firstly, let me say how sorry I am if I've caused anyone any trouble or put anyone out. I really didn't mean to. Please pass on my apologies if I've made a nuisance of myself – that wasn't my intention.*
>
> *But I wanted to explain things.*
>
> *Obviously, I'm not happy, but it's* why *I'm not happy that really bothers me. It's that I seem to make the people around me miserable. I don't mean to, I just do. The people I'm supposed to be closest to actually feel*

the farthest away. I do care about them, but they just regard me as an inconvenience. I think they'd prefer it if I was dead, to be honest.

It used to be so different. I was at an art college once. I had dreams; I knew what I wanted to be. But somehow I've lost sight of all that. My daughter talks to me now like I'm an idiot – when I can get her to talk to me at all. She doesn't respect me anymore. No one does. I think that's what hurts the most.

Losing our son tore us apart. When Christopher died, it pretty much ended our marriage. We don't communicate now, not really.

It's funny, because I feel I have so much love to give, but no one seems to want it. It's like money, I suppose – you always think you want more of it, but if you keep it all for yourself, it just becomes a burden. You really need to be able to give it away, and if you can't, then frankly, what's the point? You don't have anything to live for if no one wants your love, do you?

Sorry again. Please make sure my daughter knows that I do love her. This wasn't about her; I want her to know that.

Thank you.

Barry looked up at the officers in stunned silence. It didn't make sense; it just didn't make sense.

"We believe, from her driving licence, that the note may have been left by Julie Todd. Do you know if that's her signature?" asked Gemma.

Julie Todd. He rolled the name around his mind. It seemed familiar, and yet also somehow strangely distant, like the memory of someone he used to know. But it was unmistakably her signature. It wasn't wholly legible, but Barry would recognise its flamboyant swirls anywhere. After all those years he'd seen it so many times.

"Yes, that's her signature."

"Sorry," Gemma said. "But there's some paperwork I need to complete, Mr Todd. Can you confirm how you were related to Julie Todd?"

Barry looked at the note in front of him and its explanation of a person he never knew. "They try and focus your attention on someone who's not important or only very peripheral, so that you're not looking at the people who seem unimportant but are actually central to the whole thing. It's how deception works." It appeared that PC Worrall was right.

"How are we related?" Barry had to ask himself the question because the answer no longer seemed obvious. Eventually, it came to him.

"By marriage," he said. And suddenly something his father had said didn't seem like a joke after all. "Only by marriage."

AUTHOR'S NOTE

Acts & Monuments is a work of fiction. There is no Monument Housing Association; there is no Barry Todd. The events and characters portrayed are wholly fictional. Any similarity to actual events and/or actual people is purely coincidental and unintended.

However, the legal framework outlined in the novel is based on the actual legal framework in place in England at the time in which the novel is set. The financial and other processes described are a reasonable portrayal of practices that were (or could reasonably be) employed by real organisations at that time. The figures and reporting procedures for fraud are taken from the latest publicly available information at the time of writing.

Buildings described as being owned by Monument Housing Association are fictional composites based on a variety of real buildings. Other buildings mentioned in the text are actual buildings and their descriptions are intended to be historically and architecturally accurate. Similarly, all works of art described herein are real works of art and any historical information related to them is intended to be true. Works of art described as being on display in Birmingham Museum and Art Gallery were on display there at the time ascribed to them.

For the avoidance of doubt, at the time of writing, The Edwardian Tea Rooms did indeed contain *"examples of great cake"*.

@AlanKaneFraser
#ActsAndMonuments

ACKNOWLEDGEMENTS

There is a myth that persists in the popular imagination, which is that the construction of a book is an essentially solitary process; that a hermitical genius locks themselves in a garret, or similar, and only engages with the world once their *meisterwerk* is completed. In this conception, all everyone else has to do is wait for the writer to produce their novel and then gasp in astonishment at its brilliance. The writer then retires to their boudoir, whilst teams of people disseminate it uncritically to the reading public.

If this was ever true (which I doubt), it is certainly not true now. Today, the production of a book is a team process in which the writer is supported, steered, cajoled and sometimes simply bossed about by a great many other people whose job it is to see that the novel that the writer has written is the very best that it can be. These people do not get their name on the front cover and so the reader might suppose that they are unimportant. They are not.

And so the last task of the novelist, once the final draft of their novel is completed, is to publicly acknowledge the contribution of others toward the finished work and to thank them for helping to make it better than it would otherwise have been. In my case, this first involves acknowledging the contribution of Paul Harris at Real Success in making sure that there was a finished work at all. Without his encouragement, I wouldn't even have got to the end of draft one.

But, equally, the task of getting from the virtually unreadable 192,000-word first draft of *Acts & Monuments* to the somewhat more streamlined final draft has been aided by a number of people who have provided helpful, firm and occasionally downright brutal editorial advice. Firstly, this came from Alison Williams, but there was subsequent substantial input from Haydn Middleton and Doug Johnstone. This wasn't always easy to hear, but it all helped to tame the unwieldy beast that I started with.

If they did the editorial heavy lifting, the finishing and polishing was provided by an army of volunteer readers without whom any aspiring novelist's job would be immeasurably harder. So I also want to thank Cerys Howell, Malcolm Clifford, Fiona Bullock, Kay Dashti, Lewis Fraser and particularly Rowena Wilding and Jenny Warbrick, who all provided invaluable feedback at various stages of the book's development. Some of it I even listened to.

Of course, the plausibility of a book such as this is dependent in large part on getting crucial details right. As someone who has worked in and around the field of social housing for many years, I am well versed in the world that *Acts & Monuments* inhabits. But the world of police procedures is largely unknown to me, so it was hugely helpful to be able to call on the services of Mark Watkins at crucial points to advise on such issues. Malcolm Clifford also cast a helpfully beady eye over the process by which the fraud is perpetrated.

All of these people have contributed in some way toward improving *Acts & Monuments* as a novel. Responsibility for its shortcomings, however, remains firmly with me.

Finally, I also want to thank Sharon Fraser, who has stood by my side throughout the whole process and who kept me going at all the points when I thought of giving up – and got me restarted on the couple of occasions when I actually did give up. Living with a writer is a thankless task, which she has borne with good grace, for which I am ever in her debt.

A.K.F.
The Feast of the Annunciation, 2018